THE PF … AL

Costs dearly…

With his brother, Ma … relli has one chance to get enough men together to take back possession of his firm and his life.

Locating previous loyal members of his firm before Marco took the reins is proving easier said than done and although Zane is prepared to wait for a certain amount of time to ensure things are right, Erin can't.

Each passing day unable to take revenge for Marco's past deeds as well as putting a stop to the abhorrent ventures that are now being carried out is a further twist of the knife – one which threatens to slice through Erin and Zane's fledgling relationship.

Something has to be done but at what cost?

And how will Marco's new wife, Hazel, react when she realises the man she's just married isn't the true heir to the Morelli empire after all?

What readers are saying about *The Price of Betrayal*:

- *"Absolute corker…"*
- *"Shocks galore, fast-paced, exciting…"*
- *"WOW what a slap bang book two…"*
- *"This author never disappoints me…"*

Also by Edie Baylis

Scarred Series
Mirrors Never Lie (Scarred #1)
The Price of Betrayal (Scarred #2)
Trusting Blood (Scarred #3)

Allegiance Series
Takeover (Allegiance #1)
Fallout (Allegiance #2)
Vendetta (Allegiance #3)
Payback (Allegiance #4)
Judgement (Allegiance #5)

Retribution Series
An Old Score (Retribution #1)
Finders Keepers (Retribution #2)
The Final Take (Retribution #3)
The Retribution Series Box Set

Hunted Series
The Status Debt (Hunted #1)
The Family Legacy (Hunted #2)
The Target of Lies (Hunted #3)
The Hunted Series Box Set

Downfall Series
Until the End of Time (Downfall #1)
Escaping the Past (Downfall #2)
Vengeful Payback (Downfall #3)
The Downfall Series Box Set

THE PRICE OF BETRAYAL

SCARRED #2

EDIE BAYLIS

ATHAME
press
- LONDON -

First published in Great Britain in 2023 by Athame Press.
This paperback edition published in 2023 by Athame Press.

Front cover photography: KrisCole/depositphotos.com;
Stetsik/Depositphotos.com; bruno.passagati/depositphotos.com
Back cover photography: bruno.passagati/depositphotos.com

Paperback ISBN 978-1-7393009-1-3
Hardback ISBN 978-1-7393009-5-1
Large Print ISBN 978-1-7393009-9-9
e-ISBN 978-1-7398114-9-5

Athame Press
Unit 13230 - PO Box 6945 – London – W1A 6US

Prologue

2001

SITTING AT THE DESK of his now closed Starlight film studio, Trevor Grimes visualised the moment when his daughter walked down the aisle. The pleasure he'd taken knowing he'd ensured Hazel would be more financially secure than ever, as well as being granted kudos and protection, was gratifying. Plus, his girl's joining with the head of the Morelli firm had given *him* a payout above and beyond what he'd imagined. And that had been the main factor.

The agreement was worth selling his moneymaker of a daughter and winding up his profitable and successful adult film business to the opposition, because the opposition was no longer the opposition... Marco was now *family*. A family that Trevor was part of too, courtesy of the nuptials that he'd cleverly arranged.

Now he could finally retire and use the money from the transaction to see out the rest of his life in luxury. And when the time was ripe for Hazel to cement her place in Marco Morelli's life forever, she would give him a child – a heir to the business and a further guarantee of *his* inclusion in the spoils. At that point, things would become even more lucrative.

Trevor glanced around his office for what he intended should be the last time. This furniture in itself was worth a packet, but he'd deal with those finer points once everything had been shifted off site into storage. He'd rented a warehouse to store all the film equipment in which wasn't cheap, but he'd make his money back on that once he'd sold the kit on.

Maybe Marco might want to make him an offer? There was top of the range cameras as well as the best quality lighting rigs, but then Marco had all that clobber of his own.

Trevor sipped at his whisky and shrugged. It made no difference. He was in no need of that stuff anymore – not now he'd made his fortune. It was time to retire in peace, so sorting the gear out could be done after he'd had a break.

Including all of *these.* They could wait too.

His gaze fell to the stack of boxes in the corner of his office containing each of the original films his studios had produced over the years, including the many starring his daughter.

Those now officially belonged to Marco as part of the deal they'd struck, including Hazel's back catalogue.

A small smirk spread across Trevor's face. Hazel hadn't been pleased that the rights to her films would be no longer owned by Starlight Studios, but she'd changed her mind once he'd let her in on the part in Marco's contract with which afforded her a get out clause.

Marco may have a head for certain things, but checking finer points of paperwork wasn't one of his strong points and as suspected, the man had failed to notice the clause Trevor had insisted his solicitor include.

Trevor then frowned. He should have already moved those films – especially Hazel's, to that special safety deposit box as planned, but he still hadn't got round to it.

Taking another long swig of his whisky, he shrugged. No matter. He'd do it tomorrow. Maybe even the day after? The removals firm wasn't due for another fortnight so there was no rush.

It looked like he'd have to pay one last visit to this place after all.

Anyway, the safety net of keeping those films out of Marco's hands was only on the slim chance and in the event of certain eventualities, that Hazel needed them. And that was unlikely. There was little worry that Marco's attachment to Hazel would diminish. The man was obsessed with her, but no one could predict the future so it was best to have security in place.

Anyhow, it wouldn't be long before Hazel cemented her place in Marco's life and fortune via the unbreakable bonds of offspring.

But Trevor had made very clear to his daughter, *that* should only happen when she was certain she was irreplaceable in Marco's life via his bed, as well as the profit her films would bring. Only then she could warrant taking several months off from the vigour and required perfection of being the top billed star in the adult film industry to have a kid.

Trevor just hoped Hazel wouldn't inadvertently get herself in the family way during the honeymoon. That would be stupid. But Hazel wasn't stupid. She was as determined as him to reap the full benefit from this arrangement. Probably more. Astute as anything was his daughter.

Smiling, he turned his tumbler of whisky, enjoying how the light caught the diamond-cut faceted crystal. He tipped the remains of the spirit into his mouth, his body thrumming with satisfaction. He'd done well. He'd raised his daughter to know *exactly* how to play the game and she'd done a sterling job on every level. And, he didn't doubt, would continue to do so.

It was all thanks to *him*.

Trevor shoved what was left of the bottle of whisky into the last box of desk contents. There was no sense hanging around now he'd called time on the business. All there was left to do was get home and start enjoying his retirement.

Trevor shrugged on his jacket and made to leave the office. He had no regrets. None whatsoever.

Very soon, Hazel would return from honeymoon, eager to get back in front of the camera. And this time, it would be Luna Motion Film's cameras, rather than his at Starlight Studios.

Swinging around as the office door flew open with a loud crash, Trevor thought his eyes were deceiving him with the unmistakable figure of Zane Morelli in his doorway.

'Mr Grimes?' Zane stared around the boxed up office, his voice devoid of pleasantries. 'I understand you know my brother? It also seems what I've heard is correct - you're closing down?' His eyes narrowed. 'I guess you have no need of a studio since striking a deal with Marco in my absence?'

Trevor blinked several times in quick succession. He wasn't imagining this. This *was* the older Morelli - the one Marco had assured him would not be released from prison for the foreseeable future - if ever. Yet here he was in the flesh. In this office. *Which meant...*

Zane walked over to Trevor's desk and plucked the whisky bottle from the packing box. Holding it up, he glanced at the label. 'Not the best brand…' His face screwed up with distaste as he shoved it back into the box. 'Cat got your tongue, Mr Grimes?'

'I... It's just that… I… I'm surprised to see you,' Trevor blurted. 'I thought... thought that you...'

'Thought I wouldn't see the light of day again?' Zane folded his arms across his chest and stared at Trevor with cold blue eyes. 'My brother was mistaken if he told you I would not return to London. You see, he was aware I would be coming...'

And wasn't he just! Yes, Marco - his brother – a very loose terminology of someone alleged to be his kin knew that he would be here at some point in the near future. 'Marco also knew I would never agree to incorporate a business such as *this...*' He looked disparagingly at the framed photographs yet to be packed of semi-naked women on the walls. 'A business dealing in the flesh trade is not something I want as part of the Morelli portfolio.'

A mirthless smile cracked his face. 'So, do yourself a

favour and unpack your boxes, Mr Grimes. Contrary to what my brother may or may not believe, *I'm* in charge of the Morelli firm, therefore any deal made with him does not stand.'

Trevor's mouth hung loosely as he clawed his brain to make sense of what he was hearing. *The deal was off? What on earth?* 'But Marco, he is the...'

'Oh, and by the way.' Zane leant against a box of paperwork and casually inspected his leather gloves. 'I should offer my congratulations over the joining of your daughter with my dear brother. I guess that now makes us family? Rather unfortunate in my opinion, but then again, you can't choose who you fall in love with.' *And he knew that more than most.* 'Not that I believe this marriage was anything to do with love...'

Trevor's shock at the unexpected intrusion disintegrated as the glaring truth echoed inside him. It wasn't a pleasing truth. Not even slightly. If Zane Morelli was out, which he clearly was, and still the legitimate boss of his firm, rather than his brother, then this had all been for nothing.

Fuck.

His eyes narrowed. He wasn't having it. No way. He'd put *months* of effort into brokering this deal. Hazel had married Marco as agreed, so this arrangement was not being thrown away.

Anger overtook Trevor's sensibilities. Bravado was not something he usually possessed, even on a good day, but this was too important and all-consuming not to stop it in its tracks. There was no room for manoeuvre on this subject. 'You steam into my office and tell me the deal is off? You are mistaken.'

A chuckle escaped Trevor's mouth. Hazel would not betroth herself to anyone other than the true heir of the Morelli firm. He'd seen the bloody paperwork himself. His daughter was in line for the Morelli fortunes and that was not up for discussion. *Ever*. 'The deal is *not* off, Mr Morelli. My daughter married your brother and I have it in writing from his solicitor that you are no longer the legitimate owner of the business, so I suggest you check your facts.'

Turning his back, he made to stalk past Zane out of the office. 'Now, please leave before I do something I might regret.'

'Whereas I regret nothing, Mr Grimes,' Zane growled.

It was when Trevor made the mistake of moving his hand to rest on the butt of the pistol lodged in his waistband which sealed his fate.

He could have thought about how to deal with this unexpected spanner in the works sensibly before making the extremely dangerous move towards his gun. Unfortunately, he realised this far too late.

The fleeting crack as Zane Morelli's gun discharged wasn't nearly enough warning for Trevor to avoid the bullet from entering his skull.

• • • •

RETURNING TO THE HOUSE he'd rented the previous week, Zane was still in that frame of mind - the one where all senses were on high alert, strung out like over-tuned piano wire and brittle to the point where the slightest thing would cause that extra bit of tension required in order for him to snap.

He'd always been the same.

The way the evening had panned out had also accelerated his resentment towards his current situation and his brother's actions. Not that Marco and what he'd caused was ever far from his mind, but tonight had fuelled his hatred to the point where Zane could combust within himself. And he probably would be unable to hold the growing rage were it not for one thing.

As he shrugged his leather jacket off to reveal his blood-soaked clothes underneath, Zane's deep scowl faltered seeing Erin Langley's eyebrows raise.

Her expression was not a sign of shock or a signal that she was about to freak out. Neither did it mean she was about to question him to the nth degree. It was none of those things. It was a sign that he'd got lucky in his odd pairing with this remarkable woman because she was looking at him with sardonic amusement. And with this, his rage was defused - at least temporarily.

'What now?' Erin eyed Zane knowingly. 'I thought you went to talk?' She ran her eyes over Zane's T-shirt, the darkness of the blood obvious against the material.

It wasn't the blood which bothered her. Or even why it was there. She could hazard a guess at that. There was very little that surprised her with this man or the life she was part of.

She knew her way of thinking wasn't usual in comparison to most people, but to *her* it was. At least, it had been since her father was murdered in the name of 'business'. Since setting her mind to do anything and everything to take revenge for that there was nothing that could faze her, or more importantly, distract her from objectives.

Apart from perhaps Zane himself...

Pulling a cold bottle of beer from the fridge, Erin used the metal bottle opener to remove the cap, rather than letting Zane use his teeth - a habit of his that always made her cringe. 'I'm guessing you didn't stick to the planned agenda?'

She held the beer out, pausing as he pulled his T-shirt over his head, leaving it to fall onto the tiled kitchen floor. Her gaze ran over his defined chest and abdominal muscles, his sheer power never failing to ignite a spark deep within her.

Zane flipped the T-shirt into the washing machine and took the beer from Erin's hand. 'It was going fine until the twat thought about pulling a gun on me.'

'Only *thought* about?'

There were the eyebrows again, Zane mused, his foul mood neutralising more every minute. Erin was one hell of a woman - someone whose own anger with the injustice of the situation matched his. She was a woman that, if anything *did* faze her, he was yet to witness it. She was also someone who he'd immediately clicked with on a level that was difficult to explain. Despite until finally believing the truth about who had really murdered her father, Erin had been hellbent on killing him, but against all the odds, including the driving factor in bringing them into each other's orbit in the first place, they were meant for each other.

Yep, a woman unlike any other - capable of killing and who *had* killed someone, Erin was the only person in the world who understood him. They were a match made in heaven. Or hell, depending on which way it was looked upon.

Zane fought the need to pull her into his arms and take her right now. Whether he wanted to discuss this or not, there were things which had to be said.

He tipped the beer into his mouth, savouring the bitter taste. 'Grimes won't be discovered. Not before I regain control of my firm. Starlight Studios is closed, so no one will go in there until the removals and developer goes in. By that point, I'll be in control and no one can touch me.'

Erin nodded. She knew Zane's plans were to have control of the firm before Marco returned from honeymoon, but every second that piece of shit remained away meant another moment forced to live with the knowledge that the man was still breathing. In her opinion, that bastard shouldn't be on honeymoon. He should be in little pieces inside an incinerator somewhere.

But no matter how much it grated, Marco was out of the country and couldn't be dealt with until he returned and she could do nothing about that but wait. There was little point in fixating on something she could not change, but she didn't want anything further slowing up the end result either.

'As long as no one discovers the body.' Erin stepped forward and traced her fingers down Zane's bare chest. As usual, Zane's presence pulled her deeper like a high-powered magnet.

Determined not to remain stuck on facts that plagued her, she instead concentrated on the one thing she *could* deal with.

Him.

'As I said, no one will find Trevor Grimes until it's all over,' Zane murmured, his lips grazing Erin's. 'Even then, they'll have a job proving anything. Starlight Studios will be razed to the ground soon enough, but that needs to wait a while. It can't be done too early as it could get back to Marco. It will be done though.'

Putting his beer to one side, he effortlessly lifted Erin up and wrapped her legs around his waist. 'Now, enough of talking shop. I need my fix of you!'

She was the only thing to detract from the grinding rage running through his veins each day. And right now he needed a reminder of that. Since getting wind from Sonny Mitchell that certain people he needed to put his plan into action had been located, it was all systems go.

But that began tomorrow and this was *now*.

ONE

Three days later

IN A PRIVATE BACK ROOM of the White Saddle pub in Dalston that had been rented for the evening, Tiger Shoreham fixed his steely glare on that of his boss - or should he say, *had been* his boss. Now Zane was back, he'd become his boss once again.

Tiger was very glad about that, but had barely been able to believe his ears when he'd received a message that Zane Morelli wanted to see him. Initially, he hadn't believed it at all - especially as the messenger had been Sonny Mitchell.

Zane's side of staff had either been dispatched or binned off the second Marco took the reins. Sonny however, had remained and was therefore held with short shrift by the rest of who had once been Zane's men.

It wasn't difficult to deduce why. All those loyal to Giuseppe and then Zane after him, knew Marco's changes weren't how the firm operated. But those questioning the unpalatable direction the firm took were quickly removed one way or another. Many, permanently.

The men who had been under Marco's side of the business

- the majority being unimportant, had no cause for alarm or to jump ship. But for others, such as him and Leo Holland, who were loyal to Zane, could never give Marco Morelli credence to run the gaff. The man had never been a contender to do that in the first place, but that was before Zane got banged up.

The majority of Zane's loyal inner circle had their own version of why *that* had happened. But for the few who *did* jump ship, there had been no love lost towards how those traitors turned their backs on what Giuseppe and Zane stood for and arselicked their way into retaining their jobs by agreeing with Marco's warped way of thinking.

Bill Wainwright being one of them. That man being on Team Marco was no surprise. He was Marco's wing man on the enforcement arm from the off. But Sonny Mitchell?

His abandonment of right from wrong was a surprise. And that was why Tiger was convinced Sonny's message must be a set up.

However, it wasn't. And that's why Tiger was here now. In the three days since getting that message and touching base with Zane after all of this time, things were starting to move. And Tiger vowed to do everything in his power to help the man regain his rightful place and put the firm which had previously treated him so well until that psycho cokehead took the helm, back on track.

But it would take a hell of a lot of sorting out.

However, none of this meant he was comfortable with Mitchell being back in the know. As far as Tiger was concerned, that cunt had more faces than Big Ben. 'Is Sonny not joining us tonight?' he asked, not looking forward to receiving an affirmative answer.

Mulling over how best to answer the question, Zane pulled his cigarettes from his top pocket and lit one. He knew Sonny was not held in good stead with his men. Sonny's original choice has surprised him too. The man had never shown preference to him *or* his brother and had been loyal to the firm in general. But to choose the side of the brother intent on trashing the long standing hard work, and worse, being aware of Marco's plan to frame him for the murder of David Masters was difficult to bypass.

Zane pursed his lips. He now realised that Sonny had gone along with Marco's plans out of all-encompassing and terrifying fear, but that did not excuse the man's part in Zane's long incarceration, nor the unrest that followed. But when Zane had been on the cusp of killing Sonny for his involvement, he'd instead taken the standpoint that the man was more use alive than dead.

Sonny was the only person on the inside of Marco's version of the Morelli firm who could help Zane get where he needed to be - to deliver revenge on the brother he'd loved and protected his entire life and retrieve what was *his*.

Despite his initial cynicism over whether Sonny could be trusted, the man had put his neck on the line during Marco's wedding, so for that alone he should be given the benefit of the doubt.

Besides, it was the only option.

Raising his eyes to Tiger's, Zane gave a quick nod. 'Sonny isn't joining us tonight. He's at the studio.'

'More like he knows his presence ain't wanted,' Tiger muttered.

Zane gave Tiger a warning look. 'I'm aware you don't have time for him and I understand that, believe you me, but he's our only option until we get things sorted.' He tapped his cigarette against the ashtray. 'He passed my test, so this is how it's going to be and whether you agree with it or not, I expect you to respect my choice.'

Tiger inclined his head in acknowledgement. Zane was the boss and Tiger respected him more than anyone, but no, he didn't like it. Not one bit. 'Understood,' he muttered. 'But the less I have to do with that snake the better.'

Zane sighed. He knew this wouldn't be easy. Neither were things moving as quickly as he wanted, but they didn't have the numbers for another method. Not yet, anyway.

His thoughts were interrupted by a tap on the door of the small room. 'Yes?'

The door opened to reveal a man of equally big build as Zane and Tiger, sporting a face to turn the most congenial of moods to withering fear.

'Leo!' Zane grinned, jerking his head for the man to enter. 'What's the low down?'

Dropping his muscled bulk onto the chair, Leo waited as a barman skittered into the room to deposit fresh pints on the table. It was only after the man left, shutting the creaky door behind him, did he speak. 'I've found a couple more of the original crew, but I've yet to touch base with them.'

Zane nodded. Things had to be done without alerting suspicion. Without being 100 per cent sure who could be trusted, keeping a low profile was vital. It was a far cry from the days when everybody recognised him around his usual haunts. This was the main reason why he remained under the radar. It was frustrating, but necessary.

Being reduced to lurking around the backstreets of territories that weren't his was difficult. He was limited in what he could do and where he could go, but all of that would change soon.

Once he'd got the numbers to deal with Marco's minions - and there were lots of them, then he'd act. The men under the banner of the 'Morelli' firm might be nobodies, but numbers were numbers and within certain areas, these nonentities could be anywhere.

Zane's impatience rose. 'When do you think you'll be able to touch base with the people we need?'

Leo shrugged his large shoulders. 'I need to weigh up their surroundings more before I risk it. I haven't seen enough yet to warrant making that move. Give me a day or two, max.'

Zane nodded. Though the men in question were loyal, approaching them in a place that could contain others who *weren't*, would expose them all. So for now, at least, they had to tread carefully.

Five men, including himself and Sonny on the inside, was the bare minimum to have a chance of pulling this off. And until they got two more into the fold they were short.

Even then it would be a push.

No, he had to wait until everybody was in place, but that didn't make it any less frustrating.

Two

SONNY MITCHELL strutted down the corridor at Luna Motion Film studios acting like the confident stand-in boss of the Morelli empire in Marco's absence.

And he *was* confident. Not in this place or the people within it, but in the ability of the one man who could succeed in getting the firm out of the hands of the lunatic that was Marco Morelli and back to where it should be.

Sonny frowned. If Bill had lived to see the day when Marco was stripped of his power he would have been relieved.

Whatever Zane's opinion was of Bill remaining on Marco's side until his death, it didn't change that Sonny knew deep down that Bill would be glad about this turn of events.

Even though Bill had been Marco's man from the off, he'd seen the cracks forming. Everyone had. They all knew Marco was losing it. He was a liability and a danger to all.

Okay, Sonny understood why Zane had killed Bill. Bill would have killed Zane had he not got in first, but whatever Bill's faults, Sonny didn't half miss him. He missed him a lot. At least ousting Marco would go a small way in honouring Bill's memory. Bill's life had been lost, but what was happening now would help to stop the same thing from occurring to anyone else. Although it was a tall order - especially in the available time frame, Sonny had faith that if anyone could pull this off, it was Zane.

He tried but failed to stop the shiver from running through his body. He'd really thought his time was up when Zane cornered him the other week. He'd believed he was on his way to join Bill's unclaimed and unidentified body on a mortuary slab somewhere in the Midlands, but fate had something else in store.

And he wasn't messing up this second chance.

Sonny continued towards the room where he'd called a meeting for some of the staff. Taking a turning down the labyrinth of corridors, he suddenly noticed how quiet it was.

Unusually, there was no hustle and bustle of actresses and cameraman rushing from set to set.

A wisp of wariness crept into his veins. He hoped things hadn't gone awry with production. He knew many of the young actresses and actors were nervous over the increasing frequency of Marco's legendary rages, as well as the spate of 'accidents' which happened to some under Marco's employ, but if the cameras stopped rolling Marco would get to hear of it - even from a sun-drenched tropical island.

And if that happened, the man would return from honeymoon a lot sooner than expected, thwarting Zane's plans for a timely takeover.

Suddenly spotting Damon Sandler, Sonny breathed a sigh of relief. Not that he liked the man. In fact, he vehemently *despised* the bloke, but being as Damon was now in charge of the filming schedule he should know why it was so thin on the ground today.

'Damon!' Sonny shouted, catching up with Damon down the corridor. 'Where is everyone? I haven't seen the usual crowd here today. Is there a problem?'

Damon grinned. 'Problem? No! Everything Marco wanted to happen today is running like clockwork.'

Sonny masked his confusion. *What had been arranged?*

And furthermore, why wasn't he aware of it?

Worry bristled, his instinct screaming that whatever it was, wasn't good. 'What with having to step into Bill's shoes, I've lost track of what day of the fucking week it is,' he deflected.

'I know the feeling.' Damon said. 'The good news is there's been no whining from unions. Not that Marco allowed those silly cunt actors to be part of one. As for the cameramen, they're just glad for a couple of days off.'

'Yeah,' Sonny agreed, still not having the first clue what was going on.

'You want to see them? They arrived an hour ago. We can test them out when the first shipment arrives in a couple of days. Marco will be well chuffed. Oh, sorry, I forgot you've called a meeting. Afterwards, maybe?'

With interest as well as mounting dread as to what Marco had planned, Sonny decided the meeting could wait. 'No, it's fine. Show me.'

Grinning, Damon jerked his head at the opposite corridor and strode off.

Sonny followed, the general quiet of the usually loud studio becoming more and more disconcerting. *How could he have not noticed the silence?* And what did Damon mean about unions? Furthermore, the cameraman *never* got time off. Why would Marco allow that?

Damon stopped outside a room sporting a heavy metal door. 'I've had them put in this recording studio. It's one of the only soundproof places!' He rolled his eyes. 'Hope you've got a pair of ear plugs because I suspect we'll need them at first until they accept their obligations.'

Sonny frowned, even more confused. *Had he missed something?*

As Damon unlocked the door and slung it open, Sonny balked at the rows of metal cages, each one reaching the ceiling, the thick metal frames and doors strong enough to withstand the angriest of animals. A horrible feeling descended. 'What the fuck?'

'I know there's lots of the bloody things,' Damon laughed. 'I must admit I didn't expect there to be quite so many, but don't worry, the use of this recording studio is only temporary.'

Sonny's eyes fell to Damon proudly patting the gun secured at his hip.

'There's only so long the fuckers will think it clever to make a racket. Taking out a couple to hammer home the importance of obedience will do the trick. There's bound to be a few ugly ones too, so I'll offload those first.' Damon laughed heartily. 'Like Marco says, you never know what you'll get doing business with foreigners!'

Fighting from revealing his shock, Sonny pulled his mouth into the expected grin. He couldn't make Damon aware that he hadn't been party to this plan. 'You'd best fill me in with the details. Marco only gave me a quick rundown,' he lied.

Leaving the room housing the claustrophobic cages, Sonny led the way back to his office. Or rather, Marco's. He'd reschedule the meeting. It was more important to find out what the fuck had been organised because as well as *him* not liking it in any way, shape or form, he was sure that Zane would like it even less.

• • • •

ERIN LANGLEY had been watching out of the window for an hour. It had achieved nothing, apart from confirming there was no sign of Zane. There was only the usual procession of random people en route to the small bank of shops at the end of the road.

This place Zane had rented in Dalston was all right, as far as run down housing estates went. The area was busy, with a lot of people coming and going. It was easy enough to blend in without anyone taking a blind bit of notice. But most importantly, it was the other side of the river from territory the Morellis held. Although this cut down the chance of Zane being recognised, it did run the risk if anyone of note *did* spot him, they would ask the question why a Morelli was on foreign turf.

Actually, they wouldn't ask the question - they would *react* and that was not a good prospect. But they'd had to pick somewhere to stay and this was as good a place as any.

Erin stared at the replacement mobile phone in her hand. She didn't expect it to ring. Why would it? No one, short of Sonny had their new numbers. On his advice, they had both ditched their previous mobiles. After Zane's contact with Anthony and Bill, their whereabouts could be tracked. Although Sonny usually dealt with such things, it didn't mean someone else couldn't. Sonny's change of job from tech wizard to Marco's right-hand man meant another person could now be undertaking his previous work. Especially if Marco harboured suspicions.

She frowned. Sonny had assured Zane that Marco suspected nothing, but it made sense to prevail on the side of caution. Although Erin agreed with that, she remained unconvinced about Sonny. Why would Zane offer his trust to someone who had been part of his downfall? She didn't like Sonny Mitchell on any level, but Zane was insistent the man held the key.

Erin drummed her fingers on the rotten wood of the windowsill. Tracked phones or not, she was the one stuck here day in, day out, whereas Zane was out and about busy putting his plans into motion. She'd barely seen him for the last couple of days and she was going stir crazy from sitting around waiting.

And waiting for nothing because she wasn't part of anything.

The throb of resentment stirred. She didn't want to wait. She wanted to act. Zane's plans made sense, but it didn't make her feel better. The gulf between what she and Zane wanted to achieve from this differed. She wanted revenge on her father's murderer, nothing else.

Erin bit down on her bottom lip. The way she felt about Zane was something she'd never experienced with anyone else before. It was something she hadn't believed she was even *capable* of. But was it the real deal?

Yes, they had chemistry. *Lots* of it, but things were blurring around the edges. The question had returned more than once during the long days of waiting in the wings, whether what she and Zane had was true or whether it had spawned only from the circumstances of how they'd been thrown together in the first place.

Was what she felt really love or merely a shared need for revenge? Even their versions of that now differed.

Shaking her head, Erin stood up and paced the length of the sitting room. It took all of three seconds. Too much time to think didn't help either. The endless stretch of hours manifested unwanted questions and she was driving herself mad.

She'd already killed the man who had tortured her mentally and physically for six years and she had no regrets about that. But it hadn't escaped her notice that she'd only been granted the option of doing it because Zane decided it should be that way. He'd *allowed* it.

Had he taken the option to kill Anthony Walker himself, like he'd planned, then she'd be living with the resentment of being robbed of doing what had kept her going all these years. The only thing which had allowed her to cope with her parents' deaths and the turmoil and grief which followed.

Was it normal for a couple to argue over who killed who?

Definitely not, but nothing about her and Zane's life was normal.

More to the point, were they even a 'couple' in the real sense of the word? She'd thought they might be, but now she wasn't so sure and a real fear was developing that without the shared revenge and wrongdoing, their relationship wouldn't exist.

Erin hoped that wasn't the case, but it played on her mind more and more each day.

How could she tell? When would she know?

It was an impossible question.

A bit like the one she kept asking Zane: *When is your fucking brother going to die?*

THREE

ERIN HEARD ZANE'S MOTORBIKE arrive long before she spotted him pull up. Eager to finally see another living soul, especially him, after a whole day of being stuck inside, she rushed into the hallway to wait. But the usual urge to press her lips to his and fall into bed was slowly replaced with frustration. *How long did it take for him to walk from his bike into the bloody house?*

As the front door opened, she darted forward, only to be warned off – Zane's raised hand demanding silence. She noted the mobile pressed close to his ear, along with the livid expression on his face.

'Yeah, get yourself round here as soon as possible. I need more information about this,' he snarled as he stalked past towards the kitchen to dump a carrier bag on the table.

Following Zane, Erin watched while he ended the call and then stared at the blank screen of his mobile. 'Who was that?'

Zane looked up, his blue eyes flashing dangerously. 'Christ, Erin! More questions? What do you want to know now?'

Erin tensed, Zane's attitude igniting her fuse. 'For God's sake! I only asked you who it was!'

Shrugging his leather off, Zane dumped the jacket over the

back of a kitchen chair. He pulled a bottle of beer from the carrier bag and ripped the metal top off with his teeth. 'Sonny's coming over. I need to talk to him.' He nodded to the bag. 'I've brought back some stuff for dinner so rustle something up for him as well, would you?'

Erin's hands clenched into fists. 'What am I? A fucking skivvy?' She peered into the bag. 'Two chicken breasts? Is that it? What am I supposed to make with those to feed three people when there's nothing else in the house?'

'You'll think of something,' Zane muttered. Why couldn't Erin understand that he needed to concentrate? What did he know about cooking? He'd bought something to eat, hadn't he?

Erin yanked the chicken from the bag and stared at the small pieces of meat. This wasn't much different to Anthony barking orders at her. Another example of what was preying on her mind. She and Zane hadn't *chosen* to live together. Although they shared a bed and did so willingly, their relationship hadn't progressed in a standard way.

Being kidnapped by the man she'd wrongly believed to have murdered her father and then being forced to work with him to rid the world of her fiancé wasn't a natural course for any new relationship, if it could be called that. And now living together in this second house whilst waiting to remove Marco Morelli from the world might be sensible where logistics were concerned, but it didn't mean they should forge a relationship which otherwise would never get off the ground.

Was this not a case of too much, too fast?

The red hot chemistry which had evolved between them from the start was one thing, but that alone was not enough to sustain anything else.

Her fears may be proved right. Their attraction was just that. *Attraction.* Whether anything deeper would develop remained to be seen and it wasn't looking promising. Zane had started to blow hot and cold. One minute he couldn't get enough of her and other times it was like she didn't exist.

Yes, she knew he had a lot on his mind with this business

with his firm and scheming to kill his own brother, but it wasn't like *she* hadn't had a fucked up life!

A twinge of regret twisted Erin's heart. Despite its difficult inception she'd really thought they had something, but maybe not. Whatever happened, she wasn't being a slave to anyone again. For *anything*.

Erin watched Zane kick his boots off, leaving them in a messy pile in the centre of the kitchen and then scowled with irritation as he flopped down in the chair with his beer. 'If you reckon I can make something with this and extra for one of your mates who, I might add, was part of setting you up, then I'm sure you can do just as well!'

Zane rolled his eyes. 'Give it a rest! I've got important things to deal with.'

Erin launched the packet of chicken across the room in frustration. 'I'm sick of being spoken to like a piece of shit! I've had enough of that in the past and I'm not taking it off you or anyone! I'm trapped in this house whilst you go off here, there and everywhere and I won't put up with it.'

Zane watched Erin's chest heave with anger. After what he'd just learned, he could do without her having an outburst, but then again, she *was* stuck here and he may have been guilty of speaking to her like a kitchen maid…

He accepted this business with Marco was overtaking his whole life. He knew he had a tendency to fixate on certain parts instead of looking at the whole picture. He'd promised himself he wouldn't lose sight of other things – things he'd never imagined would be open to him. Like in the form of Erin Langley.

A smile inched onto his face. Erin was definitely a picture he liked looking at. Aside from anything else, her display of temper reminded him exactly why everything about this wildcat, crazy enough to match him, ticked his boxes. The way they'd met hadn't been the best, sure, but it was what it was, and he'd be damned if his fucking brother and the ensuing aftermath would ruin anything else.

Slamming his beer down, he got to his feet and strode over to Erin, her defiant eyes meeting his. 'Have you finished?'

'You don't scare me,' Erin spat as Zane towered above her. 'I'm sick of waiting for that bastard brother of yours to get what's coming to him and I'm sick of *you*!'

'That's why I want you, Erin Langley,' Zane growled, effortlessly pulling Erin towards him. He needed to remind her as well as himself, that he still wanted and needed her desperately, regardless of how he may act.

Crushing his body against hers, the corner of his mouth twitched into another knowing smile. 'I love that you're not scared of me.' His hand traced the length of her side. 'You might be fed up with waiting, but you're not sick of me. Not yet, anyway.'

Crushing his mouth to hers, Zane lifted Erin up and deposited her on the kitchen table.

Erin couldn't stop the moan from escaping her mouth as Zane pushed her knickers to one side. He was right. She wasn't sick of him and doubted whether she ever would be. She just hoped the additional pressures surrounding their less than conventional relationship wouldn't scupper things between them before whatever they had became properly established.

Because when all was said and done, she believed they had something worth hanging onto.

• • • •

'IT'S, ERM... CURRY,' Erin said, watching Sonny tentatively poke a small piece of chicken floating within the sea of sauce on his plate.

Sonny smiled, wishing he was anywhere else but here. Was it not bad enough to have dumped this news on Zane in the first place, without coming round here only to get no answer and proceed to make the fatal mistake of peering through the window to see this pair going at it like rabbits on the kitchen table?

Worse than that, Erin had spotted him looking through the

crack in the curtains like a pervert. Red-faced, he'd been let in to quickly recount what he'd discovered today, whilst Erin busied herself making, well, whatever this was on his plate...

He glanced across the table, convinced his face still remained the colour of a tomato. 'The dinner's lovely, Erin. Thank you,' he mumbled awkwardly.

'What's not lovely, is what's going on at the studios,' Zane grunted.

'I don't understand why you haven't already shut the place down!' Erin cried. 'If adult entertainment isn't and won't be part of your firm, then why is Luna still operating?'

Her frown deepened. The day they had arrived in Battersea to discover the firm's headquarters now operated from little more than a jumped-up porn shop, Zane had said he was shutting Marco's brainchild of Luna Motion Films down. But nearly a week later the studio was still going strong. 'From what I've just heard it's worse than ever! You can't allow this place to continue! Trading in people's fucking lives is different to smutty films with willing participants!'

Zane slurped the mainly liquid curry into his mouth. 'I want nothing to do with that shit, but I have little choice but to keep the studios going for the time being. If I shut it, then everyone will know I'm here and they'll disperse. I have to bide my time.'

Again? Erin thought bitterly. The session Sonny had rudely interrupted may have served to remind her that Zane owned a piece of her heart, but that didn't remove the nagging resentment that Marco was still breathing. And trafficking people? Planning to keep them in cages to use against their wishes? It was disgusting! 'Your brother has extended his ways of making money to one of the worst kind.'

Zane rubbed his hand over his chin. He couldn't disagree and the concept of allowing Luna to remain operating even for one day longer grated. Flesh in films was one thing, but trafficking *people* was another! And he wasn't quite sure how to deal with it.

'You should see the state of those cages,' Sonny added. 'It

took all of my power not to react. Damon sees no issue with the instructions Marco issued before his honeymoon.'

Not for the first time Zane regretted not grabbing the opportunity to take his brother out on the day of the wedding when he had the chance.

'You've got to sort this, Zane.' Erin slammed her fork down on the table. 'It's not right. You must stop this!'

'You think I don't know that?' Zane roared, his eyes flashing. But how could he 'stop it' without blowing his cover? In addition, if he did that, then the unexpected human cargo due to arrive could be dispatched in order to remove the proof. 'Like it or not, we're stuck with the studios for now.'

Sonny looked at Zane, then Erin and then back again. Considering this pair were forced together, they did a good job of acting like they'd been married for years. The unusual fact for someone in Zane's position and line of work to speak openly about the firm's business in front of a woman spoke volumes too.

Zane clearly trusted Erin and by all accounts she was far from a standard woman. But it didn't change that Zane was stuck with moving on this for the time being. 'You can't go to Luna yet anyway,' he said. 'Marco's not due back for another week and you know we haven't yet got enough men to warrant the takeover.'

Zane cracked his knuckles, his frustration growing by the second. 'Then Sonny, you need to move onto the film side of things full time. A close eye must be kept on those women due to arrive. Do anything required to stall them from being utilised. I don't care what it takes. I will not be party to *that* happening to these people, whoever they are.'

'How can I do that as well as run the rest of the business in Marco's absence?' Sonny exclaimed. 'If I suddenly start dealing with this over Damon Sandler, then he for one will get suspicious. He knows I have little to do with filming and scheduling and he'll report it to Marco, honeymoon or not!'

'For fuck's sake!' Zane screamed. 'I don't give a shit what

that cunt Sandler thinks! Trafficking people puts a different slant on things. A completely different slant!'

Sonny began to panic. 'But… but I can't! I'll never get away with it!'

'No, you won't,' Erin agreed. 'But *I* will. I can do it. I'll go in there full time.'

'What?' Sonny gasped. 'That's insane. You'll…'

'Absolutely no fucking way!' Zane's fist crashed onto the table, his plate jumping an inch into the air. 'You think I'll let you go into that filthy fucking porn-hub of my brother's making to be screwed by God knows who, along with the poor bastards in cages? You must be mad. I won't allow it!'

Erin stared at Zane incredulously. 'Allow it? I don't need *your* permission! Besides, I'm not planning on starring in their bloody sick films! I mean to *work* there!'

Sonny fully expected Zane to react to Erin's blatant dismissal of his words, but there was nothing. *This had to be an all-time first!*

Erin turned to Sonny. 'You say there's no suspicions on you, right?'

'Yes, but...'

'Then employ me. I don't know what as. How about admin? Or a bookkeeper, film scheduler, whatever. That way I can keep tabs on what's going on and we get the upper hand. If you're acting as the boss whilst...' She could barely bring herself to speak *that* man's name... 'Marco is absent, then you have the clout to employ someone to work in whichever area you see fit, do you not?'

'Well, yes… I…' Sonny glanced at Zane. 'It could work. There's no admin staff anymore. Marco got rid of everybody apart from the cameramen. His paranoia convinced him that they were all talking about him and speculating abo...'

'No! It's too dangerous,' Zane barked. 'You said before that Marco has seen a photo of Erin. If I remember rightly, it was *you* who showed him one of her and Flame from the paper.'

Erin glared at Sonny with renewed dislike. *Had he indeed?*

And Zane still felt able to trust this man?

'It's highly likely Marco won't recognise her. You have no idea what he's like these days, Zane,' Sonny sighed. 'He's snorted so much shit his brain is fried. He can't even remember what day of the bloody week it is!'

'That's sorted then!' Erin said triumphantly.

Zane shook his head, his anger intensifying. He gave Sonny an extra glare for encouraging the situation. 'So, you reckon I've been off the scene long enough to assume I don't know the state of my own brother these days? Okay, let's suppose you're right and it's doubtful Erin will be recognised... But whatever you "presume", it's not *definite*. Neither does it mean someone *else* won't recognise her. It's too risky.'

Erin rolled her eyes. 'No it's not!' This was her chance to get out and do something to speed this shit up, as well as stop people being forced against their will to perform for that wanker's bank balance. 'For God's sake, Zane, you said yourself things are moving too slowly. This way I can be there as well. Two sets of ears and eyes are better than one. Have you any better ideas?'

'It was only Marco and Bill who saw the photo of Erin and Flame,' Sonny added, unwilling to throw more fuel on the fire but *something* had to be done.

Meeting Zane's icy-cold stare, Erin continued. '*I* think it's worth the risk and it's the only feasible idea that we have to keep control under the circumstances. You can't let this trafficking happen, Zane.' She moved her gaze to Sonny. 'I'm doing it.'

'You're *not* doing it, Erin,' Zane barked.

Sonny nervously glanced between Zane and Erin, conscious of this new battle of wills. This woman was either crazy or had a genuine place in Zane Morelli's heart.

When Zane said no, no one dared to argue, short of *this* bird. Maybe there really was more to their pairing than he'd first thought. Either way, he wasn't hanging around to experience the fallout.

Standing from the table, he forced a smile. 'Thanks for dinner. I'll leave you both to it. Let me know what's been decided.'

The loaded silence as Sonny left the room leaving Zane and Erin glaring at each other was deafening.

FOUR

GRABBING HIS CRASH HELMET, Zane wrapped the bandana over his mouth and nose and made his way to his bike. It was unlikely anyone would recognise him under the helmet, but as he was venturing onto his own turf again today he had to be extra vigilant.

Slinging his leg over the Yamaha FJ1200, he fired the engine, the throaty roar collecting looks from people along the street where he now lived.

Pulling back on the throttle, Zane sped up the road, glad to be out of the distinctly frosty atmosphere of the house. Since Sonny left last night he and Erin had done nothing but argue. Half the bloody night it had gone on and he was knackered.

Erin was a stubborn mare, but she did have a point…

Whatever the logic behind Erin becoming a mole and working at Luna Motion Films, he was far from convinced it was a good idea. But it was also true that he didn't have any better ones. Not that could be put into practice so quickly, anyway.

But it was still a risk. And a *huge* one.

Regardless of what Sonny believed, surely Marco or the men at Luna weren't so deranged to not recognise Flame's fiancée? Any number of them could have seen that newspaper article.

Just thinking of Flame made Zane's skin prickle. That the man was now dead did little to quell the hatred he still harboured for the bastard who'd been so instrumental in the time he'd served behind bars.

And okay, Zane now knew the setup had been under Marco's orders, but that didn't deflect from what Flame had been part of. Or that he'd treated Erin like utter dirt. That was not something he could gloss over.

Zane squinted against the bright sunlight as he sped towards Battersea. Perhaps granting Erin her wish of removing Flame herself had been the wrong thing to do? Despite her initial exhilaration, since doing it she'd progressed into not coping as well as he'd hoped. She'd become more abrasive and spiky than usual. Yes, she'd been hot-headed since the minute he'd first seen her, but on top of that, and perhaps more disturbingly, the overpowering connection they'd shared had changed.

Admittedly, he'd been brusque of late, his mind full to capacity with what he must do rather than ploughing his attention onto her. But he wasn't the sort to arrange romantic boat trips or fucking picnics if that's what she expected.

Whatever the reasons for Erin's impatience, either with him or the general situation, it had morphed into angry resentment, aimed at *him*. Could she not understand that as much as he wanted to, he couldn't just steam in, kill Marco and reclaim his firm just like *that*?

Marco wasn't even in the country. But even if he was, things must be done correctly otherwise more people would die. Enough people had become Marco's victims already.

There was also the continually nagging issue that Marco was his little brother...

Even though Zane knew the end object must be achieved, it pained him relentlessly. But now these foreign women were arriving in a matter of days, there was no choice but to allow Erin to be a new pair of ears and eyes. He just hoped that Sonny was correct with his theory because if *anyone* inside Luna recognised her, then…

Pulling into the cemetery on Swain's Lane, Zane parked up. Leaving his bike in the small car park, he made his way into the graveyard and glanced into the distance at the church where mourners surrounded a hearse.

Zig zagging his way through the graves, some new, some old with inscriptions no longer readable on the weathered stone, Zane picked his way to where Sonny said his father lay.

He gritted his teeth. If Sonny hadn't told him he wouldn't know where his father was *buried*, let alone where the grave was located. Something else Marco had promised to give him details of but despite constant reminders, had failed. Another casualty of the time he'd been stuck in nick with the stigma of everyone believing he'd been the one behind the hit on David Masters.

Zane had nothing to do with that hit. *Marco* had and passed the blame onto Flame. They'd *all* been in on it. Worse still, his father had died believing the son he'd trusted to inherit and run the firm he'd sweated blood and tears to build up from scratch could not be trusted.

Pushing away his growing rage, Zane trod carefully between the gravestones, the back of the headstone he believed to be his father's now in view.

Apprehension bubbled. He couldn't even attend the funeral.

Clenching his jaw, he turned to face the headstone.

GIUSEPPE ALPHONSE MORELLI

4th March 1928 - 15th February 1996

'Sorry I didn't make the funeral, Dad,' Zane said, the unwanted lump uncomfortable in his throat.

He didn't care if it was stupid talking to a gravestone marking the place of a body who no longer had capacity to hear. No one was around to see but Zane didn't give a shit if they were. This was what he wanted to say. *Needed* to say. He wanted his father to witness the explanation he'd spent six long years waiting to give, whatever way it could be offered.

Now, this *was* the only way.

He placed his hand on the polished granite stone. 'I hope you know I had no hand in dishonouring your wishes,' he continued, feeling like a small boy again. He forced away the threatening burn of tears at the back of his eyes.

Did his father know the truth now? Did he realise the son he'd always shared a special bond with hadn't let him down and never would?

'I intend to put the firm right and...' Zane's words tailed off as he read the rest of the inscription etched proudly into the stone underneath his beloved father's name:

Father, husband and hero
Your legacy will live on in your only son

Zane's first reaction was to rip the headstone from the ground with his bare hands.

Only son?

Marco had arranged the funeral and headstone. He'd also clearly arranged the words!

Could this slight be any more offensive?

Resolve burned fiercer than ever. Since his betrayal, Marco had been demoted to a brother in name only and even that ate away at his insides. But *this* was something else!

How dare Marco attempt to delete him from his father's memory. If the other things his brother had done over the past six years weren't bad enough, this was the final insult and if it were possible, cut deeper than everything else.

Blinded by rage and unable to comprehend the gross injustice of what he had seen, Zane was about to leave the graveside when he spotted flowers at the base of the headstone.

'You come here and lay fucking flowers, do you, Marco, you lying piece of shit?' he spat, snatching up the small bouquet.

There was still some life left in these flowers - more than would shortly be said about Marco.

Zane couldn't remove the headstone and wouldn't, but he could take *these* as a token to express his black rage and disgust.

Stomping away, about to shred the flowers with his hands, Zane paused.

Oh look! A card too...

Zane frowned. *Skye? Who was Skye?*

Slightly defeated that his small act of revenge was pointless, Zane backtracked and replaced the bouquet. Whoever Skye was, she wasn't Marco.

Pressing his lips to the top of the headstone as a final gesture, Zane whispered, 'I hope you understand why I have to do what I'm planning.'

Walking away, he replaced the bandana around his face and made his way back to his bike.

• • • •

BEING IN THE CLOSE PROXIMITY of Sonny Mitchell again so soon was not top of Erin's to-do list, but she had pushed for this. It was what was needed, despite how much Zane was against it.

As Sonny manoeuvred his way through the London traffic

from Dalston to Battersea, Erin pressed her forehead against the passenger seat window, grateful for the change of scenery.

The heavy silence in the car prompted Sonny to speak. He'd fully expected Zane to be present when he'd collected Erin. The surprise phone call first thing to say Erin entering Luna Motion Films was going ahead was also unexpected.

On arriving at the house, Sonny had braced himself for a barrage of what he should and shouldn't allow, but Zane was absent. To where, Erin hadn't volunteered, but then she'd barely uttered a word since getting into the car, her dislike for him permeating the air like a miasma. 'Zane's all right about you doing this now?' he asked.

Erin sighed. 'Not particularly, but he's agreed to it on a trial basis.'

Not particularly, was an understatement. Zane *really* didn't want her doing this. Considering the hours they'd argued about it last night, there could be no confusion over that. He'd tried the heavy-handed approach - the way she imagined he worked with everyone else, but it didn't work with her.

Too long she'd put up with orders and instructions. Too long she'd toed the line and danced to others' tunes that went against every moral fibre in order to attain her objectives. But no longer. This time, she was standing her ground. If her presence in Marco Morelli's shitty film studio sped up the process of stopping that bastard in his tracks, then she'd do anything.

Zane may be a dangerous man - a *very* dangerous man, but she wasn't sitting back and accepting everything he said. She *couldn't*, knowing women would be caged and abused for perverts' pleasure. She would do everything in her power to prevent this horrible new scheme of Marco's going any further. She didn't want anything worse happening to the women due to arrive than what had already happened to them. And she dreaded to think what that might be.

Plus, if being inside Luna Motion Films mean speeding up Zane taking back control of his firm then it was worth any risk she may face.

Erin watched a child and his mother slowly move over a zebra crossing, her determination rising further.

She didn't know how or even *if* she could prevent things continuing with those trafficked women, but she'd give it her best shot. She'd do whatever it took to end this for Zane.

And for herself.

'I know you don't like me very much, Erin, and I understand why, but if we are to work together for a while, you need to make the effort so it looks believable. We can't have anyone getting suspicious.'

Sonny's voice startled Erin from her thoughts. Her skin burnt with irritation. *Make the effort? Did he think her stupid?* 'At this precise moment, it is just you and I,' she said coldly. 'I do not need to put on an act until I get there, but do not worry, I'm adept at being whoever I need to be when the time arises. But you're right, I don't like you. I think you're fake and two-faced.'

She saw a small, yet fast twitch in Sonny's jaw. 'But I won't get you killed, if that's what's worrying you.'

Sonny remained silent, his initial respect of this woman's bolshiness and ability to hold her own to the likes of Zane Morelli, diminishing. He understood her resentment that on the surface he hadn't done right by Zane, but he'd risked life and limb to put that right since and he intended to continue doing so.

Taking his eyes from the road, he cut Erin a quick measured look. 'Lady, I get what you're saying, but acting like a spiky bitch won't help. I'm doing what needs to be done to put things right, as are you, so I suggest you meet me halfway. We need to watch each other's backs.'

'Why? Before you stick a knife in anyone else's?' Erin retorted.

'Like you tried with Zane, you mean?' Sonny fired back equally rapidly. 'Yeah, he told me of your exploits, so let's just leave things there and get on with it, shall we?'

'Touché!' Erin begrudgingly swallowed that Sonny had her bang to rights there. Her first attack on Zane with that penknife and then stabbing him with a corkscrew hadn't been her finest hour.

Sensing the ceasefire in Erin's attitude and considering they were now not far from the studio, Sonny felt it apt to push the subject onto something relevant. 'I guess I should fill you in with the story I've given to explain your "employment".'

'I guess you should,' Erin said, somewhat sulkily but civilly. Behaving like a child achieved little. It certainly wouldn't end Marco's life any quicker. If anything, it might even prolong it. However distasteful she found Sonny's past misdemeanours, he was all she had once within Luna Motion Films, so she'd best get used to it.

'I brought you some suitable stuff to wear that we had knocking around the studios,' Sonny said. 'It's in a bag on the back seat.'

Erin rolled her eyes and reached over to grab the bag. She'd have to wear whatever Sonny suggested. She couldn't afford to screw this up for anyone's sake.

FIVE

MARCO PUSHED HIS designer wraparound shades half an inch down the bridge of his nose to see who was causing the shadow to fall across his bronzing body.

The minute his eyes were exposed to the blistering sun, the shadow moved, blasting his eyeballs with searing light. 'Fuck!' he yelped, closing one eye.

With his one remaining eye, he glared at the waiter depositing fresh drinks on the table between the sun loungers and felt like smashing his beer bottle into the twat's face. 'Get out of the fucking way,' he barked. 'And what are those? I didn't order that shit!'

The waiter fumbled to place the heavily laden cocktails on the glass table, gingerly nudging the overflowing ashtray to one side. 'Y-your wife ordered them, sir,' he stuttered, wiping his wet fingers on the starched white cloth draped over his other arm.

As much as he tried not to let his eyes wander in the direction of the woman next to Marco, it was impossible. The voluptuous blonde with her oversized sunglasses and glossy fuchsia-coloured lips was difficult to bypass. Especially with breasts *that* size on show. And, as in *completely* on show. The only item of clothing she sported was the tiny triangle of sea-green metallic bikini bottoms which was barely worth wearing. 'Erm, I'll just empty your ashtray and...'

'Don't think I haven't clocked you ogling my wife. She's *my* wife, not yours, so take your fucking nosy, boggling eyes, along with your hard-on and do one! I'll have you fired if you look at her again, you pervert!'

'Sorry sir, yes sir.' Bowing and scraping, the waiter rapidly skittered away.

Marco swerved his glare back to the tall glasses on the table which held a strange combination of red and green liquid with a clear division between the colours. Crystals of sugar or salt lined the glass rims, along with a selection of fruit strategically placed at intervals. There were even stupid paper umbrellas perched on the top.

Marco felt like shoving Hazel off her sun lounger for ordering this crap. Couldn't she have got him beer or a fucking whisky?

'You didn't have to be so mean to that poor man, babe,' Hazel drawled, swivelling her long legs over the side of the sun lounger.

'Yes I did,' Marco muttered. 'People think they can stare at you? Well, they can't! I'll have them all fucking killed!'

He could see why they were looking though. His new wife, soon to be the top billing star of his porn films, was every inch the stunner her reputation dictated. And she was his. *His*.

No one should forget that. He'd paid enough for her, what with that overpriced shite Hazel had insisted on for the wedding. The fucking ring alone had set him back more than the average mortgage, but he wouldn't begrudge her that. In fact, he wouldn't begrudge her anything. He'd hankered after Hazel, or Lisa Tequila, as was her stage name, for too many years. Now she was his and courtesy of the arrangement he'd made with her money-grabbing father, he'd got everything he dreamed of.

Short of one thing...

His brother going against everything he'd put in place by getting released from jail had taken the edge off his happiness. Plus, from what he'd gathered, Zane was now aware that *he* was the mastermind behind his incarceration. This wasn't good and Marco would not be content until he'd received word that Zane was contained ready to be removed from his orbit.

Opening the leather pouch he'd had specially commissioned to clip on to swimming trunks, he fished out a small silver vial fashioned into the shape of a bullet. Unscrewing the top, he removed the tiny spoon and snorted a small, heaped measure of cocaine up his left nostril.

It wasn't the same as doing a nice fat line, but that was difficult outside. The tropical breeze around the hotel's luxurious swimming pool would blow it all over him and that would piss him off no end.

'You shouldn't be doing that out here.' Hazel's long fingernails traced an enticing line down Marco's oiled-up abs. 'Someone might see you.'

'What if they do?' Marco said, already feeling the stir in his overtight speedos. 'No one will do fuck all.'

And the reason why? Because he was Marco Morelli - the kingpin, the top of his game and the man who everyone wanted to be. Even from the other side of the world...

This self-inflated grandeur calmed Marco down a notch. He'd promised himself he wouldn't dwell on what was going on back home whilst he was away with his new wife. This was his honeymoon and Sonny had assured him things would remain under control until he returned.

When Zane showed his face, which he *would* at some point, he'd be kept under lock and key to wait like the sad animal he was until the time of Marco's choosing.

Admittedly, Marco had been tempted to put in a call to see if Zane had been apprehended. It was only a matter of time before his arsehole brother made a 'heroic' attempt to trample over his hard work, but so far he'd refrained from picking up the phone.

Anyway, there had been no calls to the emergency mobile he'd brought along just to be on the safe side, so he should switch off and enjoy his honeymoon.

But maybe putting in a quick call wouldn't hurt? The first shipment of his new venture was due to arrive tomorrow as well, so perhaps he should touch base with Damon and...

No, he wouldn't!

This. Was. His. Honeymoon!

'Ooh! This is divine!' Hazel gushed, her pouty lips sucking at the cocktail straw. 'You should try yours, babe. And…' Her hand trailed lower, her fingers following the line of hair from Marco's navel to disappear underneath the edge of his low cut trunks. 'Don't get stressed over people like that waiter. You should be flattered men find me attractive.'

It didn't take much to deflect Marco from the argument within his head. The tight lycra covering of his trunks would not conceal or withstand the pressure from his urgent arousal. 'I don't care what any other fucker thinks,' he growled, lifting Hazel onto his sun lounger. 'You belong to me and therefore I only care what *I* think.'

'Marco!' Hazel squealed in pretend horror as Marco hoisted her astride him, his thick fingers deftly pushing her triangle of a bikini to one side. 'We can't do this out here in front of all these people!'

'Why the fuck not?' Marco freed himself from the constraints of his trunks and pulled Hazel down onto him. 'You do this with a film crew watching, so you'll behave as I see fit.'

Giggling, Hazel splayed her hands on Marco's chest as he thrust his hips upwards. She winked mischievously at the man on the sun lounger opposite gaping at the spectacle in open-mouthed shock.

Unfortunately, the sun, cocktails and power had a worrying ability of enabling her to gloss over the warning signs she should be heeding from the man she'd recently married.

• • • •

'WHO THE FUCK IS THAT?' Damon hissed, pulling Sonny to one side.

Sonny shrugged his arm out of Damon's grip. Some people could do with being set straight. Men who had only joined the firm since Marco took the helm might only remember him as the firm's ex-tech guru, wandering around with a laptop under his arm, but they would do well to learn that *prior* to that, he'd been an enforcer. A competent one at that, as well as not one to be messed with.

The ability of which Sonny was rapidly recalling.

Not only that but since Bill's death, Sonny was Marco's right-hand man, so in the absence of the organ grinder he was the fucking boss.

'Let's get some things straight,' Sonny snarled through clenched teeth. He glared at Erin further down the corridor eyeing them dubiously, then held a finger up close to Damon's nose. 'One: I do not have to explain anything to you because I am the acting boss, yet I explain out of courtesy. And two,' a second finger unfurled to prod Damon's cheek. 'I've already told you what she's doing here.'

Damon took a step back; this outburst from the usually more placid member of the firm further fuelling his resentment.

'Being as we have no admin staff or anyone running the back end since Marco binned them off and after your account of the new numbers we're expecting tomorrow, I had to act on the situation.' He jerked his large head in the direction of the recording studio housing the cages. 'Unless you want to spend your time dealing with orders, working out filming schedules, cameramen rotas and the whining that we expect to get from our latest "arrivals", then I think you underestimate the fucking workload!'

Sonny continued, confident his points were hitting home. *Fuck - he was even convincing himself!* 'I for one, don't have time to deal with a tenth of that when I'm standing in for Marco.' *Oh yeah, he'd get that one in too whilst he was at it.* 'So, unless you want Marco to return to a shit show with incomplete films and unfulfilled deadlines, then I suggest you make it easier for this bird to get on with what I've employed her to do!'

Damon eyed Erin warily. 'Okay, okay, I get that, but... I mean... Can she... Is she...?'

'Can she be trusted? Is that what you're asking?' Sonny interrupted. 'No, I just placed an advert in the local rag!' He rolled his eyes. 'Course she can be trusted. Do you think me a fucking prick?'

'No! I...'

'If you must know, she's the daughter of a bloke I know from the old days. She's aware of how our line of business works and won't be a problem.' Sonny's eyes narrowed. 'So, I don't expect her to get any issues from you, nor anyone else, got it?'

Damon nodded resentfully. He'd have to swallow Sonny's shit until he'd succeeded in getting the man out of this role. Then things would be different. *Very* different. 'What should I show her first?' he mumbled.

'Exactly what you've planned so far and what's in the pipeline.' Sonny smiled, knowing Damon would find it difficult to deduce whether his smile was sarcastic or not. 'See her as your personal assistant. It's only until we get some semblance around here, or if she's really good, maybe we'll take her on full time.'

He jerked his head in Erin's direction. 'Caroline? Could you come over here, please?'

Erin moved down the corridor. She'd heard most of what Sonny said and had to admit he'd handled it well. But Caroline? Couldn't she have been given a choice of names to use as her alias?

The stilettos Sonny insisted she wore were too big and as she clacked along the shiny corridor towards the two men the leather was already chafing her heel. Wearing a suit wasn't usually in her repertoire either, but then again, she had to look the part. What bothered her most though, was where Sonny had got these clothes from. Imagining them being last worn during a seedy office scene in one of Marco's smutty films did nothing to lift her general mood.

At least it wasn't crotchless knickers and basque set.

Reaching Sonny, Erin plastered on the smile she'd become accustomed to switching on like a light during the time she'd played the part of the dutiful woman in front of Anthony's detestable business associates.

Keep telling yourself this is no different, Erin, she thought. And it wasn't. Not really. Except this time, lives of people she didn't even know possibly hung in the balance of her getting this right, as well as enabling one particular life - a person she *did* know, to be snuffed out faster.

'Pleased to meet you,' she lied, extending her hand in the direction of the man next to Sonny. 'I'm Caroline. I take it you're my boss?'

'Apparently so.' Damon crushed Erin's hand in his own and retained hold of it. 'Sonny informs me he's briefed you as to what you need to do?'

'To an extent,' Erin answered politely, wanting to pull her hand from the slimy grip, her distaste for this man immediate. 'Although he said *you* were the best person to explain in detail.'

'That I will do, Caroline' Damon said, coming to the conclusion that now he'd seen this bird close up, having her as his assistant may not be too much of a hardship after all.

Sonny clocked the glint in Damon's eyes and felt an immediate spark of unease. 'Like I said, I knew Caroline's father,' he said to reiterate the point. *No funny business*.

Erin flinched with the reference of 'father'. Sonny *had* known her father, not that he was referring to her real father, but it hit home nevertheless. Sonny had been privy to the murder, along with Marco and his bunch of trained fucking henchman.

She masked the spark of disgust and rage from showing in her eyes and pulled from the reserve of sharing only what she allowed. Her training in dealing with Anthony served her well, but it also reminded her that she should never forget what Sonny Mitchell had been part of.

Six

'I WAS AWARE OF IT,' Tiger admitted, the rage in Zane's eyes enough to stir the dead.

'Did you go to the funeral?' Zane probed, his fingers still retaining the tremor the words etched into the headstone had caused. *'Only son...'*

Tiger nodded. 'We all did. We wanted to pay our respects. I saw the headstone then. We were all shocked by what was on it.' He cracked his knuckles awkwardly. 'We didn't go to the wake though. Marco made it clear we were not welcome.' He shrugged. 'Giuseppe was good to us and we respected him too much to kick off at his funeral. It wouldn't have been fitting.'

Zane nodded. *Marco would pay for this, as well as everything else.* 'I wasn't questioning your loyalty. It's obvious the situation many of you were put in wasn't acceptable.'

Tiger inclined his head. It was even *less* acceptable that the ones who had dared to openly voice their opinions had paid with their lives, but Zane was aware of that too. Reiterating it wouldn't serve. Thanks to Marco, the man had far too many slights thrown at him already without adding more.

'Do you know of anyone called Skye?' Zane asked, his mind returning to the bouquet of flowers at his father's graveside. 'Does the name ring a bell?'

'Skye?' Tiger frowned. 'In association with who?'

'I'm not sure. Was there anyone you didn't recognise at the funeral?'

'It was a few years ago now but from what I recall, I knew most people by sight, if not by name. I mean, a lot of the firm's wives were present.' Tiger frowned. 'Why? Is there a problem?'

'No, no problem. It's probably nothing,' Zane said, coming to the conclusion that there wasn't an issue. The most likely explanation was that the flowers had blown from a nearby grave and a helpful passer-by had placed them back on his father's grave in error. This was the most likely explanation if no one knew anyone called Skye linked to his father or the firm. In addition, the flowers had been recently laid, so why would a stranger go to the effort of visiting a grave all these years later?

Zane glanced at his watch. 'Erin should be at Luna by now,' he muttered. What he'd agreed to was playing on his mind and he didn't need to look at Tiger's face to know that the man shared the same reticence about that task as he did.

'Hmm, it's risky, I grant that,' Tiger acknowledged, deciding to offer his unsolicited opinion. 'But, fuck me! Trafficking? Are there no levels that bastard will sink to? I know he's your brother and all that but...'

'He's no brother of mine!' Zane spat. That accolade had long since been stripped from the back of that man.

Even at two years old, the memory of seeing his baby brother for the first time was etched into Zane's brain. As was his vow to love and protect him. He had done that very thing until the moment he'd discovered his so-called brother - the boy he'd protected, dug out of the shit and promised to always have his back, had betrayed him in the worst way possible. And like that inscription on his father's grave, the betrayals kept on coming...

Marco had never genuinely intended him to get out of jail alive, had he? And now, even though it went against Zane's instinct, Marco had to die. As well for revenge, his brother must be killed for everyone's sakes.

The harsh reality was, if he didn't kill Marco, then Marco would kill *him*.

Seeing the strain on Zane's face, Tiger broke the silence. 'Leo's gone to do more digging on the lay of the land with the other members we want back onside. Hopefully, by close of play tonight, we'll have a yay or nay as to whether they can be approached. He'll also do the business with Grimes' studio as arranged.'

Zane nodded. Even if the members he wanted back in the helm *could* be approached, would they want to return to fight this battle? He'd like to think so, but nothing in this life was set in stone. That had already been proved more than once in the not so recent past. But if they weren't onboard then he couldn't overthrow Marco's firm because of lack of numbers.

At least the business at Starlight Studios would be completed. Removing Trevor Grimes' body couldn't be left much longer. There was a fine line between doing it himself the day he'd shot the stupid fucker, or doing it later. Torching the place at the time would have risked Marco getting wind and returning early, but by doing it now - a few days later, by the time anyone else learnt of it, Zane would hopefully have regained control and Marco would return as planned, ready to step headfirst into his trap.

• • • •

ACUTELY AWARE of Damon's presence, Erin concentrated on the paperwork in front of her, his burning gaze making itself known.

She wanted to scream for him to get out of her personal space, but that would only make things worse. Each time she asked a question he used it as a reason to close up more of the gap between them. For once, she wished for Sonny's presence, if only to divert her thoughts from plunging the silver letter opener on the desk into Damon Sandler's neck.

Stop, Erin! Remember what you are here for, she reminded

herself.

'So,' Damon drawled, his hand brushing against Erin's leg as he trundled his desk chair closer. 'How are you getting on? Have you made sense of everything yet?'

This Caroline bird really was a tasty chick. Fuck what Sonny said about her father. If the bird was up for it, then surely that was her prerogative, not her father's? Or Sonny's!

And with legs like *hers*, it was a shame she wasn't on the books for the films. Not that Marco would want anyone else stepping in as a contender once his wife graced the screens.

Damon's nose wrinkled. Everyone made such a big deal of Lisa Tequila, but that chick wasn't his cup of tea. His wasn't a popular opinion, being as most blokes around here would give their right leg for her to sit on their face, but not *him*. He preferred chicks who looked like *this*, rather than tits packed with silicon and gobs full of filler.

Damon found his eyes once again lingering on Erin's chest before moving his gaze slowly down her shapely legs.

'You asked if I had made sense of everything?' Erin said sharply, her skin crawling, aware she was being mentally undressed. 'It would be a big help if you could show me around the studios.'

She tapped the paperwork in front of her. 'It says here that you have thirty new women arriving tomorrow. Is that right?' Batting her eyelashes, she aimed to look confused. 'Thirty in one day?' *Oh, she could play the game and knew how to work wankers such as him.* 'They can't all be here for films, so...?'

'Ah, but they are all for the films,' Damon's face cracked into a sinister sneer. 'Hasn't Sonny told you that our new way of doing things is to bulk buy? It's our latest way of controlling spend.' *That made him sound good, didn't it?* Stuff like that impressed the birds, especially ones interested in how things worked and this Caroline chick seemed eager.

He ran his tongue along his teeth. He'd be happy to personally induct her into the ins and outs of what was expected of the starlets at Luna. With the exception of putting her in a cage. Not unless the idea took her fancy, of course...

Standing up, he squeezed Erin's shoulders. 'Come on then. I'll give you a tour.'

• • • •

CAV AND LEWIS FLETCHER were on their fourth pint in the Bluebell, waiting for the pool table to free up. Cav was contemplating wading to the bar to get a new round in, when a nudge to his ribs made him turn to his brother.

'That's not who I think, is it?' Lewis made an almost indistinct nod in the direction of the far end of the bar.

Despite many years of being out of a job where remaining undetected was vital, Cav hadn't forgotten the rules. He continued supping his pint and only after a couple of moments elapsed did he glance in the direction, pretending he was looking at something else.

What he saw amazed him. Never would he forget the unmistakable figure of Leo Holland. The guy was a legend, but having heard on the grapevine that the man had been one of many casualties when the firm they all loved fell under unwanted 'ownership', he hadn't thought he'd ever set eyes on him again. 'Fuck me! It *is*!'

'What should we do?' Lewis hissed. 'Do you think he's seen us?'

'He's seen us all right, therefore we do nothing but wait.' Cav picked his pint up from the sticky table and fished a cigarette from his pocket.

This was a moment he'd visualised many times, but as the years went on, the hope of it happening became less likely and the chances of things ever being put right became a pipe dream. Being reduced to doing security at one of the docks for a job had seemed, rather depressingly, to be the only thing on the cards, but now, maybe not...

A fission of excitement glimmered. Had the time come when they were all due a slice of much deserved luck? 'He knows we're here and I suspect that's why *he's* here.'

Lewis frowned. 'You mean you think th...'

'I don't know what I think,' Cav muttered out of the corner of his mouth. 'Just sit tight and remember the drill.'

Lewis nodded. All the years he'd worked alongside his brother for the Morelli firm under Giuseppe, they were well versed on putting tabs on people. Heading up that side of the business, Zane Morelli had been a master of it and both Lewis and Cav had worked well with the man, as well as Leo, Tiger and the rest. They'd been an exceptionally tight team, making it all the more gutting when Zane was stiffed and he, along with all those closest to that particular Morelli brother, were rapidly disbanded.

Some of them permanently.

'Are you going first, or me?' he asked Cav, itching to make contact with Leo Holland.

'I'll do it.' Cav pulled his large frame to his feet. 'Leo will have done his homework and know there's no traitors in here tonight. He also knows that if there was, I wouldn't be making a move.'

'I'll be out in a bit then.' Lewis watched Cav stroll out of the back door of the Bluebell without a glance at the man at the bar. Even with his back to them Leo's instinct would know the very second Cav passed him and then, exactly four minutes after, he would follow.

Lewis checked his watch. Six minutes after that he would leave too and go where he expected them to be waiting.

Fuck their shifts at the docks this afternoon. If they were correct about the reasoning behind Leo Holland's presence here today, then neither he or his brother required that poxy job any longer.

SEVEN

ERIN HAD DONE WELL by stopping the disgust and horror from flickering over her face since entering the room housing the metal cages. That this creep believed it acceptable to keep human beings or *any* form of creature in here was beyond contempt.

What made things worse was the tosser she knew to be Damon had animatedly explained the time these women would be held in here depended on whether they acquiesced to expectations or not. He'd also enjoyed explaining to her how it all worked.

She could see the whole thing excited Damon by the tell-tale bulge in his jeans. Not that she'd gone out of her way to look. The *last* thing she wanted was to come across that she was checking him out.

But even *more* offensive was having to act interested in this despicable venture, pretending she was impressed by the 'well-thought-out' plan.

This persona was one of the hardest she'd ever had to upkeep. And considering the farce of pretending to be happy with Anthony Walker, that was saying something. In comparison to *this*, masquerading as the contented other half of the freak she'd planned to marry in order to kill him was a breeze.

Her eyes fell once again to the thick metal wire of the cages. Within, there wasn't even a ledge to sit on, neither was the floor area big enough for anyone to rest. 'What's the minimum time you'll keep them in here?' she asked, her tone bright, when in real life she wanted to drain the blood from this man's body, leaving him a withered, empty shell, along with all the other people involved in this disgusting exercise.

Damon rubbed his hand up and down the thick metal edge of a cage. 'At least forty-eight hours and then how much longer after that depends how accommodating they are.' He winked at Erin. 'Perhaps they'll never get out...'

'That's really mean,' Erin said, hating herself for the coquettish giggle she forced from between her lips. 'If they're in there all night, how will they sleep?'

'Sleep?' Damon laughed. 'Why will they need to sleep? We've got a whole host of men employed here waiting to test-drive those bitches. We need to get them ready for filming, after all. The boss doesn't like slackers, so any lazy cunts will be weeded out before he returns.'

Erin swallowed down her rising nausea and feigned interest in inspecting the horrible metal cages when the real reason was to put space between her and this foul example of a human.

'I've already decided the ugly ones will be the first to act as a lesson to what happens to those less compliant,' Damon laughed, impressed with his acumen. 'Besides, no one wants ugly sluts in films.'

'You said, when the boss returns?' Erin seized the chance for a bit of digging. 'I, erm... thought Sonny was the boss? He said that he...'

'He made out that's how it is, the sneaky fucker?' Damon rolled his eyes. 'He's trying to impress you. Sonny's only standing in for the *real* boss who will be back next week.'

'Oh!' Erin feigned surprise. 'When exactly next week?'

Damon's expression changed and Erin inwardly froze. Had

she made things too obvious?

'Listen, girlie. Don't get it in your head that you can entice your way into Marco's favours. He's got himself hitched now, so save yourself the trouble. If he wants you, he'll have you, but it won't be like the old days for you birds, that's for sure.'

'I didn't mean…' Erin cut herself short. There was no point denying anything. In men like Damon Sandler's mind all women wanted the same thing, so she wouldn't dissuade him from his warped perception, no matter how much it riled her.

'Besides…' Damon sidled up to Erin so quickly she hadn't time to sidestep. His fingers twined in her hair. 'A chick as pretty as you should remember there's other contenders around here. It's not just Marco with clout, you know...' His hand fell to rest on her right breast where he tweaked her nipple through her blouse. 'Play your cards right and your luck might be on the up.'

Erin went to pull away from Damon's wandering hands when he jumped back of his own volition.

'How are you getting on?' Striding into the room, Sonny chanced a quick glance in Erin's direction, but his sights remained mainly fixed on Damon. 'Showing Caroline around?'

'We're just discussing how things work,' Damon said, confident Sonny hadn't clocked where his hand just lay. Sonny must have had a brain transplant and under the impression he had more clout than he actually did. Damon couldn't for the life of him work out why Marco had put this keyboard warrior as his second-in-command, but until their coke-loving boss saw the light, Sonny *did* have the upper hand.

Damon wasn't losing his place. Not with easy chicks about to land on his plate. Caroline would do nicely as an entrée, but he had plenty of time to get what he wanted from her, so he'd best pull his head in, especially if Mitchell kept popping out of the woodwork with no warning.

• • • •

AFTER A FULL DAY lounging around the swimming pool,

fast becoming a nice shade of golden brown, Marco had kept his steady uptake of alcohol and coke topped up.

The sun had long since begun to make its descent, but it was still pleasantly warm and he was so relaxed that even if the temperature plummeted to minus four, he wouldn't mind. Especially now a group of hot chicks had taken up residence opposite. One in particular catching his attention.

Propping himself up on his sun lounger, Marco splayed his legs either side of the cushioned base. That would give the woman in question a decent eyeful of his well-packed trunks.

He'd put his cock to good use many times already today, giving people around him a real-life view of how things *should* be done, but there was always room for more. What was in his pants never got tired and neither did he.

Stamina was his middle name and no one had ever complained. He doubted that would start now.

And - he eyed the shapely brunette opposite busy adjusting the spaghetti straps of her short sundress - neither would she if she won the chance of having some Morelli action. He knew behind those shades the woman's eyes focused on the huge bulge in his trunks, so all he needed was a bit more powder and he'd be well away.

'So, I've booked a few for when we get back.' Hazel's voice cut into Marco's singular existence.

'What?' Marco muttered, having almost forgotten Hazel's presence. The stunner opposite him wasn't a patch on his Hazel, but as he'd had Hazel plenty of times today, didn't they say variety was the spice of life?

That was his motto, anyway.

Hazel should be honoured that he'd kept his hands only on her for the last few weeks - a feat never before accomplished in his history and one that perhaps needed a shake-up. After all, he didn't want to get bored. No shagging the same chick in a two week period was his way of doing things. Until he'd got married, that was. Now Hazel expected weird shit, like him to stick just to her?

What was she thinking? Hypocritical or what? She'd be shagging all sorts in the films, yet she expected him to sit back like a puppy dog and be hers alone? That wasn't happening and the sooner Hazel realised that it was *him* who called the shots, the better.

'Marco!'

Marco winced at the harridan-like edge to Hazel's voice, belatedly recalling that he'd never met her mother. He couldn't really, considering the woman had been brown bread for years, but he should have at least checked out a photo and got some background information. Didn't people say a girl's mother gave a good indication as to what the girl herself would end up like? If Hazel's old queen had resembled a fishwife with a voice like shredded glass, then he'd definitely need a rethink in a few years from now, if not sooner.

But now was not the time for worrying about that.

Smiling, he turned to his wife, wondering if she would pop to the apartment and fetch him a new wrap of coke because he couldn't be arsed. Besides, the view was so much better around the pool... 'Sorry babe, did you say something?'

'Yes, I did!' Hazel pouted. 'Were you not listening?'

'Well yes, but...'

Hazel's eyes narrowed. 'What was I talking about, then?'

Oh for fuck's sake, Marco thought, his annoyance flickering to life. 'Don't play games, Hazel,' he said, flicking her exposed nipple. 'Just tell me again, would you?'

Placated by Marco's attention, Hazel continued. 'I was just saying I've booked viewings on some new penthouses in Mayfair for when we get back. There's one in particular that I really like. It's more expensive than the rest, but you should see the roof garden and...'

'What? Wait! You've booked viewings?' Marco spluttered. *What the fuck was this?*

Hazel's frozen eyebrows dragged into enough of a frown enough to make a point. 'We've discussed this before, Marco,' she sighed. 'You agreed that we could do with a better postcode than our penthouse in Battersea.'

Seeing Marco's expression, Hazel attempted to soften the blow. 'Not that there's anything wrong with our penthouse. I mean, it's lovely, but what with our marriage and the fact that I'll be top billing with our studio, then surely we need a relevant space for entertaining?'

'Hmm, perhaps,' Marco agreed, noticing the use of the word 'our' for both the penthouse *and* his studio. He thought not. Neither did he have any intention of going to any bloody viewings.

Zane's penthouse - no, *his* penthouse, was fine. More than adequate for entertaining. The cinema complex he'd had installed for private screenings of his films was cracking. There were several balconies and bars, so what the fuck else did Hazel want? A space station?

Furthermore, even if he was up for moving, he wouldn't out of principle. Keeping hold of what used to be his brother's was yet another way of rubbing salt in Zane's wounds.

And the more ways he could do that, the better.

Eight

NEARING THE HOUSE, Erin couldn't wait to get inside. She wished Sonny hadn't insisted on taking her home. She could have made her own way back. The less time spent in the company of those tainted with the miasma of Luna, the better. Plus, she'd wanted fresh air on her skin to remove the traces of Damon Sandler's hands.

She shuddered. As sickening as that had been, it was nowhere near as repulsive as what these women due to arrive faced. But Sonny was adamant he would accompany her home, insisting it was too risky to do otherwise.

'I know what he's like,' Sonny said suddenly. 'You must tell me if things get out of hand.'

Erin glared at Sonny's angular face focused on the road ahead. She knew who he was talking about. 'I can handle Sandler,' she snapped. 'I don't need your help. I'm getting the information required and that's what's needed.'

Sonny sighed inwardly. *This girl was hard work.* 'I know that, but I won't have him thinking he can do what he likes.'

Erin laughed sarcastically. 'From what I've heard, he and other people there do *exactly* what they like!'

Sonny frowned. It was true Marco had succeeded in getting

just about everyone with questionable morals that side of the river under his employ. And yes, firms like this needed people with a certain type of 'personality' as well as the ability to not have problems veering over the line, but there were some things that did not include. Marco's latest venture being one of them. However, it appeared he was one of the few who didn't share the general enthusiasm for Marco's business sense.

Guilt rolled deeper that he himself had been party in helping Marco reach his present position of power, but hopefully that would soon be remedied. 'They won't be doing exactly what they like soon,' he muttered.

'You have less sway than you think,' Erin said, enjoying taking Sonny down a peg or two. 'Damon might say what you want to hear in front of you, but he doesn't hold much respect once you're out of earshot. Although, being two-faced isn't uncommon for you lot, is it?'

'That's as maybe, but most of them don't know what I *used* to do. They see me as someone that only has experience of hiding behind a screen, but I know different. As will *everyone...*'

Holding anything further she wanted to say in check, Erin chewed the inside of her cheek. Being an abject bitch wasn't helping. She must control herself. It made her no better than the rest otherwise.

'Don't mention anything about Damon Sandler to Zane,' she said quietly. 'I know you saw him grope me, and that wasn't the last time he did it.' She watched Sonny's jaw clench at this information. 'If you tell Zane, he'll pull me out and let's face it, I need to be in there. That's the only thing I admit to agreeing with you about.'

Sonny begrudgingly nodded. 'Okay, but if the twat goes too far, then forget Zane, I'll deal with Damon myself! I won't have him taking liberties.'

'As I said, I can handle him,' Erin muttered. If Sonny Mitchell thought she needed a man who had betrayed Zane being her knight in shining armour, then he was mistaken.

Glancing ahead, she smiled tightly. 'We're back now. I'll see you tomorrow.'

Sonny pulled up outside the house. 'I'll come in for a moment. There's things I need to speak to Zane about.'

Getting out of the car, Erin made her way up the path. She wanted to close the door on this day as well as Sonny and gather her thoughts, but that wasn't an option now. And she resented that.

• • • •

ZANE GLANCED UP as the front door shut. *Erin was back?* Getting up from the chair, he moved into the hallway. 'How did it go?'

Erin noticed straight away that Zane was looking at Sonny when he spoke. Clearly she didn't warrant the question being put to her. She brushed past, but Zane blocked her way by putting his arm across the narrow hallway. 'Are you okay?'

'Yep, I'm fine,' Erin said, ducking under Zane's arm. 'Sonny can update you about things from my side, if you're interested, that is? I'm going to take a bath.'

Zane frowned as Erin moved swiftly up the stairs without a backward glance. He beckoned Sonny into the kitchen. 'What's the score?'

Pulling the kitchen door to behind him, Sonny gratefully accepted a cold beer. 'Erin did okay. She's been picking Damon's brains. He spills more to her than he does to me... Marco's due back two days before we expected.'

'Not on Saturday? I thought we had a full week before he returned? Are you sure?'

'That's what Erin said,' Sonny confirmed. 'Damon also told her that the women are arriving tomorrow.'

Zane's hands clenched, his blood simmering in his veins. He needed control of the firm when his brother returned, not *as* he returned. 'For fuck's sake. We won't have enough time to get things in place before Marco gets back now.'

'Not necessarily.' A small smile formed on Sonny's mouth.

'I heard from Leo. He's got Cav and Lewis Fletcher on board.' He glanced at his watch. 'And by now, Grimes and his studio should be ablaze.'

Zane returned the grin, hope returning. 'That brings our number to five. We need to call a meeting for tomorrow.'

'If the women are due tomorrow we'll have to arrange the meeting on the fly. I can't leave Luna with that happening or Erin alone with the rest of them.'

Zane bristled. 'Has something happened that I should be aware of?' If anyone had dared to play silly devils or laid a hand on Erin, then he'd be in there like a shot.

'No, not as far as I know,' Sonny lied, keeping his promise to Erin. 'Erin can handle herself.' *At least he hoped so.*

'The mood she's been in the last few days, everyone's probably better off giving her space!' Zane muttered.

Sonny laughed, but inside he didn't like what he'd seen today or what it could lead to. He didn't trust those fuckers, but the problem remained. Erin didn't trust *him* and Zane was so focused on everything else to see that things weren't quite as palatable as he'd like to believe.

NINE

DAMON EYED SONNY with bad intent, wishing the prick would fuck off. He didn't need him hanging around.

Holding his mobile under the table, he covertly tapped out a text:

```
Park in layby a couple miles away + wait. I'll let
u know when 2 come
```

Pressing send, his beady eyes moved to Erin sitting at the desk in the corner. He wanted time to work on her before Marco returned and decide he wanted first dibs.

'What's on your agenda today, boss?' he smarmed, making sure to use the word 'boss' without sarcasm. *It was difficult.* Sonny Mitchell wanted reverence during his fifteen minutes of fame, so he'd sport the shit the man wanted to hear, but he had other plans. Ones which didn't involve Mitchell. It was only a matter of time once Marco became wise to his error of giving this man this job.

Luckily, Damon had everything ready to underline that *he* would be the perfect choice when Marco was forced to rethink his second-in-command.

'I'm hoping to pop out for a meeting at some point today,' Sonny answered, hoping information would be volunteered as to when the truck load of women was due.

This wanker had told Erin it was definitely today, not him, so he'd have to careful how he worded this. He was also aware of what he and Zane had discussed last night and taken heed of what had been suggested should the opportunity arise. Marco had not made a secret that his brother was on the loose and would prove detrimental. He had many pairs of eyes on the lookout. *Too* many.

'Oh? You've got a meeting?' Damon feigned interest. The sooner this prat fucked off out of here, the quicker his delivery could arrive.

Sonny being here when those chicks rolled up would balls things up. The twat was a spoilsport and would piss on his fun. That would not go down well with the other blokes who had been promised time with these chicks for a small payment.

His eyes narrowed. He hoped Sonny's meeting turned into a long one too. 'It sounds like you're planning to go off site? Anything interesting?'

'It could be. I hope so, anyway.' Sonny casually flicked through Damon's desk diary. Enjoying Damon's irritation at his personal items being perused but not having the clout to complain, he felt this an apt opportunity to continue. 'I've had word that Zane's been spotted, so I'm meeting the scouts and checking it out.' He ignored Erin tensing in her seat out of the corner of his eye. 'I may be some time though. Didn't you say those women were due today? I'll have to postpone the meeting.'

'You really should check it out. We all know what the instructions are,' Damon urged. Everyone knew to keep a lookout for the elder Morelli and that Sonny was tasked with intercepting Zane should he show up, so this was the perfect excuse to get Sonny out of the way so he could enjoy the delivery. 'Marco would expect you to go,' he pushed. 'We know that wanker, Zane, will show his face sooner rather than later.'

That was another example of Marco's bad judgement by assuming Mitchell had the balls to take on and apprehend Zane Morelli.

But *he* would, Damon thought with a glint of rising anticipation. Being as Zane got banged up before Damon had joined the firm, he'd never met the bloke, but he'd *heard* enough. He didn't give a rat's arse about the eldest Morelli's fearful reputation. Being butt-fucked for years in nick removed a man's fight, so he'd heard. It was doubtful the bloke was the same as what he'd once been.

He smirked. Whereas, *he* was fit, eager and on the ball with what he wanted to achieve. He'd happily take on the wannabe heir who was past it and used ideas from the dark ages, like his father. There was only the call for up-to-date attitudes which made money. Zane Morelli with his old-school ways was a fossil.

Damon would have nothing scupper his position here. Thanks to Marco he'd never had such a good gig. Birds on tap 24/7 and coke freebies too. Nope, nothing would screw that up. 'This info you've received could be a kosher lead. What did the intel say?'

'That there's been sightings around the Mayfair area,' Sonny added, knowing exactly what Sandler was doing, the devious cunt. He wanted him out of the way.

Erin felt she should make the effort to ad-lib. Zane had previously mentioned steering these people off course should his name crop up, not that he'd said much to her personally last night, but it was worth adding something into the mix. 'What's all this? I thought the other Morelli was imprisoned?'

'Yeah, he was,' Damon shrugged. 'But apparently, he's not anymore. Marco's expecting him to return at any time to lay claim to the firm, but no one wants that. The guy's a cock. Old-fashioned and past it.'

Erin swallowed her choke. Zane was very much *not* that. She instead acted like none of this made a blind bit of difference.

'It's strange though,' Damon continued, hoping Sonny took the bait. 'We've got people with their eyes peeled everywhere, yet there's been no word or sightings, apart from this one you mention in Mayfair. I'm starting to think Zane's lost his bottle and ain't showing up at all.'

'Hmm, but on the same vein we can't afford to be complacent,' Sonny said, grateful for Erin's addition to setting the scene.

'Then you should *definitely* go to this meeting,' Damon pressed. 'We don't want anything screwing up Marco's plans.'

'No we don't!' Sonny agreed. 'So when exactly is this "delivery" due? You still haven't confirmed anything. Is it today or not?' He fixed Damon with a steely glare. I can't leave until it's arrived or until I know what's going on.' He wasn't fucking around any longer. He'd force the fucking times from Sandler if he had to.

Damon scowled. 'Oh, erm, yeah… it's today. Come to think of it, it should have been here by now,' he lied, pulling his mobile from his pocket. 'I'll ring the driver and see what the fuck is going on.'

Pretending to scroll through his contacts, Damon paced up and down the room. 'Gav? Yeah, it's me. Where the fuck are you? You sh… What?' His eyes shot to Sonny's, confident he'd done a good job of looking suitably surprised. 'Oh, Jesus Christ... Okay, right, when? Oh, for God's sake... All right, yeah... Well, it will have to do, won't it? I'm not happy though Gav, not happy at all.'

Pressing the end call button of a conversation that never existed, Damon raked his hands through his hair. 'For fuck's sake!'

Sonny raised his eyebrows. 'Problem?'

'The lorry's held up in some shit down in Dover. It's been stuck there hours.' Damon said, deciding his story was brilliant. 'Don't worry, it's not customs. It's something to do with a strike. The container's fine, but the driver is parking up. He's been on the road for thirty hours and too knackered to continue. It will be here tomorrow morning instead.'

'What about the women? What will happen to them?' Erin cried, horrified.

'Nothing a blast of water with a hose into the back of the container at a fucking truck stop won't fix,' Damon snapped. 'A pisser it might be, but it's the only way. We don't want them getting killed on the way because the driver's too tired to function or being stopped by the rozzers for swerving all over the gaff. Either of those things would be a disaster and would waste tons of cash!'

'I agree,' Sonny said, hiding his joy that now he could safely go and have this meeting. Not with any scouts from Mayfair, but with Zane and the rest of the newly-formed crew ready to tip over this shit heap. 'Looks like I can check out this sighting after all.'

• • • •

HAZEL STARED from the top floor balcony over the superb view of the azure ocean, courtesy of the best apartment the hotel had to offer.

This was the most luxurious hotel the island had. She'd made sure of that when booking the honeymoon. Being as it was invoiced to Marco there was no reason to account for cost. And why should she? It wasn't like she couldn't command only the best.

She slammed her Tequila Sunrise on the glass table and inspected her newly painted toenails. The shade matched that of her false fingernails and also went a dream with the brand new jewel-encrusted sandals she'd treated herself to from one of the hotel's designer boutiques. The beautician who'd arrived at the apartment first thing this morning to do her hair, nails and makeup had said so, anyway. And yes, okay it was only 11 a.m. - some may say a tad early to be on the fourth cocktail of the day, but this was her honeymoon.

Or it was supposed to be...

Her eyes drifted from the beautiful view back through the four double doors leading back into the pristine apartment.

Still no sign of Marco.

Hazel's botoxed face struggled to screw into the frown she desperately wanted to form. If Marco thought she was a pushover and would accept being treated less than the star she was, he was in for a sharp shock.

It might have been her father's idea for her to wed Marco as part of a business deal to catapult her further into stardom of the industry she was already the most sought after leading lady in, but with Marco's position as the owner and more to the point, *beneficiary* of the profits of his *own* film studio, as well as a well-established firm dealing in things that she had no particular wish to know about, Hazel agreed her father's suggestion was a lucrative one.

The power Marco held as a notorious and feared gangster in many parts of London hadn't gone unnoticed either and Hazel was all for the additional kudos being married to such a man brought.

And no, she hadn't initially been too impressed with the pairing or of the man himself. But once Marco's position had been confirmed after the rumours doing the rounds that his elder brother would be released from jail, making her place in the marriage pointless proved unfounded, she'd reached the conclusion that Marco wasn't as offensive as she'd first thought.

And the way he'd striped that man who'd bought her drinks on her hen night had impressed her too. It was nice to be fought over by a man of such immense physical power. Plus, Marco knew his way around in bed, so it had turned out a good decision all round.

Marco's obsession with her was another bonus because she could wind him around her little finger. There was nothing he wouldn't do for her. Or more importantly, *pay* for. She was born to live a life of luxury and now she had exactly that - more so now than ever.

But there was one more thing that she insisted on and expected with no argument: full, unequivocal worship from the man who she'd agreed to marry.

Hazel opened a packet of cigarettes and lit one. This was her tenth today. She didn't usually smoke. Everyone knew it played havoc with the skin and she didn't want to fork out for a facelift earlier than necessary, but she was stressed. *Really* stressed.

And fucking offended.

At first, Marco had been attentive - he couldn't get enough of her. For Christ's sake, she gave him a hard on just by being in the same room! But barely a week on and his attention had wandered. Since when did she - Hazel Grimes, or, as the general unwashed knew her, Lisa Tequila, ever take second place?

She didn't. *And neither would she.*

Yet she'd seen Marco giving that brunette by the swimming pool the once over yesterday. She'd seen it as clear as day. Nor had he listened to a word she'd said about the Mayfair penthouse. Buying her what she wanted was the very least he could do, as well as acting the way a husband hell bent on keeping his wife happy should. Wasn't that what all men wanted if they were fortunate enough to land a woman belonging to a league such as *she* resided in?

Yes, it bloody was!

Hazel's eyes narrowed. *So where the fuck was he, then?*

Her eyes tracked back to the empty bed visible from the huge glass doors of the balcony.

'I'm just going to get some more ice,' he'd said as they'd fallen into bed last night.

It had been her who'd ordered the magnum of champagne via room service, but Marco being Marco, wanted more ice. She told him to call room service back, but he'd insisted on going himself.

And that was the last she'd seen of him...

Her husband had been gone *all* night. And there was still no sign.

And to where?

Hazel crushed the half-smoked cigarette into the crystal ashtray, imagining it to be the face of the brunette from yesterday. *If that was where he'd been, then...*

Hearing the click of the apartment door, Hazel jumped to her feet. Storming into the suite, she glared at the dishevelled figure of Marco, his red-rimmed eyes barely focusing as he swayed against the bathroom door.

'Where the hell have you been?' Hazel screeched, launching herself forward, her claw-like nails on target for Marco's unshaven face. 'You've been shagging that bird, haven't you? How dare you! I'll ruin you, Marco Morelli. I'll...'

'Stop!' Marco's large hand blocked Hazel from gouging his eyes out. 'What the fuck is the matter with you?' Thinking on his feet, he pulled on a hard-done-by look. 'How on earth could you think I'd ever look at anyone else but you? We've just got married, for God's sake. I've been after you for ten years, Hazel. Ten!'

Hazel blinked. 'Where have you been then? You said you'd gone to get ice but you never came back.'

'Oh, I got chatting at the bar – to a man, before you ask!,' Marco lied. 'I ended up getting involved and put it this way, a bottle of whisky later, I only woke up ten minutes ago!'

He bent to kiss Hazel's hand, hoping that Shelley chick who had run her nails down his back as he'd fucked the life out of her, hadn't left visible marks. 'I'm really sorry, babe. I didn't mean to fall asleep.'

Hazel pouted. She wanted to believe Marco, she really did. She couldn't bear the humiliation of divorcing her husband for cheating after a week! That would be mortifying.

Her eyes narrowed. She must think about this. He *had* put away loads of alcohol yesterday, so if he'd knocked a bottle of whisky back on top of that, it was feasible he could have crashed out. 'How do I know that you're...'

'You know I love you, babe,' Marco whined. 'Who couldn't? And you're mine! You think I'd risk losing you? If you don't believe me, ask the waiter. He saw me and even fetched me a coffee just now!'

And the scrawny shit had best say what he'd told him to if asked. He'd better, considering it had cost him the equivalent of £300.

As for Shelley, well she'd broken his boredom of being stuck in bed with the same woman for over a week, therefore he could now bear just shagging Hazel again for another few days. At least until they got back. Then he'd see if there was anything worth picking from his imported collection that should be at his studios.

'Come here, you silly girl,' he growled, pulling Hazel towards him by the tie of her sheer cover up. 'Get your kit off and let's make up for lost time.'

Relieved that she still held pole position, Hazel smugly let her cover up fall to the floor and stepped out of her bikini. She'd been silly jumping to conclusions. Everyone knew Marco realised he was onto a good thing.

TEN

AFTER WATCHING ERIN leave for Luna Motion Films for the second day in a row and then waiting to hear whether Sonny would make a meeting today, Zane was at a loose end.

Sitting on his hands waiting to commence with the many things he needed to do - all of which had tight windows of opportunity was becoming increasingly frustrating. Not to mention aggravating. Everything was linked to another thing and one couldn't be done without the other.

He couldn't bear feeling impotent, especially with so much riding on the outcome.

Now Cav and Lewis were back on board, which he was grateful for, it meant that although their numbers were many less than what Marco had at his disposal, Zane knew the handful of men he had back onside were the best of the best. Each man was the equivalent of thirty of Marco's brainless robots. And, although it was tight, he now had just enough manpower to do what was required. But *nothing* could go ahead until he'd got everybody together and had thrashed out exactly what would happen. There was no room for anything but exact precision with everybody knowing their part. This hinged on when Sonny could risk leaving the studios and that in itself was a double edged sword.

Sonny had to be present at the meeting, but that could only happen if things ran to plan at the studios. There was no way Sonny could be absent when the trafficked women arrived or for Erin to be alone there. Her being at Luna at all bothered him more with every passing second.

Erin had blanked him last night and blanked him again this morning. Something was going on in her head. He could sense it and didn't like it. Were things doomed to failure with her?

Zane frowned. He didn't know what it was, but *something* had changed. Was it something in addition to her resenting how long this was taking?

His face set in steely determination. Whatever he felt for Erin, which was a cut above what he'd ever had before with anyone, things still had to be done the right way. A way which meant they weren't looking over their shoulders for the rest of their lives.

Leaning back against the tree, Zane closed his eyes and raised his head towards the sky, the summer breeze pleasant as it brushed his face.

He didn't know why he'd come here again. Hanging around graveyards wasn't a usual spot to pick, but he'd found himself heading here despite knowing to spend minimum time the wrong side of the river. But the quietness of the surroundings acted like a calming balm on his fraught mind and helped still the tumultuous thoughts swimming around his brain. He still had no answers nor did it change things, but it was peaceful.

Sometimes it was a benefit having only the dead for company.

It sounded stupid admitting that being in the proximity of where his father lay bought a modicum of solace, but whether it was daft or not, he didn't care. Being here dropped his mind down a notch below frantic.

And by God, he needed that.

Zane pulled his mobile from his pocket and brought the screen to life.

No texts. No phone calls.

Nothing.

Not sure what he'd been expecting, Zane shoved the phone back in his pocket, deciding it was time to get back on the road. If this meeting was going ahead at some point, he at least needed to be waiting in the right area.

Pulling himself up from the tufty grass, Zane tensed with a sudden strong sense of foreboding. Placing his shades on, he glanced around.

Foreboding was the wrong word. It was more like the sense of being *watched* – the hairs on the back of his neck standing up. He could feel eyes focused on him, but from where?

Without wanting to make it obvious, Zane casually scanned the area as he made his way across the graveyard to where he'd parked his bike. Apart from an old lady the other side of the churchyard stooped over tending a grave, there was no one around. There was a lone car in the car park opposite his bike - probably the old lady's. Aside from that, there was nothing.

Shaking his head to himself, Zane continued walking. He must have been imagining it. Having time on his hands did him no favours.

The buzzing of his phone jerked his concentration and he swiftly pulled it from his jeans pocket.

...SM calling...

'Sonny?' Zane wedged the phone in his neck, freeing his hands to undo his crash helmet strap. 'What's going on?' He frowned as he listened. 'Okay... When?' He glanced at his watch. 'Yep. I'll be there.'

Ending the call, Zane put the phone back in his pocket, but as he did so the unmistakable burn of eyes seared into him once again. He glanced up just in time to see someone duck out of view behind the window of the only car in the car park. The one he'd thought to be empty...

It couldn't be that old lady because she was still over the

other side of the churchyard, so who the hell was it?

He hadn't been imagining it after all. Someone was watching him and whoever it was, had been doing so for some time.

Increasing his pace, Zane hastened towards the car park. Was it one of Marco's men? Had he been spotted and then followed?

Shit! He'd put himself in the territory and wasn't wearing his crash helmet or bandana.

As the engine started, he squinted, unable to see through the car window because of the sun's reflection on the tinted glass. From this distance he couldn't even deduce whether it was a man or a woman at the wheel.

Breaking into a run, his hand clasped around the butt of the gun in his waistband.

Fuck! The car was driving off.

Out of breath, Zane reached the gravelled car park only to be left with the dust kicked up from the car tyres as it sped out of sight down the lane.

• • • •

IT HAD BEEN over five minutes since Damon had left Erin to her own devices under the pretext of making a call and she was sick of looking at the bunch of scripts, if they could be called that, for the next set of films due to be made.

Sonny had left to go to Zane's meeting and there was no one else about. Thankfully, the rest of Marco's men resided over in the opposite end of this building.

'We'd never get any filming done if that lot were this side of the place,' Damon had said when asked, one of those smarmy smirks on his ugly face.

Yeah, hilarious, Erin thought. *Prick.*

Getting out of her chair, she left the office. Seeing the corridor clear, she made her way along it. This was the best chance yet to gain extra information about Luna. She didn't know what she was looking for, or what use it might be, but surely anything to speed up the end of this shit was worth searching for?

Stopping outside a room further down from the recording studio holding the cages, Erin hesitated. She looked at the shiny new plaque on the door sporting the name 'Lisa Tequila' with a gold star either side of the lettering.

Marco's new wife?

Erin shuddered. How proud the woman must be...

Inwardly wondering whether a woman deluded enough to marry a man such as Marco was aware of her new husband's business dealings and exactly what they involved, she hesitatingly reached for the gold door handle.

Pushing the door open an inch, she saw straight away that it was a dressing room. And newly kitted out, by the looks of it.

Slipping inside, Erin flicked the lights on, the room illuminating like a circus. She quickly took in the rows of tacky bulbs around the huge mirror atop the dressing table – the glass top festooned with a range of top-quality makeup products.

She ran her hand over the fluffy pink cover of the heart-shaped seat. Everything was brand new and ready for the latest star. Racks of clothes hung on rails to one side: dresses, jackets, every colour of lingerie set imaginable and ewww - boxes of sex toys in all shapes and sizes.

Marco certainly hadn't scrimped on expense when it came to Lisa Tequila, she thought with a wry smile.

And that must be her...

Erin's gaze fell on a framed print of a resplendently naked blonde with pumped up lips lounging seductively on a chaise longue, her hand strategically placed between her splayed legs to cover her modesty.

Well, the woman was certainly attractive in a surgically enhanced way, no one could argue with that, but what did this woman - this Lisa, *really* think about what she did for a living?

Did she enjoy it? Hate it? Was she forced into it or did she do it willingly?

That was an answer Erin doubted she'd ever know, being

as the chances of her meeting this person was remote. Not that she particularly wanted to.

Meeting anyone who chose to share a bed with Marco Morelli wasn't top of Erin's guest list. But with sudden realisation, she admitted her fake life with Anthony Walker beforehand had been a means to an end too. She'd slept with that foul creature for years to place her in a position where she could seek revenge for her father. Was what she'd done all that different?

Feeling nauseous at the memory, Erin pushed it out of her mind, but it grated nonetheless. She'd been doing what she'd been doing for *genuine* reasons, not for money. That made a difference, didn't it?

Besides, that was over now. It had been pointless anyway and...

'What the fuck are you doing here?'

The growling voice came from nowhere and the hand painfully gripping her forearm shocked Erin to the core. As she was slammed face first into the wall, her panicked brain questioned how she could have been so stupid to get so involved in her thoughts not to keep an ear out. 'I… I erm… I ran out of scripts, so I thought I'd take a look around.'

'Did I say you could wander off without me?' Damon snarled, his sense of power only heightening the urge to relieve his sexual frustration inside this pretty chick he now had in an enviable position. 'But seeing as there's no harm done...' His fingers trailed a line down Erin's cheek, along her neck and then down to her waist, inching closer to the waistband of her skirt and underneath it. 'Why don't we take this opportunity to get to know each other a bit better?'

Pulling from her reserve, Erin pushed backwards, catching Damon off guard. 'That's not a good idea.'

Impressed by the strength of this slightly built woman, Damon's eyes danced with both lust and amusement. 'Why's that then? You got some kind of thing going with Mitchell?'

With Sonny? he had to be joking, Erin thought bitterly. 'No,

I don't but don't push your luck!'

With this, the amusement died in Damon's eyes and his lip curled in irritation. 'Listen, bitch. I don't know why Mitchell employed you, aside from to shag you, but you need to start being nicer to the hands that feed you.' Grabbing a fistful of Erin's hair, he yanked her head down. 'You can make up for your misdemeanour by putting your mouth to better use than coming out with snarky comments. Then in this instance we'll say no more about it.'

Overriding the searing pain in her scalp, Erin's eyes darted around the strange angle she was being held at for anything she could use to render this bloke incapable. *Shit. There was nothing.*

Bile rose as Damon's free hand undid the zip of his jeans mere inches away. *Right*, she thought, steeling herself. *I'll use my mouth all right... I'll fucking bite him. I'll bite it clean off.*

Erin had all but accepted her fate, along with the retribution Damon would receive as he pulled himself free from his jeans, when the shrill ringing of a mobile shattered the man's efforts.

'Fuck!' Damon hissed, fumbling to pull his phone from the jeans halfway down his thighs. 'For God's sake. Now of all moments?' With one hand still wound tightly in Erin's hair, he glanced at the screen. If it was Sonny, he could do one. He had better things on right now.

Bollocks. it was Gav.

Gritting his teeth, Damon reluctantly answered the call. 'Great timing…' he muttered. 'What now? Round the back, I hope? Okay... One minute.'

Ending the call, he begrudgingly tucked himself back into his jeans. 'We'll continue this later. For now we've got more important things on.'

Erin stared at Damon, unable to mask her hatred. He expected her to help him out of whatever crap he was in after that stunt he'd just pulled?

'Wipe that snotty look off your face, bitch!' Damon spat. 'This is important. You've got thirty unhappy women to placate!'

Erin blinked in surprise. 'What? What do you mean?'

Damon came to the conclusion that this Caroline chick must be a sandwich short of a picnic. The silly cow really had no clue how things worked, did she? 'That lorry is here with the women. Now get your arse into gear and help me get them in.' *At least having another bird on site might make them pull their fucking heads together sooner.*

Erin gasped. 'But Sonny? You told him th…'

'Wise up, you silly cow. Mitchell is a boring fucker and cramps everyone's style. Are you trying to tell me you didn't realise I blagged that shit about the lorry being stuck in Dover?' He rolled his eyes and yanked the door open. 'Get a move on.'

Erin reluctantly followed Damon into the corridor. No, she hadn't realised. But she *should* have. She should have known better. And now in Sonny's absence she would have to keep a lid on things here.

Rounding the corner, spotting for the first time a collection of thugs avidly waiting for the women to be unloaded from the container, Erin realised with a rapidly sinking heart that it was unlikely she'd be able to do much to ease these poor women's entrance to this shit show.

ELEVEN

TURNING HIS CIGARETTE PACKET around in a circle on the table in the White Saddle, Zane looked around the faces of the men in the back room. What the landlord of this boozer thought about his frequent bookings of this tiny and barely used function room, he had no idea, but Zane *had* made it clear that these meetings were private and the man would do well to ensure no mention was made of them being here. *Ever.*

Whether the bloke knew who he really was or not, Zane didn't have a clue, but it was neither here nor there. People in places like this knew the lie of the land well enough. In vicinities such as this they were aware certain things went on. They also knew to maintain the silent rule that applied to all. *If you want to live, keep what you know or speculate upon to yourself.*

On plenty of occasions over the years folk from this side of the fence had seen what happened to those investing in idle gossip, so Zane felt it unlikely there would be issues, even if his identity was suspected. Firms operating the wrong side of the law were commonplace and always had been, therefore anyone worth their salt knew the rules and adhered to them.

There was little choice in using this place as a temporary

base anyway. It wasn't like he had his own headquarters. *Not yet*. But when he did, they wouldn't be at that fucking place Marco now used.

Once he got the firm back under his control, *proper* headquarters would be chosen – ones like they used to have. But for now, the White Saddle would suffice. It wasn't like he could bring meetings to the house he shared with Erin. He wanted no business ties with that address, especially when things were so volatile and anyone could be watching.

Which it seemed like they might be...

Zane passed his stare back around the small group, realising each man was waiting for him to speak. He'd contemplated saying nothing about this latest event, but now he'd changed his mind because it could be relevant. And if it *was*, then these men who had chosen to put their necks on the line for him should be warned.

'I have a suspicion I'm being watched,' he said simply.

'Watched?' Tiger frowned. 'By who?'

'I don't know.' Zane turned to Sonny. 'Does anyone else at the studios know we had a meeting planned?'

Sonny shook his head. 'Only Damon, but he's under the impression I've gone to Mayfair. He doesn't know I'm here.'

'You saw this person you believe was watching you when you arrived *here*?' Cav pushed himself to the edge of the wooden settle in readiness. 'If there's someone in this boozer then we need to...'

'It wasn't here. It was at the graveyard. I went there again this morning.' Zane looked at each of his men in turn. 'It was someone in the car park. I couldn't see who it was because they were inside a car which sped off. All I know was that it was a silver car - something like a VW Golf.'

He could see by the flicker on the men's faces that the question as to why he'd unnecessarily returned to the territory which had once been his, was silently brewing. None of them would voice it though. They all knew a risk had been taken when it wasn't needed. He knew it too, but that's as far as it went. 'I just wanted to make you aware of what happened,' Zane said.

'Everyone at Marco's headquarters are watching out for you,' Sonny said. 'Sandler said there's been no sightings of you at all, but Marco has eyes everywhere, so it's feasible you could have been spotted.'

Just the mention of Marco's name and headquarters made Zane's skin bristle. 'What someone like Sandler says means shag all! They're all fucking liars!'

'But if they believe the last sighting was in Mayfair, that's good,' Tiger said. *At least Sonny had managed one thing right.*

'Ah well, it is what it is,' Zane shrugged. 'If they're watching me, then we need to act quickly and now you gentlemen are all here, we can put the plans into motion.'

He wouldn't tell his men that the concept of being watched unnerved him, but it *did.* He didn't want those bastards who sided with Marco getting warning of when he would strike.

If someone was watching, they could follow him. And if they followed him, they would learn where he lived. And who with…

They would see Erin, which would expose that she was also the spy within Luna, which would place her in grave danger. And as Sonny had been the one to bring her in, it would jeopardise him too. Every single one of the men sitting around this table knew this.

'So!' Zane slapped his palms down on the surface of the wooden table. 'We now know the container of the trafficked women is delayed until tomorrow. We also know that Marco is returning from honeymoon on Thursday, rather than Saturday. It's now Monday, so this is what we're going to do.'

• • • •

ERIN FELT LIKE she'd been plunged headlong into hell as she watched the men pulling terrified women from the back of the container. It was taking all her power not to scream for them to stop and do whatever possible to hold off this dreadful spectacle, even if that meant calling the police.

But she could do none of that. One wrong move which exposed her of having an issue with this, let alone involving the Old Bill, and she would be killed before the phone even connected. It would also underline her as a traitor, plus expose Sonny's part in it. Although she immensely disliked the man, and whether he deserved a lesson in betrayal or not, she would not do that to him. Furthermore, if they were exposed, then Zane would be too and that she would *never* risk.

Her only choice was to remain unquestioning and keep a mask of cool indifference in place on her face as to what was happening to these poor women.

In reality, it felt like her brain was melting from the inside out.

Erin continued watching with impotent horror as the men continued pulling women from the back of the urine-soaked container, many losing their footing and falling from the container to the floor.

Damon snarled as one woman hit the deck with a scream, her knee ripping open on the concrete of the loading bay. 'You stupid bitch!' he roared. 'You'll now be useless for filming until that gash on your leg heals.' He snatched a handful of her hair and yanked her to her feet. 'Ain't you got eyes?'

Erin instinctively rushed forward, then stopped, her eyes moving from the woman's torn knee to the unmistakable swell of her belly. 'She's pregnant!'

'What of it?' Damon dragged the whimpering woman forward. 'There's three like this. Special requests for a particular film Marco has planned.' His ugly face broke into a savage grin. 'Hey, tart! At least you've kept the brat where it's supposed to be. Not much use to us if you'd had the fucking thing on the way!'

Damon's comment earned laughter from the rest of the men as the woman fell back to her knees, but sickened Erin further.

'She's hurt!' Erin protested. 'At least let me clean her up.' She risked laying her hand on the terrified woman whose frightened eyes conveyed a thousand words.

'I doubt she's as hurt as she'll end up!' One man jibed. 'Christ, Damon. Why have you employed this do-gooder? It's the last thing we need!'

'I ain't employed no one. Anyway, Caroline knows the score.' With his free hand, Damon pinched Erin's chin between his fingers, forcing her head up. 'You *do* know the score, don't you, sweetheart?'

Erin nodded, biting down on her tongue to keep the words she longed to scream at this man to herself.

'But they do stink of shit,' Damon acknowledged, his nose wrinkling. 'Maybe you should clean them up.' Shoving the heavily pregnant woman towards Erin, he clapped his big hands together. 'Listen up lads! Caroline here will oversee this lot and give them a wash and sheep dip.' He silenced the disgruntled murmurings. 'Yeah, yeah, I know you all want first go and *that* you'll get, but...' His face cracked into another one of those hateful sneers. 'I don't know about you lot, but I'm not sticking my cock in a smelly cunt, so let's get them clean. We don't want to catch owt from the dirty bitches. Besides, we've got all day.'

Holding her breath, Erin locked eyes with the pregnant woman. Getting these poor women away from these bastards, even if it only delayed the inevitable for an hour was something. And after that, well, she didn't know.

How she wished, not for the first time, that Sonny was here. Sandler had lied. He'd lied on purpose so Sonny would leave, believing the women were delayed. Whatever Sonny's faults, he wasn't an animal. He'd have pulled rank and stopped this despite what the women would subsequently be exposed to in order to fill Marco's purse.

Taking a deep breath, Erin squeezed the pregnant woman's hand and with a voice as loud and clear as she could muster, she turned to face the other women. 'Okay then, girls, come with me. The showers are along here.'

Facing Damon, somehow refraining from spitting in his face, she appeared business-like. 'I'll get them sorted and then they're all yours, okay?'

'That's more like it!' Damon sneered. 'Just don't let any of them take fucking liberties. Quick as you can, too. There's impatient fellas here. You might also want to point out to any of these chicks who understand English that they should be grateful for a bit of fun before being locked up.'

Nodding tersely, Erin turned away, not trusting herself to give an acceptable response. It was unlikely there would be a way out for those women. Just like she'd suspected, whenever Zane stepped in would be too late. Resentment burned. He should have shut this place down from the off.

Releasing them at a later point was all very well, but the damage would have been done. And that alone sickened her to the very bone.

TWELVE

HAZEL HAD WAITED for as long as possible without risking Marco getting suspicious enough to come and look for her. Although, being as he was happily involved in a game of roulette at the hotel casino, he may not have noticed how long she'd been gone.

She smoothed down the satin of her blue cocktail dress and afforded herself another gratifying glance in the cloakroom mirror.

Stunning, as always, she thought proudly. Marco would never get better than her.

The wobble this morning that her new husband could ever be so deluded to think about even *looking* at another woman had been ridiculous. Why she'd even entertained such possibility flabbergasted her. All this sun was messing with her head.

Marco's explanation for last night's disappearance must be true. Where else could he have gone? He had no reason to stray. Why the hell would he when he had *this* to wake up to?

Putting on one of her most celebrated poses, Hazel studied the perfect moue her lips formed in the mirror, then pushed her enhanced breasts together to form a killer cleavage under the tight bodice of her dress. With these babies to gaze at any time he liked, who could want for more?

She smiled, her white teeth shining in the bright lighting. She hadn't been remiss enough however, not to confirm with the waiter what Marco had mentioned. It proved he'd been telling the truth. Not that she needed confirmation, but men liked their women to believe they could be led astray. It made them feel important and Hazel was happy to make Marco feel like a king.

All men needed worship and being as she stood to gain plenty from this marriage, she'd happily stroke Marco's ego.

Applying another coat of lip gloss on top of the last eight layers, Hazel focused on the closed door of the cubicle behind her, hearing a faint rustle coming from within.

How much longer would this stupid bitch be? Had she got dysentery?

Hazel's lips curled into a feral snarl. With any luck, the cow had the fucking plague too, but if she didn't hurry up, then making her point would have to be deferred.

But she wanted to make the point and rarely failed to achieve what she desired. In fact, she couldn't remember a time when she hadn't. On the same vein, she couldn't hang around here forever.

Hearing the toilet flush, Hazel grinned. *See? As if by magic. What Hazel desired, Hazel got. It was the law of the land and the way of her world.*

Popping open her sequinned clutch bag, she slipped her lip gloss back inside, her fingers moving to the other item placed inside for one purpose alone.

Marco had been innocent with his attentions but *others* weren't.

As a beautiful brunette exited the cubicle and moved towards the sinks, Hazel's eyes narrowed in the mirror's reflection.

Her usually plump lips flattened in contempt. That wasn't even this season's Dior dress. Urgh!

No, she had no worries with Marco. Her man wouldn't look

twice at anyone else, but this slag had given him the once over, thinking she stood a chance of enticing her husband away! It was laughable, but tarts like this must learn they couldn't behave in such a way. Not with anything belonging to Hazel.

It was irrelevant that nothing had happened. It was enough that this bitch had *wanted* it to and for that she'd be sorry.

Ignoring the awkward smile the brunette afforded her, Hazel's fingers found a comfortable grip on the item in her clutch bag.

It was such a shame that the jar accompanying her continental breakfast this morning had 'slipped' from her hand to smash into pieces on the balcony, wasn't it?

Whipping the small piece of glass out of her bag, careful to hold it at the blunt edge, Hazel quickly sliced at the brunette's cheek. It happened so effortlessly, she wasn't sure contact had been successfully made until the hairline cut spanning from the edge of the woman's eye down to her jawline widened and then bloomed with blood.

It was fascinating how something as innocuous as a small piece from a jam jar could inflict such impressive wounds.

Hazel stared with satisfaction as the brunette who, momentarily unsure what had happened, gaped at her reflection, before letting out an anguished scream.

The woman's hands flew to her cheek, the now fiercely flowing blood tracking over her hands and down her forearm to drip in a steady flow from the tip of her elbow onto her tight white dress. 'What have you done?' she shrieked. 'You've ruined my face! Oh my God!'

Hazel felt no need to lay another finger on this woman. Apart from not wanting blood on her own hands or dress, she'd made her point. One which would last… Instead, she glared into the ruined face of the sobbing brunette. 'Don't make a play for my husband ever again.' She casually handed the woman a tissue from the gold dispenser next to the sink. 'Here, take this. Although I think you'll need a few stitches.' *Like thirty...*

Chucking the shard of glass underneath the sink, no longer

useful now it had served its purpose, Hazel tossed her long blonde extensions over her shoulder and smiled coldly. 'Oh, and a word of advice... I wouldn't mention our meeting to anyone or my husband will have you killed. He doesn't like me getting upset.'

Turning on her heels, Hazel stalked from the cloakroom, not a hair out of place and with a wide smile, made her way back towards the hotel casino.

• • • •

ERIN REALISED that she couldn't protect all of these women. In reality, she couldn't protect *any* of them, but for what it was worth, she'd had to make a choice. It was difficult. Impossible really, but the heavily pregnant woman still bleeding profusely from the deep wound in her knee had to be treated, as did another girl, all of sixteen - possibly even younger who had sustained a blow to the head, either during transit or from tumbling from the container.

Her instinct was to help every woman and stop those depraved bastards from doing what she now knew would happen. *Was already happening...*

As the women emerged from the showers, one of Sandler's henchmen had dragged them off to do their 'duty'.

'It's only right to test them out,' they'd laughed.

Sickening.

Despite herself, Erin felt the burn of frustrated tears in the back of her eyes. She was powerless to stop it. The only reason she'd kept hold of these two was because they were more injured than most.

She reached out to apply a cold compress she'd fashioned for the younger girl's head, only to get batted away.

'Get off!' the girl spat, her eyes flashing with venom.

Erin flinched. 'You've taken a nasty bang to you head and y...'

'Help? You are one of these same people!' The girl glared at Erin with open malice. 'I'd rather die than accept your help!'

Erin caught the eye of the pregnant woman, who she now knew to be called Sonia.

'You waste your time,' Sonia mumbled in her broken English. 'This girl get us killed with her attitude, but I appreciate you help.'

Nodding sadly, Erin turned back to the young girl. 'Are you from Poland too?' This girl's spiky attitude was similar to her own and her heart went out to her - to *all* of them. She couldn't blame them for their assumptions. If *she'd* been manhandled into a container and shipped to be used as sex fodder, then she too would presume anyone the other end was part of it. There was no point trying to change this perception, but if things could be put into place with the minimum amount of damage then hopefully this girl and all of these women, would come to realise that not *everyone* were animals.

'You won't get answer with her,' Sonya repeated. 'But yes, most of us are from Poland. The agency told her she be nanny – like care for children.'

Erin's anger burnt brighter. 'And you?' She nodded at Sonya's huge belly. 'What did they tell you?'

'I tell I have live-in place with job. Place where baby and I live and look after three other children.' She rubbed her bump protectively. 'I know now that not happening.'

Erin bit her lip, her heart breaking. How she hated Marco for this. For *everything*.

Why didn't you stop this, Zane? she thought again. *Why?*

Erin wasn't entirely sure just how low things would sink for these women, but she suspected that judging by those cages, it would be worse than she thought.

'This woman lives in dream world,' the young girl snarled, prodding the blackening lump on her temple over and over, like the constant pain deflected from life - or rather than the life they now faced. 'I know what is plan. They take our passports. We are to be prostitute. Sex with fat, ugly men,' she spat, her hatred palpable. 'I kill them. I not care. I will not sleep with fucking pigs. I not sleep with *you*, either.'

She cut a glare so violent that Erin felt her own temper spike. 'You're not expected to sleep with me!' Reining in her rising fury, she tried once again to calm this youngster down. 'You must be calm. I'll help you in any way I can.'

'Liar!' the girl spat. 'You all fucking lie.'

Damon suddenly burst into the room. 'Are these two good to go?'

Erin paled. Had she failed to even keep these two safe? She gestured to Sonia. 'I can't stem this lady's bleeding. I think she needs stitches. And this one has concussion and needs rest.'

'You fucking what?' Damon roared. 'That's not an option. This...'

'You bastard pig!' The young girl lurched towards Damon. 'I kill you and all you fucking…'

Erin jumped to her feet to intervene but she was too late.

Pulling his gun, Damon planted a bullet in the centre of the young girl's forehead as she ran towards him. A split second of shock passed over her face before she crumpled to the floor, dead.

Erin blinked. 'What the...' She didn't get chance to finish her sentence before the second bullet left Damon's gun to extinguish the life of Sonia who hadn't even moved from the chair.

Heart thumping, Erin's breath caught in her throat, horror outweighing her burning rage.

Hawking, Damon spat phlegm on the pregnant corpse and glared at Erin. 'I told you not to waste your time with these ungrateful foreign cunts! These people are of no use if they can't work. Now stop pissing around and come with me. The rest of those fuckers can come and look at this pair. It will show them what happens if they don't play nice.'

Damon stalked from the room leaving Erin to drop to her knees to heave up nothing but bile from her empty stomach. *He'd killed them both for nothing.*

And there she was thinking she could make things slightly more palatable for two of these women, yet she'd ended up aiding in their demise.

Damn Damon Sandler and all of the rest of these bastards to hell. This cunt had to be taken down, along with Marco. But how long before that happened?

Wiping the back of her hand across her mouth, Erin forced herself to her feet and left the room. For the rest of those women's sakes she had no option but to follow Sandler. But that would not last forever and then if she got a chance, she would make him pay.

• • • •

ERIN SEARCHED FOR AN EXCUSE not to remain in the room with the men so she could get a message to Sonny and tell him what had happened.

Her hand brushed against her mobile phone concealed in her waistband underneath her blouse.

Sonny was at that meeting with Zane and if she could get a message to them about what had happened then surely Zane would act and storm the place?

But there hadn't been one moment to risk getting her phone out. Damon Sandler hadn't taken his eyes off her, relishing in the perverse enjoyment of forcing her to witness this spectacle.

Erin glanced at Damon standing against the wall overseeing his men violating the women. It had been bad enough helping to shepherd these women past the room where Sonia and the other girl lay dead. She'd had to witness their expressions at the grotesque scene and with it, the dawning realisation that this would be *them* if they didn't comply with what this filth wanted.

Now the women were complying – led like lambs to the slaughter. The human capacity to grasp any shred of hope in order to survive.

But Erin suspected that now they wished they hadn't. *And this was only the start...*

She couldn't stop her eyes from returning back to the scene she'd tried so hard to switch off from. Seeing these women being grossly and forcibly violated made it increasingly difficult to stay expressionless and not attack every single one of these bastards.

But that was half of the problem. Even if she threw her and Sonny's cover out of the window and with it, Zane's plans, she couldn't take on fifteen men. Not without a machine gun. And that, she did not have.

Furthermore, from what Damon said, there were plenty more men within this building in addition to those here. Did Zane have any concept of how many men he and his small group would be taking on?

Feeling ever sicker as a man dragged his unwilling victim mid-copulation from one part of the room to the other to slam the woman's head onto the table right in front of her, Erin saw fear and pain spilling from the woman inches away - her clear blue eyes conveying the obvious. *Help me!*

Language wasn't required when eyes did the talking, yet not a flicker of emotion passed over Erin's face. Resenting herself past the point of no return for her lack of courage in standing up to these monsters, she genuinely wondered how much more she could withstand before she reacted and by doing so, bringing everyone else down. It wouldn't help these women though. Nothing would.

Was being impassive a lack of courage or the best thing to do?

The arguments within her own head rushed faster, her temples pounding. Turning away from the beseeching eyes of the woman impaled on the table, Erin's nausea rose higher.

Everywhere she looked, men rutted on the women like animals. Some of them two on one.

She avoided looking in the direction of the other two pregnant women where a pair of men goaded each other to slam into the women as hard as possible, jeering about which one would go into labour first. And as much as Erin tried to delete the image from her brain, the snapshot of the women she'd watched lose their lives to Sandler remained emblazoned in her mind.

That unborn baby left to slowly die within its mother's womb...

She shook her head as if it might dislodge the slow-motion shock that fleetingly crossed Sonia's face as the bullet entered her skull before the life seeped from behind her eyes.

'Why do you look so pissed off.' Damon reached out to grab both of Erin's breasts. 'Are you jealous you're not getting any attention?'

Erin stuck her nails into the fleshy parts of Damon's hands. He relinquished his grip, but seeing his eyes narrow with rage, she realised she should not have done it.

'You fucking whore!' Damon spat, globules of spittle spraying into Erin's face. 'You just won't learn!' He lunged towards her and grabbed her waist.

Erin's heart lurched. Forget what else Damon might do - if he found her mobile phone everything would be worse. 'Damon, I...'

When the door suddenly crashed open, Damon's head shot up giving Erin a moments respite. Her first thought was that Sonny and Zane must have got wind of what was unfolding and made their move. But that was impossible unless her thoughts transmitted through the ether.

They hadn't.... It wasn't them...

With Damon distracted enough at this interruption to concentrate only on the skinny man bursting uninvited into the room, Erin took her chance and inched away from his reach, scanning for something to use to knock the bastard to the floor.

'What the fuck do you mean by barging in here?' Damon yelled, seeing the man's eyes light up at the orgy in front of him. 'Runners aren't invited to this particular perk, so fuck off!' Grabbing the runner by the arm, his face twisted in fury. 'Did you not hear me? You've got two fucking seconds to get ou...'

'I've just come from the Blacksmith's Arms,' the runner gasped, coming to his senses. 'I've legged it all the way over here to te...'

'I said, get the fuck out!'

Erin edged towards a bunch of keys on a nearby table. If she could reach them, maybe she could stab Damon in the hand. Or the eyes… Then it would only take a few seconds to raise the alarm...

Her hand hovered over the mobile phone underneath her skirt. Could she call Sonny or Zane by pressing the buttons through the material? They were the only two contacts on there, but could she guess which buttons would unlock the phone without looking?

Perspiration beaded underneath her hairline, her headache growing.

'I'm not fucking interested what happened at the Blacksmith's Arms!' Damon barked, dragging the skinny man to the door. 'Now bugger off!'

'But Starlight Studios has been torched and a body's been found!' the man blathered. 'Isn't that Lisa Tequila's place? Doesn't Mr Morelli have interest wi...'

'It's *what*?' Damon froze, as did Erin, her fingers hovering nearer the bunch of keys.

'It's burnt down,' the runner continued, gratified to have Damon's attention. 'Some bloke in the pub - his brother's a fireman. He said a body was found this morning by kids who'd broke in. They think it's Grimes. They also think it's no accident.'

Damon's jaw clenched. *Fuck.* Marco would go batshit. Now he had to deal with this which would balls up his men's fun. Suddenly an idea formed. 'If that's all you have to say, then you've said it. Off you go.'

'The young runner blinked. 'But don't you want to...'

'I said, off you go, didn't I? You've already had enough of a look in here to not need wank mags for a week!' Pushing the runner from the room, Damon leant against the closed door, his mind whirring.

If he called Marco and told him what had happened before Sonny got the chance, then *he'd* be the one rewarded for his resourcefulness. This would give Marco another obvious reason to realise that Sonny Mitchell was about as much use as second-in-command as a chocolate fire guard.

Straining to hear over the loud grunting of men around her, Erin clocked every word of Damon's conversation. Starlight was the studio where Zane had offloaded Trevor Grimes – Marco's new wife's father. She knew the plan was to torch it but no one was supposed to come across the body yet.

Feeling Damon's full attention back on her, she tensed as he approached. She quickly resumed the look of being fixated on the disgusting goings on.

Damon slapped Erin around the face. 'Wakey wakey, Caroline! Men don't like desperados and you sitting there like a left-out wallflower isn't a turn on. If you want action, you need to change how you portray yourself,' he chuckled. 'I'll break you in, but I need to make a quick call first. Something's come up that the boss needs to know about.' He dragged his calloused finger over Erin's lips. 'Now don't move. I'll be back in a moment.'

Erin nodded like the obedient dog she pretended to be and waited as Damon slipped out of the room before her hand moved to her phone. With him gone, she might get away with *this*.

Turning to the side, she inched her phone from under her waistband, her fingers shaking as she unlocked it. She had to get word to Sonny or Zane right now. She couldn't risk calling so a text would have to do. She could only hope they were in signal.

THIRTEEN

MARCO WAS PLEASED to have found a member of the hotel staff offering a better price on coke than that dodgy bloke in the hotel's entertainment troupe.

He should have known better than to think he'd get a good deal from a poxy fire-eater in a shitty circus, but he'd had little choice unless he wanted to stray from the luxurious confines of the hotel resort and venture into the backstreets of the surrounding cities. And that he did not want. It would be like a busman's holiday. Even then, since becoming head honcho sourcing coke himself wasn't something he'd dirtied his hands with for the best part of six years.

Considering he had enough coke back home to supply half a country it was a bit of a shit to buy more. But even with his connections, the chances of getting enough to last him two weeks through customs had been impossible.

Anyway, this new guy had offered a much better deal and judging by the buzz in his head, it was purer stuff than the other crap he'd sourced.

He glanced with satisfaction at the healthy mound of gaming chips piled on his section of green velvet. He was on a winning streak tonight. Maybe on more than just roulette if he played cleverly.

Being careful not to accidentally brush anyone else's leg, Marco's hand snaked underneath the roulette table, his fingers tracing a line down the velvety thigh of the redhead seated next to him. From the double flutter of her false lashes, he deduced that she did not object.

Bonus.

All he had to do was be more sensible this time and not spend the whole night away from Hazel.

Suddenly noticing his wife's lack of presence, Marco's eyes narrowed. Where the fuck was she? Hadn't she just nipped to the bog? Fell down it, had she?

The pumping in his hands signified the urge to form a fist. Was Hazel taking the piss? Had she gone to flirt with another man to get him back for last night?

That was stupid. Hazel had no worries that he'd disappear permanently. Not whilst she commanded such a following of her films. But if she tried to make him look a mug, she'd learn the hard way.

With cocaine making Marco's brain turn at three times the normal speed, his paranoia cranked up a notch. Maybe several. And as the redhead's hand found its way to his crotch, he pushed it away. There was no point her doing that now. She should have reciprocated thirty seconds ago before his mind was elsewhere.

Ignoring the woman's look of personal affront at his rebuff, Marco peered around her flamboyant hairstyle to see if he could lay eyes on his errant wife. *If Hazel was playing him, then...*

Slipping soundlessly between Marco and the redhead, Hazel cut the woman a suitable withering look to underline where her territory began and others ended. Turning her back, hoping her left buttock was suitably uncomfortable on the woman's thigh, she draped herself possessively over Marco, her pumped up lips brushing his earlobe. 'Have you won?' she purred.

'Where have you been?' Marco growled, the lips against

his ear going straight to his cock. This had the effect of considerably reducing his paranoid angst and instead gave rise to toying with the idea as to Hazel's interest in a threesome with the buxom redhead. After all, didn't she owe him something for going off the deep end this morning?

'I haven't been long!' Hazel raised her plucked eyebrows at the other women around the table staking possession on their husbands the moment she'd sat back down. She felt like laughing.

Gratified the redhead she'd squashed into the chair made a petulant huffing sound and extracted herself from the table, Hazel smiled benevolently, her hand finding its way onto Marco's crotch.

Unperturbed, Marco pulled his concentration back to the roulette table and pushed a huge pile of chips into the centre. 'Number twenty-one,' he muttered. He'd already won 30K, so his luck was in. Even the redhead's disappearance failed to dampen the chemical rush in his brain. He was on a roll and nothing would stop him.

Marco watched the croupier spin the wheel and focused as the ball bounced around the numbers. He willed it to land on number twenty-one.

It was going to. It was going to!

It took a couple of seconds of his emergency mobile buzzing in his pocket before Marco's speeding brain put two and two together. He wasn't answering that now. It could wait.

The ball's path slowed as the roulette wheel began to grind to a halt. *Go on, go on...*

Red - five, black - twenty, red – nine, red - eighteen... Not the green zero, not the zero. Come on...

Black – fifteen. Yes, go on...

The phone continued buzzing.

Fuck off, Marco thought. His concentration couldn't slip now.

Red - nineteen, black - four.

Fuck!

Yes! Red – twenty-one! Stop! STOP!

Yes!

'Red twenty-one!' the croupier announced.

'Yay!' Marco whooped, proudly puffing his chest out as Hazel squealed with delight. That would bring a pretty penny.

'You've won, babe,' Hazel purred, already clocking up how many filler injections this windfall would cover.

'Don't I always?' Marco grinned. *Fuck, he was good.* The phone had stopped ringing too. He'd check to see what that was about in a minute. He'd just have one more go here because he was definitely on a roll.

Scraping his pile of chips towards him and ignoring the other players' disgruntled faces, Marco readied himself to place his biggest bet yet. When this one came in, it would net around 150K. There was no question that he would lose.

'Excuse me, sir.'

Marco flinched at the hand on his shoulder. He hated being touched uninvited. Only when *he* said could anyone touch him. Swinging around, he was all set to slam his fist in the face of whoever possessed the audacity to step over the line, but paused on seeing the casino manager.

'I'm truly sorry to interrupt you, sir, but an emergency call has come through for you on one of our telephones.'

'For me?' Marco's mind worked overtime. Only certain people knew of his exact location and they had no need to ring him here. That's why he got a fucking emergency mobile, was it not? *But then again, he hadn't answered it...*

Pushing Hazel off him, he snatched the receiver from the manager's hand, the phone pulling tightly on the wheeled trolley next to him. 'Yeah?' *This had better be important. Why the hell couldn't this have waited until...* 'What? What did you fucking say? FUCK!'

'What is it, babe?' Hazel exclaimed as the general noise around them died to a hushed whisper with the sudden blast of expletives.

Scowling at his wife, Marco waved Hazel's question away.

'Just fucking wait! I'll be back as soon as.' Slamming the phone down, he nodded tersely to the manager and then jerked his head to signify his dismissal. Almost chucking Hazel off her chair, he lurched from the table to scrape his chips together. He'd cash this lot in tout suite and then get the hotel straight onto booking flights.

This had to be his bastard brother's doing.

'What's going on?' Hazel's fingers grasped at Marco's tuxedo. 'Who was that?'

Marco shrugged Hazel's hand away. 'That was Damon from work,' he growled. Not that Hazel would know who the fuck Damon was. Even *he* barely knew who Damon was. 'There's been a problem. We're going home.'

'Home?' Hazel yelped, skittering after Marco as he stormed towards the cashier. 'What do you mean, home? We're not due to leave for another four days!' She wasn't having her honeymoon cut short. What did that look like? Furthermore, she still had a couple of tan lines she needed to get rid of. 'I'm not going back early! I...'

'We're going home!' Marco snapped. 'Your father's fucking dead!'

But it wasn't Trevor Grimes he was returning for. It was for whoever had done this. And furthermore, to find out why Sonny hadn't been the one to let him know rather than Damon Sandler.

• • • •

ZANE STUDIED EACH of his men in turn. Making sure everyone from the top to the bottom of an organisation were happy to go ahead with whatever was asked, no matter how big or small, was the way he'd been taught to do things.

A flashback of his father sitting in his leather chair in the office at the original headquarters flew into his mind. He could picture Giuseppe - immaculate in his dark, tailored suit, not a hair out of place regardless of the time or day or what had gone on. He'd fold his arms across his chest and study Zane for several minutes before speaking. He always had.

His father's cold blue eyes, the same penetrating ones that both he and his brother inherited, would scrutinise him intensely. *'Respect, son,'* he'd say. *'Respect for all members of the firm. These people will risk their all on your say so, therefore the very least you can guarantee them is respect by double checking they understand what's being asked of them. Those ones will never let you down. Manners and consideration is a small price to pay for loyalty.'*

Zane thought that never a truer word had been spoken. These men sitting in front of him right now had returned to back him, despite the odds and risk to themselves.

He wouldn't treat them like commodities.

'Are we all clear as to how this will go down? Everybody knows their part and happy with what's been instructed?' he asked. Happy was undoubtedly the wrong word for a situation such as this, but thanks to his father's advice, it was the way Zane always confirmed matters of importance with his staff.

Seeing a unanimous acknowledgement by the nodding of heads, Zane pulled forward his notepad containing his men's suggestions to his plan. Although he called the shots, he wasn't switched off to input.

Sparking up a cigarette, he finished the last of his pint. What was planned was all good and just in time. 'Right, so when Sonny collects Erin to take her to the studios it will be business as usual. He'll leave me the key to the lock-up near the old headquarters.'

Despite binning off the headquarters themselves, Marco still used that lock-up. Another example of his arrogance. 'There I'll meet with Tiger and Leo. We'll load up the guns and head to Luna.'

'I'll ensure no men have been briefed to go to the lock-up,' Sonny added.

'We'll know the exact time the container will arrive by close of play tonight. Erin will get that out of Sandler today,' Zane glanced at Sonny, receiving a nod confirming that part had been put in place. 'I'll text you all the time as soon as I have it.

Me, Tiger and Leo will be admitted to Luna at a yet to be confirmed time tomorrow by Sonny.'

He then turned to Cav and Lewis. 'You Fletcher boys will watch my penthouse. We'll shoot as many muppets as necessary at Luna and those remaining will raise the alarm.'

'The guards at your apartment complex will leave their posts to rush back to the studios to help intercept,' Cav added.

'But we'll leave them to it,' Lewis said, wanting to make clear he understood the brief too.

Zane gave a small shake of his head. 'And we need to keep it clean. There are too many civvies around the penthouse to gloss over shit happening. We need to keep that place out of it, especially after the stunt Marco pulled with that bird on the balcony. We don't want to be lumbered with a clean-up there.'

'Those guards will then storm Luna where I'll be waiting to take them out.' Leo chucked his tuppence into the mix, already salivating with the prospect of getting his hands on a decent weapon. *And using it.* It had been far too long.

'Cav and Lewis will take possession of my penthouse,' Zane continued. 'All the usual shit applies – swapping locks, etc. Once it's fully secure, they'll join us at Luna to clear out any leftovers.'

The appreciative murmuring continued as Zane ran through the rest of the plan. It was all pretty much sorted. 'All that's left is to deal with any remaining staff who could have slipped the net. They'll have to be culled. There won't be time to weigh up the small off chance that there's any who could prove loyal.'

That was the slightly uncomfortable part of something such as this, but there was always a certain amount of collateral damage. 'After that, we get moving with putting the firm back to its old self and then it's merely a case of waiting for Marco's return.'

The nerve in Zane's jaw twitched. *That* part would prove difficult. Despite what his brother had done, it didn't change that Marco was his brother and a small chink still remained of seeing him as the small lad who'd always looked up to him. But there was no room for sentiment. Nor was there time to dwell. This was happening for the greater good. Marco was a threat and would remain one. The line had been crossed too many times to backtrack. 'My brother is a liability and him remaining alive isn't conducive to anyone. Even less so now he's made the decision to go down the road of trafficking women.'

'What's the plan with those women once they arrive?' Sonny asked. 'What do we do with them? We can't let them go. They could run straight to the police and lead the Old Bill to us.'

Zane nodded. 'No they can't be let go. Not for some time anyway, so I'm unsure about that one at the moment. Whatever happens, they'll be looked after.'

'I'm just glad they won't be there when we storm the place,' Tiger muttered. 'I don't want birds' blood on my hands.' Collateral damage including a shed load of women was one of the few things that would seep under what little moral conscience he possessed. Men, sure, but women - no fucking way.

'That's why it's important we get the exact time of the drop from Erin. Women must not be present when this kicks off.'

'Amen to that!' Leo banged his fist on the table.

Zane smiled - a rare sight lately. 'Then I think we've got everything. As said, confirmation of the finer details will happen later.'

Hearing an unexpected 'ding', Zane pulled his mobile from his pocket. Perhaps Erin had got the time from Damon already?

The notification did indeed confirm the text was from Erin. She'd taken a risk using her phone whilst at Luna. If anyone spotted her with it, that could be a disaster.

Opening the message, his eyes scanned the hurriedly typed text. He sucked in air through his teeth.

`The women are here. Things are awful. They know about Grimes too. Sand calling M.`

'Shit!' Zane hissed, getting to his feet. 'Change of fucking plan.'

'What? What is it?' Tiger and everyone else scrambled to their feet.

'A text off Erin. Unless I'm mistaken, Damon Sandler fucking lied. The women have arrived and worse, Grimes' body has been found,' Zane spat.

'Shit!' Leo cried. 'This changes our timescales somewhat.'

'I'm not sitting here fucking around.' Zane grabbed his crash helmet. 'We have to intervene now.'

He rushed to leave the room. He didn't need to look at anyone else's faces to know that this was not good. Neither would he hang around longer than necessary. He had to move on this and move on it now. Especially as Erin was there on her own.

If Damon bastard Sandler had hurt one hair on her head, then that man would be first in line to be dispatched.

'Whoa! Hold on!' Tiger yelled. 'We need the guns first. We also need to think about this.'

'Think?' Zane stared at Tiger incredulously. 'You want to sit on this and think? No way!' He made to rush past Tiger to the door only to find his way blocked. Eyes flashing fire, he glared at Tiger and Leo. 'Get out of my way!'

'You need to wait,' Tiger said slowly, fully expecting a headbutt to the nose. 'Reacting off the cuff will do more harm than good.'

'He's right, mate,' Leo said. 'Now the women are on site, they'll end up getting killed. Either by us or by Marco's cunts. Without a new plan, anyone could get caught in the crossfire.'

Zane paused. Breathing heavily, his shoulders sagged slightly as he leant against the door. 'Anyone' being caught in the crossfire included Erin. With no means of warning her, she'd be in the middle of it. It would be a bloodbath.

However strong his urge was to immediately react he knew they had to pull back. 'How the fuck do we do this?' he muttered, to himself more than anyone else.

'We do what we planned,' Tiger said. 'Business as usual in the interim. It's the only way.'

'I agree,' Sonny added. 'I'll head back to Luna now and act normal. I'll bring Erin home at close like usual. I'll also make sure Marco isn't made aware of this extra shit with Grimes. It will be me who has to tell him and I won't be doing that for as long as possible!'

Zane's cold blue eyes burrowed into Sonny's. 'But that's the other problem. Erin said Sandler's gone to phone Marco. He's probably already done it by now.'

FOURTEEN

MARCO STARED VACANTLY at the blood on his starched white shirt cuff in confusion until he remembered he'd dug his nails into the palm of his hand purposely until they broke the skin. His nails were short and manicured, so it was some feat to achieve, but he'd hadn't relented until he'd experienced that slight release only self-inflicted pain could bring. He needed it to deflect from the urge to throw Hazel over the balcony to smash into pieces onto the pool terrace many storeys below.

It wouldn't have been the first time he'd been responsible for launching a woman to her death off a balcony and doubted it would be the last, but it *wouldn't* be Hazel.

Plus, he wasn't in his suite, but waiting in the hotel's lobby bar.

If he killed Hazel, he'd have wasted ten years' worth of fantasies over her for nothing. He didn't like the thought of putting time into something, yet gaining nothing. By marrying her, he'd got what he'd wanted, plus the lucrative addition she'd bring to his films.

But her wailing was driving him to distraction. He wished she'd shut the fuck up because he couldn't think straight.

Wiping the blood off his hand down his tuxedo trousers,

Marco wished the hotel staff would get a fucking move on. Twenty minutes he'd been sat here like a spare prick waiting for them to find him a flight. He was on his fifth rum and had heard nothing. He didn't appreciate Hazel's loud sobbing and moaning making them a tourist attraction either.

Glaring in the general direction of the booking desk, Marco watched the staff rush around behind the counter. Busy on the phones, they took it in turns to sneak nervous glances at him, only to then rapidly look away.

They'd better get him those flights. Right *now*.

Marco stared at his watch, his blood pumping. He'd also issued clear instructions for the apartment to be packed up so that he'd be ready to leave the second the confirmation of the tickets to fly back to London tonight came through. What the fuck was the hold up?

Now the pain in his palm was easing, the scraping sound as he wore the enamel down from grinding his teeth helped further in distracting from Hazel's whimpering. He had to keep his mind occupied.

Christ, he needed a line. A fucking big one. And he didn't care who saw him.

Pulling the bullet-shaped vial from his inside pocket, he bypassed the attached spoon and instead snorted it directly from the silver bottle.

Sniffing loudly, he relished the burn behind his eyeballs. He glared at an old woman staring at him as she tottered past in her high heels. She should wear flats. And a longer skirt. That ensemble only emphasised the varicose veins on her calves. 'Buy yourself some support stockings, bitch!' he sneered loud enough for her to hear.

Dragging the back of his hand underneath his nose, Marco jumped to his feet, his pulse crashing in his veins. Not bothering to say a word to Hazel, he barged past the older woman gaping at his comments and stormed over to the reception desk.

Slamming a young couple waiting to check in out of the way, he didn't give anyone the chance to say a word before he dived over the counter and grabbed one of the reception staff by the throat.

Dragging the man back with him so he was spread over the shiny marble surface of the reception counter, Marco pushed himself into the man's face. 'Where the fuck are my flights, you bastard? Twenty minutes I've been sat here like a cunt!' His eyes bulged from their sockets. 'What time is the plane leaving and from where?'

The reception manager scuttled from a small office behind the desk, took one look at the commotion unfolding and rushed to the counter. 'Mr Morelli! Please unhand my staff! I'm aware of your distressing news, but rest assured my staff are working flat out to secure you and your wife tickets, but...'

'Jesus Christ! If you lot worked for me I'd have you killed, you useless bastards! Where are my fucking tickets?' Marco raged, increasing his grip on the terrified man in his grasp.

White-faced, the manager dashed around the other side of the counter waving his hands theatrically. 'Mr Morelli! That's what I'm trying to tell you! There aren't any tickets to London available tonight. My staff are trying other airlines. Now please let this man go!'

The manager then made the horrible error of laying his hand on Marco's arm.

Marco paused, a slight grin akin to hysteria sliding across his face. Releasing his grip of the spluttering man on the counter, his eyes slowly slid down to stare at the fingers clutching the sleeve of his shirt.

He waited patiently until the manager realised his mistake and rapidly withdrew his hand. 'Do you know, for a moment then I thought I heard you say something ridiculous.' Marco's cold glare moved to meet the eyes of the now trembling reception manager. 'I was convinced you just said there were no flights available, but that's preposterous, isn't it?'

The manager blinked, a horrible sense of doom growing. 'Well, I erm... I'm afraid there really aren't any flights with your airline leaving tonight to Lo…'

Amidst a collection of horrified shrieks and gasps from others in the reception bar area, Marco's fist connected with the manager's nose with the power of a jack hammer, the force flicking the man backwards to land on the floor at his feet.

Panting, Marco reined in his escalating temper. *Control, control.* 'Being as this incompetence was an unintentional error of yours and I'm a fair man, I won't take this any further at present. I trust the problem will be immediately rectified?'

Two other staff skittered from behind the counter and cautiously approached their manager to help him from the floor under the watchful eyes of this lunatic.

'I'll be waiting in my apartment. Ring my room when flights are sourced,' Marco instructed, his voice steady. 'It has to be tonight. Any class and any airline will do. Got that?'

Storming back across the hushed lobby, Marco grabbed Hazel's arm and yanked her to her feet. 'Come on, sweetheart. We'll go back to our room until this situation is rectified. You don't need to get yourself any more upset than you already are.'

Pulling Hazel towards him, his arm locked possessively around her shoulders as he steered her in the direction of the lift.

What had Hazel got to be upset about? It wasn't like *her* brother had torched her moneymaker.

And there was another thing that had seeped into Marco's mind during the drawn-out wait in the reception bar... Whether Hazel's entire back catalogue of films, as well as all the other movie Starlight Studios had created over the years were still in that place which was now allegedly a pile of ash...

If Grimes hadn't shipped them out for safeguarding as instructed when they'd struck the deal, then thousands of pounds in royalties would be lost. No. Worse than that... *Tens* of thousands of. Possibly more.

The nerve in Marco's jaw twitched as he reached the lift. He jabbed at the button, Hazel's whining down his ear becoming even more insulting. She didn't have the first clue about the meaning of the word 'upset'. But she would if she didn't stop fucking bleating.

His brain felt like it was bleeding.

Drip, drip, fucking drip.

Inside the lift, Marco dialled Sonny's number. He wanted information that the entire stock of Grimes' films had been received at Luna. They'd better have been. Sonny could fucking find out. And he could do it right *now*. The cunt had best answer this time. Four times he called now and the wanker hadn't answered once.

Taken the night off had he? This slackness was something *else* he'd have to deal with when he got back. Perhaps he'd been premature by believing Sonny Michell a suitable replacement for Bill Wainwright? Bill wouldn't have fucked off and not answered his phone. Neither would he have failed to immediately inform him of the latest events, leaving a jumped-up fucking toerag to do the job instead.

Marco's face twisted into a ferocious scowl. He *would* be going home even if he had to charter a fucking plane himself.

• • • •

IT PUT SONNY OFF HIS BEAT meeting Damon Sandler down the corridor. He must not give the slightest inkling that anything was other than normal. *Remember - he'd been at a meeting over Mayfair and was allegedly unaware Damon had lied and that the women were now on site.*

Luckily, many years of training of wearing a neutral expression gave Sonny the upper hand. He rarely displayed emotion, good or bad, unless he chose to. And it wasn't often that happened, It was more than his life was worth.

And right now that ability served him well.

Needing to make sure Sonny couldn't go anywhere before he'd weighed up the situation, Damon blocked the corridor. It was unfortunate he and his men hadn't got a few more hours with the whores before Sonny returned. Now the twat was here he'd insist on toning things down. Worse still, he hadn't got chance to put the delectable Caroline to use before he'd received the nod that Sonny's motor had entered the compound. Still, at least he'd successfully reached Marco before this dickhead had chance. 'You're back early. How did the meeting go?'

'The scouts were adamant they'd seen Zane, but the more they told me, the less I think it was him.' Sonny shrugged. 'It was worth checking out though and just to be on the safe side, I'll send a couple of our men over to the area in question and see if they spot anything.'

He stared at Damon, wondering how long the lying prick would drag this out before mentioning the women were here or about what had happened to Grimes. The women's presence would be obvious the minute he turned the next corridor, but would Damon conceal the knowledge about the fire at Starlight?

Sonny batted away the relentless itch to plough his fist into Damon's face. It didn't take rocket science to work out this guy wanted his job, but purposely withholding information for his own gain could only backfire.

His veins thrummed with the need to ensure Erin was unharmed too, resentment that he'd unwillingly left her in such a precarious position bubbling. Zane would flay him past the point of death and beyond if anything untoward happened to her.

Fuck, he'd flay *himself* if she'd been touched. Given half a chance, these men here would take all manner of liberties. *This* one had already overstepped the line where Erin was concerned and keeping that knowledge from Zane was not something Sonny was comfortable with.

He kept his eyes on Damon, the ability to maintain his neutral expression becoming harder by the second. 'Where's Caroline? Is she in your office?'

'Nah, she's in the studio helping,' Damon said casually. 'The container turned up after all.'

Sonny raised his eyebrows in mock surprise. 'Oh? I thought the driver was parking up until the morning?'

'Change of plans,' Damon shrugged. 'The driver decided to wing the extra miles. It turned out he wasn't as far away as we'd thought. I tried to call you but you must have been out of signal...'

'Oh, right...' Sonny muttered, keeping his rage hidden. *Tried to call? Of course he had...* 'Let's see them then. Any good?' Acting interested sickened him, but it was unavoidable. He pushed past Damon. 'I take it they're in Studio One?'

Damon kept pace with Sonny as they headed towards the studio. 'Most of them ain't bad. 'There were a couple who proved a problem but they were dealt with, if you get my drift?'

'Yeah, well, we expected that,' Sonny muttered. *So, this cunt had already killed some?* 'How many needed dealing with?'

'Only two,' Damon said, matter-of-factly. 'There will probably be more by tomorrow. You know how flaky tarts are. I'll arrange to dispose of those other two shortly. I've left them in situ for the time being in case we need to issue another reminder. The others have already been treated to one.' He laughed. 'It worked a treat like it always does.'

Sonny shoved his hands deeper into the pockets of his donkey jacket to conceal his forming fists. *Two dead? How many more before this situation was contained?*

'It has to be said that little girl of yours, Caroline, has been of use,' Damon continued. 'She put the whores through a sheep dip, so they're clean enough if you fancy having a go on one of two of them?'

Sonny tensed. *He knew it.* He knew Damon and his men would be on those women like flies around shit. 'No. We need to keep them in good order for filming.' *Hopefully there would be no filming...*

Damon draped his arm around Sonny's shoulders in fake camaraderie. 'What's up? You're not usually so coy! You ain't shagging that Caroline, are you? You check up on her a lot, so is that why you employed her in the first place, you sly old dog?'

Sonny clenched his jaw, the urge to lay Sandler out becoming overbearing. 'Nah, she's a bit plain for my liking.' *Erin certainly wasn't that.*

Reaching Studio One, Sonny pushed open the door. His face remained passive at the scene which met his eyes, but internally he was fuming. Catching Erin's eye, he shot her an unfathomable look, hoping she possessed the nous to play the game.

He held his breath, waiting for her to rush forward in a state of angst, but she remained overseeing the goings on with an expression as impassive as the one he himself wore.

Yes, she had the nous.

And now for Sandler...

Allowing his rage to make an appearance, Sonny turned to Damon. 'Why the fuck have you allowed these men in here?'

'Ah, come on, boss. It's the done thing to give our men first dibs on new meat. It's what we always do.'

But that 'meat' was usually willing, Sonny thought. 'Not this time we don't. This is different.' Banging the butt of his pistol on a desk, he succeeded in getting the rutting men to pause. 'Your jolly is over, boys. Get back to your day job!'

Damon cringed with embarrassment. This slimy cunt had overridden him? 'You could have let them finish, boss,' he grumbled.

'This is the first time we've brought women in this way.' Sonny eyed the bruised and battered women scrambling to their feet. Clearly these bastards had put them to heavy use in the few hours he'd been absent.

He didn't dare look in Erin's direction for fear of seeing raw distaste reflecting in her eyes for this whole thing and for *him*. Instead, he concentrated on Sandler. 'I'm pissed off that you sanctioned this. If these birds aren't fit for filming because you've allowed these dolts to mark them, then how do you think that will look to Marco?'

Marco would have been all for it, Damon thought, but kept his opinion to himself. He'd have to swallow this dressing down no matter how bitter the taste. He could do fuck all about it until *he* was in charge, which after today wouldn't be long.

'I'll not have it appear like I've allowed things to happen in Marco's absence that will negatively impact the business,' Sonny raged, looking Damon up and down. 'I'm not impressed.'

Turning to face the men busy stuffing their cocks back into their jeans, Sonny yelled at the top of his voice, 'Don't ever come in here again unless you are specifically asked to. Now fuck off!' He then turned his glare to Erin. 'Don't just sit there. Get these bitches cleaned up again and do it quickly.'

Hopefully, Erin would understand what he aimed to achieve by his actions.

FIFTEEN

'JUST DON'T!' Erin spat, flinching when Zane's leg curled over hers underneath the duvet.

She stared at the limp blue bedroom curtains hanging from a wooden rail. Being as she hadn't got much sleep, she'd been looking at them most of the night, her stomach churning with what she would find at Luna today and wondered what had happened to all those women since she'd left last night.

But then, what would have happened if she'd remained?

What good could she have done on her own against those men hell bent on taking whatever they wanted?

None, that's what.

Zane begrudgingly untangled himself from Erin's body. He'd never pushed himself onto a woman in his life and he wasn't about to start now, but he didn't appreciate her acting like this situation was *his* fault. How the fuck could it be his fault? He wasn't in the mood to deal with blame games. Not when he'd got a hell of a day to get through.

He knew what was bothering her. She hadn't needed to go into details about what she'd witnessed at Luna yesterday. The stilted, cutdown version of what she had told him gave enough of a hint as to what had happened. 'This part of the situation will be over today,' he said quietly.

'Over? For who?' Erin turned to face Zane. He was on his back, arms folded - staring up at the ceiling, his chiselled jaw hard in the early morning light. 'Over for me? For you? It won't be over for those women though, will it? What I saw yesterday, let alone what's happened since will never be over for them! That's if they live!'

Zane's jaw clenched, the tell-tale nerve twitch beginning. 'I don't possess psychic powers to foresee my brother's decisions, Erin!'

If he did, then he wouldn't have been set up in the first place. He wouldn't have gone to jail for something he hadn't done and he wouldn't have had both his home and his firm stolen. No. He would have seen it coming and stopped the lot in its tracks.

'You *knew* those trafficked women were due to arrive. You could have acted then, rather than waiting!' Erin sat up in bed, her temper rising. 'I texted you with what was going on and that Damon had lied, yet you still did nothing. *Nothing*!'

Her eyes flashed with frustration. 'Instead of doing what you should have done at the start - you know, like killing your brother, you allowed Luna to continue. Why? I'll tell you why. Because it was easier!'

Zane swung his legs out of bed. 'Easier?' He glared at Erin, her defiant blue eyes facing him off. 'That statement alone shows how little you know if you believe everything is so fucking easy. Lucky life has been straightforward for you!'

Erin's mouth fell open in shocked rage. 'How is any of it easy for me? You dragged me into this shit in the first place by kidnapping me! I should have killed you when I believed you'd murdered my father. *That* would have been easier. But I didn't. Now you're making excuses for your bloody brother?'

As the words left her mouth Erin regretted them. She didn't mean them. She didn't mean them at all. She saw the flash of hurt on Zane's handsome face before he masked it, but her stubbornness refused to let her offer the apology he deserved.

Zane pulled his jeans and T-shirt on, then did up his boots. He studied Erin coldly, his face like stone. 'Yeah, you're right. You should have just killed me.'

Turning on his heels, he left the bedroom before he said something he may regret. There was no point having a shower. He'd be covered in shit and blood before this day was done.

Hearing Zane thunder down the stairs, Erin jumped out of bed. Pulling the long T-shirt down over her hips, she raced after him, her agile form making quick work of the staircase.

Catching up with Zane she grabbed his arm. 'Doing what you usually do? Running away? You think I don't have the ability to kill you? I killed Anthony, didn't I, so I can kill you. I *should* kill you!'

Biting down on his lip, Zane shrugged his arm from Erin's grip. If her plan was to make him lose his temper, she was going the right way about it. But he wouldn't. He *couldn't.*

Erin was unable to stop the diatribe spilling from her mouth. 'You could have stopped all of this. You *chose* not to. You...'

Grabbing Erin's shoulders, Zane forced her down onto a stair. Bending, he levelled his eyes with hers. 'Kill me if you wish,' he growled. 'You'll lose... Remember, you only killed Flame, or Anthony, as you called him, because *I* let you.'

'You *let* me? Oh my God! You really believe you control everything?' Erin shrieked, her hand scrabbling to prise Zane's grip from her shoulders. 'And look at you now! Resorting to force because you're losing the argument? Isn't that what people like you do? Like all of those men in your brother's firm do? Kill and rape women!'

Zane stiffened, his ice blue eyes darkening. *That was it. She'd gone too far.* A sneer tugged the corner of his mouth. 'I don't force anyone, Erin. I didn't force you and nor would I. I'm not the one who sold my body to further my aim and then blame everyone when my plan screwed up! You should have stuck with Flame. My initial perception was correct. You two were perfect for each other!'

That was as far away from the truth as it got and he knew

it. His sneer dropped. 'Erin... I...'

The olive branch Zane was about to utter jammed in his mouth when Erin delivered a stinging slap to his face. He hadn't seen it coming and the force surprised him.

With angry tears burning, a wash of cold flooded Erin at the black rage sliding over Zane's face. As quickly as it appeared, it evaporated, but she'd overstepped the mark. And by a longshot.

She tensed, bracing herself. Zane Morelli was dangerous but she wasn't scared of him. She would *never* be scared of him. If that happened, they would have nothing.

But did they have anything now?

Zane silently scrutinised the woman in front of him. He'd never raise a hand to her. The concept of hurting her was anathema, but he *wanted* to. He wanted to slap the taste out of her mouth for what she'd just said. He wanted to slap the taste out from his *own* mouth for the hurtful things he'd retaliated with, but she'd beat him to it.

It was a bad idea ever getting involved with Erin. A *very* bad idea. He should have stuck to his guns and not gone there. But...

His eyes couldn't help from tracing Erin's long bare legs as she sat on the staircase. She still made him hard as fuck even during a bloody argument. He needed to get out of here and put some space between them. Too much was riding on today and he didn't need anything clouding his judgement.

He snatched his crash helmet from the hallstand. 'I must get on. I have things to do.'

Erin panicked. He wasn't leaving things like this, was he? Not today! None of this was Zane's fault, yet she thrown every ounce of her own frustration in his face. He might be killed during what would unfold today. He'd explained as much of what was planned as he could last night. Not that she'd taken in everything he'd said as her head was whacked out.

She wasn't the only one suffering and finding it hard. There was also one other rather large factor she hadn't given adequate consideration to: Zane would shortly face the prospect of killing his own brother. Marco was the lowest of the low by anyone's standards, but he'd been Zane's brother once and whatever else had changed, *that* hadn't.

As Zane reached the front door, Erin jumped up. 'Zane! We...'

'Not now,' Zane said coolly. 'Today we concentrate on what's going on and nothing else.'

'But...'

Ignoring Erin, Zane opened the door to reveal Sonny approaching up the path.

Sonny began to smile but stopped at the thunderous expression on Zane's face and a dishevelled and strange-looking Erin standing in the doorway behind him. Instead, he held out the keys to the lock-up.

Nodding his thanks, Zane took the keys then glanced over his shoulder back to Erin. He held her eyes in his cool blue stare. 'Sonny will brief you on everything you need to do today. Whatever happens and however this ends, be careful, okay?'

Unease mounting, Sonny stepped to the side to let Zane pass. Whatever had occurred here didn't give much encouragement that the day was starting off with everyone in a stable frame of mind.

• • • •

HAZEL STARED BLANKLY over the balcony at the beautiful vista in front of her, but the stunning scenery of the ocean did nothing for her today. She'd barely slept a wink last night.

She rubbed at her sore, red-rimmed eyes, swollen from crying.

This was like a horrible nightmarish dream. *How could her father be dead?*

Her father had always organised everything. Not only had he worshipped her, he'd got her the best business deals, made sure she always got paid what she deserved and on top of all of that, she'd been able to wind him around her little finger.

The onset of a new flood of tears began. It was surprising there was any left.

Hearing movement, Hazel turned her heavy head to see Marco pacing up and down inside the suite, his mobile in his hand and his jaw set like it did when he didn't get what he wanted.

He'd been no help. He'd delivered the news of her father's demise so bluntly, like he was remarking on the price of bread. On top of that, he'd made no effort to comfort her.

Yeah, last night he'd tried to shag her, coked out of his head after chucking his phone across the room because one of those idiots back home hadn't answered his call, but that didn't count.

Despite being upset, Hazel still possessed the energy to glare at Marco. Her father had made her feel important and special. He'd been the one who'd made her believe she had what it took to be a film star. And look at her - the top adult film star in the country! Yet Marco was more interested in his phone?

Now Marco was all she had, so therefore she expected him to make her feel just as priceless as her father had. He'd started out so well too, but now what with that business over the brunette and other stuff, Hazel was beginning to wonder. Either way, he needed to pull his socks up.

She pursed her lips. If Marco didn't treat her with the reverence she desired then she'd divorce him. Now they were married, she was entitled to half his money so if he couldn't be bothered, she'd start again elsewhere.

A glimmer of hope spawned. That was another thing her father had made sure of. *Security*. He'd kept hold of her entire back catalogue of films from Starlight, so if she left Marco she'd just cash them in.

Hazel suddenly faltered. It was all very well thinking of a backup, but she just wanted to go home. Her blotchy tear-stained face screwed up like a prune. Last night, Marco had promised they'd fly out immediately, yet they were still here!

Tugging the double doors open, she strutted back into the

suite. 'Marco, you said we'd be gone long before now. I want to go home.'

'So do I,' Marco muttered, his concentration still on his mobile phone. He'd have a heart attack if he couldn't get out of this poxy place and back to London. How could it be so difficult for someone such as *him* to get a flight when chavs on their cheapo package holidays got flown out with red carpet treatment immediately if one of them so much as hinted that they were stressed or one of their hundred state-funded offspring was about to give birth to their tenth child and a bigger council house was required?

Whereas *he*, who could afford to hire or probably even *buy* Air Force One, couldn't even secure two tickets in peasant class. Even just one bloody ticket would do. Hazel could find her own fucking way back.

Flopping into the chair, he slammed his mobile on the table and raked his fingers through his thick hair.

'Marco! I said I want to go home!' Hazel demanded, her bottom lip wobbling. 'I want to see my daddy.'

'Daddy?' Marco scoffed. 'How old are you? Who calls their father 'daddy'? Are you some kind of weirdo?' Yeah, he was being mean, but he didn't care. Hazel was getting on his tits. He had important things to think about. Like *proper* stuff.

Trevor's death made no difference to him. But what *did* make a difference was whether what had happened to old man Grimes was courtesy of his brother. If it was, then why the fuck had Sonny not apprehended Zane? He'd made it clear what needed to happen and the cunt was supposed to have eyes trained everywhere, so how could this have occurred in the first place?

Marco glimmered with rage. He still hadn't been able to get through to Sonny, so remained none the wiser about whether Zane had been apprehended or the whereabouts of Grimes' films. It wasn't good enough. Sonny was proving to be a useless bastard.

Hearing the none too dulcet tones of Hazel commencing yet

another loud sobbing session, Marco's teeth began grinding again. He couldn't stand much more of this. It was like being in purgatory.

How could he stop his brother in his tracks from wrecking his reputation and business if he was stuck here with this whining bitch? He had films to make and brothers to kill. 'For fuck's sake, Hazel,' he roared, his voice vibrating the balcony doors. 'Give it a rest! I've got enough on my bloody plate!'

'What have you on your back that is so pressing, Marco?' Hazel snapped petulantly.

'Fucking answer!' Marco yelled at his phone, stabbing at the buttons after another call to Sonny went through to voicemail. He'd have to call Sandler the way this was going.

But how would that look? Calling some random fuckturd from the film side of things because he couldn't get hold of his alleged second-in-command?

Seeing red, Hazel snatched the phone out of Marco's hand. 'Leave that fucking thing alone! I'm talking to you! I want to know when we're leaving. You're supposed to hold power, but I'm seeing very little if you can't even get a plane ticket!'

Marco turned on Hazel with an icy look. 'Give. Me. My. Fucking. Phone.'

'Why should I?' Hazel goaded, holding the phone above her head. 'I've lost my father and all you can do is ponce about with your bloody mobile?'

'I've already told you. I've got things to sort out,' Marco hissed. If she didn't give him the phone back he'd... He'd tried to be nice, but if she continued pushing...

'I'm more important than your phone!'

'For God's sake!' Marco barked. 'What's your problem? Is this tantrum because your dad's karked it? Your father was a greedy cunt, so you should be glad to see the back of him.' His eyes glinted with malice. 'Did you know that he was taking a percentage of your cut for himself?'

Hazel's eyes widened in shock before her face crumpled. 'How could you, Marco? How could you say such things?'

Marco rolled his eyes as Hazel dissolved back into sobs. 'Turn the fucking waterworks off, for Christ's sake! Have you not seen the state of your face? You look like a burnt fucking badger!'

Hazel's howling grew louder and Marco knew he was nearing snapping point. Her screeching vibrated every single nerve ending.

Hearing the sudden shrill peal of his mobile, Marco's heart leapt. *Finally*! Now maybe he could find out what the hell was happening. Being as none of the useless bastards here could manage it, Sonny could charter a private plane from London and once he'd done that, the man could explain exactly where he'd been for the last twelve hours instead of answering his bloody phone. He could also answer the rest of the questions he needed answers to.

Forgetting Hazel had possession of his mobile, Marco searched for it on the table, momentarily confused.

Hazel snivelled, her anger mounting. She had a good mind to chuck the phone over the balcony. Her father hadn't been using her. He wouldn't.

She'd make Marco wish he hadn't said those things. She would divorce him. She'd embarrass him in front of his important associates. She'd walk out of his studios and refuse to star in his films. She'd make him wish that...

'Give me that phone, you stupid woman,' Marco roared, lurching towards Hazel.

Hazel stared at the ringing phone and with a flash of inspiration, poked her long fingernail on the end call button.

'You've cut the call off!' Marco screamed. 'I needed to take that. It's important!'

'More important than *me*?' Hazel's tears quickly dried up. '*Nothing* should be more important than me!'

She realised that wasn't entirely true when, with a look of animalistic rage, Marco's fist connected with her face.

Knocked from her feet, Marco's phone clattered to the floor, followed by Hazel.

SIXTEEN

MARCO PULLED AT TUFTS of his hair, yanking as hard as he could as penance for his lack of control. What had he been thinking of to hit his wife? Anyone else was fair game, but not Hazel. Not his beautiful Hazel.

Getting to the floor, he scooped Hazel into his arms, mainly so he didn't have to look at the swollen mess of her cheekbone. 'I'm so sorry, baby,' he soothed, cradling her against his chest.

Fuck. If her cheekbone was broken it would be *weeks* before she looked decent enough for the camera. How had he been so remiss and allow Zane's actions to get the better of him again?

This was Zane's fault. Everything was Zane's fault. The stress his brother caused pushed him out of his orbit.

'Please don't cry,' he begged. 'I'm not myself. These past couple of days have been awful.' He had to make Hazel believe him. He'd fantasised over her for so long, he couldn't lose her now he'd got her. Not while she still made his dick dance and would coin it in for his films.

Damn his temper and damn Zane. If he didn't turn this around and make things right it would screw everything up.

He pressed his lips to Hazel's trembling fingers and traced

a line of kisses up her arm. She liked that usually so why wasn't she responding now? 'Don't ignore me, baby, please,' he continued, hoping he was laying it on thickly enough to convince her. 'Tell me you forgive me. I don't know what got into me.'

The throbbing in Hazel's face was constant, but not enough to override that she had just been punched in the face by her own husband. Her initial shock and the resulting pain were all-consuming. Marco might be contrite for losing his rag and belting her, but that didn't make it all right.

'Sweetheart, *please*,' Marco whined. 'You know I'm crazy about you. I'd never do something like that on purpose. I don't know how it happened.'

Actually, he did. She wouldn't give him his bloody phone and that was the last straw in a long line of piss-take bullshit. Regardless, he had to make her see what everyone pushed him to.

'I'm not thinking straight,' he blagged, determined to absolve his guilt. 'All I wanted was to spend time with my beautiful wife on our honeymoon, and then what with your accusations about me and that woman...' *It was always good to lay part of the blame back...* 'And then the shock of hearing about your father…'

'B-but you hit me!' Hazel whimpered. 'I don't know if I can forgive that, Marco.'

'Please! You have to,' Marco cried. 'I didn't mean it. I swear, *swear*, baby that it will never happen again. I always get blamed for things that aren't my fault. People take, take, take and it pushes me to extremes. When you wouldn't give me my phone, I saw red. I know it's not an excuse…'

Releasing Hazel from his arms, he put his head in his hands, desperate for another line and to finish the dregs of the whisky bottle. 'I shouldn't have drunk so much. It's only because I'm so fucking stressed. It must have been Zane who torched and killed your father. It *has* to be. He'll do anything to get back at me because he's a jealous bastard and can't stand that I'm more successful than him. Don't let him ruin what we've got.'

Hazel had been quietly enjoying Marco's grovelling until he mentioned his brother - the brother who would never be released from jail...

If Marco believed Zane killed her father, then it meant he *was* out of jail. And if Zane Morelli was out, didn't it stand to reason that *he* was the true heir to the Morelli fortune, not Marco? 'What was that you said about your brother?'

Marco flinched. He'd been so entrenched with his rambling he'd almost forgotten she was there. *Shit.*

Had he mentioned Zane? Bollocks. If he'd let that slip, then he'd screwed up.

Fuck. Fuck. Fuck!

'Say you forgive me for raising my hand to you? I need you to forgive me.'

'I want to know what you meant about Zane,' Hazel pressed, the pain in her face now fading into the background as her senses heightened with the prospect of the life and security she'd been assured of disappearing down the toilet. 'You believe your brother burnt my father's studios? Are you telling me he's out of jail when you said he wasn't?'

Marco felt like he was drowning. 'I'm not thinking straight, babe. You heard the rumours. I didn't mean he'd been released... I just meant it wouldn't surprise me if he *was* out and that he was behind what happened to your father.'

He was digging a bigger hole, he knew he was, but he had to say something to gloss over his faux pas.

Hazel pushed Marco away in disgust. Not because he wasn't sure whether his brother was out or not, but because he *did* know. And if he knew Zane was out, that meant he'd lied.

Her eyes narrowed. She'd been tricked into this marriage and married the wrong fucking brother.

Quickly. Think. How did she play this? The only decent part about this was that Marco was still suitably obsessed with her to be of use, but she'd only need to count on that until she'd put this right, Zane must be out and therefore she would be doing something about this predicament.

'You don't need to worry, sweetheart,' Marco said, pulling Hazel back into his arms. 'I'll call Sonny back now. He'll charter us a plane. I don't care how much it costs. If Zane *is* out, then he won't be for long. It changes nothing for us, okay?'

And yeah, he knew full well that Zane was out, but it was a question of whether he'd started moving in on his territory. From what had happened to Grimes, he suspected that Zane indeed had.

Hazel nodded and smiled, wincing at the pain the movement afforded her swollen cheekbone. She'd pretend to agree. *For now.*

But Marco was wrong. It changed *everything.*

And if he thought she would accept that, then he was very much mistaken.

• • • •

ERIN HOVERED in the doorway of Studio One. She'd expected to see caged women, but it was more harrowing than expected.

Glancing up the corridor to make sure no one else was about, Sonny beckoned Erin into the room so he could close the door. This was the only place no one would overhear what was being said and where he was certain there were no bugs set. He wouldn't put anything past Sandler, especially now the man had more of an axe to grind.

His mobile began buzzing again. Although he'd dealt with the dressing down after finally answering one of Marco's calls not long since, this one he couldn't ignore either. Besides, it was part of the plan.

Putting his finger to his lips for silence, Sonny answered the phone. 'Hey boss, yeah... I've checked with every firm I could find, but no one can privately charter a plane for you until Friday, so you might as well hang onto your original flights.' His eyes remain on Erin as she witnessed the conversation. 'Like I said, things are in hand here… No, we've found no link with your brother with what happened to Grimes yet. No, no sign of him either. The films? Yes, like I said, a box from Starlight arrived last week. Oh, and the women are here… Yep, all okay. I will… Okay, I'll keep you posted.'

He checked the call had disconnected before he spoke to Erin. 'I presume you guessed who that was?'

Erin nodded. 'Zane still has until Friday to sort this? Will that be enough time?'

'As long as Marco doesn't realise I've phoned no one about flights and gets one himself, it's long enough.' The first hint of a smile twitched at the corner of Sonny's mouth. 'I'm fairly sure Marco will be too busy shovelling coke up his nose to do anything, so fingers crossed we'll be fine.'

Erin scanned the rows of cages spotting vague outlines of figures crunched on the metal floors. The room was quiet, short of hushed sobbing coming from within the wire prisons, but every single woman was aware of their presence and on tenterhooks as to what was coming next. She could hardly blame them.

'They've been in here since last night and will remain so until later,' Sonny said, seeing straight away that Erin was less than impressed. 'I've taken Damon's keys after what he pulled with his men yesterday so these women will be safe enough in here.'

'I can't believe you're not letting them out! It's disgusting!' Erin snapped. 'Don't you lot think of anything but what's easier? I'm releasing them now.'

Sonny slammed his bunch of keys on the table and grabbed Erin's arm. 'Don't be stupid! If you do that, they'll go berserk. You'll never round them up without drawing attention. Listen! They'll be released when the time is right and not before. Until the gunfight goes down, Marco's men have been cleared and there's is no risk to the women, only then will they be uncaged.'

Satisfied Erin was no longer thinking of undoing the cages, he frowned. 'I don't know what's gone on between you and Zane and quite frankly I don't want to, but whatever it is don't take it out on me.'

Erin stared at the floor. Sonny was right. She was taking things out on him and she shouldn't be.

Much to her surprise she'd found her opinion was gradually changing about Sonny Mitchell. Last night she'd watched how he'd handled that bastard Sandler. He'd dispersed the men and insisted the women were immediately caged.

Initially, she'd been horrified and even more resentful of him for doing that. That was until she'd realised it was to protect the women as much as physically possible without blowing the operation. And with Sonny now being in possession of the keys to the cages and the studio itself, it meant although these poor women were trapped, it also meant no one else could get in here without his say so.

Regardless of what she'd first thought, she was starting to believe that Sonny wouldn't abuse his power. He'd pulled rank to protect the women, even if it appeared the opposite. Now it was her turn to do likewise.

'When should I let them out?' she asked quietly. She wasn't going to apologise for her outburst but this was the next best thing.

'Not sure. I need you to shadow Sandler. Keep him in his office for as long as possible. Do whatever you need to keep him there.' His eyes narrowed. 'Within reason, of course.'

Erin nodded. She knew of one very good way to keep Damon Sandler otherwise engaged, but that was not happening. 'I'll engage him with discussing which women are going in what films.' She didn't hold much hope of *that* pacifying the mood she expected Damon to be in today, but she'd try her utmost.

Sonny suddenly grabbed her arm again. 'Don't put yourself in jeopardy.'

Erin stared at Sonny's cragged face and felt the strange urge to fall against his chest and sob to release the frustration and devastation of the last few days. 'I'll be fine. Don't worry about me.'

'But I *am* worrying about you,' Sonny continued, his voice low. 'We all are. You shouldn't be in this situation. It isn't good.'

Erin blinked. She'd hated this man from the off and hoped Zane would have nothing further to do with him, but Sonny understood how she felt about what she'd witnessed yesterday. Zane did not.

Dropping his hand, Sonny cleared his throat. 'The desk phone will ring once and once only before it cuts off. That will be your signal that things are about to kick off.'

His eyes morphed back to a steely gaze. 'Under no circumstances are you to leave that office until the second call and keep these with you at all times.' Picking up the bunch of keys on the table, he placed them in Erin's hand. 'When the phone rings the *second* time, that's your cue to go and release the women. Lead them out of the fire door at bay B.'

'Bay B?' Erin exclaimed. 'Where will they go?'

'No idea yet, but we'll move them somewhere short term. I'll be in the building but I can't be seen hanging around you. Damon is suspicious enough as it is. I'll head back to my office now, so leave it a minute before you leave and lock the door behind you.'

Walking to the door, Sonny glanced over his shoulder. 'Good luck and be careful.'

SEVENTEEN

'BLOODY NICE DRUM this!' Cav stared up at the looming façade of the executive apartment complex overlooking the Thames. 'Fuck knows how much a place here costs!'

Lewis eyed the numerous balconies scattered along the upmarket riverside apartments with a tinge of envy. 'Probably twenty times what my two-bed flat cost. The perks of being the head of a company, I guess!'

'If I remember rightly, Zane purchased this out of his own brass rather than the company,' Cav corrected. 'That makes it doubly insulting that Marco's helped himself to it, along with everything else.'

Lewis nodded. 'Yeah and used it to wang poor tarts off the balcony while he was at it. We all know it was Marco who did that, not some freak accident.' Everyone had seen the news about Pauline Albiges falling to her death from the penthouse. Plus there weren't many who hadn't heard the rumours about women being butchered in the name of 'select' films…

Marco was a lunatic who had to be removed.

He crushed his cigarette end out in the van's ashtray and stared back at the building. 'The place looks like Fort Knox. How feasible is it that we'll get in there even once Marco's monkeys have toddled off to deal with the shit soon to kick off at Luna?'

Cav fished a piece of paper from his top pocket. 'We've got the code for the penthouse floor, so unless it's been changed, I can't see there being problems.'

'But that was the code Zane set,' Lewis frowned. 'Wouldn't Marco have changed it?

Cav laughed. He tapped his temple. 'No way would Marco think of that. He's untouchable, remember? Fucked in the head, that one!' His smile then evaporated. 'But his original right-hand man could have changed it. Bill Wainwright was a lumbering thug but not stupid. And if he *did* change it, this will prove difficult. These kind of places have alarms linked directly to the Old Bill.'

Lewis and Cav exchanged glances, not needing to remind each other that their instructions were for the complex to remain free from requiring 'clean-ups'. If push came to shove, they'd find a way to deal with what any required action could bring, rather than risk an under-the-counter button alerting the police and bringing them all down before the takeover had barely begun.

Pulling up the cuff of his sleeve, Lewis peered at his watch. 'When do you think we'll get the nod?'

'They'll be at the lock-up by now, so if things go to plan I expect to see movement within the next hour,' Cav said. 'Oh, and Lewis… Whatever happens, we do what's needed, okay?'

Lewis pulled his bag of locksmith tools closer. Picking locks might be his specialty, but if this code still worked he'd only need to change the locks, rather than break them. If the codes *didn't* work, they'd be dealing with a bigger mess than changing bloody locks.

The most important thing was to secure the penthouse with minimal civilian casualties and *no* interference from the boys in blue.

• • • •

ZANE TOOK A GOOD LOOK around outside the lock-up before giving Leo and Tiger the signal to load the guns into the back of the Transit. The van had been reversed tightly up to the warehouse doors, but he wanted to double check no one was watching who shouldn't be.

Surveying the area and the cars in the forecourt of the neighbouring warehouse took longer than it should, but that was because he wasn't sure what he was looking for.

If only he'd clocked the reg plate of that silver car the other day.

Tiger's voice came from behind. 'Problem?'

'Nah,' Zane muttered. 'It's fine.'

And it was. There was no sign of anyone. Why would there be? The packaging warehouse next to this unit had a strict clock in-clock out policy, insisting no workers to be allowed out in between breaks. Judging by its rules it was run by Nazis, but a factory was a factory and their way of working was one of the main reasons the Morellis took the lease on this particular lock-up in the first place. The Morellis line of work had not changed in all the years they'd rented this place and fortunately, neither had the factory's work ethic.

'I'll get these loaded.' Tiger hefted the first case of ammunition into the back of the Transit, leaving Leo to bring up the rear with a collection of weapons. With the number of men requiring culling today they needed heavy duty gear. Semi-automatics were the name of the game here, rather than handguns or shotguns.

Standing to one side to allow his men clear access to the van, Zane continued scouring the neighbouring car park, as well as the one the other side. That car park was empty, like the warehouse itself.

The car he was looking for wasn't anywhere to be seen. At least he didn't think so. He was normally good at spotting things most people missed, but the way things were left with Erin this morning meant his mind was overcrowded. He had to be sure he'd missed nothing.

Because he certainly hadn't missed it this morning...

Turning his back on Erin in the doorway, he'd got on his bike. He'd been arguing with himself to retrace his steps and tell Erin that he loved her; that things would be okay; that they'd get through this and the pressure wouldn't drive them apart. But he hadn't said a thing and the unpleasant way things were left between them muddied his concentration. So much so that he'd almost missed that motor.

Zane frowned. He was sure that silver Golf parked a few doors down from his house was the same one which had been watching him at his father's graveside.

He'd overshot the motor, but wasted no time in doubling back. U-turning his bike at the end of the road, he'd opened up the throttle. It had taken less than twenty seconds to get back, but in that short space of time, the car had vanished.

Again...

Desperate to eyeball the driver, he'd sped off in the direction he presumed the car had taken, but it had gone without a trace.

He'd have spent more time looking if timescales weren't so tight, but they were so he'd had no choice but to head off to meet Tiger and Leo here at the lock-up. It was imperative they got this show on the road bang on time.

That motor this morning was definitely a silver VW Golf, but as for anything else, he'd learned nothing.

It was plausible it could have been a different car. After all, there was more than one silver Golf in London, but his instinct screamed it was the same one. It being outside his house meant whoever was driving it knew where he lived. They would also have seen Sonny on the path and Erin in the doorway...

Zane's heart pounded.

They could have followed him to this lock-up. Or worse, now having evidence of a link, gone to Luna in pursuit of Sonny and Erin.

The person watching could even have returned to the house after he'd ridden off and Erin could be lying dead in the hallway...

Feeling sicker by the second, Zane snatched his phone from his pocket.

'Are you all right, mate?'

Tiger's low voice made Zane start. 'Yeah, I'm fine,' he muttered. *No he wasn't*. Until he knew Erin was safe, there was no way he could concentrate. Going ahead like this made him a liability.

'We're ready when you are.' Tiger raised his eyebrows at Zane's unusual behaviour. Zane on a mission saw nothing but the task in hand - that's why he was so good at what he did and why both he and Leo had faith they'd succeed with this seemingly unsurmountable job. But if Zane wasn't 100 per cent on it, it was dangerous. 'Boss?'

'Yeah, I heard you.' Zane nodded. 'Get the van started. I'll be two ticks.'

He hastily tapped out a text:

`R u okay?`

Zane pressed send and hoped to God that Erin was a) able to receive it and b) didn't ignore it out of stubborn petulance. *Not today*, Erin, he thought, his jaw tightening.

He stabbed at the open text button before the staccato buzz of the notification even completed.

`All okay. R u?`

`Sorry for earlier`

Zane exhaled with relief. *Now* he could concentrate.

He tapped in his reply:

`I'm OK. I love you`

There. Said it.

Pressing send, Zane scrambled into the van's cab. That was

the last text he would send before seeing Erin again. That's *if* he saw her again... But now his head was clear his confidence in pulling this job off reset and his eyes shone with the determination Tiger and Leo were waiting for. He slapped his hand on the plastic dashboard. 'Let's get this shit done!'

The silver car wasn't here. Erin was safe and so therefore whoever was intent on watching him could just fucking wait until today was over and done with.

EIGHTEEN

WINCING, HAZEL DABBED another layer of thick concealer on her blackened cheekbone. Being on holiday, she hadn't thought she'd bought it with her, but luckily there was a tube lurking at the bottom of her makeup bag. It was a good job because it would be embarrassing wandering around looking like a cheap slut who'd just been whacked by a jobless boyfriend for misplacing his Giro.

She turned her head from side to side and stared at her reflection in the bedroom mirror. Sweeping a section of her hair extensions to one side, she strategically teased the nylon strands into place across the damaged side of her face to offer a bit of camouflage. Makeup could only deflect from a swollen face so much. And with one cheekbone three times its usual size, she looked like she'd had botched surgery.

She glared at Marco sprawled out on the bed, his complimentary white towelling robe open revealing his muscular body and semi-erect penis.

Always horny that man, Hazel thought, her anger rising. Well, he'd be getting no shags from her ever again once she'd got her life in order.

Her lip curled in contempt as Marco hoovered up another

line of cocaine like he hadn't a care in the world.

Marco glanced up, a grin on his face. 'You did well organising a flight so quickly, babe.'

Hazel smiled tightly. This time last week - even a couple of days ago, she'd have revelled at a compliment from Marco. Not anymore. 'I'm not sure why everyone else found it so difficult,' she said, pretending to inspect her manicured fingernails.

It hadn't taken much effort, but fancy having to resort to booking the flights herself! Marco allegedly had all these people at his beck and call, yet no one had achieved in a day what had taken her a minute? It was almost like he didn't want to go back at all.

But *she* did.

Hazel's brows strained to form a frown. She was going home one way or another. She wanted to know what had happened to her father, but more importantly, where this eldest Morelli was now he'd been released from prison. That was imperative.

No matter how much Marco attempted to gloss over the slip up he'd made, she *knew* those rumours were true - Zane Morelli was out and she'd been royally turned over.

But not for long...

Her marriage to the wrong brother would be rectified the moment the plane she'd just booked touched down in London.

Solving this issue wouldn't be too hard, but Zane Morelli would be. For *her*...

Hazel had yet to find a man who didn't want her and this was no different. Apart from this time she had more riding on it than ever. No wonder Marco didn't want to go back. It would be obvious that he'd lied and manipulated everything for his own gain.

That's what he thinks, Hazel thought, eyeing her husband suspiciously. 'Yes it's very strange about the flights... There were several spaces available on the first airline I tried, so I can't imagine why nobody here or none of your people could manage it. I guess it depends who's asking...'

Marco pretended to be nonplussed but inside he was steaming. The ineptitude of those tossers in the hotel didn't surprise him, but Sonny was adamant there was nothing available *anywhere* until Friday. What the fuck was going on?

If the man that he'd handed the kudos to of being his new right-hand was messing about, then heads would fucking roll. Furthermore, if it was that easy, why hadn't Sandler the foresight to book a flight? The bloke fell over himself to wheedle his way up the ladder, so why hadn't he sorted it?

The minute Marco stepped off that plane tomorrow he'd be asking those very same questions.

• • • •

Erin stared at Zane's text under her desk, the hollow in her heart filling. She wasn't alone or adrift. They would get through this.

'What are you doing?'

Her head jolting up, Erin's blood thundered in her veins. 'Nothing. I'm not doing anything.'

Shit! Turning her phone to silent with just enough vibrate to feel notifications from inside her pocket was one thing, but not being alert enough to remember Sandler was in the same room was another. She'd promised herself only a quick glance at the phone if she got a message, not to stare at the bloody thing and open herself up as a target.

'You were staring into your lap like a fucking donut,' Damon scowled.

'I've got a stinking headache and I'm trying to shift it,' Erin blathered. 'Sometimes tilting my head eases it.' *Oh Christ, that sounded rubbish!* Willing her escalating panic to stay put, she edged her phone along her skirt line and slid it onto the office chair, under her thigh.

'You were looking at something.' Suspicion brewing, Damon got to his feet and moved towards Erin. 'What were you looking at? I don't trust you so show me your hands. You're too fucking pally with Mitchell. Tell me, why the hell are you *really* here?'

Erin slunk back in the chair, praying her phone was completely hidden. *She'd been stupid. Stupid!* 'I don't understand what the issue is,' she said as she raised both her hands to prove they were empty. 'I admit that I don't like what you're doing here, but it's not my business. Anyway, thanks to my father, I'm aware of how things work.'

Guilt bloomed as the words tripped from her mouth. Her father, like Zane's, would never have dirtied his soul with what was going on at Luna.

Her eyes narrowed, an idea forming. 'Anyway, what the hell has Sonny Mitchell got to do with this? Why are you so obsessed with him? He knew my father – so what? Why does that mean I'm involved in some way with Sonny?'

Damon sneered, his ugly features becoming more repugnant. 'Because he's too interested in where you are and what you're doing for there not to be something going on.'

Not missing a beat, Erin immediately hit back. 'I expect he's keeping an eye out for me out of honour to my father.' Even though the story was untrue, the sentiment wasn't. *Had* someone been in cahoots with her father, then her welfare would be important. But he wasn't here anymore…

Shaking away the distracting thoughts, Erin pushed on. She had to move off this topic. Damon must not spot the phone because then he'd know that all along she was the mole. 'Personally, I think the way Sonny speaks to you is out of order.'

She hated herself for wearing a suggestive smirk. 'You'd make a much better boss than him. There's more about you and you're more organised than Sonny. You have the company's best interest at the forefront and isn't that what a second-in-command should do?'

She saw the flicker of uncertainty on Damon's face. *Oh, the vain bastard - she'd got him! Come on, Erin, you can turn this around. Zane should be here soon and then this shit will be over.*

'For instance,' she continued. 'I don't know how you kept

your temper when Sonny dismissed those men yesterday. It was unprofessional to override you. He spoke to me like a piece of crap in front of them too, but then I'm not in a high-up position like you.'

High-up position? Damon's ego buzzed. Yeah, he was, wasn't he? Head of Filming *was* a fucking high-up position and soon he'd have a *better* one. Maybe this Caroline chick wasn't a two-faced cunt after all? 'Trust me - Sonny won't be around for long,' he winked. 'Marco will rethink who's who around here.'

As Damon leant on the desk, his bulbous head leering horribly close to Erin's, it was difficult not to recoil from the foul smell of his breath. Instead, she feigned interest in his self-importance. 'Well, perhaps Mr Morelli will do just that when he gets back.'

'That won't be long now either,' Damon grinned, his uneven teeth forcing another blast of foetid breath in Erin's face. 'He'll be back anytime now.'

Erin masked her shock into delighted surprise. 'Really? I'm sure I heard Sonny stressing because he'd been unable to get earlier flights booked for Mr Morelli.' *Shit. Marco would be back at any time?* 'When is his flight exactly?'

Seeing Damon's suspicion flicker to life, Erin grinned. 'I'm intrigued to meet the man. I've heard so much about him.'

Damon scrutinised Erin. 'As I said, don't be getting ideas. He'll make it obvious if he wants you. Anyway, I'm not sure exactly when he's back. His wife organised the flights.' His face resumed its usual sneer. 'Something else Sonny failed to do.'

Erin smiled again, but inside worry churned. *If they were due back today...*

She dare not ask further questions. Steeling herself, she patted the chair next to her. 'I have some ideas to get the best use from the women. Being as they've had a night off courtesy of Sonny, we don't want them getting too comfortable, do we?'

Again, her words sickened her, but she had to keep up this act. *Come on Zane*, she willed. *Where are you?*

NINETEEN

HEART POUNDING LIKE A DRUM, Sonny moved down the corridor to loading bay A. Although Sandler was in the office two corridors away, he couldn't be sure the man hadn't wandered off and Erin was unable to warn him.

It was bad enough leaving her alone with that man. The prick was volatile and twisted, with no regard for anyone. A perfect Marco Morelli in waiting. Nor could Sonny be sure the rest of the men were out of the way. It was impossible to cover all bases when it was only him in here overseeing this part of the operation.

Zane was undertaking a massive risk and time was short. Only three days before Marco returned to home turf and three days to remove London of his minions.

It was almost impossible.

Wincing at the muffled wailing from behind the door of Studio One, Sonny continued. As soon as things were ready for the off he'd get the signal to Erin.

Reaching the heavy metal door of loading bay A, he took another furtive glance over his shoulder. Satisfied he was alone, he slid the heavy metal security bar off the latch and freed the locks. Gritting his teeth, he pushed the bar down and held his breath as he applied pressure to the door. *This had to open without a sound.*

All he could hear was his own heartbeat pounding in his ears.

Cringing as the door suddenly clanked open, sweat dripped down Sonny's back. He froze, reluctant to release his breath until he was certain no one had been alerted.

All good. There was no sign of anyone.

Carefully pulling the door back into place, he checked it was as closed as it could possibly be without being shut and locked.

Now Zane and the others had their entrance set, as agreed.

Rapidly making his way back up the corridor, Sonny glanced at his watch.

Five minutes.

He and Zane had agreed to make no calls to each other to avoid being overheard. They were relying on timing alone, but with no way of checking Zane had been able to stick to exact time scales, Sonny had to continue regardless.

He had high hopes Zane would be second perfect. He had been at Marco's wedding. Zane had delivered on the dot at every stage, so with any luck this would run the same way.

With his brow furrowing, Sonny entered his office and closed the door. Leaning up against it he exhaled slowly.

Now for the next part.

Picking up the phone, he dialled Damon Sandler's office praying Erin was waiting there as planned. If Sandler had made her do something else, she'd miss the signal and be in the line of fire. On the flip side, if she received the signal and acted, but Zane was running late then not only would that put her in the shit, but those women too.

Not to mention *him.*

The phone rang out twice and Sonny cut the call, replacing the receiver.

Done.

He hurried to the cabinet at the back of the room. With

fumbling fingers he unlocked it, tugging the metal door open ready for when he needed to retrieve the loaded gun inside. The pistol in his waistband was not enough for this.

Ready for the off, Sonny hovered in his office waiting for the time to move.

• • • •

ERIN'S RELIEF that the ringing phone had forced Damon Sandler out of her space was immense. She didn't know how much longer she could have lasted.

Busy running through her fabricated ideas for the caged women, Damon had placed his hand on her thigh and stroked her leg. This unwanted manoeuvre had gradually moved higher until there was minimum time before he reached the place where she would rather hell freeze over than him touch.

But now the phone had rung twice it meant Zane was ready and things were about to start.

'I fucking hate it when that happens,' Damon grumbled, glaring at the phone. 'Bloody cutting off before you get to it.' He frowned as he checked the last received number. 'It was Mitchell. I bet he's checking up on me.'

Erin smiled, hope surging. 'Are you going to see what he wants?'

'Nah!' Damon spat. 'It will be something and nothing like usual. I'll wait until he comes to find me.'

Erin nodded. *Damn*. She'd hoped he'd go to Sonny's office, giving her the excuse to leave. Now she was left with finding a way to slip out of here. None of the ideas she'd entertained so far were great but one would have to do. And it was *this* one.

With Damon's attention still on the telephone, Erin rose from her chair and snatched her mobile from under her thigh. Shoving it back in her waistband, she masked the movement by doing up her suit jacket and then headed to the door. 'I won't be long.'

'Where are you going?' Damon asked. 'I want you in here.'

Yeah, you've made that quite obvious, Erin thought.

Gripping the door handle, she glanced over her shoulder. 'I'm just popping to the loo.'

It took all of her power to act casual when really she wanted to bolt from the room. She had only minutes to reach Studio One and explain to the women what was about to happen and pray she could keep them under control.

Erin's eyes fell to Damon's desk as he opened the drawer to shove his diary inside.

Passports! There was a whole load of them in there. They must have been taken from the caged women. If there was a way to get her hands on those and take them before the women were moved out of here, then…

Her train of thought promptly cut off when Damon jumped up from the desk and moved across the office.

'I might join you in the toilet...' Damon leant against the door, his tongue running slowly over his bottom lip. 'I'm sure we could use a bit of privacy…'

Erin quelled the rising nausea at this suggestion and instead forced her eyes to sparkle with mischief. 'Perhaps... but not on this occasion. Us girls require the use of facilities for "certain things" on a monthly basis, if you get my drift?' Hopefully this prat wasn't so thick to miss *that* insinuation.

'I don't mind if you've got the painters in,' Damon laughed, his messy teeth in Erin's face.

'I do!' Erin playfully nudged Damon in the ribs. 'You'll just have to be patient.' *Over my dead body...* But while he believed he had half a chance, playing on that sickening prospect was the best way of manipulating him. But if it didn't work...

'Hurry up then. I want to get back to where we were. You have some good ideas for those tarts. You're not just a pretty face, are you?'

I'm a lot more than that, Erin thought, her plastered-on grin sliding from her face the second she crossed the threshold to the corridor outside.

She touched the keys Sonny had given her safely stashed in

her jacket pocket. Now to get to Studio One without anyone seeing her.

She had to act fast.

TWENTY

THROUGH HER oversized sunglasses, Hazel stared out of the window as the taxi made its way towards the airport, still irked that she'd had to tell Marco several times to load her suitcases into the car.

How dare he just stand there staring at his bloody phone and expecting *her* to do it. Did he want her to break her nails?

Oh yes, for all the words of endearment he spoke when he felt like it - or rather, words of endearment that he'd barely offered these past two days, he was now showing his true colours.

Her new husband had smacked her in the face and was acting like everybody else, including his phone, were more important than her. He'd also lied about his brother.

Her overfilled pink lips thinned. For Christ's sake, she'd just lost her father, yet it didn't cross Marco's mind that she'd be upset?

Actually, she *had* been upset. She still was to a degree, but not quite as much since Marco pointed out she'd been turned over with the cuts from her films all of these years.

Hazel couldn't believe it. She just couldn't. Her father had always been loving and caring. Nothing he'd ever done had been for his own benefit. She came first and he wouldn't have dreamt of ripping her off.

That thought remained steadfast until Marco forced her to look at the paperwork of both the documents from the deal her father had signed with Marco, as well as photocopies of her royalty percentages from the Starlight films. It was like Marco had bought these with him on honeymoon purely to rub it in her face that her father had been turning her over since day dot.

Had Marco known her father was going to die? Had he set up the murder in order to get possession of everything? Including *her*?

Well, Hazel thought, the tug of a tiny smirk pulling at the corner of her mouth, she still had her original films that her father promised to ship out to a safety deposit box. That she *did* know. And now, although her father's betrayal stung, her brain was otherwise engaged in planning on how to rectify her situation. It was *that* which took priority now.

Glancing up, Hazel noticed the taxi driver staring at her intently in his rear view mirror. The minute she met his eyes, he spoke.

'Excuse me for asking, but aren't you that one in those films?'

Despite her predicament, Hazel glowed with satisfaction. Recognised everywhere, like the star she was. Oh, Marco had been a very silly boy throwing her away and giving that prize to his brother.

She twirled a nylon curl around her finger. 'It depends which films you mean...' she answered mysteriously, ensuring she gave those big eyes of hers the trademark sparkle. *Yeah, she could turn on the persona of Lisa Tequila whenever the need arose.*

The taxi driver's mouth split into a wide grin. 'I knew it! Lisa Tequila! Wow! I loved "Night of the Arabian Prince!" You know that film where that man took you fr…'

'Just fucking drive, will you!' Marco barked, his concentration jolted away from his phone. 'My wife's stardom is shag all to do with you. Count yourself fortunate to be sitting in the same car with her!'

'Marco!' Hazel cried. 'You don't have to be so ru…'

'How much longer before we get to the fucking airport?' Marco banged on the back of the driver's seat. 'It would be quicker if you stopped perving on my wife and drove. Now get a move on!'

Snatching his silver vial from his top pocket, Marco hoovered a loaded spoon of cocaine up his left nostril, further resenting leaving the majority of that decent coke he'd recently bought behind. He'd chug as much of it as possible before getting on that plane. If they *ever* got on the bloody plane...

Ignoring Hazel's glare, Marco refreshed his text messages, his face folding into a snarl. *Still no response.*

He'd spoken to Sonny not long ago, so why the bloody hell was he now being blanked? Five text messages he'd sent since they'd got in this taxi, yet he'd received no reply to any of them.

What was the matter with that retard? Fucking deaf and blind as well as bastard pointless?

With the coke slamming around his brain to top up his last eight lines in the past hour, Marco's fingers moved swiftly over the phone's keypad.

`Answer the question damn you.`

`Are there films in that box from Starlight or not?`

Marco frowned. It wasn't a difficult request. Sonny had said a box had arrived from Starlight last week, but hadn't confirmed what was in it. Wasn't that the important bit?

Yes, it bloody was, so why did Sonny presume he'd turned into Paul McKenna?

Marco frowned again, his headache growing as the cocaine upped his heart rate further.

Was McKenna a mind reader or one of those hypnotist people?

He shrugged. It didn't matter. Sonny just had to look in the box. If those films had been left to burn at Starlight...

Open. The. Box. And. Look.

Marco stabbed the send button, hyperventilating with stress. 'Come on! Reply, you bastard!'

'Who are you texting?'

Hazel's voice seeped into Marco's mind but he ignored it and instead dragged his silver vial back out of his pocket for another top up.

Open the box.

He counted to three.

Open it.

Sniffing hard, Marco banged on the back of the driver's seat yet again. 'How long now? Drive faster, you cunt!'

'*Marco*!' Hazel gasped. 'What's the matter with you? We're almost there now.'

Marco couldn't answer Hazel. If he answered her then he'd have to punch her again and he'd already clocked this wanker driver sneaking looks at the swollen flesh of Hazel's cheekbone which her hair hadn't fully concealed.

Was she determined to make him out to be the bad guy?

'You need to slow down with that powder,' Hazel nagged when Marco unscrewed the little vial for the second time in thirty seconds. 'They won't let us on the plane if you're off your head.'

Marco snatched his arm out of Hazel's reach before she had chance to make contact. Her voice was grating, grating, *grating*.

Have you got Zane?

Is that why you're not answering?

Marco made a loud hissing noise as he sucked air into his lungs.

Answer me or you're fired.

Fired? Sonny was fucking fired anyway after this!

Marco's temper spiralled dangerously close to blowing. He'd kill the bastard for this fuck up. If there was a fuck up?

There *had* to be a fuck up.

'Is that why you're not answering me? Because you've screwed up?'

'What?' Hazel frowned. 'Are you talking to me?'

'No. Nothing,' Marco muttered. Had he said that out loud? He didn't know but if Hazel kept questioning him and moaning, he'd throw out of the car.

He tightened his hand around his mobile, feeling the plastic case begin to bend with the strain.

This was *her* fault. He should have stuck to his guns and delayed honeymoon until he'd dealt with Zane. He should have put his foot down and insisted they remained in London. Going so far away was a ludicrous thing to do. Why on earth had he been so stupid?

Bloody Hazel nagging, nagging and nagging about going here, there and everywhere! Now look what had happened. He leaves his firm for five minutes and it all goes Pete Tong.

If he'd had to pick somewhere to go after the wedding purely to keep Hazel off the scent that things were amiss with Zane lurking around, his very presence threatening to lob his plans out the window, then he should have insisted on Clacton-on-Sea. That would have done for a few days. He could have placated her with a month-long holiday afterwards.

Even a shopping trip to New York on Concorde for a weekend would have shut her up.

But no.

Stupid, stupid.

And still no response from that useless piece of shit, Sonny

Mitchell.

In frustration, Marco started banging his mobile on the inside of the passenger door and when this failed to release his snowballing stress, he moved onto slapping himself around the face with it. Over and over and over.

It didn't even hurt. Come on!

'Stop! What are you doing?' Hazel's fingers clawed at Marco's shirt sleeve.

Marco ignored her. He also ignored the annoyed look in the taxi driver's eyes from the mirror when he slammed his forehead into the car door window. If he didn't get on the plane within the next four seconds and return home to find out what the hell was going on, then he'd shove his head through this window *entirely*.

• • • •

'YOU MUST LISTEN to me and listen well,' Erin said, her voice low. Now the wailing and sobbing had reduced after her arrival into Studio One, she stood a chance of being heard and hopefully, understood.

Most of these women could speak English and would explain to the ones who couldn't. That was the idea anyway. She hoped that would happen because she had to keep their attention. The moment she received the signal from Sonny giving her the go ahead to open the cages she'd have her work cut out.

There would literally be *minutes* to unlock the women, keep them manageable and get them out of here. It would be difficult, so it was vital they understood what was going on. If they panicked it would likely result in them all being dead.

Erin met eyes with one woman - a tall blonde who appeared less jittery than the rest. Anyone able to meet her eyes was a decent bet. 'I know no one trusts me and I understand that, but it's important to do what I say. Help is coming but the only way to get out of here is to trust me and not panic.'

'Why we trust you?' the blonde hissed. 'You people lie!'

Erin understood the woman's reticence. She'd clocked her blackened eyes and the crusted blood in her hair. 'I and my people aren't like those others.'

My people? It sounded bizarre. Erin didn't know who Zane had with him. She barely even knew Zane, for Christ's sake. Plus, she was still unsure of Sonny and he was paramount for this working. But it was all they had. All *any* of them had. 'Please! You must listen carefully. I'm going to undo these cages but you need to remain where you are until I say so and then follow me.'

'Follow you where?' The woman's eyes narrowed. 'Why?'

'There will be a lorry,' Erin continued. 'It will take you t…'

'No lorry!' the woman shrieked. 'You think I stupid? No. NO! That not happen! We...'

Erin's jaw clenched. Sure, she understood after how these women were transported in the first place that being put back in a lorry wouldn't go down well, but it was their only hope. Panic mounted. Time was ticking and that they didn't have. 'We're wasting time arguing. Just trust me!'

The blonde made a strange sucking noise. 'Pssspht! I no trust you. I not trust you or any of them. I rather die!'

Erin gritted her teeth, her patience wearing thin. 'Die, if you so wish, but don't assume everyone else wants to! I'm trying to get you out, you stupid bitch so let me get on with it!'

At the blonde's silence, Erin sighed with relief. 'Good! Now we wait until it's safe to go.'

The second she got the call she'd open these cages and hope these women didn't let her down. She also had to pray that call came soon because Damon would be looking for her before long. There was only so much time he'd buy she was in the toilet and if he went walkabout before Zane and the others were in place, everything would go wrong.

Twenty One

SONNY WAS ON TENTERHOOKS. Clockwatching, his hand remained poised over his phone as the minutes counted down to when he could signal Erin to release the women.

Come on, come on.

His pulse raced and his heart thundered.

'What was it you wanted?' As Damon entered the office, he saw Sonny's hand jump away from the telephone like it carried leprosy. 'About to call me again? What is it, Sonny? What have I done this time?'

Sonny could barely comprehend that he'd omitted to conceal this number when dialling Damon's office. How could he have been so remiss?

'Or were you after Caroline, like you usually are?' Damon's rubbery lips twitched with amusement. 'I don't think she's interested, mate. In fact, she doesn't have much time for you at all!' *That would piss on Sonny's chips*. Caroline had said herself that he was better than Sonny. And he'd prove that on every *single* subject once he'd had his way with her. Painters in or not, he'd take his chance.

The bird might have played hard to get at first. Didn't they always? Well, not anymore. He was well in there now and

Sonny didn't stand a cat's chance in hell, the stupid cunt.

Damon sneered. Sonny didn't have the decency to answer his question either because the fucker knew he'd been had bang to rights. 'Hello? You called my office but it cut off.'

'No, it didn't cut off. I misdialled.' Sonny muttered. 'I meant to call the crew room to reschedule that meeting with the men. Sorry if you've had a wasted journey.'

Fuck, fuck fuck. Damon was on walkabout at the worst time possible. Now there were only minutes to go until the off he'd have to keep the man here.

Damon made no effort to hide that he didn't trust this shithead. It was utter bullshit about misdialling. Sonny had something up his sleeve.

His eyes narrowed. The twat was setting him up and making out he was crap at his job to scrape back merit when Marco saw the shite job that had been done of running the gaff. Yeah, that was it. Sonny had worked out he'd brought Marco up to speed with what had befallen Grimes, as well as everything else.

Tough shit. It was Sonny's own fault.

Damon wouldn't let this dickhead know that Marco would be back earlier than planned either. It would only give the tosser time to cover his tracks or push his fuckups onto everybody else.

And there it was again… That was the fourth time Sonny had looked at his watch. 'Keeping you from something, am I?' he snarled. 'Best I leave you to it.'

Caroline should be back by now. She'd already been gone ages. Bloody women. No doubt flapping about not having the correct change for the Tampax machine. Aside from wanting to get his hands on her, he wasn't giving her the excuse of rifling through his office. She had a tendency to be a nosy bitch, so he should head back.

Sonny tensed as Damon moved towards the door. 'Before you go, there's a few things I'd appreciate your opinion on.'

Damon turned, his sneer blatant. 'You want *my* opinion?'

He felt like laughing. Sonny Mitchell had best get used to

hearing his opinion because very soon it would be the only one he'd be obeying. That's if the turd even had a job by then. 'Okay, so what do you want to know?'

• • • •

ZANE LEVERED OPEN the fire escape door at Luna and tried to get his bearings whilst Tiger and Leo followed him into the corridor. He pictured the route Sonny had given him. Having never been inside here, he didn't have a clue about the lie of the land. *Talk about working blind!*

Where was Erin in relation to where they were? Sonny said she'd be in Studio One with the women, three corridors to the left.

Craning his neck, Zane peered down the corridor in front of him that forked off in several directions – left, right and straight ahead.

Tiger flattened himself against the wall, his gun moving in various directions. 'This place is like a fucking rabbit warren. With this layout it will be difficult covering all angles.'

Zane frowned. 'Sonny said the men will be down that end of the building.' He gestured to the corridor on the right-hand side, then squinted down the far end of the corridor barely visible in the windowless passageway. 'Apparently, there's stairs to the first floor over there. All the men are located on the ground floor over the far end, so we kick the shit off as far away from the women as possible so Erin can get them out safely. Then we move to the next floor and take the men out from there.'

Leo glanced at his mobile. 'The text's just come in saying the lorry is in position at bay B.'

Zane double checked they had entered through bay A. 'Erin knows where to take the women. Tiger - me and you move to the first floor and then in exactly five minutes from now, Leo puts a shot out from the right-hand corridor to bring the men running.'

Leo nodded. 'Then I'll block off the corridor on the left so no one can slip down there. The women will have free passage.' He glanced around once more. 'This place reminds me of a lab. I don't like it.'

Zane's lips thinned. The floor to ceiling metal walls and passageways did have the appearance of a laboratory building - the type where everything looked identical and the metal doors to the rooms were randomly numbered to confuse animal rights protesters. 'I reckon it probably *was* a lab or testing centre prior to Marco. The cunning bastard would have chosen this place because the layout is perfect to scupper anyone's chances of escape.'

'We'll pick off as many of these wankers as we can, mate.' Tiger locked eyes with Leo, his expression fierce. 'The rest is down to you.'

'Not a problem,' Leo grinned.

Zane stared at his trusted men. 'We need our wits about us at all times, boys, okay? I don't want any casualties from our side. That prize is *theirs* to have.' He tapped his watch. 'Four minutes now, so let's go.'

Leo watched Zane and Tiger move up the corridor to the stairs. The galleried landing allowed a free range on the corridor below. Receiving a thumbs-up, signifying they had found a good position, he slipped around the junction of the right-hand corridor and stared at his watch. The minute he fired the shot to bring the bastards running, he'd move into the other corridor to wait.

He adjusted the heavy semi-automatic in his hand. These beauties would take rows of men out, so by the time Zane and Tiger had shot a few rounds there would be little remaining by the time anyone got to where he'd be lurking.

Three minutes to go...

Leo readied his gun and positioned himself against the wall. It was then that he heard someone whistling.

Fuck! Who was that?

His head darted in the direction of the tune as it became louder and his finger hovered over his trigger. He couldn't fire.

It was too early. The timing had to be exact.

A thickset man rounded the corner and the whistling abruptly stopped. The surprise on the man's face morphed to anger. 'Who the fuck are you?'

Leo saw the man reach for the gun and risked a manoeuvre of his own. Surging forward, his forehead crashed into the man's nose, his free hand slapping over his mouth. 'Don't move a muscle.'

With blood streaming from his nostrils, the man crumpled to the floor. Leo accompanied him down with a crash.

Hearing a loud and very unmistakable sound, Leo tensed, the ringing in his ears from the deafening crack only dwarfed by the stinging in his arm.

Grappling with the gun still held in the man's hand, Leo glanced down at his own arm, his heart sinking to see blood seeping through the sleeve of his jacket. *Fuck! The fall had discharged the gun and the stray bullet had copped him?* He flexed his arm. It was still moveable so hopefully it was only a graze. But everyone must have heard that shot.

The man beneath him began to struggle and with dread, Leo realised that reinforcement would soon be here. One shot had been fired, so a second would make little difference.

But he was too late…

The man's eyes bulged through his bloodied face as he flailed, forcing his pistol into Leo's belly. There wasn't time to aim his own gun before this bastard fired. *Shit!*

With all his strength, his hand started crushing the windpipe of the man underneath him, his other hand applying as much force as possible to release the fingers off the trigger of the gun whose barrel pressed into his stomach.

Suddenly, the sound of heavy boots - lots of them - were heard stampeding in his direction.

Fuck, fuck, fuck!

If he couldn't get this gun from this bloke he was a goner either way. He couldn't prise the man's fingers away from the trigger. One millimetre more and it was over.

Sweat trickled between Leo's shoulder blades, the thumping of his heart banging in his ears.

The second gunshot was loud.

The man's face exploded, showering Leo with gloopy pieces.

In shock, he scrambled to his feet and blinked away the blood and flesh slithering into his eyes. Whoever had fired hadn't hit *him*. Panting heavily, he glimpsed the barrel of Tiger or Zane's gun pointing through the railings above.

Thank God for mates, he thought. Pulling his own gun into position, he wiped the gunk from his face with his sleeve, then darted around the corner into the other corridor to prime himself for the off.

• • • •

'PLEASE BE QUIET!' Erin yelled, aware the very act of shouting wasn't helpful in maintaining silence. But calming these women down when they were convinced they had just heard a gunshot was easier said than done. It hadn't helped they had gone into overdrive the second word spread of their impending release either.

She glared at the blonde woman whose outburst had acted as the instigator for the melee. Picking her to speak to about this had been a bad choice.

And yes, Erin had heard the noise too. It might have been muffled behind the shrieks and frantic clamouring of the women rattling the bars of their cages as they lurched between excitement and frustrated desperation, but it *did* sound like a gun...

The second shot that followed was unmistakeable. It was also louder and *closer* than the first one...

It was a gunshot, loud and clear.

Her eyes darted around desperately as the screeching and banging of the women became further frenzied. She had to do something but she hadn't yet received the next call from Sonny, so what should she do?

Fear loomed. Something had gone wrong. There wouldn't be gunshots before time if things remained on plan.

'Shut up!' Erin yelled, unable to hear herself think. Sweat dripped freely down her back, her blouse sticking to her clammy skin.

As she hadn't received a second call, that shot could have been for Sonny.

Or worse, *Zane...*

If that was the case then they would be all dead, including these women.

Fuck. Should she wait for the call or get the women out regardless?

Erin pulled out her phone, her fingers slipping over the buttons. There had been no new texts or missed calls. Unable to keep herself steady enough to press the correct keys and several failed attempts later, she shoved her phone back.

She grabbed hold of the bars of a cage, the metal slick in her sweaty hands. Wincing as someone's nails dug into her fingers, she snatched her hand out of reach.

Shoving her hand back into her pocket, she fumbled for the keys. She couldn't wait for the call - if there even would be one now. She had to take the chance to get these women out of here.

Her heart pounded harder. There was no way of knowing whether the lorry was in situ either. She knew nothing of what was going on outside of this room, but it made no difference. Something had to be done.

Forcing the thoughts of what was happening elsewhere, Erin shoved the key into the first lock. How she would undo all these cages in time she didn't know. Neither was there a guarantee when the women were released they wouldn't turn on *her* or rush out into the corridor drawing more attention. Every single one of them could be killed, but there was nothing else to do but take the risk.

Twenty Two

HAZEL BUSIED HERSELF browsing through the selection of perfumes on offer in duty free. She'd treat herself to a few items in here. Considering her honeymoon had been cut short and things had now changed from the life she'd been promised, Marco could take the hit on his credit card.

Picking up an extra-large bottle of Chanel N°5 in its limited edition box, Hazel glanced at the price tag with slight disdain. How disappointing. It wasn't quite as expensive as she'd hoped.

But...

She ran her hand along the crocodile skin vanity case she'd asked the assistant to remove from the display cabinet for her to inspect. *This* would bump up the price.

Throw in a few Dior makeup palettes and that would round things off nicely. *To start with, anyway.*

A bit like the effortless task of upgrading the seats on their flight to business class. It was amazing what a platinum credit card with a unlimited level did in making people more amenable.

Marco would have a problem with it if he noticed being as he had a problem with *everything* lately, but she didn't care.

Hazel's eyes narrowed at Marco's well-built frame in the

middle of the duty free shop like a sore thumb. His full attention was centred on the phone clutched in his hand, oblivious to being in the way of anyone browsing. No doubt texting again...

And who he was texting, Hazel would *love* to know. She would bet money that it was another equally slimy man from the firm – the firm which turned out not to be Marco's anymore.

And any money she would bet would come out of *his* coffers, just like these high-priced unnecessary items she would shortly buy.

The cash she spent from now on would no longer cut into what she was owed. *Her* pool of money would soon come from a different source - from the man she should have married in the first place before she was duped by that coked-up lunatic.

And that was exactly what Marco was - no more, no less.

The way he'd behaved in the taxi was downright embarrassing. They were just lucky the driver was placated by her autograph. Had he pressed for the damage Marco caused to his taxi it could have been different. They could even have ended up missing the flight if the police were called, like the driver threatened after Marco had broken the bloody window with his stupid head.

If Marco behaved the same way on the plane, then Hazel didn't know what she'd do. She had to get back and put her life straight.

'Have you decided yet, madam?'

The sickly-sweet voice of the meticulously dressed sales assistant tugged Hazel from her burgeoning worry. Flicking on her stellar smile, she trailed her fingers over the scaly, but very expensive skin of the vanity case. 'I was just thinking it's a shame you haven't a matching handbag and makeup bag to go with this. It would make a perfect set...'

'How amazing that you should mention that,' the assistant gushed, her nude lip gloss enhancing her pouty mouth. Flicking her wavy auburn tresses over her shoulder, she stooped behind the counter.

Momentarily distracted by where this woman had got her

lips done being as they were slightly better than hers, Hazel's concentration lurched back to the counter as the woman placed a handbag, makeup pouch and matching compact next to the vanity case.

'These pieces only arrived this morning. Aren't they divine?' the woman exclaimed. 'I haven't even had chance to put them on display yet.'

Imagining the hefty amount this would shunt onto Marco's card, Hazel's eyes lit up. 'They're absolutely perfect!'

'I tell you what...' The assistant leant closer to Hazel over the mirrored counter and lowered her voice. 'This handbag is £3500, but if you'd like the whole set, then I'll can knock off £500.'

Hazel flapped her hand dismissively. 'No, don't worry.' She waited for the woman's face to show the expected crestfallen expression at the loss of a huge sale before she continued. *Ah ha - there it was...* 'I wouldn't dream of cutting into your commission. I know how hard you must work,' she lied, not caring a jot about the woman or her piffling salary. 'I'll pay full price and take the lot. Oh, and don't forget the Dior palettes and the limited edition Chanel.'

The assistant hurriedly rang up the items through the till, scarcely able to believe her luck. 'Beautiful choices madam. They'll go superbly with your perfect style.'

Yeah, yeah, cut the shit, Hazel thought, but smiled all the same. Now all she had to do was wait for the price. Holding Marco's credit card between her long, slim fingers, she watched the assistant's eyes widen as the total price displayed on the till, before a smile as well-practised as her own replaced her fleeting surprise.

'That will be £14,975.' Taking the card from Hazel's outstretched hand, the assistant casually swiped it through the machine.

'Perfect,' Hazel muttered as she keyed in Marco's PIN number. *That was money well spent.*

Taking the two thickly embellished carrier bags from the

overjoyed assistant, Hazel strutted from the shop. Walking past Marco on her way out, she called over her shoulder, 'The plane is about to board.'

Within a few hours she'd be home and then Marco could get stuffed.

• • • •

DAMON SHOT OUT OF HIS SEAT quicker than if it were on fire. 'What the fuck was that?'

Sonny had heard the gunshot. He'd heard the second one too. His hand darted to his mobile. It couldn't be Zane or his men. It was too early. They wouldn't fire before time – not without good reason. The only explanation being they must have been sprung.

He stabbed at his mobile to release the screen lock. Whatever had happened wasn't good. He had to get the signal to Erin to release the women.

Suddenly, two text notifications pinged and echoed around the room. *Shit! Marco again?* He'd already had loads of messages since Damon had come into his office and he hadn't been able to look at any of them. But Damon had clocked every single one.

'Did you not hear that?' Damon screamed, yanking the door of the metal cabinet at the rear of Sonny's office. 'It was a fucking gun! I know there's weapons in this cabinet, so hurry the fuck up and grab one! We need to investigate.' His eyes narrowed. 'It could be Morelli. Hey! Why is this cabinet open?'

'No idea.' Sonny jerked himself to a standing position, his brain lurching between continuing to play the game or taking Damon out here and now. But if Zane and his men weren't casualties of that shot, killing Damon now could scupper things further.

Quickly pushing his phone into his pocket, Sonny grabbed the gun Damon shoved in his direction. Pretending to remain on Damon's side was the only way. 'Quickly!' he panted. 'There's no time to waste.' He checked his gun was loaded and released the safety catch.

Damon steamed towards the door, his face twisted into a fierce snarl only for Sonny to pull him back by a tight grip of his arm. 'Wait! We have to tread carefully. If it *is* Morelli, he's clever. You know he is. We don't want to walk into an ambush.' He jerked his head towards the door. 'We must go slowly and quietly.'

'Shit!' Damon hissed. 'This is...'

'Have you put the alarm out?' Sonny interrupted, nodding at Damon's mobile. 'We don't know for definite it's Zane, but we should presume that it is. Call the guards from the penthouse back here. We need all hands on deck.' *Oh yes, it most certainly was Zane. And he would rid the world of these fuckers.*

'But Morelli will go to the penthouse too. You know that place is on his list.'

Sonny frowned. *Come on, you useless fuck. Cav and Lewis are waiting for those guards to vacate so they can take possession.* 'If Zane is here, then he can't be there at the same time! Look, the business and men take priority over the penthouse.'

'I guess you're right.' Damon fumbled with his phone to locate the prearranged text instructing staff to return to base in the event of a storm. And this *was* a storm.

This *had* to be Morelli. They all knew he'd show his face eventually. Now he had and it had to be dealt with. And Damon would make sure it was. It meant another feather in his cap guaranteeing his standing when Marco returned.

Yet another 'ding' from Sonny's direction signified more texts. Pressing send on his own phone, Damon frowned. Sonny had received countless messages – sometimes one after another, yet he hadn't looked at any of them. 'Who *is* that?' he asked. 'Why aren't you reading your messages?'

'It's just bullshit from spammy firms. I get them all the time.' Sonny shrugged. 'Have you sent *your* text yet? Isn't that the important thing?'

'The alert's been sent,' Damon said. He'd get to the bottom

of what Mitchell was hiding sooner rather than later, but first *this* had to be dealt with. 'Let's go and find that fu…'

A long barrage of furious gunfire stopped Damon mid-sentence. 'Shit the bed! Let's get the hell out of there.'

Without waiting for agreement, Damon ignored everything Sonny had previously said about being stealthy and stormed from the room, leaving Sonny little choice but to follow.

'Hold on!' Sonny gasped, catching up. 'Head this way. We'll cut them off from the other end and catch them unaware.' Springing into action, he jerked his head in the opposite direction, relief flooding him as Damon took heed and changed course.

Succeeding in leading Damon away from where Zane, Tiger and Leo were was one thing, but would it make a difference? It might already be too late...

He hadn't got the signal to Erin yet either. She must have heard those gunshots. The question was, what had she done about it? Had she stayed put or started to get the women out? Or had she and the women been the recipients of the gunfire? He shuddered, but kept his pretence of being on Damon's side in place.

'Over here!' Damon rushed in the direction of the galleried landing at the opposite end of the corridor. 'We can weigh things up better. We'll lie in wait. Morelli or whoever these wankers are will be visible from there regardless which way they take.'

'Good thinking,' Sonny puffed, rushing to match Damon's long strides. *It wasn't good thinking at all.* Not for him or Zane. He'd given his word that Damon would remain contained and also that all other men would be over the other side of the building. From what he could gather from the direction of the gunfire, the men, or at least some of them, were now the *opposite* side of the building - the very end where Zane was. If Zane and his men remained alive, they would be heading into Damon's line of sight. They'd be walking into a trap and there was nothing Sonny could do to warn them.

But there was one thing he had to do. Sonny didn't know Erin well enough to deduce how she would react to this and she could be sitting tight waiting for the signal, so he had to get it to her.

• • • •

'LET'S GO!' Cav cried, prompting his brother to grab the bag of locksmith tools.

Scrambling from the van the minute the two cars containing the enforcers from the penthouse left, adrenaline pumped in Lewis's veins. 'They've been summoned,' he said as a statement, rather than a question. It proved the mission was successfully underway at Luna.

He followed Cav towards the entrance to the penthouse complex. 'You're sure they've all gone?'

'We don't know exactly how many were there, but with two full carloads leaving, I'm guessing so,' Cav said, raising an eyebrow at the glass double doors in front of him. He could have a shave in this reflection the glass was so clear. Pity he looked like utter shit, otherwise he might have enjoyed the pristine shine.

Whether all the enforcers were gone or not, it was a risk they had to take. Getting the penthouse back into possession of its rightful owner was necessary in order for Zane to gain control of his life, as well as his firm.

Not needing to spell out to his brother to act like they had the right to be heading to the penthouse apartment, Cav yanked open the door and made his way across the polished marble flooring towards the lift.

Following closely behind, Lewis didn't glance at the man watching as they made their way across the lobby. He drummed his fingers on the shiny gold surround as Cav summoned the lift.

He could hear the mechanism whirring from within, but the descent was taking an excruciatingly long time. The longer this lift took, the heavier the weight of the eyes boring into his back from the reception desk became. It also became harder not to gawp at the opulence of this expensive complex.

'Come on!' Cav hissed under his breath, jabbing at the button for the second time.

'Excuse me, sir.'

Both Cav and Lewis ignored the voice and willed the lift to hurry up, but they couldn't ignore it for a second and then a third time.

Cav glanced at his brother, then turned around. 'Are you talking to us?'

'Yes, sir,' the concierge said. 'May I ask who you're here to see?'

'Do you ask everybody who comes in here that question?' Cav spat, immediately riled.

'Well erm, no, sir,' the concierge stuttered. 'It's just that...'

'Just that this is the lift goes to the penthouse floor and *we* couldn't possibly be heading there?' Cav snarled, ignoring the nudge from his brother.

The concierge fidgeted in his seat. 'That wasn't how my question was intended, sir,' he spluttered. 'I haven't seen you before and we have strict security for...'

'For Mr Morelli, who is out of the country at present?' Lewis interjected before Cav punched this guy in the face. 'I understand your concerns because our boss is tight with security, but as you may have noticed, our other staff have been unexpectedly called away, so we are standing in until they return.'

'My apologies, sir. I didn't realise you were part of Mr Morelli's staff,' the concierge said.

It was Cav who noticed the man's hand drop below the desk. And he knew what was there: a silent alarm to both the cop shop and the Morelli firm. Before the enforcers raced back to headquarters they could have briefed this dickhead on reception to let no one up to the penthouse under any circumstances. And if he pressed that button they'd all be screwed.

Whipping his revolver from his waistband, the released bullet made little sound thanks to the attached silencer.

'Shit!' Lewis yelped as the shot hit bang on target through the concierge's skull. He stared at the blood-splattered wall behind the reception desk and then at the man still poised in his chair, his glassy eyes staring unseeing across the quiet lobby. 'What the fuck have you done? We're supposed to keep this place clean! He was letting us through!'

'Was he bollocks!' Cav shoved his pistol back in his waistband and hastened over to the concierge desk to scan the list of controls and buttons underneath the shiny countertop. 'Just as I thought.' He nodded towards the silent alarm button. 'He was about to signal the alarm. We'd have been fucking swarmed within minutes!'

'What?' Lewis gibbered. 'The Old Bill would have come running?'

'Either that or Marco's bunch, if they weren't otherwise engaged.' Cav jabbed a button on the door control panel which emitted a high whining noise and then a loud click. 'Check to see if that's locked the entrance doors.'

Lewis hesitated, still in a state of disbelief that he had stupidly fallen for the show the concierge put on.

'*Now*, Lewis!' Cav jerked his head back in the direction of the doors. 'Check they're locked.' Raising his boot, he kicked the body off the chair to land on the floor with a thud. 'We need to get this cleaned up before anyone shows up. It won't be long before someone wants to get into their apartment.'

'The doors are locked,' Lewis confirmed, glancing back at the mess on the wall behind where the man had sat. Now they had an unexpected corpse to get rid of. 'Loads of people live in this complex. If you shove the body out the back and clean this up, we can then release the doors. In the meantime, I'll change the penthouse locks.'

Cav grimaced. He wasn't happy undertaking this clean-up alone, but not having Lewis's lock changing skills, it was the only solution. They had to get this place cleaned and secured quickly.

Pulling the corpse by the feet into a small room leading off from the reception, Cav grabbed some cloths and got to work on the wall behind the desk, leaving Lewis to scramble into the lift that had finally reached the ground floor.

TWENTY THREE

OVERRIDING THE RINGING in his ears from the constant gunfire, Zane tucked himself behind a jutting wall which acted as the bridge between life and death.

Wiping a sheen of sweat from his brow that threatened to drip down and obscure his vision, his eyes darted to Tiger lying on the floor. Propped up by his elbows, Tiger's head was the only thing in view from the floor below, short of ricocheting bullets - but there were plenty of those. His head was the most important thing, but so far they had both avoided being hit by the never ending volley of shots.

Sliding the muzzle of his gun back around the edge of the wall, Zane remained tense waiting for the opportunity to fire again. Doing so meant exposing more of himself and elevating the chance of getting shot, but they had to advance from this current position and gain ground. That must be achieved quickly because the men below were making fast work of heading to where Leo waited, but at the moment gaining ground was impossible because they were surrounded.

This was bad. They had to reduce the numbers of men. There were far too many for Leo to handle on his own despite him being a crack shot. The sheer numbers of the men below outnumbered them at least ten to one.

Marco's men were not as competent as them with their shooting capabilities, but still better than expected.

As a bullet flew past the muzzle of Zane's gun, narrowly missing hitting or at the very least, grazing his shooting hand, he retracted, his heart pounding.

Shit. If only that man hadn't appeared forcing the first shot to be fired before time they would be in a much better position.

Taking a deep breath, Zane whipped out from around the protection of the wall and fired off several rounds before ducking back behind the meagre protection which was becoming cheese-like with bullet holes. He'd added a few more bodies to the pile mounting up on the ground floor, but there had to be more. A *lot* more.

His ragged breath rasped in his lungs. Marco was better prepared than any of them realised.

Zane's teeth clenched so tightly his jaw ached. As quickly as they took men out, they were replaced by others. The supply seemed endless. At the moment every man's sights were centred on them, but it wouldn't be long before some splintered off to look for other possible intruders.

That would mean Leo would be done for. And if Leo was done for, it would expose Erin.

Nausea bubbled in Zane's gut.

'We're losing control!' Tiger hissed, hoping Zane heard him over the deafening chaos.

Zane did hear. What Tiger said was true and there was only one way to rectify this. He wouldn't have his men lost. They were only in this situation because they were helping *him*. His plan was an almost impossible task, yet they'd still chosen to put their lives on the line.

Even Sonny –who yes, had previously betrayed him, had put his neck on the chopping block for weeks in the hope of rectifying his previous bad choices.

And then there was Erin… After all this firm had done to her and her family, her heart was big enough to allow herself to accept him.

As well as fall in love…

Zane's face twisted into a scowl. And what was he doing? Waiting up here until he and his trusted men got blasted to bits, leaving Erin to fend for herself?

No. That was not happening. Whatever came from this, it wouldn't be because he hadn't made the ultimate sacrifice.

Taking a deep breath, Zane jumped from behind the wall, leaving his entire body open to the relentless gunfire. His eyes shone with determination. Nothing but the end result hammered in his mind as he opened fire, his spray of bullets moving backwards and forwards along the rows of men below.

'Get back behind the wall!' Tiger screamed in disbelief. 'Don't do this! Get back behind your fucking cover.'

As before, Zane heard Tiger. At least he heard *something*, but his concentration was solely on removing the bastards who threatened the life of everyone who had stood by him. Protecting them was his only aim, whatever that meant.

Like his father had always said: *Loyalty is everything.*

• • • •

REGARDLESS OF HER USUAL hardcore attitude towards things most people would recoil from in terror and disgust, Erin discovered that she also had a limit to what she could withstand without plummeting headfirst into unbridled panic.

And this was it...

'Get away from the door!' she shrieked, the uncontrollable shaking coursing through her body making unlocking the remaining cages impossible.

Her focus remained on the women she had previously released who hammered on the door of Studio One in a joint effort to find freedom.

'Don't!' Erin screamed, her throat raw. 'Just wait. WAIT!'

If they succeeded breaking the door down, then God only knew what would befall them. The gunfire close by had reached an excruciating level. It sounded like there was men with guns everywhere - and only a handful being those Erin knew to be on her and these women's side.

And there was a high chance those particular men on side were no longer capable…

Erin shook off the stabbing dread that Zane had been mown down and instead pulled air into her lungs, willing her crippling panic to subside.

There were only four more cages left to unlock. Only after achieving that would she worry about where to go from there.

Forcing her stricken gaze away from the women who were now tipping a cabinet on its side to use as a battering ram to knock the door clean off its hinges, Erin willed her trembling hands to calm.

She stared at the woman in the cage as she fumbled to insert the key. The base fear in the woman's wide eyes spoke volumes. 'It'll be all right,' Erin said, finally jamming the key in the lock. 'Please stay calm.'

She had no idea whether this woman understood her, but what difference did it make? They would either get out of here or they wouldn't. The longer this went on and the more commotion made cut down their percentage of success. If they didn't leave this studio and get to bay B soon there was no chance at all. The gunfire was getting closer and louder with every passing moment and time was running out.

With a jolt, the lock gave and the woman burst from the cage to land heavily on the floor.

Erin didn't bother helping her up. She didn't have time. Lurching towards the next cage, she forced the key into the lock, grateful to find it went straight in.

Three cages to go...

Keep calm, she repeated to herself. If she was quick, there was still a chance they could get out of here.

• • • •

DAMON WANTED TO ASK Sonny why he was fiddling with his mobile whilst they raced to where Morelli and the other intruders could be cut off. Shouldn't the only thing on the man's mind be to pick these wankers off? One of whom he suspected was Zane…

Plus, further text notifications had been heard coming from Sonny's person, even through the gunfire.

And with this, Damon reached the only viable conclusion: Mitchell was part of this setup. He was receiving texts as to what was going on by the very people who were picking off Marco's men.

Sonny knew who was behind this and had arranged their entry into the building. That was what the misdialled call was about.

Now it all made sense.

It was a signal.

A signal to *Caroline*.

Which meant that whore was in on it too...

Overcome with rage, Damon halted his rapid path along the corridor. *He'd kill the cunt.*

Sonny slammed into Damon's back. 'What the fu…'

'You fucking traitor!' Spinning around, Damon's eyes glistened with malice. 'You let them in! You let Morelli in here! And that Caroline bitch - she's part of this too. Those texts you've been getting – they're to do with this as well!'

'What?' Sonny barked as Damon's gun jammed into his chin. 'What the fuck has got into you? Are you mad?'

'I ain't mad,' Damon raged. 'You're in with Zane Morelli, as is that Caroline bitch. And for that I'll kill you both!'

Pushing his fear to one side, Sonny knew there was only one way out of this. He jabbed the barrel of his gun into Damon's belly. 'I'm in charge here, Sandler, not you. You kill either of us and you're fucked. Marco won't appreciate his right-hand man being picked off by a deluded wanker who runs the films!'

Grabbing the muzzle of Damon's gun, he wrenched it away. It was a gamble, but the mention of Marco's wrath should have an effect on this egotistical bastard's brain.

Even if Sandler didn't quite realise it, he wasn't the brightest of sparks and known for second guessing his own decisions. The man believed what he wanted to believe and in this instance, that trait might just save Sonny's skin.

'Stop fucking around, Sandler,' Sonny continued, turning up the rage behind his eyes. 'You're pissing about with bullshit whilst our men get shot to fuck by whoever's behind this – who, I might add and despite what you think, isn't *me*!'

The flicker of uncertainty in Damon's eyes may have only been slight, but it was enough. Retracting his gun, Sonny pulled it into a normal position. 'Stand there if you want, but I'm sorting these wankers out. Are you with me or not?'

Damon raced after Sonny, his brain firing on all cylinders. *The cunt was lying. He had to be.*

Sonny was acutely aware of Damon behind as he neared the end of the corridor where the gunfire was deafening. Zane, if still alive, was metres away. 'They must be just around here.' He glanced over his shoulder. 'We'll wait and ambush them the second they come around the corner.'

Damon flattened himself against the wall. From here, he had a thin line of vision onto the floor below. The corridor was strewn with Marco's men. Others were firing up to the floor above - the floor *he* stood on and the floor Zane Morelli and his men were also on.

The man he could see firing with precision into the men below *was* Zane Morelli. A fiercer and fitter version of Marco. Similar looking, but without the manic, jittery behaviour. Surrounded by gunfire, he was calm as anything.

From his reduced view, Damon watched in horror as another line of men scrambled into position, only to be cut down in a hail of bullets, leaving others to retreat behind their minimal cover. A few, however, broke away and moved further down the corridor only to get gunned down in the process.

His jaw clenched in fear as well as rage.

Marco would have no one left at this rate. He may be 'only in charge of the films', as Sonny relished informing him, but he wouldn't be for much longer. It was possible that Damon may be able to get the angle to hit Morelli from here, but confessed he wasn't the sharpest shot. Unless he caused a fatal wound with the one and only shot available before his position was exposed, he'd be fucked.

He didn't like the look of the savage lying on the floor, poised like a jungle sniper either.

Nah, he was better off waiting here.

Sonny pretended to wait for the intruders to round the corner. But he wasn't waiting for that. He was waiting for Damon to get into the correct position so that he could be shot without his body tumbling to the floor below. There was no choice but to do remove Sandler now because when Zane rounded this corner, Damon would shoot him. It was either that, or proving Damon right all along and then he'd end up dead too, along with Zane.

A vein pulsed rapidly in Sonny's neck as his fingers crept towards the trigger of his gun.

Damon surreptitiously watched Sonny, hearing the man's phone ding once more. Someone was watching the proceeds from a different location and relaying the info. It was a shame Sonny was so shit that even looking at his phone for the required info was out of his remit. Because if someone was watching, they would work out something was about to happen that Sonny could do with knowing…

Damon swallowed the laugh that inexplicably formed in his throat. None of this was funny but the laugh built nonetheless.

Sonny Mitchell didn't fool him. Damon may have acted like he'd taken the man's rebuff on the chin and would also admit that he had, for a small amount of time, thought perhaps he *may* have jumped to conclusions about Sonny's involvement in this nightmare.

But now he knew differently…

He wasn't wrong. Sonny *was* behind it. The man's traitorous miasma oozed from his pores like poison. And that was all Damon needed to know. He swung towards Sonny.

'You're a fucking liar!'

Before Sonny could depress his own trigger, Damon pulled his. The bang which extinguished Sonny's life was lost in the noise of the surrounding gunfire.

Damon grinned. Now all he had to do was to get the hell out of here and wait for this shit to burn itself out.

He wasn't risking being gunned down by some outrider for one minute longer. Sonny had probably led him purposefully to a prearranged position where Zane waited, ready to exterminate him.

Fuck that. He'd sidle out of here and weigh things up from there.

But just before he exited stage left, he'd get *that*!

Stooping over the body, Damon shoved his hand into Sonny's pocket and extracted the mobile phone.

He'd keep hold of this. It would serve as another piece of evidence to prove more of Sonny's wrongdoings to Marco.

TWENTY FOUR

LEWIS WASN'T SURPRISED the key code Zane had given them failed to open the penthouse apartment door. It stood to reason that someone in Marco's inner circle possessed enough brain cells to change it, especially once Zane was released.

He glanced up the plush corridor. Only this apartment resided on this floor but he still needed to be careful.

Lewis placed his bag of tools on the floor. With his knowledge he could break the lock and gain entry easily enough, but although Cav thought all of Marco's enforcers had rushed to Luna, he wasn't so sure. There was something about it up here which made the hairs on the back of his neck thrum with the warning that he wasn't alone.

Being as Cav was busy clearing up the impromptu but necessary deletion on the ground floor many storeys below, not having anyone covering his back made things worse.

But *that* looked promising...

Spotting a small box in the shadow of a fire extinguisher, Lewis slid to the left of the penthouse door. To the untrained eye it looked like a mailbox, but he knew differently. And *that* he could break into quickly and silently.

In a matter of seconds, he slipped one of his smaller tools

into the tiny lock of the box and applied the correct amount of pressure to release the casing. The metal box flipped open as simple as clicking his fingers.

Grinning, Lewis removed the key card from the bottom of the box and moved back to the side of the door, pressing himself against the wall. Leaving his big gun safe in the tool bag, he pulled his pistol from his jacket's inside pocket.

Keeping the gun aimed ahead, he presented the key card to the door sensor and waited for the click signifying the lock release.

Bingo.

Nudging the door so it swung open just enough to slip inside, Lewis held his breath, focusing for any hint of another's presence within the apartment. The sense of not being alone amplified, the vibrations of his instinct travelling along his veins.

Everything was silent. Perhaps he was imagining it? After all, so far things hadn't gone to plan and considering his astuteness had already failed by missing that concierge's plan to stiff them, Lewis felt unable to fully trust his instincts.

But right now, instinct was all he had and they screamed to be on guard.

As he edged along the hallway, Lewis's throat constricted.

Fuck - this part alone was bigger than his entire flat, so Christ knew how massive the rest of the place was. Think of all the rooms he'd need to check to ensure the place was clear...

He faltered, pausing on the marble floor.

Was he being daft? Cav said the enforcers had left, so perhaps he shouldn't waste valuable time creeping around looking for someone that wasn't here?

The brief was to change the locks and secure the place. They had no way of knowing whether everything was going to plan at Luna. If it wasn't and something had gone wrong or happened in a different order, then the enforcers or at least some of them, could return here at any time.

Even Marco himself might show up. They knew he was

inbound en route back, just not *when*. It could be anytime. *Like now...*

Enough time had already been lost by that shit kicking off in the lobby so he should get a move on.

He'd change the locks. If there was someone here, surely they'd have been lurking in the hallway, not in one of the many other rooms having a kip or watching the TV?

Pushing his bag of tools along with his foot, Lewis shook his head at his overactive imagination. It would take aeons to properly check the apartment. Aside from his own breathing, there wasn't a sound to be heard, so it was all good.

As he placed his pistol back in his inside pocket, he eyed the lock on the front door. It was a fucking fancy lock and one which would take longer than most to remove and replace, but he could do it, no problem.

Stooping down to pick the tools required from his bag, a tune he'd heard on the radio this morning filtered into his head. He'd be humming that in a minute like he always did when working. It helped him concentrate.

With his hands full, Lewis held the final tool in his teeth and stood up to start work. As he began humming the tune in his head, the man slipping from the hallway cloakroom had an easy job in running the blade across Lewis's throat from behind.

• • • •

FINDING HIMSELF STARING close up at the corridor's concrete flooring. Zane blinked in confusion. The force of the unexpected impact and subsequently hitting the ground had completely knocked the air from his lungs.

He blinked again, the pounding in his head and the noise surrounding him serving as a reminder that he wasn't dead. It was then that he noticed the gunfire had died down and Tiger was lying on top of him.

'I had to stop you, mate. We can't afford to lose you.' Tiger scrambled back into a crouching position to take aim. 'You'd have been party to more holes than a fucking sieve by standing there. What were you thinking?'

Zane pulled his jumbled head into order. He knew what he'd been thinking: that if needs be, he'd sacrifice himself to finish this.

And he still would.

But Tiger was right. Leaving his loyal men a body short in the name of misguided loyalty wasn't the way to achieve a palatable outcome.

This was no longer just about the past insults of his firm and standing being inveigled off him by his brother's betrayal. It was now also about watching the backs of the people around him who had put their necks on the line. Like Sonny, Leo and Tiger - the man who, thankfully, had reminded him of his priorities in the nick of time.

It was for the people who had lost their jobs at the firm and suffered because of Marco's greed. It was also for the woman he loved, whose life the Morelli family had wrecked, who was somewhere in this building holding her own after risking all to be a mole in this hellhole.

And last but not least, it was for the container load of women Marco had shipped here like animals to fuel his own and others' perversions.

It was for *all* of them.

Being a fucking martyr wouldn't help, but then nor would doing fuck all and whilst he was not manning his gun, it gave Marco's men time to get up the stairs. If that happened, then both he and Tiger really would be sitting targets.

Scrambling to his feet, Zane threw himself back behind the peppered wall and readied himself to continue to fire, when to his horror he saw Leo appear around the junction of the corridor below.

• • • •

LEO ROARED AT THE top of his lungs. Storming the corridor wasn't a difficult decision to take. Since the second that fuckturd had stumbled across him and forced things to kick off prematurely, things had gone pear-shaped. But remaining down the other corridor as instructed and hearing the lull in the gunfire, left only one option.

The gunfire diminishing to all but nothing meant Zane and Tiger must have been taken out. And that prospect was enough to ignite the touchpaper on Leo's control. The incendiary point had hovered on a fine line since this had been going on. It felt like years, but in reality it was minutes.

With his concentration fixed on offloading as many rounds as possible into the men as he weaved and zigzagged his way up the wide corridor, the adrenaline pounding through Leo's veins made him feel immortal to the numerous bullets zipping past. Each one missed, but passed so close he could hear the whooshing noise even over the crack of the discharge.

So ramped up was his altered state of awareness it took a couple of seconds before he took in the amount of bodies lying on the floor, riddled in bullets. The men's faces frozen for eternity in twisted grimaces, their mouth and eyes wide open in eternal shock or rage. Possibly both.

It was only at this point did Leo acknowledge the number of men available to defend Marco's stolen castle of perversion. It also showed there were plenty left who *weren't* dead and whose sights were aligned between him and that of the galleried floor above.

Suddenly, a man scooted past, his red hot trail of bullets a blur.

Leo felt the sting in his arm. He also felt the sting in his leg. It barely hurt but he knew he'd been hit again. Three bullets now, but nothing would stop him.

He wasn't dead yet, so crack on.

Leo let off a round in the direction of the man who had got past him but it was to no avail. He'd disappeared.

Shit. That man had gone towards where the studio was located – the one that Zane said Erin and the women were in.

Still firing, Leo faltered over following the man or covering Zane and Tiger. Where they alive? After all, the lull in the firing was what made him break his cover in the first place.

Seeing a new hail of bullets spill from the top floor answered his question. His eyes darted up to see both Tiger and Zane. Relief pooled.

But Zane was gesturing something to him.

Leo frowned. *What was it? He was waving his arm.*

Zane wanted him to go?

Go where?

To the women?

Leo suddenly realised his presence in the middle of all the targets wasn't helping Zane or Tiger to remove the men skittering in all directions along the maze of corridors. They would lose track of these bastards and it would only take one to pick all three of them off.

Seeing Zane frantically swiping his arm to the left once again, Leo turned on his heels and raced in the direction the lone shooter had gone.

TWENTY FIVE

HAVING SUCCESSFULLY cleared the lobby and released the lock on the main entrance doors to the complex, Cav rushed to the lift. He took a quick glance at the reception area behind before stepping into the golden enclosure which would take him to the penthouse floor. It looked good. There wasn't a trace of anything untoward. Certainly nothing to alarm the untrained eye.

There was still the concierge's body to dispose of but that was safely hidden and could wait. The absence of anyone on the desk might raise questions with some residents, but luckily none had attempted to gain entry. No doubt they were busy having after work drinks at some swanky wine bar.

Cav's foot impatiently tapped on the lift floor as it slowly ascended.

Lewis was taking his bloody time changing the locks. They had to get to Luna and help the others out, so what was keeping him? There hadn't been a lock yet that his brother was unable to either break or fix.

The lift doors opened and Cav stepped into the penthouse level corridor. His hackles immediately rose. He opened his mouth to call his brother's name and then stopped, his hand moving to his gun. *It was too quiet.*

Creeping along the edge of the corridor towards the apartment door, the rustle of Cav's jacket brushing the wall was amplified in the uncomfortable silence.

His heart raced. Lewis would be humming a song as he worked. He always did, yet there was nothing...

As the door came into view, Cav's stomach lurched with trepidation. *It was open...*

Flattening himself against the wall to the side of the door, he waited, his ears primed for movement. He slipped his head around the doorjamb and glanced into the immense hallway of the apartment, finding it empty.

With his gun in front of him, Cav stepped inside, then stopped, his eyes moving to the floor underneath his boots. A whimper escaped his mouth as he realised he was standing in a pool of blood.

Whose blood? Lewis's? An enforcer's?

His heart thrashed in his chest. It was someone's blood, but where was the person who it had spilled from?

His eyes scoured the marble floor. The pool of blood had no obvious trail leading from it. Someone had leaked blood - an immense amount, but left no hint of where they had moved to afterwards. The pool was localised in this one place.

Apart from *there...*

The arc of blood sprayed onto the high ceiling made Cav go cold.

Fuck! It couldn't be Lewis's. Not his brother. No!

With a clenched jaw, he moved further into the hallway, his boots imprinting size twelve bloody footprints in his wake. It was then that he heard the voice - a voice that didn't belong to his brother.

It was a one way conversation. Someone was on the phone.

And it was coming from in there...

Cav moved swiftly and silently towards the large double doors at the end of the hallway. Stopping, he held his breath so not to miss a word of what was being said.

'I'm telling you, some fucker was swapping out the locks... Yeah, deffo a good plan for me to remain. Nah, he was alone.'

Cav stiffened. *Was? Was alone? Past tense...*

Dread pooled. The blood he'd trodden in was his brother's?

His hand tightened around his gun.

'No, there's no one else... They'd have showed themselves by now...' The voice then chuckled. 'Silly fuckers, eh? Sending one man with no backup? Yeah, it's all good... No... I'll leave it here for now... Oh, you do? Okay, I'll stay then just in case... Yeah, okay...'

Rage burnt at the back of Cav's eyes. It burnt so hard it stung the inside of his nose. This cunt had killed his brother, yet he was fucking laughing?

His fingers trembled with rising adrenaline.

And no backup? Lewis had had backup all right. *Him*. But where had he been? Downstairs, in the lobby, that's where.

Cav's teeth clenched, the crack as one of his back teeth split loud in the silence.

Fuck. Lewis! I'm so sorry, bro. I should have been here, Cav thought, his fury reaching incendiary levels.

Cav kicked open the doors in front of him to see a man leaning against a huge leather sofa swing around with a mobile pressed to his ear.

Cav pulled the trigger and the mobile in the man's hand clattered to the floor. Sporting a hole in his chest, the large man fell backwards over the sofa to crash into a glass table which promptly shattered into fragments.

Rushing into the room in the wake of his bullet, Cav stood over the man and fired again. *Once, twice, three times...*

Blood and flesh spattered the beige rug and over the panoramic glass windows offering a vista over the Thames and the London skyline.

Cav continued to fire and he didn't stop firing until the chamber of his gun was empty. It was irrelevant that the man had been killed from the first bullet.

His gaze then fell on a hastily wrapped tarpaulin on the

floor in the open plan kitchen area. A thin trail of blood seeped from one corner to form a small pool on the tiles.

Lewis…

Tossing his spent gun to the floor, Cav stamped on what was left of the man's face over and over, the crunch of shattering bones underneath his boot not even slightly diluting the raw pain that his brother was no more.

• • • •

'PLEASE DON'T LEAVE ME HERE,' the woman wailed, tears streaking her cheeks.

'I won't leave you. I'm getting you out,' Erin promised, shoving the key into the lock for the third time. Christ, why wouldn't it open? It *had* to open. This was the last bloody one. Once this cage was open, they could all make a run for it.

Her head swivelled towards the women still hellbent on hammering at the door. Raw fear had overtaken their logic. It wasn't surprising. Fear was infectious and it only took one or two to panic before dragging everyone else into it. It was only a miracle they had failed to break the door.

'Please hurry!' The caged woman's plaintive, desperate voice jarred all the remaining nerve endings Erin possessed.

'Nearly there,' Erin said, relief firing as the key finally seated into the lock. 'I'll have you out in just a m…'

An almighty scream filled the room along with a crash which stopped her in her tracks. She barely had time to turn her head before the door burst from its hinges.

Her first fleeting thought was that the women had succeeded in ripping the door off, until she saw the blood blooming from underneath a thin brunette crumpled on the ground.

Blinking wildly, Erin's brain failed to process how this could have happened.

Then it became obvious…

A strange guttural roar drowned out the terrified screams of the women darting around in a pointless dash to escape the rain of bullets unloading into them.

'Get down!' Erin yelled, taking to the deck herself. The noise around her; the screams; the roar and the deafening sound from the semi-automatic firing into the room merged into one. Underlying this cacophony was the loud pounding of our own heart.

It was over.

It was fucking over.

Yet they'd been so damned close.

Fuck. *FUCK!*

She'd never see Zane again. She couldn't explain her recent attitude. She'd never get chance to say that for so many years she'd felt worthless; a commodity - not capable of anything, except hatred and revenge. Sometimes - *most* of the time she still felt that way.

But meeting Zane and despite the strange and unnatural circumstances, he'd made her feel that things *could* be possible.

The way he looked at her - that fire behind his eyes for her and her alone; the way he touched her like she was the most important person in the world had lit a small flame within her, that if nurtured, could grow into her becoming a *real* person. A person whose sole thoughts and acts were not driven by what she *had* to do or what she'd promised she must do to justify remaining in this godforsaken world.

But the more that spark ignited and the more it grew, then so in tandem did the fear. The fear that everything was fake – from the way she felt; what she believed her and Zane had together - *everything* was a collection of holograms. Being together in the first place had been borne from necessity and a shared hatred. How could anything good come from that?

Surely it was only a matter of time before the dream she'd cultivated and ramped into being reality would shatter? And this time she didn't think she possessed the strength or will to recover. Not after knowing that true happiness - or the prospect of it, existed.

Plus, Zane had been distracted of late. He couldn't function without his 'fix' of her, as he put it. But that 'fix' was not as strong as it had once been. Was that because he'd realised his feelings for her weren't true?

Erin had told herself time and time again that Zane had too much on his mind and his distant behaviour was down to that. She understood it.

But it made her panic, nonetheless.

She'd been pushing him away, she knew that. Doing so was easier and less traumatic. Zane walking away from her and the baggage and hangups she carted around was better than throwing herself deeper in, only to be ripped to pieces beyond reconstruction down the line.

But now… now she knew she would die, how she wished she'd stopped Zane from leaving this morning. How she wished she'd taken back her harsh words and instead sent him off by telling him she loved him.

Because she did, even though that terrified her.

Zane had even texted her those very words himself, yet she'd been unable to bring herself to return the sentiment. Stupid, stubborn cow!

Now she wished she had more than anything.

Aside from her impending death, Zane was most likely dead by now too. Why would this lunatic with the gun be shooting them all to fuck otherwise?

Erin's jumbled thoughts moved rapidly, morphing into one continuous stream that made little sense. Time took on a strange continuum as she willed her concentration to kick in.

Another woman fell, landing inches from Erin's head and from her floor level view, all she could see was the crimson pool spreading from the woman half-lying on top of her to soak the front of her blouse.

Jesus Christ. What could she do?

Nothing. She could do *nothing*.

Remaining motionless, it took every ounce of power not to scream as feet moving in all directions passed millimetres from her face, along with the heavy boots of the man with the gun.

He would shoot them all. Any who were left... The screaming of the women had already halved, showing a lot were already dead.

Erin forced her gaze to fall on the one woman remaining in the cage. The one she'd been about to release. Now she wished she hadn't looked to see that woman contorted in the bottom of the cage with several holes in her back.

She'd promised that woman she'd free her. And she'd failed…

Vomit rushed into Erin's gullet. That woman had died trapped. Not that any of them weren't trapped here. But *caged*?

Those bastards had done all of this. And *this* one randomly shooting had delivered the final, unnecessary insult.

How she hated these men and the person running it. How she hated this whole thing. How she despised this life.

What had any of it been for?

Fuck all, that's what.

This was *her* fault. She should have opened the door and let the women take their chance. Even if they'd been gunned down outside, they'd have been free, rather than being exterminated like caged animals in an abattoir.

Because that's all they were. Caged animals. A bit like she, herself, had been in one way or another since her father was murdered.

Erin's face twisted into a snarl. She was going to die, so she may as well not take being extinguished without showing a trace of resentment.

TWENTY SIX

THE MOMENT several volleys of shots resounded from a room further down the corridor, Leo knew he was too late.

Fuck.

Sweat drenched the front of his shirt as he hammered down the corridor cursing himself for hesitating before following this cunt of a lone gunman.

Until the rest of the men were successfully removed, Zane and Tiger were trapped on the upper floor surrounded by gunfire, so it made sense that it should be *him* who gave chase.

So why the fuck had he not done so immediately?

Spotting a sign on the wall that read 'Studio One', Leo's heart slipped further into his boots. This fucker had gone to kill the women and the anguished screams from within backed up this theory.

Shit. Aside from the poor bitches who'd arrived on that shipment, the bird Zane loved was in that room too. And the wanker with the gun was still firing…

Rounding the broken doorframe of Studio One, Leo dreaded what he would find but what met his eyes was worse than even a seasoned pro, used to scenes of carnage could imagine.

His eyes flicked over piles of broken bodies on the floor, the expressions of the lifeless women mirroring the terror they'd experienced in their last milliseconds of life.

Leo then stared at blood and pieces of flesh pebble-dashing the walls before his gaze rested on a woman lying in a twisted heap at the bottom of the only populated cage.

For fuck's sake!

That woman of Zane's had almost succeeded in freeing everybody before this wanker cut short their lives, but which one was she? He'd never set eyes on Erin Langley before and it was difficult to make anyone out, let alone any still retaining a trace of life.

The need to gauge this grotesque scenario took less than a second before logic overtook.

Spotting the perpetrator, Leo raised his gun.

The thickset man standing with his back to him was the same one who had darted past taking pot-shots in the corridor. The two bullets which connected still hurt but were fuck all compared to what these poor women had suffered. And now the initial enjoyment of blasting the hell out of these birds had gone, this prick was taking his time casually moving his gun around from woman to woman.

Even from the back, Leo could see the ridges of skin wrinkling through the man's crew cut as he smiled. The sick fuck enjoyed playing 'will I, won't I' with the few women left alive.

Not anymore...

But wait! There was a woman standing behind this man. She was facing him off and the only one not running around in panic.

The man raised his semi-automatic level with her face, ready to shoot.

'Oih, cunt!' Leo roared, wanting this bastard to know he was about to die rather than it be a surprise. He wasn't giving this turd an excuse to shoot another woman.

The sound of Leo's voice caused an inexplicable silencing

of the screaming and the remaining women froze from darting around. As the man turned, his deep set eyes meeting with Leo's, Leo was about to pull the trigger when the spell rendering the women motionless broke and they rushed forward blocking his line of sight.

'Move!' Leo roared, desperate to regain a clear shot. He couldn't fire with them in the way. 'Fucking move!' he screamed again, wincing as sharp fingernails raked at his face.

Feeling tugging on his gun, he grimaced. *Bollocks. The women thought he was one of Marco's men.* He should have shot the gunman in the back straightaway.

A gun fired and Leo tensed, his muscles taut.

He was too late. Shit, shit, shit!

As the screaming around him reached fever pitch, the woman gripping Leo's gun crashed to the floor at his feet - the recipient of that latest bullet.

Not wasting another second, Leo fired into the newly-opened narrow space between the flailing women and the target, hoping none of them moved into its path again.

His bullet hit spot on and the man fell and Leo was relieved until the women's onslaught resumed. 'Stop!' he yelled, as another grabbed his gun. 'You'll fucking fire it at yourselves!'

Erin leaped over the dead man at her feet, her feet sliding on the bloody pools on the floor. 'He's one of us! He's on our side!' She yanked the woman's fingers scraping against Leo's gun away. 'Him!' She pointed at Leo. 'Our side. Understand?'

Or at least she presumed he was. He *was* one of Zane's men, wasn't he?

Leo shook off the one remaining woman clinging to him. 'Erin?'

'Yes. That's me.' Erin's eyes darted around, panic swirling. 'Zane? Where's Zane? He's dead isn't he. Fuck! Everyone's dead!' She knew it. She just *knew* it.

Her eyes moved to the butchered women around her, the few remaining alive a tiny percentage of their original number. She swayed with shock and revulsion.

'You need to get any alive out now,' Leo said. 'There could be more men coming here soon.' *Especially if Zane and Tiger hadn't succeeded in surviving long enough to remove the remainder...*

'But Zane?' Erin pushed. 'Wh...?'

'He's out there still. He's okay.' *Or he was...* Leo bent to check for signs of life in the woman at his feet. Finding none, he sighed. 'Check the rest. We'll get all the living in the lorry.'

Pushing her need to see Zane to the background, Erin sprang back into action and started checking every single woman on the ground, whilst Leo rounded up the now subdued women remaining standing.

Erin moved from one body to the next. Some were clearly gone, others were not so obvious. But the more she checked, the quicker it became apparent that most were dead.

Her hands clenched into fists, the pain of her nails digging into the softness of her palms diluting the urge to take a gun and storm out to shoot any fuckers belonging to that bastard Marco Morelli, herself.

She placed her fingers on the side of another woman's neck desperately searching for a pulse, when she realised something else. 'Sandler?' she asked Leo, worry bubbling. 'Have you killed Damon Sandler?'

Leo shook his head. 'No idea. It's fucking chaos out there. Where was he?'

'He was supposed to be in the office with me, but I don't know where he went after I slipped out,' Erin cried. 'If he's not dead, then he needs to be.'

Leo nodded. 'I'll get back out there as soon as you lot are safe. If Sandler isn't already dead, I'll see to it.'

How Erin would love the chance to do that herself. Her loathing of Damon Sandler almost matched her hatred for Marco. *But not quite...*

She suddenly detected a faint pulse in the neck of the next woman she checked. 'This one's still with us!' she exclaimed. Her relief to find a sign of life amid all of this death was so immense it overshadowed that she hadn't yet wondered where Sonny was.

• • • •

'THAT'S IT. WE'RE DONE.' Zane wiped the dripping sweat from his brow with the back of his arm. He stared at Tiger busy surveying the pile of bodies on the level below. 'Done as much as we can be for now, anyway. As for where the stragglers have gone, we'll have to wait to find out.'

The handful of men who had dodged the hail of bullets and escaped down the corridor, if Leo hadn't picked those ones off, they would have escaped via bay A.

Vaulting the rail, Zane lowered himself to the floor below, dropping the last six feet. Waiting for Tiger to follow suit, he kept his gun aimed and scanned all directions.

As Tiger dropped to the ground next to him, Zane nudged one of the bodies with his boot. 'What a fucking mess! But the area's clear. Now we have to find Erin.'

And all he could do was pray that Leo had reached Studio One in time. Because if the gunman heading in that direction had got there and...

'Come on.' Tiger jogged down the corridor, his eyes searching every possible crevice as he went. It was doubtful that any of these pricks had the nous to lay in wait now that 99 per cent of their number had been dispatched, but he trusted no one.

Reaching the studio just before Zane, Tiger froze in the doorway. 'Fuck!'

Zane felt sicker than ever hearing Tiger's exclamation. *It could only mean one thing.* His whole body trembled with a combination of rage and fear of entering the room only to see the one woman who made him feel whole, butchered.

That and the body of Leo - one of his few trusted men.

Rounding the corner, Zane pushed through his dread and with a roar, sprinted into the room, his eyes feverishly searching the myriad mangled bodies.

Where was she? Where was Erin? 'I'll kill the bastards!' he spat, his voice strangled in his throat. 'I'll fucking kill them!'

There was a man on the ground over there too...

'It's not Leo.'

Tiger's voice came from somewhere as Zane frantically rolled over butchered and bloody corpses in a frenetic need to find Erin, but the words didn't register.

Christ! There were loads of dead women here. That bastard must have killed every single one of them. Fuck!

'Erin!' Zane roared, panic threatening to render him senseless.

'That wasn't Leo!' Tiger repeated, grabbing the scruff of Zane's jacket. 'Do you hear me? That man - it's not Leo!'

Zane heard, yet didn't hear. He continued to turn bodies over, his hands thick with congealed blood.

His heart suddenly lurched.

Over there. A blonde. Erin?

'No!' he yelled, dashing over to the corpse. Grabbing a handful of blonde hair soaked with blood, he gingerly turned the body, the thrashing of his heart in his ears threatening to deafen him.

It wasn't Erin.

'Listen!' Tiger yelled. 'If that man isn't Leo and you can't see Erin, it means they've got out!'

Tiger's words seeped into Zane's mind and his frantic searching paused. *Was it possible?*

With a renewed sense of hope, he sprinted to the door of bay A, finding it open.

'Tyre tracks.' Tiger nodded to the dusty tarmac. 'And no fresh blood. The lorry was here and it's gone.'

Zane moved back towards Luna. 'Get back inside.' Pulling his mobile from his pocket, he tapped in Leo's number with shaking fingers. His temples throbbed as the call rang out.

'I've got her! And a handful of others.'

Hearing Leo's voice down the line, Zane dropped to the floor, the concrete jarring his knees. 'Thank fuck! Where...'

'I didn't call before in case it gave away your position.

We're heading over the river. Where do you want the women taken?'

'I don't know,' Zane gabbled. 'I can't think. I...'

'Is Sandler dead?' Leo continued. 'I couldn't return inside. I had to get the women out. Some need urgent treatment.'

'Okay, okay. I'll make a few calls. I'll call you back shortly. But Erin? Let me speak to her. I want to speak to Erin.'

'Zane?'

If it were possible, the relief would have floored Zane. 'Erin?' he gasped. 'Thank fuck you're okay. Listen. I'll see you soon. I love you.'

Hanging up, Zane managed a smile, even though this situation was far from joyful. But Erin was alive and so was Leo. He'd work out where to put the other women when his heart rate stilled. But there was one thing he had to move on. 'I've got to call the surgeon my father had on the books. We'll need him to treat some of those women. Then I need to find Sonny. He was the last one to see Sandler.'

Tiger nodded. 'I've had a missed call from Cav too. I'll bell him back now and then I'll look for Sonny whilst you get hold of that quack.'

Now wasn't the time to voice this, but he wasn't hopeful of finding Sonny. As there had been no sign of Mitchell since this kicked off, Tiger could only presume the man had pulled another two-faced fucker stunt and exited when the coast was clear.

Or was dead.

• • • •

DAMON HAD NEVER BEEN so glad to get home in his life. He was never usually in a rush to get back to the shitty dump he rented in Battersea. A shitehole surrounded by glue sniffers and drug addled trollops was hardly fitting for someone working for one of the most high-powered men in London. This fact was even more galling when first seeing the palace Marco lived in. By all accounts, even Sonny Mitchell's place was in a better neighbourhood than this.

But once Marco returned he'd be out of this dump soon enough.

Marco would now have to appreciate his choice of second-in-command had been a bad call. *He'd* be handed the position and then, with the accompanying rise in pay, could afford somewhere better.

All of this was even easier now Sonny was dead - something else Marco would thank him for when it was known why the man had been dispatched.

But at this precise moment, living in a squalid neighbourhood surrounded by the scourge of society did Damon a favour. No one around here would bat an eyelid hearing a gun go off.

He placed both his own phone as well as the mobile he'd taken from Sonny's body next to the pistol in the centre of his pull-down table in what had been marketed on the rental particulars as a 'kitchen'. A kitchen for what, Damon couldn't guess, but it wasn't useful for anything other than somewhere to house a bin bag for takeout cartons.

Still, that was the least of his problems.

Damon reached for his cigarettes and then necked his third glass of cheapo vodka he'd bought on the way home. He'd need a painkiller.

Doing this wasn't something he was looking forward to but it was unavoidable.

He picked up the pistol and stared at it, then put it back down.

He'd do it in a minute. He'd just have another drink first.

Damon was in the middle of unscrewing the top of the vodka bottle when his own mobile rang. Sighing, he glanced at the screen. It was one of Marco's men.

There was someone left? That was a good sign.

Snatching up the phone, he answered gruffly. 'Yeah? What? And you fucking left? You left them in there? Are they not dead?'

What the fuck was this? He had no doubt there had been enough of Marco's men left to pick Zane Morelli and that other bloke off in the end. How that pair had escaped being riddled by bullets for so long was nothing short of a miracle.

But this was bollocks and changed things somewhat.

No, actually it was okay. *All of this was Sonny's fault, remember?* 'How many of you got out?' Damon asked. 'Okay. Well, you all need to regroup. Go to Marco's penthouse.'

At the question from down the other end of the line, his face morphed into a snarl. 'No, Sonny is not! *I'm* calling the shots for now.' And people had best get used to that. 'Marco will expect us to reassemble and that place is to be the penthouse. I'll be in touch later.'

Ending the call, Damon stared at the phone and then the gun.

Shit. So no one knew for certain whether Zane and whoever he had with him were alive or dead because those yellow-bellied shitheads had legged it out of Luna once they'd got thin on the ground?

Damon's eyes fell back to the gun. At least no one had asked where *he'd* got to. But it was only a matter of time. Marco would *definitely* ask. Even more so if Zane had succeeded in getting possession of Luna after all. And whether he had or not, no one knew.

Fuck.

At least Damon had until tomorrow before Marco returned. That was partly the reason he'd told the remaining men to regroup at the penthouse. There was still a body to remove and the place would need putting right. It had to be spick and span for when Marco got back.

Which reminded him, he'd better call back that enforcer at the penthouse and let him know to expect reinforcements. At least whoever the cheeky fucker was who'd been attempting to change the locks had been offloaded. *No doubt another one of Zane's cronies.*

Damon topped up his vodka. 'Sorry Zane. I'm too smart for

you. You're out of touch with reality, mate.' He chuckled at his words.

Slugging back the glass of vodka down in one, Damon took a deep breath and picked up the gun. He had to get on with this and hoped he managed only a graze.

Holding the gun at an angle so it skimmed the top of his left arm, Damon winced, his teeth chattering uncontrollably. *What if he screwed this up?*

He had to stage an injury, granted. And a real one to justify why he hadn't overseen the end of the chaos at Luna. But he didn't want to *seriously* hurt himself, for God's sake! What if he misjudged and the bullet did more than graze him? He could even have his own arm off.

Fuck this!

Slamming the gun down, Damon jumped up from the chair.

Moving swiftly over to one of the two cabinets the kitchen possessed, he rummaged past a few bent cans of baked beans and a strange crystallised thing that at some point could have been a naan bread and fished out a little tin containing a box of bandages and plasters. Putting it on the table, he stooped to reach for his toolbox from the floor level cupboard.

Without pausing to think too hard about what he was about to do, Damon lined a thick nail against his forearm and whacked it in with a hammer.

He didn't do it too hard, but enough to puncture the flesh and make it bleed.

Yowling with pain more severe than he'd intended, Damon grimaced as blood flowed onto the table. Gritting his teeth, he pulled the nail from his burning flesh and stared at it, wondering whether he should have disinfected it first.

Christ, that hurt but didn't doubt it was lot less painful than using the gun.

Wiping the sweat off his head, he tore open a bandage with his teeth and bound it around his throbbing forearm. Admiring the blood soaked material, Damon poured himself another vodka.

Job done.

Now he had a hole in his arm and a bloodied bandage. Surely no one would insist he removed the bandage to check?

Nah, they'd accept he'd been shot. And that was *exactly* what he'd be telling anyone who asked.

Swigging from his glass of celebratory vodka, Damon picked up his mobile to call the enforcer at the penthouse when it rang before he got the chance.

He grimaced. He didn't recognise this number, but would warrant it was one of the men from Luna again. For God's sake, he'd said he'd get back to them shortly. Could no fucker wait around here, or what?

'I told you I'd get back to y… Marco? Is that you?

• • • •

MARCO SHOOED THE HOSTESS out of his business class cubicle. 'Fuck off, will you? I don't want no dinner and I'm trying to have a private conversation here!'

He waited until the woman made herself scarce before continuing. 'Yeah, I'm on the plane… Nah, mid-flight.' He peered from the window, forgetting it was the middle of the night. 'Dunno… somewhere in the air... Yeah, business class has proper phones.'

He stubbed his cigarette out on the floor. He couldn't be arsed to use the ashtray. It was over on the table – far too much effort to reach. 'Look, I can't get hold of Sonny. The cunt won't answer the fucking phone. He's been ignoring me half the bastard day!'

Sniffing loudly to shift the cocaine wedged at the top of his nostril, Marco hawked and spat green phlegm onto the curtain. He picked up his crystal tumbler of finest whisky and was about to take a swig when the colour drained from his face. 'You what? When?'

He raked his fingers through his hair, his agitation building to double what he'd experienced in the taxi. *Sandler was telling him that his studio had been stormed? Fucking stormed? And by his bastard brother?*

A low growl emanated from the back of his throat. 'You're sure it was Zane? You saw him? Fuck me, Sandler, if you saw the fucker then why didn't you shoot the cunt? And those women had best still be there!'

Hearing how Sandler had been shot himself and that scores of his own men were dead pushed Marco over the edge.

Hazel quietly watched Marco crushing his tumbler in his hand and stared benevolently as whisky and glass covered the crotch of his trousers.

'I told you and every other man in my firm to watch for Zane. We *knew* he was out, for Christ's sake. We knew he'd be planning something!' Marco raged. 'Where was Sonny during this? Where was the cunt? Why hadn't he already apprehended Zane? That was my specific instruction! Not to wait until the bastard attempted a takeover!'

Hazel casually inspected her fingernails as Marco jumped from his seat, showering her, the chair and the floor with glass. She didn't react. That way Marco would continue forgetting she was right next to him and carry on thoroughly exposing the truth...

Which was, as she suspected, was that he'd known all along that his brother - the true heir of the Morelli firm and fortune, was not in prison and had returned to push the cuckoo out of the nest.

That cuckoo being Marco...

All along Marco knew he was a fake and not the genuine article.

Bastard!

Thankfully, the amount of botox Hazel had in her face hid the deep scowl that wanted to fold her expression into double what a professional gurner could achieve.

Let Marco rant. Let him spill all of his lies. It provided additional reasons to hate him more than she already did.

'Wait!' Marco screamed, now having progressed to pacing up and down the plane's business class corridor, his voice loud enough to raise the dead. 'That wanker, Mitchell, was part of this? You're seriously telling me th… Good! I'm glad you shot him fucking dead! When I get back, I'll shoot him again myself. I'll keep shooting him until there's fuck all le… No... It will be hours yet. Fucking hours!'

Hazel waited with bated breath. Did Marco not realise that everybody in this plane could hear him talking? With any luck, the captain would radio for Marco to be intercepted by the police the minute they touched down.

Her lips flattened slightly - a difficult feat to accomplish being as they were jam-packed with filler.

Of course, no one would *dare* touch Marco Morelli - not even the police. The captain of this bloody plane had probably been paid off too. But that was okay. Soon - *very* soon, when everybody realised Marco had no real clout, but his *brother* did, he would be worth shag all.

And Hazel desperately needed the location of this brother so that she could stake her claim.

She concentrated on the rest of Marco's conversation. Not that his side of it was hard to pick up, but one-way conversations were difficult to piece together. Luckily, Marco was so mashed in the head he'd continue muttering about this long after the call ended. It wouldn't cross his addled mind that *she* was supposed to be unaware of it.

Hazel smirked, her lips tugging against the painful swelling of her cheek bone.

Sometimes it paid to be irrelevant. And this was one of those times.

TWENTY SEVEN

ZANE PULLED ERIN close, crushing her into his chest. He buried his nose into her soft blonde hair and inhaled deeply, the scent of her shampoo somehow untainted by the horrors she'd witnessed.

It was now the middle of the night - a new day and soon a new dawn. He was exhausted but there was still much to do. And a *lot* more that was unanswered, as well as unfathomable.

Deciding Leo should take the trafficked women to Mr Solenzo's Harley Street practice was a good idea. It was safe there and the minute he'd received word that they were inside, he'd instructed Leo to bring Erin, along with his men, home.

Zane couldn't bear one minute longer without seeing her. He had to witness with his own eyes that she was unhurt and alive.

And she was.

But her mind was a different matter. There was a strange hollowness behind her eyes that wasn't there before. He suspected a similar haunted look was mirrored in his own eyes. What had happened at Luna had been off the grid compared with how he'd hoped things would pan out.

Zane knitted his fingers in Erin's hair, reluctant that if he didn't touch her, she would evaporate or fade to grey.

Zane looked at Leo lying on his kitchen table, surprised the rickety thing held the man's weight and watched as Tiger rummaged for the lodged bullets. Not a sound escaped Leo's mouth, the only hint to his pain an occasional twitch in his thick neck.

Erin clutched tightly to Zane's T-shirt. She cared little that it was stiff with sweat. All that mattered was that his arms were around her and that his heart still beat in his chest. They'd all got through this.

Well, most of them.

Guilt bloomed over Sonny. He'd been the real deal after all, yet had been cut down by none other than Sandler. 'I can't believe Sonny's dead,' she whispered.

'Two seconds the other way and Sonny would have shot Sandler,' Zane muttered, his rage at losing one of his men to that toerag burning brightly.

Tiger had found Sonny's body after he went searching, convinced the man had done a runner.

Sonny had paid his dues, there was no doubt about that.

But what about Lewis...

Uncomfortably aware of Cav slumped in a chair, a shadow of his former self, Zane kissed the top of Erin's head and released her. He had to say something to Cav other than 'shit', which had been his reaction hearing Lewis's throat had been slit...

Not a sight anyone would want to find to have happened to their own brother.

Zane's eyes narrowed.

Aside from Marco...

He slapped his hand on Cav's beefy shoulder and gave it a reassuring squeeze. 'I'm really sorry, mate,' Zane said. *If it wasn't for him... If his men hadn't been trying to secure his future, then...*

'I failed him…' Cav's voice was hollow and broken. 'I should have had Lewis's back.' The words he'd heard that enforcer utter – 'with no backup' would haunt him until the end of time.

'No, mate, there was nothing you could have d…'

'Yes, there was,' Cav snarled, his eyes flashing. 'We always stuck together. I shouldn't have let him go up to that bastard penthouse alone.' His big hands formed into fists. 'It was all for nothing. I killed the fucker who took Lewis's life, but didn't succeed in securing your place, so what have we gained? Fuck all!'

Zane shook his head. 'That's not true. You made the right call to take Lewis's body out of there. If you hadn't, you'd have been dead too.'

'I deserve to be!' Cav spat.

Zane sighed. No words would make Cav think differently right now, but he would see that all was not lost. *Eventually*.

'Marco's lot still have possession of the penthouse, but they haven't got Luna.' Tiger triumphantly chucked the last bullet plucked from Leo's leg into the bin with a tinny clatter. 'But it looks like Sandler did a runner and we don't know for sure how many of the other men got out either.'

'From what Cav said, we know that at least eight of them managed it,' Zane agreed. 'But Marco's men returning to the penthouse could work in our favour. The penthouse is the only place - or rather the place of *choice* for Marco to go on his return. His enforcers and therefore Marco, will be unaware we know they're back in the apartment and will expect us to arrive. They'll expect us to walk straight into a trap.'

The nerve in Zane's neck twitched. 'And we *will* be arriving. There's no doubt about that, but it isn't *us* who will be walking into a trap...'

Tiger grinned. 'We've got a couple of days yet to secure Luna, rebuild the firm and get everything sorted for Marco's arrival.'

Zane grinned, despite the horrific events of what had happened. He pulled Erin back into his arms. Marco would soon know everything that happened last night, if not already, but even if his brother jumped on the next plane out from that tropical island it still gave them twenty-four hours.

Erin stared into Zane's rugged face in relief, but also trepidation. There was one major thing which still needed resolving. 'We have to locate Sandler. He's more canny that anyone thinks. He wants Sonny's job and now he's killed him, he'll be first in line to grab it.'

Zane brushed a lock of Erin's hair from her face. 'Sandler will be dealt with for several reasons – no more so than for offloading Sonny, as well as setting the scene for Lewis to be murdered. We have time.'

If only Zane had realised that Marco was an hour away from landing at Heathrow, he might have thought differently.

• • • •

'MARCO!' Hazel yelled aa Marco's got out of the taxi and headed towards the entrance to the apartment complex. 'How am I supposed to carry all of these bags?'

His face twisting with irritation, Marco retraced his steps and snatched up the suitcases from the pavement. 'I presume you can cope carrying the crap you treated yourself to?' He jerked his head at the fancy duty-free bags containing Hazel's purchases.

Hazel picked up her carriers, hiding her smirk. Marco would discover it had been *him* to had treated her to these expensive goods soon enough. The same as when he shortly realised that she wouldn't take his lies lying down.

Oh, how she would enjoy filing for divorce, stating the reason as unreasonable behaviour and whatever else fitted to give her a get out clause. His name would be even more mud than ever when everyone realised he no longer had a position within his firm.

'When are we putting things in motion for my father's funeral?' Hazel asked. Her father may not have been the man she thought him to be, but it would reflect badly on her if she didn't arrange a send-off.

'There's little point talking about that,' Marco muttered. 'He was torched to a pile of fucking ash remember. The police have to formally identify him and all that bollocks before anything happens.' And if Hazel thought he was forking out for a send-off for that bastard, she had rocks in her head.

Hazel flinched. Marco's base acidity and thoughtlessness giving her a sudden reminder who the man she'd married was.

Entering the lobby, Marco ignored the man stationed at the concierge desk and stepped into the lift, not caring if Hazel got in before the doors closed. He hoped that someone - even Damon Sandler, was in the penthouse waiting to brief him with *exactly* what the hell was going on.

His brow creased. He'd dump his stuff and then deal with the aftermath of Luna. 'Those fucking women had still best be there,' he muttered. 'I haven't shelled out thousands getting those fuckers shipped in only for them to escape!'

Hazel's ears pricked up, a new flutter of unease sparking. Marco had referred to something to do with women when he was ranting on the phone in the plane, but she hadn't been able to piece together what it meant. 'No women would want to escape your studio, surely?' she said sweetly, pretending that she knew what this was about.

Marco swung towards Hazel, his manic eyes flashing with fire. 'What the fuck would you know about importing women? That cunt, Mitchell, was on side with my brother, so he could have let them out of the cages for all I know. Then I'll have wasted thousands! Christ!'

Raking his hands through his now unkempt hair, Marco slammed his fist into the gold metal door of the lift. 'I'll kill Sandler if he's allowed that to happen! I might kill him anyway. No one's fucking with me. This is a joke, the whole bloody thing!'

As the lift juddered, nausea grew in Hazel's stomach. Would she fall to her death at the bottom of a lift shaft?

Suddenly, the previous satisfaction of adding a hefty chunk to Marco's platinum card, the plan of embarrassing him to his firm and the need to keep up appearances with the splendour of a large funeral for the father who had turned her over, diminished in their level of importance.

Things were worse than she thought. A *lot* worse.

Imported women?

'A-Are you saying that you... traffick women? From where? Marco, you...'

'Shut your bleating, you stupid bitch!' Marco roared, slamming Hazel against the lift wall. 'Trafficked? Imported? What difference does that make? You don't know shag all about *anything*. I'm making money here, so concentrate on doing your job which is opening your legs for my cameras.'

Hyperventilating, he shoved through the lift doors before they'd fully opened. *Zane would be coming here next. And he'd be waiting.*

Hazel scuttled after Marco, her heart thrashing in her chest. She didn't want to accompany him into the penthouse. She didn't go want to go *anywhere* with him. Marco had trafficked women and kept them in cages?

In a blinding epiphany, suddenly everything became painfully clear.

Screw everything else. She had to get away from this man. And she had to do that quickly.

For the first time, the lure of money and status crumpled into meaningless tatters.

It hasn't escaped Hazel's notice that Marco had just laid his hands on her again either. She was also fairly sure that if the lift hadn't reached the penthouse floor, he'd have hit her again too.

But what could she do? She had nowhere to go. *Not yet.*

Desolation enveloped her like a heavy shroud.

Her friends were right all along. Marco wasn't the full ticket. The man was a psycho and regardless of his supposed clout – that would soon not exist, or his alleged fortune - again now no longer his, none of it was worth *this*.

Yeah, like he'd just relished pointing out, all *she* did was to 'open her legs for the camera'… But raising his hand to her?

Keeping women in cages?

No, no, no. This was too fucked up.

Struggling to keep pace up the corridor with her new husband, Hazel found herself in a place she had never been before. She was frightened. *Genuinely* frightened. Now her father was dead, not that he'd ever had her best interests at heart and Starlight had burned down, she was on her own. She was trapped with a violent psycho - one who she now knew without a shred of doubt *was* also behind those other women's deaths after all. She'd been quick to write off those incidents as nothing to do with the man she'd been due to marry but now she figured differently.

Worse than everything, she'd gone ahead and married the man regardless.

Fear trickled down Hazel's spine. If she took steps to divorce Marco now, he'd kill her.

She was trapped.

With Marco still shouting expletives to himself as he opened the penthouse door, Hazel recoiled in horror and emitted a strangulated shriek at the sight of men all over the penthouse. Especially the two in the hallway dragging a body loosely wrapped in a tarpaulin towards the door, leaving a trail of blood smeared on the marble tiles.

'What the fuck is this?' Marco roared.

Stepping out from the open-plan lounge, Damon nodded at the body. 'That's the twat who was attempting to change your locks. The one who was despatched by the man *I* asked to remain here just in case.' Not that he'd had chance to catch up with that particular enforcer, but when he'd previously spoken to him on the phone he'd mentioned he'd wrapped the body in a tarp.

Damon hadn't bothered unwrapping the tarp just to look at the mug of one of Zane Morelli's low-lifes. Nor had he wanted to get dirty blood over him. Sod that.

Seeing Marco's rage immediately placate on realising who the body in his penthouse belonged to, Damon glowed with satisfaction. He moved to take Marco's luggage with his undamaged arm. 'Let me take those and then I'll fill you in with the details of everything.'

No one acknowledged or noticed Hazel as she swayed in the doorway, her gaze unable to move from the body-shaped lump being dragged closer and closer to where she stood. The last memory she had before passing out and toppling to the floor, was that the only way out of this, aside from being murdered, was to locate Zane Morelli.

This time her reasons were for more than the money.

If she were to survive an escape from Marco she would need Zane's protection.

TWENTY EIGHT

DAMON EYED MARCO WARILY. The man was wired to fuck. It didn't look like he'd slept for weeks, as well as like he'd snorted half the coke stash the firm kept at the warehouse.

In all truth, Marco probably hadn't slept, not with the amount of gear he put away on a normal day. And these past couple of days had been far from normal...

Damon cracked his knuckles, wincing at the sparking pain in his self-inflicted wound. He'd seen Marco clocking the bandage still conveniently caked with dried blood on his forearm. Definitely a good move, that. It explained his lack of action at Luna. It also earned him brownie points for personally overseeing the clean-up at the penthouse, despite his injury.

For good measure, he winced again - more dramatically this time just in case the initial display had been missed. This would work out fine if he played things well. There was no reason why he wouldn't achieve all he set out to do. He knew what Marco expected and what he was looking for in a replacement second-in-command.

The only fly in the ointment was *her...*

Damon's eyes moved to Lisa Tequila - or Hazel, as Marco strangely called her, lying on the floor. She didn't fool him.

Pretending to swoon at a body and a bit of blood? *Stupid bitch.*

But something had shifted in Marco's absence, Damon thought, his brow knitting. Marco hadn't rushed to his fainting wife's side like he would have done before. He hadn't even bothered seeing if she was okay. And because he'd shown no heed for his new wife lying face down on the floor, no one else had either.

It also hadn't escaped Damon's watchful eye that the woman had copped a whack to the face during the time away. Judging by the colour of the bruising underneath the fading concealer, it looked recent.

But *he* had no wish to rush to her aid. She wasn't his cup of tea in the first place and the groans now coming from her mouth made him want to kick her in the tits.

Instead, he would concentrate on *this...*

'We'd hoped to have this place fully cleaned before you arrived. Unfortunately, *this* hasn't helped my ability to pitch in.' Damon took the opportunity to draw attention once again to his injured arm. 'We'd have had more hands on deck here if I hadn't had to make the decision to send half the men back to secure Luna before a further takeover attempt was made.'

Marco's hand holding a rolled-up twenty-pound note paused over the fat line of cocaine. He'd balanced it on a book on his lap being as his glass coffee table had been a casualty during the scuffle which had gone down here. It had screwed his leather sofa up too, which had pissed him off, but his eyes lit up at Damon's words. 'You mean my brother hasn't got possession of Luna after all? He's dead, then?'

Damon shook his head. 'Dead, no. At least, not as far as I'm aware, but he'd have been short on the ground. He had no choice but to retreat and so therefore we've got possession back of Luna. But he'll return and that I don't doubt.'

He shrugged, taking charge of relaying the facts the way they needed to be presented like he'd practiced several times. 'They attempted to possess both Luna and here, but failed on both accounts.' Damon rubbed his hands together, unable to contain his happiness at the impressed look on Marco's face. *The man was finally seeing him in a different light? About fucking time.* 'They'll know by now that *we* have regained control of Luna, but they won't have a clue we have the penthouse. They believe it's been secured by *their* man. I hope I did the right thing by splitting our remaining men to cover both places?' he continued, eager for praise.

Marco snorted the cocaine and tossed the rolled up twenty on the sofa. His face broke into a grin. 'You did the right thing. I'm impressed.'

Not as quite as impressed as hearing that his brother's mission had failed. And better still, Zane would come here expecting to find it empty, rather than *him* lying in wait.

He laughed loudly. He could afford to laugh now he knew he still had the pleasure of personally snuffing out Zane's life.

Damon glowed. Anytime now he'd be officially offered the coveted second-in-command role. Despite Zane's efforts, Marco was still head honcho around here, whereas Zane was scrabbling around in the dust somewhere, not realising his life would shortly be extinguished.

'Oh, and I must show you this.' Making a big deal of how difficult it was to extract the mobile from his pocket with his bad arm, Damon brought up the text messages on Sonny's phone. He handed it to Marco. 'This proves Mitchell was in on it.'

Growling, Marco snatched the phone from Damon's hand. *This wasn't the one the firm had issued Sonny with - this was a burner phone.*

His jaw clenched as he scrolled through the last few messages.

Me:

Are u still there?

Me:

Erin?

EL:

Yes. Here.

EL:

Sandler has gone.

Me:

Go. Go now. NOW.

His eyes narrowed. 'Who the fuck is this?' Marco snarled, jabbing his finger on the screen over Erin's name.

Leaning over to view the text, Damon frowned. 'Never heard of her. Maybe a bird Sonny was involved with?' His mouth curled into a sneer. 'I thought he had a thing going with Caroline, being as he was obsessed with her, but now judging by Caroline's disappearance, the reason that wanker employed her was because she was a diversion tactic and clearly part of their scheme.'

And that was even more galling. He'd been just about to have his turn with the tasty chick when she showed herself to be a two-faced bitch. 'All women are traitorous whores. It underlines why they should never be anything other than utilised for enjoyment.' Damon sniggered at his own words until he saw the expression on Marco's face change from gloating indifference to downright rage. *Shit! Had he said something wrong?* 'What is it? If Caroline wasn't a mole, then...'

Marco stared at the phone, hatred oozing from his pores. 'I don't know who the fuck Caroline was, but she was a mole all right. But I don't reckon her name was really Caroline…'

Damon frowned, confused. *Marco hadn't lost it again, had he? Now was the worst time for that to happen.* 'But wh…'

'Caroline is Erin! Erin and "EL" – Erin Langley! How did you not work that out, you thick cunt!' Marco yelled, jabbing at the text messages.

'What?' Damon gabbled. 'I don't know who that is. I've never seen her before and...'

Marco's cold eyes glittered maliciously. *He remembered now...* His breathing became ragged as the rage for this stupidity increased. 'A short blonde with a body to die for and big blue eyes, by any chance?'

Damon fidgeted on the spot. 'Well, yes, but...'

'I knew it!' Marco shouted. 'Like I said - Erin. Erin fucking Langley!'

'I still don't kn...'

'What do you mean, you don't know?' Marco screeched, throwing the phone across the room, the plastic casing smashing as it hit the wall above where Hazel still lay. 'You saw the photo the same time Mitchell showed me! Erin Langley was Flame's fiancée - the one Zane kidnapped, yet she's been under my roof at Luna busy feeding all the information my bastard brother needed for a takeover? Jesus fucking wept! I thought for a minute there that you knew what you were doing, yet you didn't remember that?'

Zane had put Flame's bird – the one by all accounts he was cosily shacked up with, into Luna a mole?

The sly cunt.

Well, being as Zane thought himself clever for pulling that one, he'd soon realise he *wasn't.*

Marco's eyes narrowed. Wherever that bitch was, Erin Langley was next. She meant something to Zane – that much was clear and his brother would sorely regret putting a tart he had a thing for in the firing line. 'I want her gone. Find her and remove her. No one fucks with me, so get the hell onto it!'

As Marco paced the room, pulling at his hair and muttering more scathing diatribes about useless attitudes, Damon wondered if now was the time to point out that he had never seen this woman before Sonny hired her. It must have been Bill Wainwright who had seen the photograph of Flame's girlfriend, not *him.*

And yes, Damon had heard about Flame. Everyone knew

about that man's part in getting Zane sent down for David Masters' murder. But whoever Erin Langley was or wasn't, now everyone knew she was Zane's mole, she was on borrowed time. There was no escape from her fate.

It was a shame she was destined to die being as he hadn't got his go with her, but shit happens.

But where did he start in tracking the woman down?

Damon's mouth twisted into a sneer. He'd enjoy offloading that little bitch. She'd played *him* and for that, he it would be gratifying making her suffer.

Deciding he'd inform Marco of his mistake in confusing him with Bill Wainwright once he'd calmed down, Damon poured his boss a large whisky from the bottle in the illuminated display cabinet. No doubt the man would be grateful of a drink being as he was now also about to learn that this Erin Langley woman was responsible for freeing the few caged women who hadn't been caught in the gunfire. And worse, no one had a clue to where any of them had gone.

Hazel had been watching the two men carefully. Sensing Marco and Damon's concentration was on everything but *her*, she pulled herself to a sitting position, keeping up the same pitiful groaning noise she had been making for the last ten minutes. The movement of propping herself up to lean against the wall masked her hand scooping the damaged mobile phone Marco had thrown, underneath her leg.

She'd find a way to slip that into her possession and hope it still worked. Whilst pretending to be out for the count, she'd gathered that Sonny Mitchell had been in contact with Zane and so therefore, somewhere on this phone was the number of the very man she needed to find.

• • • •

ERIN HAD DONE as best as she could to find something to double up as blankets and pillows for three extra men. Sleeping on the living room floor was far from ideal, especially for Leo with gunshot wounds, but at least he'd finally conceded to her insistence to take the sofa.

Zane had offered Leo their bed, but the man wouldn't hear of it. Despite this, Erin still felt incredibly guilty for having somewhere comfortable to lie when the rest didn't. She could have easily grabbed a couple of hours standing up she was that exhausted. There wasn't a part of her body that didn't ache.

Even so, being as there was so much to do, a couple of hours sleep was all of them could afford. And now the list was longer than ever since Zane decided to change his plans.

Erin turned over and rested her hand on Zane's chest. He still slept soundly. Her eyes traced over every detail of his face, grateful that she still had the option to do so. It could have been so different. Zane could have been Sonny. Or Lewis…

She bit down on her lip to quell the forming tears. Cav had got his brother's body out, but Sonny still remained cold and dead somewhere within Luna. She knew there had been no choice but to leave him, but the plan had never been not to return.

Yet now it was…

'Morning.' Zane pulled Erin over him. 'Did you get any sleep?'

'Sort of…' Erin ached for Zane's hard body on hers but knew that would have to wait. 'My mind was stuck on running over your change of plans.'

Zane stroked Erin's hair. His mind had churned over and over the situation too and no matter how many angles he looked at it, the options remained the same.

'I thought when you said last night about having two days left to resecure Luna and rebuild, then it...' Erin's voice trailed off. There was no point in going on about this. The men's discussion had sounded achievable initially, but it rapidly became clear that wasn't the case.

Zane shifted to prop himself up against the headboard and ran his hand over the stubbly growth on his chin. 'Yeah, things didn't pan out as I'd planned.' *Nowhere near, after an unknown number of men escaped, the women getting shot up and two of his men down.*

He grabbed his cigarettes off the bedside table and sparked one up. 'We had no option but to shift. We didn't have enough men or ammo left to guard Luna when Marco's men returned.'

Erin frowned. 'I know, but they'll be back in there by now. Especially since Sandler is still on the loose.'

Zane blew a steady stream of blue smoke towards the ceiling. 'Yep, but the rest of what I said still applies. They'll expect us to arrive at my penthouse not realising we know they are in there. Look on the bright side - at least I don't have to deal with the clean-up at Luna!'

But it wasn't funny. None of it was. 'I never wanted that filthy place as Morelli headquarters anyway and like I said last night, if I can't kill my brother right now, then I'll do it another way. I'll run against him and take him that way.'

Erin's stomach churned, her dream of wiping Marco off the face of the Earth getting further and further away.

Zane reluctantly got out of bed. He'd prefer to stop talking and pull Erin underneath him. Hearing her gasp his name as he made her body sing was what he needed to deflect from this nightmare. Instead, he walked to the window. 'Everyone will be watching for us now - especially you.' He glanced over his shoulder at Erin, barely able to contain his rage that she had become a major target.

Erin swallowed dryly. *It was true.* By now Sandler would have worked out that she was a mole via Sonny and therefore, Zane. She was in a dangerous position, but then weren't they all?

Zane turned back and looked up and down the road. It was unusually quiet despite the early hour. 'Until we offload Sandler you must be extra careful. With no one on the inside now Sonny is dead, it will be diff...'

Seeing a silver VW Golf turn into the street, Zane paused, his whole body tensing. *It was that car again.* Was it the same one? This was too much of a coincidence not to be connected.

'What is it?' Scrambling out of bed, Erin rushed towards

the window. 'Is it them? Have they found us?'

'No, I...' Zane paused once again, his concentration homing in on the silver car. *It was definitely the same one. And the driver?*

Erin followed Zane's piercing gaze. 'Is that them?'

'No.' Zane let the curtain drop back into place and steered Erin away from the window. 'I thought... It doesn't matter. It's not them.'

Erin reluctantly allowed himself to be led away but not before she'd seen that car and the driver. Worry churned. It wasn't the expected fear of it being one of Marco's men having located where they were. It was that the driver was a *woman*: a dark haired, young woman. And from the short glimpse she'd got - a remarkably beautiful one.

Why had Zane been so eager to dismiss who he'd been watching? Why would he hide it?

Erin opened her mouth to ask when the shrill ring of Zane's mobile punctuated the silence.

Zane snatched up his mobile. 'Hello?' Frowning, he stared at the phone as the call cut off and then scrolled through the call log.

Number withheld

'Who was that?' Erin asked, her nervousness gaining pace.

'I don't know.' Zane shrugged. 'They hung up. It must have been a wrong number.'

Erin forced herself to keep the words she wanted to say to herself. They had burner phones with untraceable numbers - not the sort to receive spam calls on.

Only Zane's men and Erin had his number. Sonny and Lewis were dead and everyone else with his number were downstairs. Was it a coincidence that the woman Zane didn't want her to see drove past and then he received a mysterious call?

Had he cut the call because he didn't want her to know who

he was speaking to?

Was it possible the real reason of Zane's recent distance towards her was staring her in the face?

No. *Don't let your past hang ups control you*, Erin told herself.

But telling herself that didn't stop it from playing on her mind.

TWENTY NINE

SHOVING THE PHONE back in her knickers, Hazel flushed the toilet and washed her hands.

'Did you hear me?' Marco continued thumping the bathroom door from the outside. 'I told you to hurry up!'

'I'm just coming now,' Hazel squeaked, making her voice sound as normal as possible. She stared at her reflection in the illuminated mirror of the marble bathroom - the opulence of this penthouse now having lost its glamour.

A bit like her...

She focused on her straggly unwashed hair and the yellowing bruise covering her cheekbone. She looked like shit and had aged ten years this past couple of days. But at least she now had one thing to work with - that number on Sonny's phone.

Within the voice which answered her call, she'd recognised the hint of an accent identical to Marco's.

The voice belonged to Zane Morelli.

There were several numbers on that phone - none with any hints as to whose they were, but Hazel was confident she'd struck lucky.

She was sure the name of 'Anli' stood for a combination of

'An' – taken from 'Zane' and 'li', taken from 'Morelli'. A wild guess perhaps, but then again, she'd always been a dab hand at anagrams and cryptic crosswords. It passed the time between takes on film sets.

She hadn't spoken when the call connected. How could she? Marco would have heard. She'd have to call back and do so quickly before he or his creepy sidekick realised the smashed-up mobile had gone walkabout or the bloody battery ran out.

But when would she get the chance to do that while she was being watched like a hawk?

'HAZEL!'

Hazel jumped at the voice snarling through the door. 'Coming!' Taking a deep breath, she unlocked it and smiled at her husband. 'I feel less dizzy now I've washed my face,' she said, deciding the only way she would achieve anything was to pull on every single one of her acting skills and behave like she'd forgiven Marco for everything.

She'd need more acting ability than she possessed to manage that but she had to try. She *had* to speak to Zane Morelli properly. She'd make him listen and believe what she said.

'What can I do to help?' Hazel trailed her nails down Marco's chest, her experience of acting out hardcore scenes with male actors she'd taken an intense dislike to serving her well.

Admittedly, any dislike for her co-stars in the past was a drop in the ocean compared to the suffocating revulsion she had for the creature whose name she'd stupidly taken, but if playing the game granted her leeway in getting the hell away from Marco then it was a small price to pay.

Marco's eyes narrowed suspiciously at Hazel's change of attitude. 'Seen the error of your ways? Remembered that you belong to me?' Not caring one way or the other, he hitched up her dress.

Aware the phone was lodged in the front of her knickers, Hazel span around and adopted her most sought after Lisa

Tequila pose - bent over the sink unit with her buttocks raised in the air. 'Yes I have. You were right,' she purred. 'I've been silly. The shock of my father's death knocked me sideways, but I forgive you for hitting me, babe. I know you didn't mean it.'

'I should think so too,' Marco snarled. 'You know I'm crazy for you, but there's no room for anyone who doesn't understand their place. Even *you.*'

Hazel thought for a moment that Marco had seen through her lies, but he hadn't. As for forgiving him… She'd *never* forgive him - not for any of it.

Ever.

But she knew somewhere underneath his anger, Marco's obsession with her remained. That, coupled with his straining cock and the bag load of coke up his hooter would win the day. Telling this man he was right, powerful and that she was beholden to him, also had an equal effect.

Hoisting Hazel's dress up around her waist, Marco unzipped his trousers and took himself in hand.

'I like it when you leave my knickers on,' Hazel whispered, pretending to be turned on.

Marco paid no attention. 'I think you'll find that I barely need to move anything where *I'm* heading.' Pushing Hazel's thong an inch to one side, he slammed straight into a place she least expected.

'Marco!' Hazel squeaked. 'That's not...'

'I know *exactly* where I've put myself,' Marco grunted. Now Hazel had finally accepted her place, it wouldn't hurt to remind her in *other* ways who called the shots. Well, it wouldn't hurt her in *any* way. This woman possessed no orifices which weren't frequently utilised like bus routes and on days she wasn't working, she needed to remember that every part of her belonged to *him*. If she didn't, she soon would…

Choking back the burning pain, Hazel kept one hand holding the phone in place at the front of her knickers, her other arm steadying herself as she was slammed repeatedly against the mirror.

The nausea brewing deep in her belly was strong, but worsened considerably spotting Damon Sandler's reflection in the mirror as he watched with a sneer across his repulsive face.

• • • •

MAKING SURE HIS MOTORBIKE was flanked by the van, Zane took one last look at the house. Clocking Leo's standard nod of assurance from the window, Zane opened the throttle and sped off.

Being as Leo was injured and Cav in no fit mental state, it made sense for them to remain guard at the house whilst he and Tiger risked going to one of Marco's lock-ups. Leaving Erin alone was not an option ever again. Neither was her riding pillion. For her, travelling anywhere from now on would be via car or van with him or one of his trusted men.

Thankfully, Zane still had Sonny's set of keys to the lock-up and all he could do was hope Marco's enforcers weren't here. Not only would he and Tiger be outnumbered, but Marco's men would have noticed by now that their gun stash had been pilfered and they'd have shifted the rest of the weapons, plus the remaining ammunition.

Zane desperately needed to restock both.

The other reason for visiting the lock-up was that there was something located within it which he needed if he was to start over. And he had every hope that what he required was exactly where it had been placed over ten years ago – somewhere purposefully away from the original Morelli headquarters or any of their residences.

This had been his father's idea should an emergency backup ever be needed. Not for the first time did it cross Zane's mind whether his father had harboured an inkling as what may come to pass at the hands of his youngest son.

Yes, Giuseppe was aware Marco was a loose cannon and not the one to hand the reins of his firm to, but surely not even his father could have foreseen the levels to which Marco would stoop in order to gain ultimate control?

Taking a quick glance over his shoulder to check Tiger's Transit remained on his flank, Zane continued making headway towards the lock-up.

Traffic was light this morning. Normally, with just the two of them they would travel in one vehicle, but with the increased risk of being targets it was pertinent to travel separately.

Approaching the industrial estate, instinct made the hairs on the back of Zane's neck stand to attention. Checking his mirrors, one hand moved from the handlebars to hover over the gun in his jacket.

He saw it as he slowed to take the turning. It wasn't another van or one of Marco's men.

It was that silver Golf...

Who the fuck was it? He'd said to Erin that it was no one, but it was *someone*. And a woman too. Could Marco be tailing him using the guile of a beautiful young woman?

Before Zane could stop and confront the driver of the Golf, the silver motor veered off down a side road, leaving him stuck in the filter lane for the industrial estate. By the time he did a loop the motor and the woman would be long gone.

Relaxing his grip on his gun, Zane continued into the maze of roads within the industrial estate. He pulled up in the lock-up's car park, glad to see the place deserted. There was still a chance Marco's men could have hidden the van and be waiting inside, but it was unlikely.

Taking off his crash helmet, Zane pulled a cigarette from the packet, disturbed to spot the slight tremor of his fingers. This silver car being everywhere bothered him more than he'd realised.

The van pulled up alongside and as Tiger clambered out, Zane hurried to the door. 'I saw that car again,' he muttered. 'That silver Golf. That's twice today. Once outside the house this morning and just now as well.'

'Marco?' Tiger frowned, concern brewing.

Zane shook his head. 'I'm not convinced it's anything to do with him. It's a woman behind the wheel.'

'A *woman*?'

'Yeah, a woman.' Shoving the keys in the huge padlock on the lock-up door, Zane yanked the heavy shutters open. 'Whoever it is, she's following me everywhere I go, but I have no idea why.' Neither did he have time to analyse it. They had to get what they had come for and get out sharpish.

Once the door shut behind them, Zane flicked a switch to bring a bank of overhead fluorescent strip lights to life. He paused, double checking no one lurked in the shadows. 'Grab more ammo. Take everything there is. If we leave them with nothing, all the better. I'll go and check the strong box.'

Although Tiger was undoubtedly a trusted loyal friend and colleague, no one, aside from himself and his father knew the exact location of this strong box. And now his father was no longer alive it was just *him*.

Zane also knew no one was aware of what the box contained.

Once Tiger left to fetch the ammo, Zane headed to a smaller stock room at the rear of the lock-up. Going inside, he shut the door behind him, his heart thumping in trepidation. He ran his finger along the plasterboard panels of the wall to locate the notch in one particular board.

During the time he'd been incarcerated, what were the chances of this secret hiding place being discovered by Marco or his minions? Slim, but not impossible.

It was a godsend Marco hadn't seen fit to dispose of this lock-up, like he had the original Morelli headquarters, otherwise he'd have been sunk. And that variable was one his father had overlooked when thinking out this backup plan. Thankfully it wasn't the case.

Ah, there's the notch...

Remembering the knack, Zane gripped the indentation and pulled the panel forward half an inch, then slid it across to reveal a small metal box sunken into the brickwork underneath.

He fished the original penthouse keys from the inside pocket of his leather jacket. All these years he'd kept hold of them. Okay, so the penthouse ones were defunct since Marco changed the locks, but *this* hadn't changed. *At least he hoped it hadn't...*

Selecting a tiny key, Zane inserted it into the padlock and a metal flap flipped down exposing a combination lock.

Yes!

Trawling the recesses of his brain for the long unused numbers, the combination rushed to the forefront of his mind. Some things were never forgotten. In fact, not many things slipped Zane's mind.

And neither had this.

With slightly clammy fingers, he rolled the numbers into position and held his breath, releasing it only on hearing the wonderful sound of the lock opening.

Quickly tugging open the box, Zane shoved his hand inside and pulled out a wad of paperwork, flicking through the documents to check the one in particular he wanted was there.

He'd leave nothing to chance. He'd take the whole lot. Not knowing what might happen to this lock-up now Marco's lot were or would shortly be aware that entry had been gained, there was no knowing what would happen. And Zane suspected that after today, access would prove impossible.

He shoved the paperwork into his rucksack and shutting the strongbox, slid the wall back into position. Leaving the room, Zane made his way back into the main expanse of the warehouse where Tiger lugged a box of ammunition to add to the many others he'd emptied from the store.

'That's the last one.' Tiger dumped the heavy box on top of another and wiped the sweat from his brow. 'And as they say in the nursery rhyme, "Mother Hubbard's cupboard is bare!"'

Chuckling, Zane pulled open the doors of the lock-up ready to help load the Transit.

Then he'd get moving with the next part of this: setting up his new firm.

THIRTY

RELIEF POURED OVER ERIN when Zane and Tiger returned. 'Did you get what you needed?' she asked, moving forward to touch Zane's sleeve.

Only the slight flicker of an unknown expression was visible on Zane's face, but it was enough to make her stop her fingers from making contact. The fluttering of worry which had sat within her for the past few days, further underlined by his reaction this morning to that car and which had festered further during his absence, sparked to life with renewed vigour. *Something had definitely shifted. But what?*

'Any more instances of being watched?' she asked tentatively, pretending not to notice Zane's lightning-quick glance at Tiger.

'No, nothing.' Zane took his rucksack off his shoulders. 'We got the rest of the ammo. And *this...*' Unzipping his bag, he dropped into the nearest chair and signalled for everyone's attention. Sifting through the paperwork, he pulled out the relevant piece and held it up. 'This is what will enable me to start again.'

Erin saw the piece of paper and heard Zane talking, but she wasn't concentrating. All she knew was the voice shouting inside her head was pointing out the obvious. *Zane was lying.* She'd seen it in the tiny glance to Tiger that spelt loud and clear: *Don't say anything...*

He'd seen that car again, hadn't he? And that woman. Was it a tail, like she'd originally presumed or were her nagging hang-ups correct? Did Zane have another woman - one he was more drawn to than her?

In reality, she didn't know. She knew little of Zane's past, short of what he'd told her and the bits she knew herself from what had happened in the past. But the harsh truth was that she had no clue whether he'd been involved with anyone else on a serious level before or not. He was six years older than her, so the chance of him having *no* past was slim to none.

Could this woman in the car be someone he'd once loved? A relationship forced to end because of his incarceration?

In contrast, *their* relationship came from necessity and unnatural situations. It had developed into what Erin felt was something real, but could a fledgling and fraught relationship trump a previous and well-established *chosen* one?

These unanswerable questions were shunted from her mind by the reaction of the men in the room to Zane's paperwork. Forcing her concentration back into line, she leant over the document on the table.

She frowned. 'What's this?'

Zane stared at Erin like she was crazy. 'I've just explained.' He sighed impatiently. 'It's the deeds for a property my father purchased. One that is now mine. The Thames Canning Works will be the new Morelli headquarters.'

Tiger slapped the table. 'It's bloody fantastic. It's back in your original territory, as well as being legit.'

'And even better that no one else, including Marco, knows about it!' Leo added.

'Yep, it's all above board. It's mine and this...' Zane poked the paperwork, 'proves it.'

'So, when do we go to this place?' Tiger asked.

'Straight away.' Zane grinned. 'From there, we'll build the

firm back up. *Properly* this time.'

'I have some news on that subject which I think you'll be pleased about.' Leo's face split into a wide grin. 'While you were at the lock-up, I received some calls. The grapevine has been on overdrive and word about last night has spread. It's known that you're back and that Marco's short on the ground. It's said that he's floundering.' His eyes twinkled. 'This news has prompted several more men from our original posse who were forced to lay low to step forward and make contact. They're back in if you want them.'

Zane leant forward in anticipation only to be interrupted by his ringing phone. Irritably plucking it from his pocket, he glanced at the screen. 'Hello?' Frowning, he looked to his group of men. 'I won't be a moment. I need to take this.'

Erin watched Zane leave the room and stilled the now familiar prickle of threat that the man she loved was harbouring a secret and plans that no longer included her.

And no matter how much she tried to tell herself to be rational and not jump to conclusions, it was becoming more and more difficult.

• • • •

HAZEL'S EYES DARTED AROUND the room like a startled rabbit, fully expecting Marco and that other man - or even one of the nameless minions who were everywhere in the penthouse which she had proudly classed as her own not long ago, to appear out of the woodwork and catch her red-handed on the phone to the man they wanted to kill.

Still no one had noticed Sonny's phone was not on the floor behind the sofa where Marco had chucked it. But they would. She had one chance to get her point across to Zane Morelli and one only. After this, she had to replace this phone where she'd found it.

'I had no choice but to call,' she said, keeping her voice as quiet as possible. 'You've got to help me. Marco is a maniac.'

Listening to Zane's brusque response, Hazel's heart

plummeted. 'Of course it's not a trap! I'm in danger! *Everyone's* in danger. Marco lied. He lied about everything. He's going to kill me!'

Although Hazel had planned to turn on the tears for maximum effect, she found they flowed without difficulty. Not everything was put on; neither was it exaggerated. Bagging Zane for herself was still on the cards, but firstly she must prove to him that her words were true and to do that, she would do anything - *anything*, to show that she was not on Marco's side.

'I know you're planning to overthrow Marco and I *want* you to,' she continued. Please! Tell me what I can do to help achieve it.'

This man - the infamous Zane Morelli, didn't sound convinced by her words and Hazel found her panic spiralling. 'Please! You must believe me!'

She'd blurted out loads already but had received nothing to indicate that Zane believed her, let alone would help her.

A horrible thought seeped into her mind - one she hadn't given any prior credence to. It hadn't crossed her mind that by laying it on thick and telling this man everything, that there could be a possibility she would not be believed, or that her words were a trap for Marco's benefit.

Her fingernails hinged against the door jam, the glue attaching the fake nails pulling against her soft nail beds.

He wouldn't disbelieve her, would he? Out of everybody, Zane must know what his brother was *really* like. Hadn't telling him about Marco trafficking women had any effect?

Perspiration formed under the creases of Hazel's surgically inflated breasts.

There was one more thing that she could add…

'Marco knows that woman of yours was a mole. He wants Sandler to offload her as soon as possible. She's in big danger.' Hazel personally didn't give two shits about the woman or what happened to her, but Zane might. Would that not be enough to give him the impetus to believe she was speaking the truth?

She'd heard that Zane was the controlled one out of the two

- the one with the brain and proper sense. But what if he wasn't? What if he was just as unhinged as Marco? What if he thought that everything Marco did was fine? Or even agreed with it? Including that this woman of his was expendable?

No. He couldn't.

But perhaps it would have been better not to have mentioned about Marco believing Zane to be the one who'd killed her father? Wasn't she as good as accusing him too? Whether he had done it or not, Hazel didn't know, but either way, he *had* to help her.

Unused to having people - especially men, not immediately agree to her every demand, Hazel almost made the mistake of voicing her displeasure at Zane's silence and abruptness, until she remembered her position.

Cowering in a penthouse, that by all accounts belonged to the man down the other end of this line, whilst waiting in abject dread for the man she'd married returning to throw her from the balcony, like he had that other woman, wasn't the best situation to be in. But that was *exactly* where she was right now.

Desperation ran over her like an express train. 'Please say something! I have to know that y…' Freezing mid-sentence, she heard Zane finally speak, but all she could focus on was the distinct sound of the door down the hallway opening.

The muffled voices...

And then the footsteps...

'I've got to go! He's back!' she hissed, her voice little more than a strangulated whisper. 'What? When? Okay... I'll try... I don't know if I'll be able to get out. I...'

Spotting the unmistakable silhouette of Marco through the frosted glass of the adjoining door, Hazel cut the call and shoved the phone down her top, pushing it around to her side. Ignoring the ragged pieces of plastic casing that snagged her skin, she lay back onto the sofa and snatched up a magazine.

'Lounging around again?' Marco sniped, raising an eyebrow at his wife. 'You'll be glad to know that the boys are busy making Luna Motion Film studios usable again, so you'll be back in front of the camera in no time.'

And she'd better be, he thought, his mouth twisting into a snarl. As well as seeing what a shithole his brother had made of the studios, as well as the pile of bodies, he'd also discovered the box containing Hazel's back catalogue of films that Sonny had insisted were on site had been another of that traitorous worm's lies. In reality, the films were ash in Trevor Grimes's dump of a studio.

And that did not please him.

On top of that, there had been no sighting of the remaining women he'd paid thousands to bring into the country, plus he needed more men to replace the ones who had been shot - again, courtesy of his bastard brother.

And last but not least, he had to make sure he was ready and waiting when Zane finally showed his fucking face.

THIRTY ONE

RETURNING TO HIS SITTING ROOM, by the subsequent stilling of conversation and expressions on everyone's faces, Zane knew straight away that no one would like what he was about to say.

The ingrained nausea at what Hazel had said festered. None more so that knowing Erin was now a *definite* target. He'd expected it and was the reason why he'd been so against wanting her going into Luna, but Sonny had been wrong. Marco *had* remembered Erin's photograph. His brother's head wasn't quite as addled as everyone believed.

And that made everything worse…

He could not have Erin hurt. Not *ever*.

Zane picked up his crash helmet. 'Leo, what you were saying before about other members getting in touch? Make contact again and arrange a meet for tomorrow at the new headquarters.' He pulled on his jacket. 'We'll go there as soon as but right now I've got to go out. Something's come up.'

'Out?' Erin jumped up from her seat. 'Out where?'

'That was Hazel - Marco's wife on the phone,' Zane said. 'She's in trouble. Marco's lost it and she needs my help.' He'd keep the other worrying parts of the conversation concerning

Erin to himself until he knew what he was dealing with. 'I'm going to meet her and hear what she has to say.'

'Oh my God, you're not falling for that bullshit, are you?' Erin gasped, unable to believe her ears. 'You're meeting Marco's *wife*?'

Zane slammed his crash helmet down. 'I think I'm the best person to judge what to do in this situation, Erin!' He needed to protect *her*. Out of everything, that could not be overlooked.

Zane saw Tiger exchange looks with Leo. 'I know what you're thinking. Is it a trap? I thought that until I heard what she said. It's not a trap. She's terrified. Her marriage was a business deal between her manager – who was her father - and Marco. She's been set up as much as anyone.'

Erin turned away, mainly to hide the roll of her eyes. She couldn't believe Zane had fallen for this! Hazel was playing him and he couldn't that the woman hadn't been set up at all. 'She's only changed her mind about Marco because she's realised *you're* out! She now knows that she's married a man with no legal claim to the Morelli empire and the person who has is now *you*!'

Unable to help it, a mirthless chuckle escaped her lips. 'You can't be *that* desperate to be a knight in shining armour after all the sacrifices that have been made for you?' Her arm waved first in the direction of Leo and then Cav. 'One's been shot, another's lost his brother. Sonny's fucking dead and twenty-plus women your filthy brother trafficked to use as sex slaves have been butchered - all in aid of your quest to regain control of your fucking firm! Yet instead of removing the cause of it, in the guise of your bloody brother, who I should remind you, murdered my father *and* got you locked up, you're running around on the word of a money-grabbing porn star, who's reached the conclusion it's not financially viable to be married to Marco?'

Ignoring the oppressive silence from her outburst, Erin slung her glass of water across the room to smash against the wall. 'For fuck's sake Zane, how much more do you want from people?'

She saw the nerve in Zane's neck twitching and the icy glare in his eyes. A fraction of her words in private would have been enough to blow his temper, let alone an attack on his decisions in front of his men. But spotting the shock and uncomfortableness behind Tiger and Leo's eyes and Cav's jaw clenched tightly from the mention of his dead brother, Erin realised she'd gone too far. *Way* too far.

Again.

Feeling a sudden sting of tears of both frustration and hopelessness, she bolted from the room and up the stairs. She'd made an already bad situation a thousand times worse.

Flinging herself on the bed, she let the salty hot tears flow down her burning face.

All she was left with now was a question she was unsure she could honestly answer.

Had her outburst been about Zane's bizarre choice of putting himself and his men in what seemed to be an untenable position or was the *real* crux over him meeting the wife of a man who wanted to wipe him from the face of the Earth? Was it *jealousy* that he might be tempted by the allure and beauty of Hazel – the woman widely known as Lisa Tequila?

Many men's dream, Hazel's exquisite 'talents' were watched far and wide.

Erin was also aware of Zane's penchant for women under threat.

Would he be tempted by? And furthermore, if she was correct with her reasonings of the *real* reason Hazel was begging for Zane's help, then taking the woman his brother was obsessed with - his *wife*, from under his nose, as well as taking the firm, wouldn't that be almost better than killing the man?

Zane had acted edgy and odd for days. He was hiding things and this was another. Maybe he'd planned this with Hazel all along?

But was any of it connected to the girl in the silver car?

Erin's brain sped faster. She didn't know the answers but

felt the connection she'd once believed to be so strong with the man who had made her feel something other than dead was rapidly slipping from her grasp.

The prospect of Zane being killed yesterday was horrific enough, but the concept of losing him *this* way was a hell of a lot worse.

• • • •

DAMON SANDLER eyed Hazel with derision. The slut was watching them out of the corner of her eye.

Oh, she might be lounging on the sofa, pretending to read a magazine whilst giving everyone an eyeful of her long legs, but she was scheming something. Judging by the amount of men finding excuses to wander through the living area, he suspected Hazel had purposely omitted her knickers too, the manipulative bitch.

He couldn't see the attraction for the tart - he never had, but every other man in the country was obsessed. Marco being no exception.

But he didn't trust Hazel one iota.

Damon's distaste grew as Marco ran his fingers up to the top of Hazel's thigh and beyond, giving the avid onlookers free view of his fingers playing with places of his wife that most men chose to keep for themselves.

Random birds displaying their wares was a perk frequently shared between them, but from where Damon came from - wives were *different.*

Another reason why he'd never married.

Furthermore, Marco was still yet to bring up the subject of who was to be his official second-in-command.

It had to be him. After all he'd done, who else could it be?

Jerked from his thoughts as Marco snapped his fingers in his general direction, Damon's gaze moved away from the figure on the sofa.

'Now you've have a good perv on my wife, let's get a fucking move on and go to check how Luna is shaping up.'

Marco shrugged his suit jacket onto his massive shoulders, then gave Hazel's nipple a tweak through her satin top for good measure. 'I want filming back on schedule by the end of the week. I've already instructed new male actors to be brought to site on Friday.'

To Damon's horror he realised his cheeks were burning. *Perving on Hazel? Hardly!* Surely dealing with Zane took priority, rather than the films? 'What about making sure that th…'

'I know what you're going to say.' Marco silenced Damon with a distinct flap of his hand. 'I'm not allowing what my arsehole brother pulled to screw up filming or anything else.' He threw his arms in the air. 'I mean, what has he achieved from his pathetic attempt to muscle his way in? Jack shit, that's what! A bust coffee table, a couple of casualties and a handful of dead tarts? How the fuck could that possibly dent or damage a firm such as *mine* or ruin someone like me? It's laughable!'

Just for added effect, Marco allowed a rumbling laugh to spill from his mouth before stooping over for a quick top-up of cocaine.

Damon's face remained neutral but personally believed that over sixty men being shot to death yesterday counted as more than a 'couple' of casualties. But he remained schtum. He wanted the second-in-command position, after all.

Marco suddenly frowned. 'Have you located that bitch, Erin Langley, and killed her yet or is that still on your to-do list, along with everything else you haven't done?'

Damon grimaced. For fuck's sake, he'd barely had a chance to take a shit, let alone locate that bitch! 'I'm working on it.'

'Make sure you do,' Marco barked, dragging his hand across the bottom of his nose. 'Come on. Let's get moving. We'll go now.'

Damon's eyes flicked back to Hazel who watched Marco with impressed rapture. 'Is it wise to leave… erm… Hazel here... I mean, she could...' His voice trailed off when Marco's face reddened with rage.

'Are you saying my wife can't be trusted or that I would let something happen to her?' Marco's hands clenched into fists.

Damon faltered, finding his next words carefully. For God's sake - Marco had clearly knocked his wife around whilst on honeymoon, then acted like he didn't give a toss about her by leaving her lying on the deck earlier. Not that he blamed Marco for either of those things, but now the slut was suddenly Miss Perfect again? *The bloke was a sandwich short.* 'Erm, no, I meant that I'm worried your brother might come here in our absence and Hazel could be hurt.' *If only...*

'I ain't leaving her on her own though am I, you thick bastard! What do you take me for?' Marco harrumphed. Turning back to Hazel, he grabbed her chin and ran his tongue across her lips. 'Hazel isn't going anywhere, are you, babe? She'd miss this too much for a start,' he laughed, grabbing at his crotch.

Damon genuinely thought he might be sick from both the spectacle and the fawning look on Hazel's face.

That woman was falser than her tits, but he couldn't say that. Not to Marco.

'There will be a couple of guards left here as well as some downstairs, so if my wanker of a brother shows his scarred fucking face, he'll be leaving like the last cunt he sent to do his dirty work - in a fucking tarp.' Which, when Sandler got his act together, would be happening to that bird of Zane's too. He slapped Hazel's thigh. 'See you in a bit, babe.'

With that, Marco strutted towards the penthouse door, leaving Damon and the enforcers accompanying them to follow in his wake.

Hazel waited until everybody had safely left the room before letting the look of adoration slide from her face. Now all she had to do was work out how to get out of here to meet Zane.

THIRTY TWO

KNOWING SHE MUST rectify the situation, Erin burst back into the sitting room. 'Zane, I... Oh!' She met Leo's questioning eyes. 'He's gone, then?'

Leo nodded, his face tense. 'He left about half an hour ago.'

Deflated, Erin looked around the room seeing Cav sitting bleakly in a chair in the corner staring out of the window, searching for the brother that would never return.

She'd been stupid. She shouldn't have left it so long before coming back downstairs. She should have put this right when she had the chance. Regardless of her crushing paranoia, she shouldn't have made things worse. Her mind was spiralling out of control and her outburst had helped no one.

Her gaze fell to the pile of broken glass in the corner from her childish inability to control her temper. Grabbing a broom, she set about sweeping it up. She moved quickly, almost violently as she brushed the shards into the dustpan, the task giving her something to focus on other than the trouble she'd caused.

Leo's gaze silently burned into her as she worked. Stopping, she turned around. 'I'm sorry for what I said. I know I've made everything worse. It's just... I...' She paused, not entirely sure what her reasoning was anymore.

'You shouldn't have said any of it,' Leo said sternly. Clocking the angst on Erin's face, he then shrugged. 'But Zane will calm down eventually.'

Leaning the broom against the wall, Erin flopped into a chair. She was grateful for Leo's undeserved kindness, but his words weren't true. 'I'm pushing Zane away. I *keep* pushing him away... I don't seem to be able to help it and it's pathetic! I should be concentrating on what needs to be achieved here, rather than selfishly worrying about what I may lose.'

Leo studied Erin. Never having set eyes on her before yesterday, he hadn't known what to expect. He'd thought that someone who had been involved for their own gain with their arch nemesis, Flame, wouldn't be top of his Christmas card list, but this woman wasn't what he'd expected.

He'd seen how she'd faced Marco's man with a gun in her face. He'd witnessed her desperation as she'd searched for life in the jumble of women's bodies in the studio, her joy to find some still alive, immense. She'd had the balls to be the mole in a situation which could have easily resulted in her death and she'd done everything required to winkle the relevant information from Sandler. Not, Leo suspected, without considerable personal cost, yet she'd done it all without complaint.

Erin Langley was something very different, but she was also clearly someone who had been damaged by the years she'd forced herself to be with Flame to place her in a position to wreak revenge.

Zane had told him a bit about that. He'd also spoken of the times this fiery woman had made attempts on his life. That was before things changed. And things *had* changed... Something this woman perhaps didn't perhaps realise...

But what *Leo* had to make sure of was that Erin went nowhere unguarded. Before leaving, Zane had slipped him the info that Marco was gunning for her and she must not be left alone for one second.

'I can only guess what is worrying you right now, but from what you've said, I think I know. You believe Zane doesn't care…' Leo watched Erin stare into her lap unable to meet his eyes. 'But you're wrong.'

Erin's eyes shimmered with a fresh film of tears. Hating herself even more for this weakness, she snatched her hand over her face. 'I *know* I behaved badly. I can only apologise and when Zane returns - *if* he returns, then I'll apologise to him too. I shouldn't ha…'

'He *will* return, but you're missing my point,' Leo interrupted, his face stern but not unkind. 'I meant that you're wrong about what you're thinking.' He folded his arms across his chest, the stiffness is his injured arm now vastly improved.

'I've known Zane for years. *Many* years. I've worked with him for most of that time and it would have been longer had it not been for... Anyway, I respect that man more than anyone. I also know him as well as he lets *anyone* know him.' Leo raised his hand seeing Erin about to speak. 'I don't know much of what happened to you in the past, but you're selling yourself short.'

Erin tensed. She didn't want to discuss Flame or what she'd endured during her time with that man.

'You've awakened something in Zane, and for that you must be special,' Leo continued. 'He loves you - I can see that. It's not something I've ever seen before. Where the firm is concerned, he gets in the zone and this shit going down is a biggie. His head is on that, but it doesn't mean you're not what he wants. You must trust what he does and by that, I mean *whatever* he does.' A small smile cracked his face. 'I've never known him to get anything wrong yet. Zane knows what he's doing. So, Missus, whatever's bothering that brain of yours, fuck it off. It's not what you think, so have faith.'

Erin felt closer to tears than before. To hear Leo speak so eloquently and kindly, especially after her pathetic outburst, made her feel even less deserving.

But he was right. She had to stop the past from clouding her logic. She should give herself more credit and especially give

Zane more credit. He had a huge amount on his back and men like Leo knew the way Zane worked tenfold, compared to her. She needed to control her speeding brain, otherwise she really would succeed in permanently pushing him away. 'Thank you.' Erin smiled weakly. 'I appreciate what you've said. I hope you're right.'

'I am,' Leo said. 'Trust me and trust Zane.'

Erin nodded. That she would. Starting from now. She only hoped her brain obeyed her instructions.

• • • •

TIME WAS TICKING and Hazel knew it was limited. Not having any idea how long Marco would spend at Luna made things worse. He could be there for *hours* or conversely, do little more than stick his head around the door, see the place was still not up to standard and turn on his heels. He'd already been gone over an hour, so he could be back any minute.

She also got the distinct impression that Damon Sandler would push to return at the earliest opportunity. It was obvious that man had an intense dislike for her. The feeling was mutual, but Sandler would love nothing more than to catch her doing something to back up his theory.

And she had the strong instinct that Sandler knew she was planning something... Why didn't that man see her in the same light as every other man in the entire world? Was she losing her touch?

At least Marco was now acting like he wanted her around again.

Hazel shuddered. Having to let Marco touch her now he made her skin crawl with a thousand ants was horrible.

Fear bubbled. And if she couldn't push Zane Morelli's buttons in the way required it didn't bear thinking about. Aside from the precarious position she was currently in, she had no intention of walking away from this empty handed. *No way.*

With growing agitation, Hazel glanced at the large contemporary clock on the wall. She was already half an hour later than the time she'd agreed to meet Zane. What if he didn't wait?

She must get out of here now and pray she'd read the signs from the monkeys remaining stationed in the penthouse correctly.

Confident she had, mainly because there was no other choice, Hazel brought Lisa Tequila to life. Pulling her top off one shoulder to expose additional flesh, she shoved a hand inside to push her cleavage up.

Satisfied, she stood up and swinging her hips, sashayed across the room towards the corridor. She looked nowhere else, apart from a quick glance at Sonny's phone which she'd placed back in the exact position it originally fell.

Heart thumping, Hazel had almost reached the front door of the penthouse when a guard appeared from nowhere.

'Where are you going, Miss Tequila?'

Hiding her shock, Hazel turned to the man. Flashing her straight pearly whites she looked up through long thick lashes. 'I'm so crazy bored. I'm going for some fresh air.'

Despite the man's close set eyes wandering to rest on Hazel's cleavage which spilled conveniently out of her top, he stood firm. 'You can get fresh air on the balcony, Miss.'

Hazel turned side on, aware a side profile enhanced the size of her bust and leant against the wall with one leg bent at the knee to expose her thigh through the long slit in her skirt. She twiddled a lock of nylon blonde extension, then allowed her fingers to hover over the man's chest.

Christ, he was ugly, but that was the least of her problems.

'I'm sick of the view from the balcony,' she giggled, the false laughter sounding like a tinkling waterfall. 'There's only so long the London skyline and the Thames can be interesting. Plus, from that side of the building the breeze is blowing the wrong way and it messes up my hair.'

Ramping up the glittering within her eyes so they sparkled like diamonds, Hazel felt hopeful from the wavering of the guard's stony expression. *Time to bring Marco into this...* 'I'm going to the communal gardens downstairs. It's for Marco, you see. He loves it when I have flowers in my hair and I want to surprise him when he gets back.'

Stepping forward, she left half an inch between her and the man without her breasts actually touching his chest. 'You won't force me to disappoint my husband, will you?' she purred, her voice velvety smooth.

'Well, I, erm...' The man fidgeted, his eyes now fully centred on Hazel's bust.

'I'll only be a few minutes,' Hazel pushed. 'Where's the harm?' *Come on, you ugly bastard. Let me out.*

'Well, I...'

'You're a star!' Hazel gushed, not waiting to hear another 'no'. Besides, no one wanted to be the cause of Marco not getting what he desired. Not that Marco liked her wearing flowers. Last time she'd worn a flower hair clip, he said she looked like a hat. Still, this guy didn't know that, did he?

Opening the door, Hazel flashed a stunning smile at the guard for good measure. 'Oh, and radio the other men downstairs, would you? I don't want to get stopped again or I won't have time to collect my flowers before Marco returns. He'll be back any minute, so I need to be quick.'

And didn't she just.

Skittering down the corridor, Hazel darted into the lift. She'd go into the gardens as planned and then nip around the side where she hoped Zane would still be waiting. If he wasn't, then this whole thing was dead in the water.

And then very possibly, so was she.

THIRTY THREE

RISKY WASN'T THE WORD in Zane putting Marco's wife on the back of his bike. Her skirt hitched halfway up her thighs didn't aid not drawing attention either, but the alternative option of hanging around the grounds of the penthouse was a death wish, so there was no option but to go elsewhere. Far enough away not to be seen, but not so far to ruin getting Hazel back to the complex before anyone got twitchy.

Zane had to admit he admired Hazel's courage for going against Marco's wishes, especially with what she'd told him so far. And for that, she must be desperate. However, as she clung to him as they sped along the road, he could do without her playing with his belt buckle.

Spotting a viaduct, Zane brought the bike to a stop. Jumping off, he helped Hazel from the pillion seat and took his helmet off, waiting while she did likewise. He watched the woman daft enough to marry his brother take in her surroundings, her nose wrinkling with distaste.

'Not the usual kind of place I would arrange to meet a man,' Hazel moved sideways to give her patent stilettoes a wide berth from the pile of dog mess and studied Zane with interest. 'You look like your brother.' Her hand raised to trace a line down the jagged scar on his right cheekbone. 'But better...'

Zane stiffened. *Was Erin right? Was this a ploy? His instinct was telling him no, but it was possible he was wrong.*

Ignoring the steady dripping from the dank Victorian arched brickwork above, he stared at Hazel. Watching her films was not something he'd done, but he'd seen photos. She was undoubtedly attractive, but surgical precision was not something he hankered over.

Whereas Erin...

Shaking away the image flashing into his head, Zane gritted his teeth. Thinking about Erin only served to aggravate and depress him. Why had she behaved so unreasonably? Her latest outburst this morning proved things were very wrong from reasons that he was unsure how to handle, fix or even understand where they stemmed from.

The thought that the burden of what he'd always stood for in Erin's mind - as her father's perceived murderer - could have finally become too tall an obstacle to climb, gained traction. If that was the case, he wasn't sure what he would do. Or *could* do.

He needed Erin. He needed the connection he had with her more than ever now, but if she'd decided the gulf between them was too wide to bridge, then...

Sensing although Zane was here in person but not mentally, Hazel inwardly panicked. She'd just given him a green light, yet he'd blanked her. Had she really lost her talent?

She hadn't entertained that a possibility but there was nothing else for it apart from to push on.

Christ, she'd lie on this rank floor amongst the needles and dog shit and open her legs for him immediately if he would ensure divorcing Marco left her alive. Before he married her himself, of course.

'You're *definitely* more attractive that Marco,' Hazel continued, determined to get the reaction she craved.

Zane bristled further, almost hearing the cogs in Hazel's brain grinding. The likelihood that she was playing him prodded harder. He was about to look behind, expecting to find a gun pointing in his direction, when Hazel flicked her hair over her shoulder, exposing the remains of a bruise discolouring her swollen cheekbone.

It looked like a bruise, but was it? There weren't many tricks in the book he'd hadn't witnessed women using to turn a situation in their favour. Hazel could have moved her hair *knowing* it would expose an injury she'd fashioned to back up fake claims.

Licking his finger, he pressed it onto Hazel's cheek and dragged down. Makeup used to forge a bruise would smear, but this mark didn't budge. Instead, Hazel winced, her surprise quickly replaced with self-consciousness as she rearranged her hair to fall back over her cheek.

Regarding her composure, Hazel coyly looked up at Zane. Stepping forward, she pressed herself against his chest, her hand sliding down to his crotch. 'So... Shall we?'

Moving with the speed of a panther, Zane gripped Hazel's wrist and pulled her hand away. He'd been tempted to give her the benefit of the doubt then, but not if she didn't drop this shit. 'Let's just get one thing clear, lady,' he spat. 'I ain't interested in bedding you. You asked for my help, but if that's not the case and you're setting me up and Erin gets hurt, then it's not Marco you should fear.'

It was at this moment Hazel realised she'd misjudged this situation. Taking Zane for herself would be a lot harder than she'd thought.

Without warning, the persona of Lisa Tequila that she'd grown used to utilising, disintegrated into pieces and fell from her to the floor.

Collapsing to her knees in exhaustion, despair and pure fear, Hazel sobbed harder than she'd ever done as the years of pent up emotions combined with the awful situation she was trapped in smashed her between the eyes.

• • • •

ENTERING THE BUILDING that his father had purchased many years ago, Zane looked around in dismay. The disused factory hadn't been touched since it had been bought at auction and it showed.

Water tracked down the bare light flexes to form puddles onto a floor heavily scattered with chunks of plaster from the ceiling.

Tiger suddenly yelped. 'Christ! A fucking rat! I hate those bastard things!'

'We'll get the place sorted,' Zane muttered. It would need a huge amount of work and was a far cry from the pristine Morelli headquarters that had once been, but having this place was also a godsend.

Between them, they could make some rooms habitable enough to run the firm from in the short term. The rest could be done as they went along. The most important thing was establishing a base and getting things up and running, as well as collecting a force to take Marco and his men head on.

Despite wanting to repeat what he'd previously attempted and take Marco on straight away, Zane's number was too depleted to succeed. Especially now Marco was no doubt busy restocking his army of cannon fodder.

Had his original plan worked, things would have been different, but it hadn't therefore a change of plan was inevitable. Thankfully, he wasn't short of money - one thing Marco *hadn't* been able to take from him, so he could afford do this place up. But having a building that Marco was unaware of, no matter the state of it and regardless of the length of time it would take, was a bonus.

'How did it go?' Tiger asked as he dragged a table into the centre of the large room. Frowning, he kicked a pile of rubble out of the way so that the table legs remained stable. 'Fuck! This will take some elbow grease to put right!'

Zane paused. The inevitable questions about Marco's wife sat like an elephant in the room and had done since he'd met Tiger here after dropping Hazel back at the complex. He'd also made it clear to leave the others at the house.

How had it gone? Not as he'd expected, but he knew *one* thing... 'She wasn't lying,' he said bluntly. 'She's terrified! One minute Marco's giving her a whack, the next he's all over her. She wants out.'

Tiger raised an eyebrow. 'That's nothing new for Marco, but what's she like? I mean, *really*?'

Zane frowned. 'Fake? Real? Scared? I don't know... Damaged? Used to playing a role? Who the hell knows! But she has to get away from Marco as soon as possible. I know my brother and he's obsessed with that woman. Out of principle he'll never let her go and if he finds out she's done with him, let alone met up with me, he'll kill her. But worse than that, from what she said, his first port of call is getting to Erin.'

Tiger nodded solemnly. 'So, now what?'

Zane shrugged. 'I said I'd help Hazel if she helps me. I've given her a phone. She can call me if the shit hits the fan. Until then, she'll keep me informed of Marco's movements and if she can somehow be privy to it, any more info of what he may be planning for Erin.'

Tiger sucked his teeth. 'You reckon you can trust her?'

Zane nodded. 'Surprisingly, yes.' *And that was unexpected.* After Hazel's initial stunt of trying it on he'd been set to walk away, accepting his instincts were way off. That was until she'd folded like a pack of cards. He was possibly the only person ever to witness it as Hazel's fake persona and bullshit fell away like a shed skin.

What he'd seen underneath was not Lisa Tequila or even Hazel Grimes. It was the *real* Hazel - the one that Hazel herself had probably never met. It was *that* person who he'd realised he could trust. 'I believe she's on the level.'

Tiger shrugged. 'I hope you're right, but I think others may need convincing.'

Zane inwardly sighed. Tiger didn't mention names, but he didn't have to. His men would run with whatever decision he made. He hadn't let them down yet and never would.

It was Erin. Her earlier outburst had left every single person with the crystal clear knowledge about her opinion, but she had to learn to trust his judgement - as in, *really* trust it. If she didn't, they had no future. That's if they had one at all now based on how her attitude had changed.

And Erin would have no future whatsoever if Marco succeeded.

Further questions Zane wanted to ask about how Erin was faring remained trapped in his throat. He could afford for no one to hold power over him like she had these past few weeks. As much as he hated to entertain the concept, if something didn't change, then he would have to accept that there was no choice but to let her go – both for her own safety, his men and the firm.

THIRTY FOUR

'THEY'VE DONE A CRACKING JOB!' Marco strutted back through the lobby, ignoring the concierge like usual. 'You couldn't tell anything was ever amiss!' Apart from the bullet holes that had all but obliterated the walls down that corridor, but the plasterers were due first thing tomorrow, so job done.

Yep, his men had done well. Getting rid of that many corpses was no mean feat. He should know – in his younger days before grunts dealt with clean-ups, he'd disposed of more than a few bodies himself. It was a messy job and not something he missed.

Killing the fuckers – yes, all day long, but cleaning up the gash afterward – nah, he was above that these days. 'The cameras will be rolling again on Friday. No more hold ups.'

He needed to recoup the money he'd lost. No point in hanging around. Hazel could get her arse into gear. Her lounging around like the Queen of Sheba was no bloody use. The honeymoon was over. It was time she earned her keep.

'I'll make sure everything is ready for Friday,' Damon said, stepping into the lift. 'Was there, erm... anything else you wanted to talk to me about?' *Like, 'being as you've done such a good job in my absence will you be my new right hand man.'*

'Such as what?' Marco pressed the button repeatedly for the penthouse floor. 'Bloody thing always sticks!' He swung back to Damon. 'Well? Like what? What else could I possibly want to say, apart from asking you when you're getting your fucking teeth fixed?'

Damon cringed, his hand moving to cover his mouth and along with it, his crooked teeth. 'Well, I, erm... I thought now with Sonny dead and with...'

'Ah! I see!' Marco slapped the lift wall. 'You're expecting me to replace him?' His eyes narrowed. 'And reckon that should be *you*?'

Cheeks burning, Damon wished he hadn't said anything. 'Erm… I...'

'Forgive me that after Sonny proved to be a traitorous bastard if I'm a little prickly about handing that title to someone else,' Marco barked as the lift ground to a halt. 'Prove you're up to the job and I'll consider it. Maybe…'

Marco strutted from the lift, leaving Damon to skitter behind him. *Prove it? Hadn't he already done that?*

'I hope Hazel is ready and waiting,' Marco muttered. 'I'm a tad low on choice now those other tarts have done a runner. Hey, finding where they went and removing that Erin bitch would be a good start with your hopes of promotion.'

Damon silently gnashed his teeth. If he could choose, he'd forget about those Polish sluts or whoever they were and Caroline/Erin too and just get rid of Hazel. He hated that woman more with every passing second. She wasn't on the level and he intended to prove it. Perhaps *that* would convince Marco that he was the right man for the job?

'Ah, you're back.' Hazel glided out of the apartment to drape herself over Marco the second he came through the door.

She'd already poured him a drink and grabbed a rose from the garden in case that dolt she'd blagged to let her out questioned her about the flowers she'd pretended she so desperately wanted to pick. She'd also reduced the puffiness around her eyes from her impromptu meltdown whilst kneeling on the floor in that grotty viaduct. But most importantly, she now had a phone that Marco was unaware of and his brother was on the other end of it whenever she needed. She'd do all she could to get Zane his information. Now she had his backup she could leave Marco. And that she would do as soon as possible.

Yes she might be still in this situation, but now there was an end in sight.

Laying her hand on Marco's shoulder, she smiled while secretly wishing he'd die and save this extra stress.

• • • •

'I'VE APOLOGISED as much as I can,' Erin said sulkily. Even though she'd told herself that she wouldn't be spiky when Zane finally came upstairs, she was doing just that.

What she really wanted was for them to fall into bed and do what they did best. She hadn't expected to *discuss* anything. A typical man, he'd do anything, other than discuss something like this, but he was discussing it now? Or trying to…

And what was she doing? Hindering things again, that's what.

It was easier than laying her cards on the table and opening her heart by admitting that she was scared. No, *terrified*, of pushing him away and losing him.

Christ, she was no good at this. It was easier feeling nothing. But that didn't apply. Not with Zane.

Erin's gaze fell to Zane's strong shoulders and to his biceps straining against the short sleeves of his tight black T-shirt. Her mouth became dry. He was the only man in the world who made her want to both scream with genuine pleasure and with fright. And that was a dangerous, yet heady combination.

But she didn't want to discuss anything. Her mind would run away with her and she'd jump on the defensive and say the wrong things again. Her paranoia and past would take control. She had too much baggage around her neck and too little trust.

If she went on the defensive it could flip the other way. It would expose her weakness – *him*. She'd end up leaving herself wide open to be attacked and abandoned; mercilessly ripped apart by the only person she'd ever wanted.

No. She couldn't expose herself like that. It was too risky.

But what if she lost him...?

Zane remained in the chair at the end of the bed. Perching on a pile of clothes was far from comfortable, but a damned sight less of an issue than getting on the bed. His urge to peel Erin's clothes off and sink himself into her would override everything and defeat the object.

To distract himself from pulling off Erin's oversized T-shirt - not the most seductive attire known to man, Zane lit up a cigarette.

She looked perfect to him. Sensational. Good enough to...

No! Concentrate!

He finally moved his gaze to Erin's face and waited while she raised her eyes to meet his. 'I need you to trust me,' he said, his voice low. 'I won't have you questioning every decision I make.'

'What, so I don't get an opinion?' Evan gaped, immediately annoyed. 'Jesus, Zane. You sound like your brother!'

Zane smashed his fist down on the bedside table, the crash making Erin recoil. 'You can't help yourself, can you? Everything you say is sarcastic or a dig about my fucking brother!' Getting to his feet, frustration flowed. 'I've run men for many years. They trust me, yet *you* don't?'

'I don't trust people like Hazel!' Erin countered. Her eyes narrowed as she tapped the side of her head. 'You men think with your dicks rather than your brains and women like her know it!'

'Is that so?' That speaks highly of me.' Zane snarled. 'And don't discuss our personal matters with any of my men either. I will not allow it.'

'Allow it?' Erin yelled. 'Wow! Something *else* you won't allow? I'll talk to who I damn well want, just like you do. It's okay for you to do what you like? You know - that stuff you're hiding about that woman in the silver car? A bit on the side, is she?'

Shut up, Erin, she scolded herself. *You're doing it again. Be rational.*

As she'd feared, her brain failed to obey the promises she'd made after talking to Leo. *Stupid, stupid.*

'Quit acting like a jealous child,' Zane barked. 'I'm too old for that shit. I stupidly allowed you to get under my skin and let things you do go, but not any longer.'

All the bravado drained out of Erin. She'd sabotaged everything again. She had to stop this. 'I...'

'No! I don't want to hear excuses anymore. I came in here to sort things out, but that's clearly out of your remit.' The nerve in Zane's neck twitched. 'I made a decision today...'

Erin's blood ran cold. 'Zane... I...'

'You dilute my concentration and that's dangerous. I want you, Erin, but I don't want *this*! The way I work - the way I *have* to work will not change. Either accept it and trust me or we have no future.'

Erin's immediate reaction was to snipe as to whether Hazel had given him a better offer, but stopped seeing Zane study her with the blank coldness she dreaded.

He was right. They didn't have a future unless something changed. She'd known what Zane was from the start, but she hadn't expected, never *dreamt* she'd fall in love with the least likely man in the universe.

Did she want him? Yes, without a doubt.

Did he want her?

He'd said so, hadn't he?

The problem here was *her*.

Maybe she was too damaged by the past to be a real person after all?

Overcome with a tumult of emotions and unanswerable questions, Erin could do little but turn over to conceal the tears seeping from her eyes, knowing Zane wouldn't join her in bed tonight.

Her brain was working against her heart, determined to ruin everything, but tomorrow was another day. She'd start over and hope this could be mended before the chasm between her and Zane widened further.

THIRTY FIVE

IT WAS SHORT – much shorter than anyone wanted, but having Lewis's funeral under the radar meant doing it fast, with none of the accompaniments such a service usually included.

Zane scowled. There hadn't even been a service to speak of - merely the vicar saying a few words before Lewis's coffin was hurriedly lowered into the ground. Unfortunately, this was the only way. Anything else opened up the chance of word getting out and leading Marco's men straight to them.

'All right, mate?' Zane clapped his hand on Cav's shoulder.

Standing rigidly over the hole containing his brother, Cav gave a slight nod and flinched as the first shovel of earth landed on the coffin.

Zane shifted his weight to his other foot, resenting this meagre spectacle was all he could offer a loyal man who had died for his cause. It was only fortunate there were trusted figures from the past that he'd been able to call upon to dress and store the body these past couple of days, as well as arranging a behind-the-scenes burial.

Another trusted man gone.

His thoughts returned to Erin. He'd said what he'd need to say last night and the fear he'd seen in her eyes when he'd stated he'd call time unless things changed only mirrored what he'd felt in his heart. There was no way he wanted to lose her, but neither could he continue like this. No matter how much it hurt, if Erin was unable to trust him and his decisions there was no way forward.

'I think we're done here now,' Tiger said, nodding towards the vicar who stood back from the grave to watch them expectantly.

'Hmm.' Zane glanced at the men who had almost finished filling the hole in the ground and then stepped forward to shake the vicar's hand. 'Much appreciated, Reverend.'

Turning around to face the small collection of men around the graveside, Zane smiled thinly. 'Okay fellas, ready to go?' He'd drop Cav back at the house to stay with Erin whilst the rest of them headed off for their meeting at the new headquarters.

As they walked towards the car park it was then Zane spotted the flash of silver moving rapidly through the exit. He didn't have to say anything because from Cav's, Leo's and Tiger's faces, they'd seen the silver Golf leaving as clearly as he had.

• • • •

MARCO HAD ENJOYED accompanying Hazel to what was left of her father's studios. The area was still cordoned off for safety, but he'd insisted she take at least a small peek into the blackened shell of what had once been Starlight Studios - the place where that two-faced fucker, Grimes, had sidelined his entire back catalogue of films rather than delivering them to Luna, as agreed.

He'd loved the horror on Hazel's face as she'd looked at the devastated building, but he couldn't quite work out from her reaction whether she'd been party to this sneaky manoeuvre or whether her fresh upset was that her father had let her down on something else. It could just be her having another diva-like meltdown over darling daddy being burnt to cinders, but he doubted it.

It made little difference because the films were gone, so Hazel had best hurry up and start proving her fucking worth. If only she'd quit with the snivelling, they might get a bit further. That was why he'd now brought her back to Luna.

Pulling Hazel along by the wrist, Marco kicked open the door of the dressing room that was now hers. 'As you can see, everything you need has been purchased with no expense spared.' *Like usual.* Her list of demands for filming at Luna had almost surpassed the amount he'd forked out for their wedding. 'I've even got the gold door plaque like you wanted.'

Hazel eyed the large box of sex toys and top-end makeup on the dressing table. There was no doubt that Marco had supplied everything she'd requested. A week ago she'd have been pleased, but now things had changed. Changed to the extent that nothing would be acceptable, apart from being as far away from him as possible.

Her hand remained poised over her handbag where Zane's burner phone lay concealed. To show willing and to give him a clear run at whatever he was doing, she'd already texted him first thing this morning listing Marco's movements for the day. She hoped it aided in moving forward so she could divorce Marco and be done with him.

She'd work out how to bag Zane later and that already looked promising because by the time he'd returned her to the penthouse yesterday his attitude towards her had changed dramatically.

But now she'd seen the ruins of Starlight Studios before being brought to Luna, it was clear she no longer had the backup of having her original films. Those films had perished along with her father.

She really would have nothing if she couldn't successfully be granted a divorce.

'Filming starts tomorrow,' Marco said, pushing Hazel out of the dressing room and through the doorway of Studio One.

'Oh my God!' Hazel shrieked, her face draining of colour

at the rows of cages within the room. *That one at the end had what looked like blood on the floor.* Her hand rushed to her mouth as rising vomit threatened to make an entrance.

'Sandler!' Marco roared. 'What the fuck are these still doing here?'

Damon Sandler hurried down the corridor At Marco's voice. His eyes narrowed as he entered Studio One seeing Hazel looking like she might pass out. 'What's the problem, boss?'

'These cages those bitches were in?' Marco swiped his arm around the room. 'I was told these were being removed, so why the fuck are they still here?'

'You kept women in there?' Hazel squeaked. 'The trafficked women?' She'd heard Marco mention cages, but she hadn't believed he was serious. Surely no one would *really* keep people caged?

This was worse than she'd imagined.

What *had* she imagined? She didn't know, but this was... And that blood... 'Marco?' she gabbled, her eyes wide. 'What did you do to them?'

'Shut it!' Marco hissed. 'Stop being hysterical. Everything's fine.' *No it wasn't, but if Hazel didn't shut up...* He swung to Damon, his eyes glowering. 'Well? Why the hell are these still here?'

Damon grimaced, further antagonised by Hazel's whining voice. 'They'll be gone by tonight. Filming isn't until tomorrow and we couldn't get a lorry until this afternoon and...'

'Get. Rid. Of. Them. And get rid of them *now*!' Marco screamed. 'Buy a fucking lorry and do it yourself if you have to!' He didn't need reminding how those tarts had done a runner or how his cleverly thought out idea had gone to pot. Neither did he need Hazel going off on one. She had to get back in front of the camera.

Giving Damon a glare harsh enough to melt steel, he steered Hazel from the room and turned the charm back on. 'Don't stress, babe. Things will be back to normal by this afternoon and tomorrow you won't even know they were here.'

Hazel stumbled along the corridor, feeling sicker than ever. Those cages might no longer be here by the time she returned tomorrow, but she would know they *had* been. Along with the proof of what had happened.

A runner suddenly burst around the corner of the corridor. 'Mr Sandler? I've got to show you... Oh! My apologies, Mr Morelli. I didn't realise...' He inclined his head. 'Good morning, Miss Tequila.'

'What is it, Connor?' Damon hissed. 'We're busy.'

'No, we're not!' Marco stepped forward. 'Connor, is it? You clearly have something important you want to tell Damon, so...' He turned to Sandler. 'Take my wife to my car whilst I find out what is so important here.'

Damon begrudgingly led Hazel in the opposite direction of the runner and Marco.

Great. Now he was even more out of the loop and to top it all, stuck with this plastic bitch. He hoped that whatever Connor had to say wouldn't take long.

It would only be something pointless. Runners invariably had little of interest to say - that's why they got all the shit jobs. Still, it would serve the prat right for taking it upon himself to interrupt the big boss. Now Connor would look an utter ass when he relayed his pointless information to Marco.

Meanwhile, he would shift with getting things in motion to find out where that two-faced lying cow, Erin Langley, was hiding. No doubt it would be the same place as Zane. And if he found *her*, then he'd find Zane. Two birds with one stone would ensure Marco had no excuses not to grant his promotion.

• • • •

'HOW ARE THINGS, CAV?' Erin asked, aware Cav was still distraught over Lewis's loss. How could he not be? At least since returning from his brother's funeral he'd seemed perkier and more himself. Laying what remained of Lewis to rest would hopefully help draw a line under the tragedy and allow Cav to start coming to terms with what had happened.

She'd have liked to have gone to pay her respects too, but Zane wouldn't hear of it and after last night, she'd thought better of pushing the issue.

'I'm getting there.' Cav gave a small smile. 'But it's difficult.'

'I understand,' Erin nodded, stealing a glance out of the window.

What was also difficult was being stuck here when everyone else had gone off again. Zane, Tiger and Leo had left for their meeting at the new headquarters and she was itching to see for herself what the place was like. She was desperate to get out of the house and be part of *something* to help move this forward.

She'd tried her damnedest to start the day on a new footing. Reiterating to herself that she wouldn't let herself or Zane down again. She needed to keep a lid on the past that haunted her and do what Leo said – trust Zane and know that whatever he did would be for the greater good.

She couldn't lose him. She *couldn't*.

But although Zane had been civil towards her as he'd left this morning, the unmistakable wall between them remained. He'd made no move to display affection towards her during the night, their interactions verging on clinical. And she couldn't help but wonder whether her being forced to remain away from Lewis's funeral was Zane's way of punishing her.

He'd been polite, but the passion - that raw connection they'd shared from day one was being held behind a steel barrier, like Zane was conditioning himself to walk away, expecting that she'd be unable to control her outbursts and lack of trust, therefore leaving him no choice but to go.

Erin raised her chin in determination. She'd show Zane that regardless of what was thrown in her direction and however much her past sabotaged her, from now on she trusted him. On *everything*.

All she could do was prove it and hope it wasn't too late.

'These men they've gone to meet - are they part of Zane's

original circle?' Erin asked. She already knew they were, but she had to keep talking to occupy her mind and stop it from going down roads she mustn't tread.

Like Hazel...

Zane had finally given her a brief outline of what had occurred during his meeting with that woman and even though Erin had been desperate for further information, she hadn't pushed for it. She wanted to know exactly what had been said. Had Hazel touched him? Had he touched *her...*?

But she hadn't asked. She'd swallowed the insecurity that the man she desperately loved wouldn't be the final one in a long line to betray her. It was what she'd promised herself that she would do to make this right.

Zane had given Hazel a phone and agreed to help her. He reckoned he believed what she'd said... Or had he given her a phone so they could meet up in secret?

Erin frowned. What if Hazel was a victim in this too? Perhaps thinking Zane planned to take Hazel for himself to get at Marco was wrong. It could be that Hazel getting in touch out of the blue was not to swap out her husband for the brother that now held the empire at all. It might be genuine.

Besides, at the moment there *was* no empire. Not until Zane reclaimed it. The plan of doing that by killing Marco had fallen by the wayside and now a different mode of achieving things was decided.

'Are you all right?'

Cav's question made Erin realise she was wringing her hands. 'I'm fine,' she lied.

Getting out of the chair she began clearing up the coffee table even though it didn't need it. Doing something shunted her mind off the ever revolving circle of doubt. Doubt about Zane. *About herself...*

Erin moved back to the window and aimlessly glanced through the net curtains. 'I wonder what these new headquarters are like? I'm interested in seeing them and...' She froze. *How long had that been there?*

'What is it?' Cav asked seeing Erin poised stiffly like a statue at the window.

'That car!' Erin hissed. 'The silver one that's been tailing Zane.' *It was also the same woman in the driver's seat...*

'The silver Golf?' Cav gasped, scrambling to his feet. He'd seen that car at the funeral this morning – they all had.

Parked only two doors down, Erin saw the woman's eyes trained on the house as clear as day. *What was she waiting for? Zane?*

Bolting, Erin ran towards the door. She'd had enough of this.

'Where are you going?' Cav yelled, racing after Erin.

'To see who the fuck she is!'

'You can't!' Cav grabbed Erin's arm. 'You're not to leave this house!' Like the others, he'd received Zane's instructions about Erin loud and clear. And *why...*

Erin snatched her arm out of Cav's grip. She knew she wasn't supposed to leave but this was her chance to find out what this stranger - this *beautiful* stranger, wanted with Zane.

Knowing she didn't stand a chance against Cav's strength and that he could easily overpower her and force her to remain in the house, Erin decided to resort to low tactics. It wasn't something she wanted to do to Cav or any of the men who had treated her so well, but she had no choice.

The desperate need to discover what threat the driver of the silver car meant, Erin kicked out, her aim at Cav's groin hitting the target.

'Sorry,' she muttered as Cav howled and doubled over. She hadn't wanted to hurt him, but her fevered brain had to know the truth. 'I'm really am sorry,' she repeated before yanking open the front door.

Flying down the path, Erin's heart crashed in her chest as she reached the silver car in record speed. Diving over the bonnet, she yanked the driver's door.

The door was locked. *Fucking locked!*

Erin hammered on the window, the shocked expression on

the gorgeous young woman inside, vivid. 'Who the hell are you and what do you want?

The woman started the engine, her eyes darting around in fright.

Erin may have thought 'woman', but this one was barely old enough to be behind the wheel. *Jesus Christ.* She hadn't been sent by Marco - this was to do with Zane. He was having a fling with a girl not even twenty years old?

Angry tears brewed in Erin's eyes, all reason deserting her. All she could see was the perfectly-shaped mouth; glossy hair; big eyes. *A stunner...*

Hurt suffocated her. 'Don't you dare drive off! Tell me what the hell you want or I'll fucking kill you!'

Hearing the accelerator revving, Erin threw herself back onto the bonnet. The next thing she knew she'd hit the deck, her knees thudding on the concrete. Flailing in confusion, she lashed out, only to find Cav pinning her to the pavement.

'What in Christ's name are you doing?' Cav growled, his body heavy on hers. 'You kick me in the bollocks and then race out here?'

As the screech of tyres thundered in Erin's ears, she pushed at Cav's chest, trying in vain to get out from underneath him. Her head twisted in the direction of the fleeing car. 'She's getting away! I need to know who she is!'

Dragged to her feet, Erin fought against Cav, wanting to give chase even though it was pointless.

'You could have got yourself killed!' Cav roared, manhandling Erin back inside the house. Sweating profusely, he shoved her into the sitting room. 'What is the matter with you?'

Erin dropped to her knees, choking sobs wracking her body. What *was* wrong with her? She'd done it again. Desperation and fear had won.

She wasn't like this - she could withstand *anything.* Anything, apart from the prospect of losing Zane.

Shaking his head in despair, Cav pulled his fingers through

his hair. Zane would not be happy about this. Whoever that woman was tailing him, Erin had just laid herself open and anything could have happened.

Now that woman had proof Erin lived here and if she *was* connected with Marco, then Erin was in more jeopardy than before.

There was no choice but to call Zane and interrupt the meeting.

THIRTY SIX

IT STARTED AS A RUMBLING RAGE within the soles of Marco's feet. The vibration pulsed against the soft leather insoles of his Italian shoes and gradually spread up the back of his calves, up through his torso, splitting off down his arms to reach the ends of his fingertips while simultaneously continuing up behind his eyeballs to buzz along every hair on his head.

He stood transfixed - frozen for what felt like months, although it was less than a few seconds before he became aware of the runner nervously scrutinising him.

The little scrote should be fucking nervous, Marco thought, because it was *his* fault.

If this skinny little shit hadn't been so desperate to show Sandler this... this *evidence*, then Marco would be blissfully unaware. However, there was nothing blissful about this.

Not knowing about it would have been worse, yet that point didn't dampen his urge to smash this shithead to the ground. *Trying to humiliate him was he?*

Marco snatched the phone out of the runner's hand, the man's arm recoiling so fast it was a miracle it didn't snap. And he might well snap it yet, depending on the answer to this question.

Slamming the young man against the wall, Marco increased the pressure on his windpipe, gaining a sliver of pleasure from the terror in the runner's bulging eyes.

How he wanted to hurt someone - *anyone.*

'Who else have you shown this to?' he snarled, his voice a low rumble emanating from the pits of hell. 'Who else has seen this?' *If this had been bandied around the pub...* 'Answer the fucking question!' Marco increased the pressure on the runner's throat with every second he was kept waiting.

'J-Just a couple of people. I...' Connor's trembling fingers searched for a space between Marco's crushing hand and his windpipe to gain a millimetre of breathing space.

'Speak up!' Marco raged, his face becoming redder. 'A couple of people? Who exactly?'

'C-Can't breathe... I...'

Tossing the offending phone to the floor, Marco wrapped a second hand around Connor's neck. 'You want to feel what it's like to suffocate, you little cunt?' he spat. 'Because you're about to find out. Answer my fucking question. And make sure you answer correctly otherwise I'll kill you!'

And he *would* kill him. If anyone thought it amusing or *contemplate* passing it along, then heads would roll. But no matter how many heads were removed, it wouldn't change that half of London would get to know about this. They probably already did...

Marco's anger reached fever pitch, spittle gathering in the corners of his mouth. 'You've had this photo since last night, yet didn't deem it important enough to show me?'

Connor's eyes rolled as he dragged air into his tortured lungs. 'Tel and Banjo said to speak to Sandler. I-I couldn't find him until just now, but I told no one else, I swear. I swear on my life, Mr Morelli. I...'

Marco quickly calculated what this meant. Tel and Banjo were enforcers and from what he could recall they were all right, but they still could have told others or people could have overheard. If they had, this would have travelled around the pub faster than the clap on a singles night.

Rage exploded exponentially in Marco's wired brain as he decided that he had to remove the possibility of this skinny twat further worsening the issue.

It didn't take much further pressure to cut off the remaining threads of Connor's life.

Connor made a couple of futile manoeuvres to grapple against Marco's massive hands, but the effort was half-baked. The moment the pressure increased and when the questions started to repeat he knew he was onto a lost cause.

It flickered through Connor's fading consciousness that this was the reason why Tel and Banjo had said to go to Sandler. Not that he'd have dreamt of approaching Marco. *No one* approached Marco Morelli uninvited, even with good news, let alone something like this.

How Connor wished that he hadn't taken that shortcut home yesterday. He wished even more that he hadn't captured the evidence that was behind removing his life.

Then his thoughts stopped.

Satisfied, Marco released his iron grip and watched indifferently as the man's body crumpled to the ground. *Sandler could clear that up, but what to do about this?*

Stooping to retrieve the mobile off the floor, Marco scowled at the scuff on the screen his hasty chucking of the device had caused. Rubbing his thumb over the scratch didn't remove it and the offending photograph remained displayed like poison on the mobile's screen.

That fucking sly cunt of a whore.

The sinews on Marco's neck were so taut he could pluck them.

There was no doubt about it. Even with a fucking guide dog he could see the unmistakable figure of Hazel in the shadows of a grotty alley. And the man in the picture with his back to the camera was Zane. Marco could recognise his brother from his shadow alone.

The bastard had his hand on Hazel's face. *An endearing*

touch after they'd fucked?

The grating noise of Marco's teeth made his already thumping head pound more

This was taken yesterday? Yesterday, whilst he'd been here at Luna making sure everything was ship shape so filming could commence that devious bitch had slipped out to meet Zane?

Marco stomped up and down the corridor, unable to pull his eyes away from the offending picture, the image burning his eyes.

Why the fuck was he paying guards to stand in the apartment if they were letting people come and go as they pleased?

More bloody useless traitors.

For fuck's sake. First Sonny, now his guards...

Who the fuck else?

Who was there he could trust? Anyone? It certainly wasn't Hazel…

Marco's teeth scraped together harder and faster.

How the hell had the bitch managed this?

Wait! This was Zane's doing, the bastard. He'd have made it his aim to go for Hazel, so what had he promised her?

Marco's face turned redder. He wanted to crush the phone and its contents to smithereens. But then he wouldn't have proof. And he was keeping this proof.

Yeah, this was just Zane's style. What else would his brother think of but this? Attempting to take over his firm wasn't enough, so now he'd come for Hazel?

Marco let out a guttural roar. Hazel was *his* property. His fucking wife. He'd bought her and she belonged to *him*. Zane couldn't be able to bear that, could he?

Because who didn't want Hazel?

Everybody wanted her.

Marco's eyes narrowed to slits. Zane might want to steal his wife as well as his firm, but neither of those things would happen.

Zane had instigated this - no doubt playing on Hazel's

vulnerability after losing her father. But by his wife's face on the photograph, she wasn't averse to the idea…

Sweating with rage, Marco shoved the phone in his pocket and made his way down the corridor to the car park where Hazel waited.

Snorting coke from his silver vial as he went, Marco manoeuvred his face into a neutral position. Acting like nothing was amiss was difficult, but the second he got Hazel back to the penthouse the slut would wish she'd never been born.

As for Zane, well, he'd be wishing for a lot more than death to take him by the time this had finished.

• • • •

SO FAR things had gone well at the meeting. Having thirty more men Zane trusted back in the fold made a huge difference.

Now with this extra muscle and the headquarters on his old turf the correct side of the river, he had enough manpower to establish a new firm.

And no, he shouldn't have to. His original one should have been intact and ready to pick back up. But it wasn't. And never would be.

But now he could make progress. *Real* progress.

This knowledge pushed the nagging worry of the presence of that silver car at the funeral earlier to one side.

Now he was getting somewhere – *really* getting somewhere. But one thing he wouldn't do was purposely become a rival in Marco's line of work. He wanted nothing to do with the seediness of exploiting women.

Folding his arms, Zane looked around his fledgling firm in satisfaction, knowing it would double in size by this time next week. Things were looking good. *Very* good.

'Right, fellas. The aim is to concentrate on what the Morellis always did best. Security and trade.' He watched his men nod. In translation, 'security' and 'trade' meant 'extortion' and 'guns'. Both of which were extremely lucrative and the mainstay of what the firm had always been about.

Marco had allowed that side of things to deteriorate and therefore it was up for the taking. It would require little effort to move in on satellite firms who had grabbed the opportunity to step in during Marco's foolish change of plans. 'It won't take us long to establish a foothold back on these quarters,' Zane continued, his enthusiasm growing. 'We'll be in a strong position sooner than expected.'

'Leaving Marco to flounder in his own shit,' Tiger grinned.

Zane nodded. 'Shortly, certain things will be put in place to take Marco out of the picture long enough to make that easier.'

His father's surgeon, Mr Solenzo, had given word that the majority of the trafficked women were recovering well. Unfortunately, a further three had succumbed to their injuries from the shootout, but that still left several to speak out and drop Marco in the shit with the authorities. And do it long enough to enable Zane to take full control.

'The police can only look the other way so much where Marco is concerned,' Zane said. 'Solenzo has also been told that for the women's part in this, they will be looked upon favourably by the Home Office when granting them permanent residence in England.'

Marco would wiggle himself off the hook eventually. He had too many judges in his pocket not to, but it would buy the time needed. When Marco got back on the street, Zane would have reclaimed the territory and the remnants of men still left at Luna would be disbanded. Or dismembered...

'Realistically how long do you think this will take?' Leo asked, voicing the question every man in the room wanted to know.

Zane chewed his lip. 'Providing we catch Marco off guard, I reckon a few weeks.' He smiled widely. 'The vital thing is that no one else gets picked off.' And that included any of them - especially Erin. But with Hazel's help over Marco's whereabouts and plans they stood a good chance compared to working blind.

Suddenly startled by the buzzing of his mobile, Zane

hurried to pull it from his pocket. The only people not present that could be calling were Cav, Erin or Hazel.

He looked at the screen, worry bubbling. *Cav.*

'Everything all right?' *If Marco had got wind of their location and the house had been stormed in his absence...*

Listening, Zane's face twisted. 'What? Are you serious? Fuck!'

He jumped to his feet. 'I've got to go. We'll reconvene later. I'll send word out as to when.'

Grabbing his crash helmet, Zane dashed from the room.

For Christ's sake! What had Erin been thinking?

THIRTY SEVEN

'NO!' HAZEL SCREAMED. 'Marco! Please! Stop!'

'Stop?' Marco roared. 'I ain't even fucking started yet!' His ferocious face pushed into Hazel's, the urge to rip the prettiness off her overbearing. 'Think I wouldn't find out? How long has this been going on for?'

'H-How long has *what* been going on for?' Hazel blathered, her eyes darting everywhere but to Marco's.

'Don't ask stupid questions, you lying cow!' Marco seethed, tightening his grip on Hazel's hair.

Hazel swallowed dryly. *Fuck. He knew.* How the hell did he know? Who told him? Was it Zane? Was he onside with Marco and their very public rift merely a scam to gain more notoriety?

To no avail, her fingers clawed against Marco's hand and she squealed as another clump of her hair extensions were pulled from her scalp.

She'd known the second Marco got in the car at Luna that something had happened. He'd roared at Damon to *'get the hell out and find that Erin bitch'*, then driven at breakneck speed back to the penthouse. Despite her attempts to make conversation, he hadn't said a word and the silence in the car remained oppressive, punctuated only by the snorting sound as Marco hoovered cocaine from his silver vial as they sped along.

With Marco's erratic driving, Hazel truly believed they would crash. How she now wished they had. At least there would have been a small chance she could have escaped with her life.

Now there was little.

She yelped with fright as Marco flipped her onto her back and sat astride her, giving her no choice but to stare into his manic eyes. He looked like a crazed rabid animal, intent on killing.

His prey being *her*.

Although his obsession with her which had run for so many years had blown hot and cold since their honeymoon, there was not one shred left of anything now on his face, apart from anger and white-hot fury.

Hazel screamed again as Marco shoved something into her face. *Was it a knife? Oh God! No! It was a phone! What the...*

'Who's this then, if it's not you?' Marco yelled, his eyes bulging. Jabbing his finger on the phone's screen, he pushed it closer. 'Are you telling me this isn't you? The whore's expression on your face is the very same face that my bastard brother is touching in this picture!'

Marco's spittle landed on Hazel's top lip. She wanted to wipe it away but he was kneeling on her hands.

'*That* is my brother,' Marco snarled.

'N-No it's not. I don't know your brother... That's...'

Smashing the phone into Hazel's mouth, her yelp of pain was muffled as she swallowed a mouthful of blood and at least one of her teeth.

'Even from the back I know what my fucking brother looks like and that is *him*.' Marco launched the phone across the living area. 'Was he a good shag? Tell me that! Was he?'

Hazel spluttered as blood continued to pour down her throat. 'Nnnngh!' she mumbled, the pain agonising.

'You could have had *everything* with me!' Marco raged. 'I

adored you. I didn't even hurt you for fucking all those men in your films. How lenient a man does that make me?' Reaching into his pocket, his eyes narrowed. 'I've killed women for less than what you've done. A lot fucking less!'

Hazel's muffled screaming became even more unintelligible. Now it was definite. Marco *had* killed that woman on his balcony, plus more besides. Now *she* would be added to that list...

Making contact with Zane had made things worse, not better.

Hazel's eyes darted around the room. There was no one about. Marco had sent all of his grunts away the minute they returned to the penthouse. Not that any of them would have come to her aid.

From where her hands remained trapped behind her back, her fingers sought for the phone in her back pocket. There was only one number stored on it. *Zane's*. If she could alert him, would he come?

Now she knew it couldn't be him to tell Marco of their meeting, but in that case, who had set her up and taken that photograph?

'Are you listening, whore?' Grasping more of Hazel's hair, Marco slammed her head onto the floor, her skull making a sickening thump on the polished surface. 'My brother thinks he can have you because he wants everything I've got.' he ranted, his words jumbling together, his brain out of control. 'And you want him? Why? To spite me? Has he got a bigger cock? Is that it?'

He laughed, the sound strangely eerie and forced. 'Let's see how much he'll want you now...' His fists began driving into Hazel's face.

Hearing the crunch of splintering bone, coupled with flashing lights behind her eyes, Hazel struggled to remain conscious and she wished she hadn't when she saw the glint of metal in Marco's hand. *Was that a knife?*

'Noooompth!' she wailed, her smashed mouth unable to

form coherent words. *Stay conscious, stay conscious*, she willed herself. There might be a chance to take Marco by surprise. It was unlikely, but it was all she could cling to rather than succumb to the warm and enticing hands of unconsciousness that beckoned, becoming stronger with each crack to her face.

'If you believe Zane will want a cunt like you, looking like *this*, then I doubt you'll find him receptive. Always been a vain bastard has my brother.' Marco slid his tongue along the blunt edge of the blade in his hand and licked his lips. 'I wonder what it would be like to cut off your tits? Would silicon pour out or doesn't it work like that? Hmm, I'm not sure... Shall we try?'

Hazel fumbled with her phone through her trousers. She couldn't work it out. It was getting darker and darker in her own mind.

'Nah, do you know what? Before I do that, I'll do this...' With his one hand holding Hazel's throat, his other hand got to work with his knife, haphazardly hacking at her long blonde hair. 'I've always wondered what you'd look like with a crew cut.'

As Marco's manic laughter resounded around the room, Hazel stopped fighting the onslaught, leaving the part of her not paralysed by pain and fright frantically searching for a way to stop him - even for a moment. Just enough to allow her to make that call and escape.

And then she saw it...

She just needed to wait for the right time.

Heart clamouring, tears flowed down Hazel's ruined face as Marco continued hacking at her hair. Then he undid the zip of his trousers…

'Time to remind you to whom you belong,' he growled, his eyes glinting with a mixture of rage and misplaced lust.

Hazel closed her eyes. She knew Marco liked it when she acted submissive. She'd give him what he wanted this last time and hope she got the opening needed to take the only chance she'd get.

If she didn't, or it didn't work, she was dead. But she would be anyway soon.

As Marco forced himself inside her, rutting on her at speed, Hazel watched through her one eye that hadn't quite yet swollen shut for him to go into the zone. Through the agonising pain, she forced her body to match his movements. *If she could move forwards slightly.*

As if plucking the thought from Hazel's mind, Marco yanked her up astride him, giving her the leverage to reach forward.

'Ride me, slut!' he growled. Throwing his head back, his sinews tightened and his eyes hooded with the approaching rush of orgasm.

Seizing the moment, Hazel lurched forwards, giving her the additional reach to grab a crystal ashtray from the table. Slamming it sideways with all the strength she had left, it connected with Marco's temple with a dull thud.

• • • •

'SORRY, MATE. I didn't want to disturb your meeting, but you needed to know.' Cav glanced awkwardly between Zane and Erin. 'I'll leave you to it.'

Nodding, Zane waited until Cav left the room, then sank into the chair opposite Erin. Resting his chin in his steepled fingers, he studied her silently.

'I couldn't help it,' Erin said. 'She just turned up. That's twice she's been here casing the house. Or you... So I took the opportunity to find out who she was. I didn't mean to cause an issue.'

Cause an issue? Zane thought bitterly. *From what Cav said, Erin had done a little bit more than that.* 'Kicking one of my men in the groin and screaming blue murder outside for all and sundry to overhear is a bit more than wanting to find out who someone is.' *Not to mention that she could have got herself killed...*

From what else he'd been told, Erin had more of an issue that this woman was something to do with *him* and him alone.

'I told you that you were not to leave the house under any circumstances.'

Erin watched Zane's hands clench and unclench into fists. He was furious. 'I'm just trying to help. Sitting here not doing anything isn't how I work. I...'

'Don't give me that shit again!' Zane got to his feet and paced the room, his hand rubbing the back of his neck 'Fuck!' he hissed between clenched teeth. 'Does it look like I want anything to happen to you? Does it not cross your mind that I'm trying to protect you? It was bad enough when I thought you'd been gunned down at Luna, yet you fight me every step of the way. For God's sake. I'm trying to keep you safe, Erin!'

Erin blinked. 'I'm a big girl now,' she sniped. 'Why wouldn't I be safe?'

'You really don't get it, do you?' Zane seethed. Despite making the decision not to tell Erin the risk to her had now heightened, after her actions today there was little choice. 'My brother's now aware that you were the mole at Luna. *And* that you were instrumental in releasing those women.'

Erin froze. 'How? Who told him that? Sandler didn't know who I was, I know he didn't.'

'Marco worked it out from your description. He remembered that photograph.'

Erin's mouth fell open. 'But Sonny was adamant th…'

'Sonny was wrong,' Zane snapped. 'My brother isn't quite as forgetful as people presume.'

'Shit!' Erin hissed. 'I didn't realise. I...'

'No you didn't, did you? But if you'd taken what I said at face value, rather than coming to your own conclusions and making me spell it out, things wouldn't be so bad,' Zane said, a nerve twitching in his scarred cheek.

Erin reached for Zane's hand but he moved it away. Crestfallen, she retreated. 'Who told you Marco knows I was the mole?'

'Hazel,' Zane said matter-of-factly. 'She heard Sandler getting clear instructions to dispatch you.'

'Hazel?' Erin failed to stop the roll of her eyes. 'And you believed her? Are you sure she didn't tell you that to gain points for herself?'

'Grow up!' Zane snapped. 'Why would she do that?'

'Why *wouldn't* she?' Erin countered. 'Besides, why would I suddenly become the prime target over you?'

Zane shook his head. 'If you can't work that out by now, there's no point in explaining.' Even if he told Erin that Marco would go for her because he'd know it would hurt him more than anything else, she wouldn't believe it. She didn't believe anything anymore. 'You're not to leave the house again. Do not make me waste more men having to guard you like a prisoner.'

'But isn't that exactly what I am?' Erin sniped. 'Forget about Hazel for a minute, if you can! Don't you want to know who the woman in the silver car is? Or do you already know? Something else you're not telling me about, perhaps?'

Sighing heavily, Zane moved towards the door. 'Fuck this!'

'Zane! Wait, I...'

Pulling his ringing mobile from his pocket, Zane turned his back. 'Hazel? What is it?'

Erin stiffened. *Hazel again? What now?*

'Fuck! Stay exactly where you are. It's going to be all right. I'm on my way.' Ending the call, Zane snatched up his crash helmet.

'What's happening? Mislaid her nail varnish?' Erin muttered. *Was this shit ever going to stop?*

Swinging around, Zane cut Erin in a look that burned her skin. 'Actually, Hazel's been badly attacked. Marco's all but killed her, so I'm going to fetch her. And you, Erin, need to stop being such a fucking bitch because it doesn't suit you.'

• • • •

'WHAT THE HELL'S HAPPENED?' Damon gasped, rushing to kneel by Marco's side. He tried not to look at his boss's flaccid penis hanging from his trousers and instead concentrated on the cut on his temple and the worrying clumps of blonde hair sitting in larger pools of congealing blood on the floor. 'Has Zane been here? Fuck! I…'

'It wasn't Zane, you prick!' Marco slurred, downing another brandy. 'It was that bitch, Hazel. She's been at it with my brother.'

Damon flinched. 'So you killed her?' This was good news, but it would prove difficult to brush under the carpet. Luna had signed several contracts with adult film brokers for new Lisa Tequila movies and if they weren't delivered there would be more than one lawsuit hitting them over breach of contract. 'Christ, Marco. We...'

'I haven't killed her. I just taught her a few lessons she was in dire need of, that's all. But the slag went and clumped me.' Marco nodded towards the glass ashtray lying on the floor. 'It must have knocked me out because when I came round, she'd gone.'

'Gone?' Damon gaped. 'Gone where? Why didn't the guards stop her?'

'Because they weren't bloody here!' Marco staggered to his feet and shoved himself back into his trousers. 'Stop asking me stupid questions. Fucking find her. You can guess where she's gone. Running to my brother!'

He paced the room, grimacing as each step jarred the throbbing pain in his head. It was difficult to take on board that the vacuous bitch he'd spent years hankering after had turned on him quicker than a tossed coin. He felt like hyperventilating. 'I want you and every man in my employ on the search. I want the location of my brother, that tart Erin, plus I want the stupid woman I married. And I want them *now*! It's not difficult, so I don't know why you've failed in locating them so far! London ain't that big of a place!'

Damon frowned. Actually, London *was* big. Being the capital city, it was hardly a rural hamlet with a population of twenty-five, but he'd say nothing. 'I'll get onto it straightaway.' He had no clue how but he had to start somewhere. 'Then what will you do?'

'I'll tell you that once you've done your fucking job,' Marco snarled. Swinging around, he cut Damon a death stare. 'Oh, and Sandler, don't think about mentioning the parts about Hazel and my brother or about her clumping me to anyone.'

He didn't want it becoming public knowledge that Zane had fucked his wife, nor the worse humiliation that he'd been floored by a bird. 'By the way, Hazel's got short hair now. She fancied a change.'

Damon nodded, his eyes tracking back to the clumps of yellow nylon lying on the floor, doubting whether it had been Hazel's choice. In all honesty, he wouldn't go out of his way to look for her. The further away that dog was, the better. He'd be concentrating on Erin because he owed her *personally*.

THIRTY EIGHT

'JESUS CHRIST!' Leo gasped to Tiger as Zane led a half-naked woman into the Thames Canning Works. *So this was the great Lisa Tequila?*

His eyes moved over the swollen mess of the woman's face and the dried blood caked around her mouth and nose. What was left of her trademark blonde hair, extensions or not, was reduced to a scraggy mess of tufts scattered between completely bald patches - the red and bloodied scalp a testament to where her hair had been physically yanked from her head.

Even though she was only wrapped in a small towel that failed to adequately cover her, Leo didn't entertain the thought of looking anywhere else over the famed body which so many men hankered over. Now was not the time and neither was it the most pressing issue. This bird was in a bad way. His senses prickled with indignation and anger. Marco had made a right mess of her. It was safe to say that Lisa Tequila's career was over.

'Where's Erin?' Zane muttered, gingerly steering Hazel who was now shaking uncontrollably, over to a makeshift bed he'd instructed to be set up in a quiet room out of the way and far from the eyes of the rest of the men. 'Did you tell Cav to bring her?'

Leo nodded. 'Yes. I called him as soon as you called me.' He glanced at his watch. 'They'll be here any minute.'

Zane's lips flattened. He hoped Erin had changed her attitude about this since earlier, but he'd had no choice but to bring Hazel in. This poor woman needed tending. Married to Marco or not, she was in a horrific state and no one here would be as good as Erin in tending to a female's wounds.

He rested his hand on Hazel's shoulder, dreading to think what else his brother had done. His anger grew, ashamed to be connected via DNA to anyone who could treat a woman - their *wife* - such as this. And to know she'd received this beating because Marco had got word they had met up made his skin crawl with guilt.

'Are you sure Erin will be able to deal with this?' Tiger frowned. 'I mean, looking at her, won't she need that surgeon bloke?'

Zane felt Hazel's body stiffen under his hand. 'The last thing she needs is another bloke's hands on her,' he spat. 'Erin will be best for now. At least until we work out if there's more damage here than is obvious.'

The other thing that was obvious - *glaringly* obvious, was that by now Marco would know of Hazel's disappearance. It didn't take rocket science to guess she would have come to *him* for protection. This meant he had to move on Marco sooner than expected. At this precise moment, his brother would have the whole city scouring for Hazel's whereabouts, as well as his. 'Up the ante with keeping an eye out for anyone watching. The risk is even higher now.'

Zane couldn't breathe easy until Erin and Cav arrived. If the woman in the silver car *was* in some way connected with Marco, then their whereabouts would already be known.

'I've already put things in motion,' Tiger said. 'I've primed all our weapons and they're ready to go.'

Zane nodded. 'Good. Brief the rest of the men about the situation and get them stationed around the place. Put them everywhere. Every possible entry point.'

And there were loads of those. Half of this building hadn't even been checked for loose windows, smashed doors - that sort of thing, yet.

No building left sitting empty for years hadn't received its fair share of kids breaking in or squatters and drug addicts using it as a place to lay low. Judging by the filth they'd waded through so far as the rooms had been slowly cleared one by one, there was plenty to prove that many people had gained access over the years. Thanks to the extra hands on deck, more rooms had now been readied but there were still lots which hadn't been touched. Thank God he'd got extra men on board otherwise this would be a hopeless situation.

Hearing the door open, everyone tensed. Even Hazel managed a strangulated shriek.

Zane immediately whipped out the pistol lodged in his waistband and then relaxed seeing Cav and Erin.

• • • •

'THIS IS A NEW BOWL OF FRESH WATER, so we'll get this bit cleaned up next.' Erin gently dabbed wet cotton wool on Hazel's swollen cheek. One eye was completely swollen shut, the blackened flesh around it developing vividly. The other eye wasn't far behind, but a small slit allowed some vision to still remain.

Hearing Hazel's sharp intake of breath as the cotton wool made contact, Erin paused. 'I'm sorry. I'm being as gentle as I can.'

And that wasn't all she was sorry about. The minute she'd clapped eyes on the woman Zane had dashed off to rescue, her guilt weighed heavily.

She squeezed the excess water from the cotton wool. She couldn't have been more wrong about this. Zane was 100 per cent right about Hazel being badly attacked. The stress and suspicion Erin had held for days fell away the minute she'd seen the pitiful, trembling figure of Hazel Grimes cowering in the corner, curled into a ball on the makeshift bed like a broken animal.

Marco so needed to die for this - for *everything*. But the most important thing now was to help this woman - even if her very presence cranked up the risk factor tenfold.

'Right.' Erin threw the bloodied cotton wool in the bin. 'That's your face done as much as it can be for now, so let's have a look at what other damage that bastard has caused.'

Hazel had been in a catatonic state the entire time Erin was cleaning her wounds. Short of the occasional wince and muffled yelp, she'd stared glassy eyed into nothing, her mind focused on something far away. She'd said nothing. No response to anything. But Erin's most recent words propelled Hazel back to the living.

Her body stiffened and she attempted to pull the thin sheet tighter around her body, the shaking of her fingers making it impossible.

'Don't worry. No one will come in,' Erin soothed. 'It's just me and you.' Tugging gently at the thin sheet, she pulled it down, her own sharp intake of breath loud in the silent room.

It wasn't just that Hazel's exposed breasts were the largest she'd ever seen which caused the shock - it was that they were covered with bite marks - some superficial, others deep. And the bites and scratches didn't stop there. They trailed all the way down Hazel's flat abdomen over her thighs to where a trail of blood seeped out, leaving a patch between her legs. 'What the fuck has that animal done?' she gasped, not expecting a response.

'He wanted to kill me,' Hazel whimpered, her voice a mere wisp. 'And he would have, had I not escaped.' She grabbed Erin's hand. 'He'll kill *you* next. That's what he wants.' Her smashed lips trembled. 'I should have listened. I-I'm so stupid... So greedy. I thought I had it made... All those women... H-He trafficked women and killed many.'

Erin nodded. 'I know.' *She knew all of it.* 'But you're safe now,' she said, knowing that not to be entirely true. None of them were safe - less now than before.

'I'll never work again!' Hazel murmured, her voice devoid of emotion. 'I saw my reflection. I look like a monster. I've got nothing.'

Erin began cleaning up the horrific bite marks over Hazel's body. 'When did you start doing this?' she asked, trying to keep Hazel talking being as the woman looked like she might pass out. 'I mean, when did you start making films?'

'Fourteen. It was my father's idea.' Hazel's voice turned bitter. 'It's all I've really ever known.'

Erin hid her shock as much as she could. *Fourteen?*

'I trusted my father. I... I thought he was doing everything for my benefit. I believed him.' Hazel winced as she attempted a frown. 'I know now it was all about him... never about me. And Marco... that was my father's idea too. My father just wanted money. He didn't care about me at all.'

Erin wanted to say that couldn't be true, but Christ! Fourteen? 'It's unbelievable that a father would want their daughter doing something like that. You... you must have hated it.'

Hazel gripped Erin's hand harder and stared at her through the slit of her one slightly open eye. 'But that's just it. I *didn't*! Until a few days ago I thought things were great. That makes me no better than my father *or* Marco.'

Erin bristled. 'That's not true.' She'd got this woman utterly wrong. 'You're as much a victim of these men as anyone. More, even.'

'No.' Hazel shook her head, stopping with a wince. 'You're wrong. I had everything planned. I didn't give a toss about anything apart from money and status.' A lone tear rolled down her bruised face. 'I didn't care about anything and after I found out that my marriage was pointless, my plan was to take Zane and cash in on him instead. Even up until today.'

Erin stiffened. *So she'd been correct about part of it?* 'Right, and…?'

'He wasn't interested,' Hazel sobbed. 'And now I see why.

Zane has you - a *real* woman rather than a plastic monstrosity. But then... then something happened...'

Erin's heart lurched. 'What?' Had Zane betrayed her after all? Had he fallen for this woman's once perfect looks? Even if Hazel classed herself as plastic, most men wouldn't turn down a chance with the fabled Lisa Tequila.

'When Zane made it clear he didn't want me, everything became clear. I've been conditioned. I was wrong. I've screwed up and made my own grave with my greed. Then… then the dam broke.' Hazel's breath caught in hiccupped sobs. 'It broke right then and there on the floor of a bloody filthy viaduct. It's never ever happened before but I realised the truth. I guess I'd always known it deep down, but shoved it away. The bullshit, the disappointment in the years of being treated like meat – the whole lot just poured from nowhere out of me. I knew at that moment I'd never be the same again. *Could* never be the same again.'

Oh God, Erin thought. There it was: the truth in black and white. Zane really *did* love her - as in, *truly*. Her own paranoid had trashed everything. She gritted her teeth. 'It's not too late to build a different life, Hazel. You can put the past behind you and start again.'

Erin hoped those words applied to *her* too. She had a lot to fix. She wasn't sure whether it was too late for her and Zane, but she would try her best. This time, she would do it like she'd promised in the first place. No more fancy dress, paranoia or hang ups, courtesy of her past.

Hazel shook her head despondently. 'It's too late for me. I've been dreadful and look where it's got me. I wouldn't know where to start anyway. I... I've never known anything but manipulating people for my own gains.'

It was Erin's turn to shake her head. 'It's *not* too late.' Whether *she* was too late in putting things right between her and Zane was one thing, but that didn't mean that she couldn't sort *this*. 'I'm going to help you. I'll get you through this somehow and make sure you can start again.'

'Y-You really mean that?' Hazel whimpered.

Erin nodded. 'Yes, I do.' *And she did.* She would put Hazel Grimes back together again and do whatever was required in order to stop Marco Morelli from doing this to anyone else again.

And to do that, she would trust Zane in whatever he needed for as long as he let her.

THIRTY NINE

LEAVING HIS FLAT and stepping into the late morning sun, Damon really didn't want to go back to Luna. It didn't feel like he'd been anywhere else apart from there or the penthouse recently, especially by the time he'd finally returned home last night. Thanks to Marco's worsening rage and erratic behaviour it had been past 2 a.m. before he'd got back. What the man thought to achieve by smashing up the living area of the penthouse, then storming around downing more brandy and cocaine whilst everyone else cleared up, Damon didn't know.

Yet the minute everything was back to normal, Marco had done it again. Not once, but *three* times...

Damon ground his cigarette butt into the pavement, thinking the mangled dogend was reminiscent of how his life felt right now. And he was *still* no closer to the position of second-in-command.

Marco had refused to get the dent in his temple looked at too. Getting clumped there was dangerous - it could cause all manner of problems. Not that anyone would notice if Marco became more unhinged. The guy was like a bag of loose gunpowder standing millimetres away from some fucker flicking matches.

Damon continued on his way along the road. He wasn't expected back at work until lunchtime, but that didn't come close to making up for his nil hours of sleep.

And if the smashed up penthouse incident on repeat wasn't bad enough, being forced to spend a further four hours driving around London afterwards with Marco sitting in his passenger seat, insisting on finding his wife, had been.

He scowled. Unsurprisingly, they hadn't found Hazel. She *had* to be with Zane. But without yet knowing where Zane was living, it was like looking for a needle in a haystack.

Did Marco understand that? No. All he'd got was a round of abuse about how pointless and incompetent everyone was. *Him*, in particular.

Well, Damon thought, sparking up yet another cigarette. *He* wasn't incompetent, regardless of what Marco thought.

He glanced up at the Blacksmith's Arms as he walked past. He had no intention of finding Hazel. If he never saw that pretentious cow again it would be too soon. But he *would* find Erin Langley. That was priority.

After Hazel's stunt, Marco had temporarily forgotten about his instructions to locate and remove Zane's bit on the side, but he'd remember eventually. And when he did, the fact that she was not dead and Zane was still out there would undoubtedly be *his* fault again.

But, Damon thought as he backtracked to pull open the door of the Blacksmith's Arms, he'd find Erin and by doing that, find Zane. And, if he was correct, which he reckoned he was - he'd also locate Hazel...

Everybody would be happy. None more so than *him*.

Damon had many men on the lookout. He'd already upped the search for Marco's elusive brother and his tart and he'd step that up further this afternoon. But before doing that he'd have a couple of pints. Marco wouldn't miss him for another hour.

Striding to the bar, Damon glared at the barman and slammed a fiver down on the grubby bar top. 'Pint of Stella.'

The barman eyed Damon warily. 'There was a geezer in

here just now asking after you.'

Damon scowled. *Not Marco?* The boss wouldn't lower himself to step foot in this shithole. But if someone had been sent to chase his whereabouts already, then maybe stopping for a couple of jars wasn't the best idea after all?

As his pint of Stella was deposited on the soggy beer towel, Damon changed his mind. *Fuck it. He needed a drink.*

Snatching the pint up, the liquid slopped over the side of the glass and up his arm. Damon took a long swig. 'Who was asking?' If it wasn't one of the enforcers then he'd chance his luck and stay for a few. 'Is he still here?'

The barman shrugged. 'It was a skinny runty-looking fella. And no, I think he left.'

Damon concentrated on slurping at his pint. By that description, it wasn't one of the enforcers so he didn't care either way who it was.

'I stand corrected.' The barman nodded behind Damon. 'He's back.'

Groaning inwardly, Damon turned around to see one of Marco's runners. He raised an eyebrow. 'Yeah?'

'Mr Sandler?' The runner fidgeted from foot to foot. 'I was hoping to catch you. Can I have a word?'

Damon eyed the nervous young man. He half-recognised the lad but couldn't remember his name. It wasn't surprising the bloke was nervous. Just about everyone at Luna had heard about what happened to Connor yesterday.

Downing the rest of his pint, Damon signalled to the barman for a top up and then jerked his head for the runner to follow him away from the bar. He sighed inwardly, supposing he'd better hear this bloke out. Bullshit like this was something he'd have to get used to once he was officially second-in-command. 'What is it, erm... I can't remember your name.'

'Russell, sir,' the runner gabbled. 'I wasn't sure what to do. I...'

'About what?'

'Well, erm...' Russell faltered. 'After what happened with...

erm... you know... After yesterday, I didn't know whether to... whether I should... erm...'

'Oh, get to the fucking point!' Damon's fresh pint was waiting on the bar and he wanted to drink it. 'If you've got something to say, then get on with it.'

'I wanted to tell you off the record, rather than erm... doing it at Luna... erm... in case...'

'Yeah, yeah.' Damon flapped his hand. *In case Marco happened to be there and took it upon himself to strangle another young runner for no apparent reason?* 'What is it then... Russell? I need to get on.'

Russell leant closer and Damon instinctively stepped back. He didn't like people in his personal space. Especially those smelling of last night's curry.

'I think I saw Lisa Tequila yesterday,' Russell said under his breath.

Damon froze. 'What? Where?'

'I thought it was her... but then again, it might not have been...'

'Christ! Was it or not?' Damon spat.

'Well, it looked like her. Sort of... Except with short hair. I only got a quick glimpse before she was lifted into a van,' Russell continued. 'I thought it strange for a van to be around the back of the complex near the bins, but then it disappeared.'

Damon rolled his eyes. 'And that's it?'

'No! I saw the driver and I'm sure it was Zane Morelli.'

Damon almost choked. *He knew it.* Zane had picked Hazel up from the penthouse and taken her into hiding, the cheeky cunt. So Zane had Hazel, but no one knew where. *Shit.* It was best Marco remained unaware of this until he had more information. 'What sort of van was it?'

Russell grinned, pleased his information was being taken seriously. 'A Transit.'

'Did you get the reg?' Damon asked. 'If we have that, then...'

'No, but I followed the van,' Russell whispered. 'It went to the old Thames Canning Works on Rydon Street. I couldn't go further than the gate, but I saw *him* get out - the brother, Zane, carrying the woman who might have been Lisa. She had a hood over her head and was wrapped in a weird towel thing. They went inside.' He began searching his pockets for his phone. 'I took a picture. It's not very clear, but...'

Looking up as his phone was snatched from his hand, Russell realised Damon Sandler had disappeared and the pub door was left flapping in his wake.

• • • •

'HAZEL CAN'T STAY at the canning works,' Erin said, watching Zane hammer out text message after text message on his phone.

He'd been more civil last night after seeing how she'd dealt with Hazel, but he was still cool towards her. Unsurprising really, considering the pressure on him to turn this fast escalating situation around. Her lack of faith about him wouldn't be put to bed overnight, either. She had a lot to prove. 'Zane,' she pressed. 'I said that Haz...'

'I heard.' Zane glanced up from his phone. 'She'll be all right. I left Cav with her last night and there's men guarding the works.' *But that was another issue*. What Cav had mentioned earlier, he also had to deal with. There were more things linked here than he'd believed.

'It's not that Hazel doesn't have enough people around her which bothers me,' Erin explained. 'Although, I suspect being in that dingy place with strange men isn't helping, but she's in a worse state than you think.'

Placing his phone down, Zane gave Erin his full attention. 'What do you mean?'

'Hazel's injuries are bad,' Erin continued. 'No offence, but that place of yours is filthy. She's got open wounds and nowhere to wash. She's got a broken cheekbone - possibly a fractured jaw and broken ribs too.' She sighed. 'I cleaned her up as best as I could, but the rest is way out of my depth. She needs to see that surgeon who's with the trafficked women. I can go with her when that happens.'

Zane's eyes narrowed. 'I don't understand you. This time yesterday you hated Hazel, yet now you're acting like you care?'

Erin had the decency to avert her eyes. 'Like I said when we got back last night, I was wrong and you were right. Hazel is broken mentally - *completely* broken. She admitted these past few days have changed her attitude and with that, her original plans.' She dared to slightly smile. 'Had that not been the case then my opinion *would* have been correct.'

Zane's face hardened. 'You have to get a dig in, don't you? It doesn't seem like *your* attitude has changed.' Seeing Erin's face drop, he softened slightly. 'Okay, I'll sort something out and get Mr Solenzo to take a look at Hazel over the next few days.'

'You don't quite understand,' Erin pushed. 'I promised her I wouldn't say anything, but it's too important not to... Hazel needs to see your surgeon now. She'll need a tetanus too, otherwise she could get seriously infected.'

'What are you talking about?' Zane frowned. 'I know Marco gave her one hell of a beating, but...'

'You haven't seen the raw bite marks all over her though, have you? They're everywhere!' Erin cried, gesturing to her chest. 'Many are deep. Plus, I think she has internal damage...'

'That bastard!' Zane hissed, his hatred for his brother multiplying.

'I suggest we take her to your surgeon's practice,' Erin said. 'I know it's a huge risk, but the state she's in we can't allow her to remain at the canning place. I'll stay here with her in the interim. If you can take me to collect Hazel, someone can take us to the surgeon. Doing that will bring no more risk to anyone.'

Zane's expression grew more solemn. 'That's where I think you're wrong. I was going to suggest you moved out and...'

'What?' Erin cried, horrified. 'I know I've screwed up and that you won't trust my word overnight, but I promised I'd trust you from now on. I don't want to lose you, Zane.' *There*. That was the most honest she'd been about her feelings for a long time, but would it be enough? Was she being selfish in expecting how she felt to come into play with everything else going on?

Zane chewed his lip. 'I need to tell you about the woman in the silver car. I haven't been on the level.'

Erin's mouth fell open, her heart thumping. 'W-What do you mean?' Was Zane about to admit that beautiful woman was who he really wanted?

'I meant move out more for your own safety. I think you were right and that the woman *is* connected to Marco.' Zane reached for another cigarette. 'I didn't think she was, but things aren't adding up.'

Erin's panic calmed. *Was it wrong to feel exhilarated about this disclosure? If Zane believed that woman was linked with Marco, then he wasn't planning to...*

'I first saw her watching me a while ago,' Zane admitted. 'I've seen her several times since on top of the times *you've* seen her. She was even watching me at my father's grave.'

'Who is she?'

'That's the point. I don't know, but she was here again last night as well as at Lewis's funeral.' Zane stubbed his newly lit cigarette out. He hadn't even wanted it. 'Plus, Cav saw her watching the house again when you both left to come to the canning works.'

Erin's eyebrows shot up. 'I never saw her. I'd...'

'Cav didn't tell you because he didn't want you accosting her again. I reckon she's watching us on behalf of Marco, therefore he knows where we are - where *you* are. That's why I need you to remain out of sight.'

'Hazel said Marco wants me killed as priority,' Erin muttered, her voice far away. 'God, I've been so stupid. I thought...'

'I'll get to the bottom of who she is, but I need you safe. I've got a bad feeling about you going to the canning works,'

Zane muttered. 'My gut is telling me that something will kick off. Something to do with the silver car. You leave this house and you'll be walking into the line of fire. *Literally*!'

'We can't leave Hazel!' Erin pressed.

'Fuck!' Zane raked his fingers through his hair. 'There's too much shit going on. This stuff with Hazel has turned things on its head. With her not being on the inside and able to tell me of Marco's whereabouts, we're blind.'

'I know,' Erin mused. 'But we must get Hazel somewhere clean and looked at properly. I'll risk it. Drop me at the works and Leo can take us to Harley Street, leaving you to concentrate on finding this silver car. If that woman is the link between us and Marco, then...'

'Then she will be removed.' Zane finished Erin's sentence, his heart feeling lighter. No, he didn't fully trust Erin's ability to remain rational but it was a step in the right direction. 'Okay, let's do it. I've already told Solenzo to arrange the trafficked women to give statements to the police and Leo's gone there to get the lowdown, but you have to promise me you'll keep close to one of us at all times. Even looking out of the window is a no-no!'

'Okay, okay,' Erin agreed, the danger of the situation steadily brewing. Creeping dread suddenly crawled over her. 'What about Sandler? Has he been removed?'

Zane shook his head. 'Unfortunately not. He's on the list. We just need more time than we've got.'

Ideally, he didn't want Erin leaving the house again until Marco was 'otherwise detained'. Or in a perfect world, had ceased breathing…

Marco's net was closing in fast and not for the first time, Zane regretted not grabbing the chance to remove his brother when the opportunity first presented itself.

'I'll call Leo and see how he's getting on and to let Solenzo know to expect Hazel,' he said. He hoped to God those women had spoken to the police by now. Marco had to be taken out of the picture for a while as soon as possible to buy more time and before he could issue any further orders.

The woman in the silver car had to be dealt with too.

Zane had to remain one step ahead. The trouble was, it was becoming increasingly difficult.

FORTY

DAMON STRUTTED INTO LUNA, glad to be here after all. Now he'd got the required information Marco wanted it was plain sailing.

Oh yes, Marco would like this. He'd like it a lot. The best part being that *he'd* be the one to gain the most from it. It was brilliant!

Damon's mouth curved into the first genuine smile his face had seen in ages. Just think about it: not only could he remove that two-faced cow who'd had the audacity to play him by lying her way into Luna and fooling him with her devious plans, he could also offload that plastic witch, Hazel. Whether Marco wanted his wife dead at this point was of little consequence – it's what would happen. He'd write it off as an accident if needs be. Or blame someone else - whichever. He could also tell Marco where Zane's new headquarters were located, as well as where the man himself was.

But the icing on the cake was the promotion which should already be his, now *would* be.

'Is Marco around?' he shouted to an enforcer further down the corridor. Seeing the man jerk his head in the direction of Studio One, Damon doubled back and yanked the door open.

The first thing he noticed was that the cages had gone. The second was the line of men standing with their trousers around their ankles whilst Marco moved along inspecting them.

Damon frowned as Marco lifted one man's penis with the aid of a ruler to peer underneath, then scrutinised the testicles. *What the...?* 'Erm, sorry to interrupt...'

Marco glanced at Damon with disinterest, then continued with what he was doing. Whatever that may be, he dreaded to think, but Marco wouldn't be quite so interested in random men's bollocks when he heard *this* news. 'I need a word.'

'It will have to wait,' Marco muttered, pulling back the foreskin of the next man. Stopping, he glared at Damon, his heavy eyebrows bunching. 'Actually, you can take over from here.' He wiped his hands down his trousers. 'Finish giving these new actors a once over for obvious diseases. I can't be arsed to get them medically checked. Besides, I haven't got time with filming starting tomorrow.'

Damon's frown grew. There was no way he was doing *that*. And there was another slight problem. 'Er, how will we film if Haz…'

'She'll be back by then.' Marco's eyes narrowed. 'Because you'll find her today, won't you!'

Damon clenched his teeth. Marco really thought it was that easy, even though now armed with the new information, it was. Aside from that, considering the amount of blood and hair on the penthouse floor last night he didn't imagine Hazel would look her best.

'I know what you're thinking.' Marco bent to snort a fresh line of cocaine off the table. 'Makeup is shit hot these days so she'll be easy to patch up.' Glancing dismissively at the half naked men behind him, he turned back to Damon. 'Get on with it then. The sooner you do this, the quicker you can get back to the *real* job in hand, being as that's what you're *supposed* to be doing today, rather than being here.'

Damon bit back his irritation. If that was the case, then why was he told to come here and furthermore, waste time inspecting these blokes' cocks? Who gave a fuck if any of the women got a dose? And Hazel would be getting shag all, short of a shallow grave.

With that pleasant thought in mind, Damon grinned confidently. 'The task I was given to do today – it's been achieved.'

Marco's eyebrows bunched in surprise. He gestured for Damon to follow into a side room, leaving the line of men standing awkwardly with their nether regions on display.

Shutting the door of the small office behind him, Damon waited. The sliver of enjoyment making Marco Morelli ask for information was gratifying. Except Marco didn't ask - he stood with folded arms and a fierce expression plastered over his face.

After ten seconds of this, Damon decided to volunteer the information after all. 'I know where your brother is,' he blurted. 'He's got Hazel and has set up new headquarters. It's a total dump, so I don't think he'll get very far wi…'

'What the fuck do you mean, new headquarters?' Marco barked. Zane had the cheek to take him on? And Hazel had run straight to him, the bitch? Zane was setting up a rival firm *and* had his wife? His blood raced through his veins. 'Where is this place? What is it? When did you go there?'

Damon faltered. *Fuck. What did that Russell prick say the name of the old factory was? Bollocks! He couldn't remember. Shit, shit, shit!*

There was no way he could nause this up. He was taking the credit for this - not the runner. *Think, think!* 'I spent what was left of the night scouring for signs,' Damon lied. 'I knew how important it was to you. I've had no sleep and I...'

'You think I care whether you got any kip? Where is the fucking place of Zane's?' Marco spat, his face colouring a vivid puce.

'It's the old canning factory off Ryden Street,' Damon said, thankfully recalling the information. 'He's in there. With Hazel.'

Marco paced up and down the small office, achieving two

strides before having to turn around and go back the same way. A nerve in his neck pulsed. 'And that Erin Langley woman? Did you kill her?'

Damon grimaced. *See? He knew Marco would eventually remember that.* 'Erm, not yet... I didn't see her. I...'

'Why not?' Marco screamed. 'You come in here with this, yet have failed to do what I asked? Are you winding me up?'

'B-But I've located Zane as well as your wife and I'm sure Erin will be there or at their house, which must be somewhere,' Damon cried. *He couldn't believe this. Was nothing ever good enough?*

'Of course she'll be *somewhere*! Get yourself over to the canning works immediately and wait until you see Langley.' Marco's eyes narrowed into slits. 'And then when you do - which you need to ensure will be today, you kill her!' He opened the office door to leave and then shut it again. 'And don't touch my wife or brother. Those kills are *mine* to have.'

• • • •

ARRIVING AT THE Harley Street practice, Leo had expected to wait a while before Giuseppe's trusted surgeon, returned. Even with a man of his standing and influence with the Old Bill it still took time to give witness statements. And with those trafficked women's English not being wonderful, if present at all, it would take longer than usual.

But what he hadn't expected was to find that Mr Solenzo here already…

Sitting in the chair in Mr Solenzo's office, Leo cracked his knuckles. The slight discomfort the shifting joints afforded offered a small diversion to this news. It was last thing Zane would want to hear.

He stared at Mr Solenzo's gold spectacles perched halfway down his nose making it appear longer than it already was. The man's thinning white hair was at odds with his olive complexion and his tweed suit seemed out of place with the dodgy work he'd been involved in for the past five decades.

Old he may be, but Mr Solenzo was one of the best, From a young age he'd worked as a distinguished surgeon at this prestigious Harley Street practice and never once let Giuseppe Morelli down in all the years he'd been called upon for off-the-cuff jobs - ones which 99 per cent of surgeons would not manage or be willing to risk anything the wrong side of the law.

But in all that time, Mr Solenzo had always delivered - and done so extremely well. Though Giuseppe was long dead and Mr Solenzo had long since scaled down his practice, now only working for select clients, his loyalty to the firm remained - or rather, to Zane.

When Marco stepped in to take the reins, Mr Solenzo bowed out of his longstanding duties, but the minute Zane returned, his services became available once again. His clout with the authorities was second to none too - always a bonus, but what good was that when there was nothing to hold clout over?

Leo leant on Mr Solenzo's desk. 'The rest are adamant they won't do it?' He must have asked this question ten times, but he still hoped he'd been hallucinating.

'Correct. I tried my best to persuade them, but they are too terrified of the repercussions.' Mr Solenzo nodded as if reaffirming this fact to himself.

Leo sighed, his lungs tight. This was a disaster. Out of the handful of women who had escaped, three had since died and only one had agreed to speak to the police. The reassurance their legal status would be looked upon favourably for providing such information had fallen on deaf ears.

In a way, Leo wasn't surprised. After what they had been subjected to, the women's trust in humanity would take longer than a week or two to fix - if it could *ever* be fixed. Remaining under the authorities' radar and avoiding reprisals from the men who had already stolen everything from them, far outweighed the promise of a 'good chance' of being granted permanent residency. 'At least there was one woman willing to speak out,' he said, trying not to think of everything being hinged on only one person.

Mr Solenzo shook his head, his rheumy eyes still imbued with deep intelligence. 'Unfortunately, that won't happen either,' he said, his Sicilian accent strong, despite seventy years in the UK. 'That woman did give a statement, but as we have no evidence to back up any claims there will be no investigation.'

Leo's whole body stiffened. 'They can't be serious? Surely the woman's account is all the evidence required?'

Mr Solenzo shook his head. 'Sadly not. Account or no; injuries or no; without firm evidence they said it would be turned around in court as an attempt by the illegals as an excuse to be granted residency.'

Leo's mouth fell open. 'But they were trafficked here illegally! By *Marco*!'

'I agree,' the old man said. 'But that's how it stands. One woman or ten, without hard evidence it's a waste of time.'

Leo gritted his teeth. *Shit*. This completely scuppered the plans. Now there was no way to get Marco out of the way in order to reconvene after Hazel's arrival upset the apple cart. *Unless...* 'What evidence is required? Would your account of the injuries not count?'

Mr Solenzo smiled. 'Dear boy, if I thought it would make a difference, I would gladly stand up in court and say that what I saw on those women's bodies corresponds with their accounts. But that isn't classed as concrete evidence.'

'Then what is?' Leo pushed, his frustration rising. *This was a complete disaster.*

'Things such as documentation from customs proving Marco ordered and stocked the container or written proof of purchase of the women. Perhaps photographs clearly showing Luna and women in cages they alleged they were held in might suffice?'

Leo's large shoulders sagged. Marco would have ensured the shipping ran through an untraceable pseudo company and there was hardly likely to be a receipt hanging around for thirty women for sex slave purposes. Nor would there be a collection of souvenir photographs. Nothing had been filmed before the shootout occurred. If even *one* film had been made...

But even then that would probably come under the banner of 'fiction' where the court was concerned.

Fuck.

He dragged his hand across his chin in despair, only interrupted by the ringing of his mobile.

Zane.

'I've got to take this,' Leo muttered apologetically. 'Yes, boss...? What, now? I think maybe we should wait bef… Oh! Right… Okay... I'll see you there.'

Ending the call, he turned back to Mr Solenzo. 'I've got to go. Zane's asked if you can take a look at some serious wounds on Marco's wife. I'm going to fetch her now.'

Mr Solenzo nodded. 'Then I will get a bed made up ready.'

Leo left the Harley Street and hurried to his van to go to the canning works. But before he took those women anywhere, he had to tell Zane about this change in circumstances and make sure he still wanted him to take the risk, being as Marco was still in circulation. And by the looks of it, he would remain that way.

FORTY ONE

PARKING MAINLY BEHIND the pillars of the gate to the Thames Canning Works concealed most of Damon's van, yet afforded him a good line of sight. It also allowed him a clear shot should he need it.

Damon found his gaze moving in the direction of where he'd stashed his gun underneath his seat. He hadn't planned on using it here. The chances of the person he wanted to receive a bullet through the head being here was unlikely, but it *was* plausible there would be *someone* showing up who he could tail to find out exactly where his target was. He hoped so anyway, otherwise the noose of Marco's unreasonable demands would be even tighter around his bloody neck.

There was only one other place around here - the fishhook factory. His old nan had worked there years ago, wearing her fingers down the bone. Aside from that, the canning works was on its own. Nothing else was around, short of waste ground where old factories had been demolished, creating a well-known spot for fly-tipping.

At least that runner's information was correct, in as much that the canning works still existed. Had it all been a load of bollocks, then he'd have looked a right cock after saying to

Marco that he'd *personally* seen everything.

And talking of cocks, having to complete Marco's task of inspecting those men before coming here had only wasted time, as well as giving him a complex over the size of his manhood. Most of those blokes were hung like donkeys!

Damon shuddered. The less he thought about that, the better.

He turned his attention back to the building in front of him and squinted against the sun which reflected off the few unbroken windowpanes on the ground floor of the works.

Jesus, this place was a shit-tip.

He stifled a snigger. If it was true that Zane was turning this gaff into headquarters it didn't give a great first impression to prospective customers. Not that he'd have any, being as his time was limited...

He glanced at his watch. Ten minutes now with no sign of movement from inside or from out here.

Worry prickled. Just because this place existed didn't mean Zane, Hazel or anyone was here or ever had been. But he'd seen the runner's photograph. Someone *had* been here yesterday and that someone looked like Zane Morelli.

But where the fuck was he now?

Damon glanced in his rear view mirror, his body tensing as a car pulled out of a gate of the fishhook factory.

This car was shortly followed by another and then another.

Damon frowned and checked his watch again. Of course - Friday lunchtime! The fishhook factory's old rules were still in place! His nan had always said that was the reason she'd worked there. Shutting down early on a Friday for the weekend was seen as a bonus, but she'd clearly missed that the sixteen-hour shifts every other day of the week outweighed that. But then, old people had weird ideas.

Damon slunk down in his seat and waited as dozens of cars passed him while the neighbouring factory emptied. He didn't want anybody clocking him. His Escort van wasn't out of place here but it didn't pay to draw attention.

As the stream of cars diminished, eventually fading to nothing, the road became deserted once again.

Frustration nagged. What if no one turned up? Even if they did, it could be *hours* before the chance came to tail someone to wherever Zane lived.

Even then it might not happen. Neither did it guarantee Erin Langley would be there...

Fuck. Marco would have his nuts for dinner if he didn't sort this today. He'd rip his *own* nuts off if he didn't sort it, being as killing Langley had been his priority since she'd played him for a fool.

No one made him look like a prat and lived.

Seething with indignation, Damon thought about his gun under the seat. It was loaded and ready to go.

So fixated on the joy of pulling the trigger and watching Erin Langley's face explode made him miss the van approaching from behind until it was almost upon him.

Freezing in his seat, Damon's eyes strained into the rear view without daring to move his head. *Remain still. Don't move.*

A white Transit. *Was it going past or...?*

Damon's breath hitched as the van slowed behind him to swing through the gates of the Thames Canning Works.

Finally! But who was it?

Risking moving, he reached underneath his seat, his fingers scrabbling for the gun. Making contact, he pulled it out then returned his gaze to the Transit now parked in front of the large doors of the canning works.

Damon inhaled sharply as the driver get out.

Zane Morelli was here. But who was with him?

He craned his neck to see past the thick brick pillars of the gates.

His eyes widened and his hand tightened around his gun.

It was her! That bitch, Erin Langley!

Right! Here was his chance. He could do it now. He'd shoot her and then speed off. He'd do it so quickly that by the time

Morelli had chance to pull a gun, he'd be down the road.

Damon checked his keys were in the ignition. Yep. In place and easy to fire the engine the minute he pulled the trigger.

Like any second now...

Focusing as Erin got out of the passenger seat and moved around the back of the van to where Zane waited, Damon raised his gun.

Ha! She was directly in his sights. A perfect shot. So perfect, it was fucking textbook!

Applying slight pressure to the trigger and feeling the resistance, he waited for Erin to move into line.

Just two more steps and...

Shit!

Damon's jaw tightened as Zane suddenly swapped position and stepped aside for Erin to walk in front of him, taking his place behind her.

'For fuck's sake, move! Fucking move out of the way!' Damon hissed under his breath. *Morelli was blocking his shot.* He squinted through the sights. There was a chance he could still get a shot. *Just.*

No. No, he couldn't. If one of them slightly moved, the bullet could hit Zane.

Damon could scream with frustration. He dare not risk it.

Christ, his life would be over if he copped Zane. Marco couldn't have made it clearer *that* was for him and him alone to do.

Fuck, fuck, fuck!

Should he chance it? If he got both of them in one go that would be even better. As for offloading Hazel, well, he didn't give two shits if that didn't happen. All he wanted was the accolade of making Erin pay.

His finger squeezed the trigger a little more, then paused.

If he hit Zane - even *clipped* him with lead, Marco would not buy the accident excuse in a million years. Not with *this.*

Damon watched with a rapidly sinking heart as Erin and Zane reached the door of the canning works, his chance well and truly gone.

Slamming his head against the headrest, Damon expelled a stale lungful of air and half-watched a silver car stop further down the road.

Sharpening his attention, he peered into his rear-view, then frowned. He had no idea who that was, but it was a bird, therefore no one of any interest so there was nothing else he could do for now, but wait.

FORTY TWO

THE RELATIVE PEACE of the night without worrying what Marco might do next should have had a positive effect on Hazel's overall state of mind, but it hadn't. If anything, being in this draughty, dingy place surrounded by men who looked more psychopathic than any she'd seen in Marco's employ, only served to shred what remained of her nerves.

As well as being wracked with pain which had considerably worsened as the hours passed, Hazel remained upright and unmoving, her heart lurching each time she heard a sound.

Each drip from the leaky ceiling made a 'plop' sound, the echo giving the impression that it came from elsewhere; every clank of old pipework; every rustle of mice, rats or spiders made her heart still and her breathing cease. And the faceless men lurking outside every doorway and within every shadow, made it impossible not to be plagued by vivid images of being back underneath Marco, the blade in his hand hacking at her hair, his teeth sinking into her flesh, him shoving items into places that…

Thinking about *any* of it made her want to vomit.

The constant round of questions circled as to why she'd put herself in this position in the first place. That she'd chosen to be linked to Marco Morelli and all that brought with it forever more, was never-ending.

Why had it taken her so long to see the wood through the trees?

Hazel shuddered, her heart lurching as a door slammed from somewhere outside her cell-like room. It wasn't even dark - she could see every detail of the drab and dank concrete walls surrounding her. There was nothing to be afraid of, yet she was terrified as well as being drained of all hope.

Hazel forced away another wave of tears. She'd truly believed she would die yesterday. She'd almost *welcomed* death until a chance to escape was exposed. But taking that chance came at a cost. Looking over her shoulder for Marco to catch up with her for the rest of time was, in many ways, more terrifying than dying.

And that would happen regardless if Zane didn't reach Marco first.

Why had she been so stupid; so false; so pathetically greedy to put material things above everything else?

It was now clear that she'd sold every shred of self-respect and piece of herself which money should never have been able to buy. And for what? A pointless bauble of one description or another?

It was a few seconds before the sound of footsteps outside the room sunk into Hazel's mind. And they were getting louder. Her broken fingernails dug into the palms of her hands. *Had Marco found her?*

Through her swollen eyelids, Hazel could just about make out the doorknob turning. Her breath caught in her throat as the door opened with a loud scraping judder and an ear-splitting shriek of terror escaped her mouth, the force burning the nerve endings in her broken teeth.

Erin stared in horror at the woman huddled in the corner, her feet slipping and pushing against the camping mat on the floor which doubled up as a place to sleep.

She rushed over, instinct pushing her to wrap her arms

around Hazel, before stopping. The woman's uncontrollable shaking exposed a terror that touch would only accelerate. 'It's okay,' she said, forcing her voice to remain quiet and level when all she wanted to do was scream every obscenity she could think of in Marco's direction.

No one deserved to be beaten and terrified to the point where mere human interaction triggered a spontaneous meltdown. Yet Hazel was only one in a long line who Marco had handed that unwanted accolade to.

'We're leaving here.' Erin risked taking a step closer. After making Zane promise to head straight off in pursuit of the woman in the silver car, she'd left him outside talking to Leo. She and Hazel would be fine with him. 'Hazel? It's me, Erin.'

Finally making contact, Hazel flinched from Erin's touch, but there was nowhere to move to because she was backed up against the wall.

Erin squatted down, able to smell the faint hint of Hazel's unwashed body. 'You must concentrate on what I'm saying,' she continued, her voice gentle but firm. 'I'm taking you to be seen by a surgeon. You need those wounds properly looked at.'

Even through the small slit remaining of Hazel's eyes, Erin glimpsed pure terror in the tiny bit of blue visible underneath the purple and blackened flesh. 'Leo will take us. We'll be fine.' This time she got a grip of Hazel's hand. 'I'll stay with you. You won't be on your own, I promise.'

A lone tear rolled down Hazel's broken cheekbone. 'I-I don't deserve your kindness. I don't deserve anybody's kindness.' The memory of the woman's face that she'd callously slashed whilst on honeymoon flashed into her mind, along with all the other selfish, manipulative things she'd engineered throughout her life.

'None of us can say we've been perfect,' Erin stated, speaking more for her own decisions that she'd sorely regretted over the years. 'It's never too late to make things right.' She smiled brightly even though she felt the opposite. 'I'll go and see if Leo's ready for us.'

Extracting her hand from Hazel's surprisingly firm and persistent grip, Erin darted from the room.

• • • •

SPEEDING ALONG THE ROAD, Zane frantically chewed at the gum he'd shoved in his mouth to stop him from clenching his jaw. It was supposed to help, but gnashing away at the spearmint gunk made the aching pain worse than ever.

As his speed increased, so did his desperation of setting his sights on what was needed. This stretch of road was notorious for coppers lurking with speed guns, but the threat of a thousand points on his licence failed to deter him.

There was only one question he wanted to know: was this woman working for his brother?

Zane's hand moved from the gear stick to brush against the gun in his belt. He'd get an answer one way or another. And if he received the wrong one, then this gun would be used. If the woman *was* working on behalf of Marco, she may be tasked with more than merely spying on him.

Cav telling him just now that he'd clocked a white van hanging around had piqued his interest, but it was when Cav added he'd been about to investigate the van when he'd been distracted by the presence of that silver car was what had sent Zane scrambling into the Transit to give chase.

The silver car had been spotted *everywhere* - the new headquarters being the latest.

Zane had immediately left. This was his chance. Little time had elapsed before giving chase, and Cav supplying the direction the car had gone narrowed down the options.

Zane scowled as he pressed the accelerator further into the floor. There was only so fast this bloody Transit would go. 'Come on!' he roared, banging his fist on the dashboard. He couldn't lose the tail now. This was the closest he'd got to catching this person and he was damned if he was missing out again.

How he wished he was on his bike rather than stuck in this

old rust bucket.

Zane peered into the distance as the road snaked ahead, catching a flash of light reflecting off something before it disappeared.

Was that it?

Leaning forward, hoping the physical movement would somehow aid the van's progress, Zane's knuckles whitened as he gripped the steering wheel. The juddering of the van from the sustained speed the old motor was being pushed to was unpleasant, but rounding the bend in the road, his lips curled up.

Got you!

With a renewed sense of hope, Zane slacked off the revs then slammed his foot back down again in the hope it would make a difference. It didn't, but it made him feel better.

And he was closing the gap.

How would he force the car to stop without shooting out the tyres or killing the driver? He needed this woman alive to answer his questions.

At least for now...

But stop that car he would. He could not rest until he knew who else he had as an enemy.

Closing the gap further, Zane spotted the woman's fearful eyes in her rear-view mirror. She knew he was there and that the game was up.

Flashing his headlights, the Transit's bumper closed in on the back of the Golf. 'Time to give it up, lady,' Zane muttered. *Would she accept defeat and pull over or would he have to force her?*

More importantly, was he prepared to wait while she made her mind up?

Was he fuck!

Slamming the Transit down a gear, the engine screamed and Zane floored the pedal again. Shooting forward and giving a slight tug to his wheel, he nudged the Golf in the left side of the bumper.

Was that enough?

Easing off, Zane watched as the VW skewed, the front of the car sliding. He repeated the manoeuvre. 'Come on!' he screamed, his eyes blazing with rage.

Seeing the woman grapple with her steering wheel to control the car from skidding off the road, Zane went in again. This time he slammed into the right hand side of the bumper. Not letting up, he pushed the car along the road at an angle, the silver motor's bonnet spinning to the left.

Zane continued with the angled pressure. The driver had only two choices: stop or tip... 'Fucking stop, bitch!' he roared.

Seeing the motor slowing, he applied the brake and with the front of the Transit shoved into the left hand side of the car, both vehicles drew to a stop.

Leaving the engine running, Zane flew out of the cab with his gun raised. He pointed it through the window into the face of the terrified woman. 'Get out of the fucking car. Now!'

FORTY THREE

'BLOODY HELL!' Leo cried as Erin barrelled around the corner to crash into his chest. 'Where the hell are you racing to?'

'What happened with the police? Have they got Marco?' Erin panted. Ever since Zane pulled up outside the canning works she'd been desperate for news. It had been so tempting to wait and listen while Leo brought Zane up to speed, but she had to get Hazel ready to leave. It was a good job she had.

'Hazel's not in a good way. Mentally or physically,' she babbled. 'The sooner we get her out the better, but *please* give me a quick rundown of what's happened first.'

Her eyes glittered with anticipation of hearing how Marco had been apprehended and was being held whilst enquiries were ongoing, but studying Leo, Erin noticed how grim his expression was. 'What's happened?' she cried. 'Where's Zane? Is he okay? Is it the silver car?'

'Zane's fine. He's speaking to Cav and then he'll be on his way,' Leo said. 'We need to get you and Hazel out of here immediately, so if you'd ju...'

'But what about the women?' Erin pushed, her brow creasing like a concertina. 'Their statements? Have the police not pulled Marco in yet? For God's sake, how long will it take them?' *This was all they needed - Marco Morelli wandering around for one second longer than necessary.*

'They're not taking Marco in,' Leo said bluntly, his disappointment over the injustice of the situation rawer than ever.

Erin's mouth formed a perfect 'O'. 'Why? When are they going t…'

'No, listen. They're not arresting him at all. Only one of the women spoke up and because there's no evidence, nothing will happen. Without concrete proof Marco was involved with the trafficking, it can't.'

'Shit!' Erin spat. 'So now what? What did Zane say? Oh God, does that mean we can't get Hazel to the surgeon? She has to get treatment, Leo. If she doesn't die from infection, she'll die from mental torture.'

'Zane's not happy, but now you're here too, there's no choice but to leave. We're going to the surgeon and we need to do so immediately before Marco orders his people to strike. The chances are he knows where we are and is planning something.'

With as much relief as possible considering the disappointing turnaround, Erin nodded. 'Okay, but you'll need to carry Hazel to the van.'

Rapidly moving back down the corridor, Erin bristled with fury. If only she'd taken those passports she'd seen in Damon Sandler's desk. *They* would count as evidence. Recording the conversations when Sandler had boasted about Marco's 'super' trafficking plans and how the women were to be kept caged at Luna would have worked too. She could have taped his words on the phone hidden under her skirt. *Christ! Why hadn't she thought of doing that?*

Leo clocked Erin's expression. 'Zane will track down the woman in the silver car. He knows you're as safe with me as you are with him. We'll find another way to get Marco. I promise.'

'It's not that,' Erin muttered as they neared Hazel's room. 'I just wish I'd recorded Sandler talking or took a fucking picture of... Wait!'

Leo watched Erin yank her phone from her pocket and bring the screen to life. 'What are you looking for?'

'There was a photo…' Erin's fumbling fingers scrolled through her files. 'I saw it the other day and couldn't make it out at first, but... Here it is. Look!' She turned the phone to Leo. 'It must have been taken accidentally when I was trying to message blind. It's a bit blurred but you can make out the 'Luna' sign on the wall and there's women inside two of those cages. See?'

'Fuck!' Leo gasped. 'You beauty! This is cast iron!' Planting a kiss on Erin's forehead, he grinned. 'Give me that phone. I'll go and show Zane.'

'No,' Erin cried. 'You get Hazel. I'll show Zane. Where is he?'

Leo wanted to stop Erin, but she was already halfway down the corridor. 'He was talking to Cav in the big tinning room at the front, but he might have left by now.'

'I'll find him,' Erin called over her shoulder.

'Don't go anywhere until I come with Hazel,' Leo called as Erin disappeared around the corner.

• • • •

FEELING HIS BLOOD PRESSURE spiral out of control, Zane cocked his gun and rapidly moved around the other side of the silver car. Out of necessity, he tried the door and as suspected, it was locked like the other side.

He kept his eyes on the woman in the driver's seat, alert for rash movements hinting she was reaching for a weapon.

It would be the last thing she did...

But she did nothing. Nothing, short of remaining paralysed with terror, her hands covering her face and her jet-black hair splayed out to cascade down over her hands and past her shoulders.

She made no move to do anything, which was odd in itself, but from experience Zane knew things should never be taken at face value. He'd been around too long to be fooled by such stunts.

From what he could see, this woman didn't look old enough to be masterful in any such devious manipulations, but appearances could be deceptive. Anyone on Marco's payroll would have been fully appraised and this girl's alleged innocence was probably the reason she'd been enlisted for the fucking job in the first place.

His eyes narrowed. Marco should have trained the stupid cow not to be so bloody blatant she was watching someone if he didn't want her shot.

Zane chewed his lip. Shooting a woman, and a young one at that, wasn't something he'd consider unless it was a matter of life and death. And this perhaps was. Although she wasn't threatening him at this precise moment, she had to be the go between - the informer spilling all to Marco about everything. *Him... Erin...*

Erin was not losing her life because he had a conscience over killing a woman! He'd been prepared to end Erin's life not that long ago when she'd attempted to take his, so he'd do what was needed.

But he wanted answers first. If this stupid woman chose to remain schtum, then she deserved everything which would follow.

Turning his gun, he slammed the butt against the driver's window, shattered the glass.

'Don't! Don't shoot!' the woman shrieked.

'Last chance to talk.' Zane shook away the urge to flick chunks of glass from her hair. 'Who are you and who sent you? Why the fuck are you watching me?'

Getting no response, he leant through the smashed window, flipped the lock and yanked the door open. Pulling the shrieking woman from the car, he shoved her against the door. 'What has Marco asked of you? Shoot me? Follow me? Kill the woman I love? What? Tell me!' he roared, pushing himself into her face. 'Fucking talk!'

'N-None of that,' the woman gabbled. 'I haven't had any contact with Marco. I-I did try, but he was strange. He...'

Zane frowned. If this was a convoluted way of setting him up, then it was confusing the hell out of him. 'Who the fuck are you, then? What's your fucking name, girl?'

The dark-haired girl muttered something intelligible and Zane's temper spiked further.

• • • •

'OH FUCK! NO!' Leo roared. He deposited Hazel onto a plastic chair as gently as he could despite his sheer panic at what he'd just seen through the large window. Calling for back up from the men in the adjoining room, he turned back to Hazel who still clutched the front of his shirt. 'Stay there. Don't look out of the window and don't fucking move.'

'That was a gun, wasn't it?' Hazel shrieked. 'Oh my God! It's Marco! He's come for me! He'll kill me!'

Ignoring the pitiful questions, Leo tugged his shirt from Hazel's claw-like grip, readied his gun and darted towards the front door.

It wasn't Marco, but it was *from* him. He'd seen that bastard Sandler take a shot through the window of the white van.

Fuck. It wasn't Hazel who was the target. It was *Erin*. When Leo heard that shot, his line of vision had tracked in the direction of the source just in time to see her topple to the ground. Now he had to get out there and shoot Sandler before the bastard fired again.

His lungs screamed as he reached the door. It had been uncomfortable enough lifting Hazel with the half-healed bullet wound in his arm, but running on a damaged leg was even more painful. Even that paled into insignificance knowing when he opened this door, he would be in prime position to receive the next bullet out of Sandler's gun. But at least that meant it wouldn't be Erin.

Leo's face twisted into a fierce snarl. He'd kill Sandler for this. Kill him stone dead.

What had Erin been thinking? He'd *told* her not to go anywhere until he got there. *If she was dead...*

Yanking open the heavy door, he raised his shotgun and gritted his teeth at the renewed surge of pain in his arm. Seeing the barrel of Sandler's gun poking through the lowered car window to take aim at the body on the concrete once more, Leo's only concern was to shield Erin. He had no idea if she was alive, but if she was, a second shot would greatly reduce that probability.

Firing at the distant figure shielded behind the glare of the Escort van's window, Leo darted out of the door, ducked down and raced towards Erin.

A volley of shots followed, showing that the men inside the canning works had reached windows. He was covered to some extent, but could still get hit any minute. *As could Erin.*

Panting with exertion, he reached Erin and crouched in front of her, his damaged thigh screaming in protest. Raising his gun, he aimed again only to see the Escort van disappear up the road amidst a screech of tyres.

Heart pounding, he heard more screeching of tyres as two of his vans left the yard in pursuit. Sweating profusely, Leo turned his attention to the body beneath him and met Erin's bewildered eyes. Although her face was contorted in agony, she was alive. *At the moment...*

But the blood rapidly soaking the front of her top left no doubt that she'd been shot. But where, and how badly, he wasn't sure.

'You're okay,' he lied, yanking her top up to press his big hand firmly on the bullet hole in her torso. At least it wasn't her heart, but there were plenty of other things around that area that could prove fatal and the blood was flowing fast.

'I'm sorry,' Erin hissed through clenched teeth. 'I know you said...'

'Shh, don't try and speak,' Leo said, using his free hand to summon Tiger to ready a car. 'We need to get you seen and fast.'

'I saw the van… I-I thought it was Zane. The white van… I thought if I caught him and showed him the photograph. I...' Erin stopped mid-sentence, her eyelids fluttering as her world grew fainter.

'Stay with me!' Leo roared, willing the car coming around the back of the building to hurry the fuck up. Erin was losing a lot of blood and they would lose her *completely* if it couldn't be stemmed.

Applying as much pressure as possible, Leo kept his hand in place as Tiger and another man gingerly lifted Erin into the back of the car. 'I'll press on the wound from the front,' he panted as he clambered into the passenger seat, leaning over to keep the pressure on the wound consistent.

He'd be like a contorted waxwork within three minutes of doing this, but it was better than Erin dying.

As Tiger jumped into the driver's seat, Leo turned to the remaining man. 'Get that phone out of her pocket. Take it to the cop shop on Plenty Road. Tell them it's from Solenzo and the evidence which corresponds with his visit this morning. Do it anonymously, but make sure they act on it!'

Nodding, the man took Erin's phone and shut the door.

As they sped away, Leo realised he now had to call Zane and tell him the news that he'd failed to keep Erin from harm, like he'd promised to do in Zane's absence.

• • • •

'I CAN'T HEAR YOU!' Zane reached out to grab a chunk of the woman's thick hair and twisted it hard. 'Your name?'

The woman's lips moved but the words were inaudible. 'Louder!' Zane raged.

The woman's shaking became uncontrollable. 'S-Skye. M-My name's Skye.'

Zane frowned. *Skye? Why did that name ring a bell?*

Hearing a car approach, Zane had a decision to make: did he keep a grip of this woman's hair and run the risk of looking like he was attacking a woman on the side of the road, or did he drop his grip and give her an opportunity to pull a gun out and blast him in the face?

Deciding it was unlikely her shaking was an orchestrated and purposeful act, Zane made the call to drop his grip. His arms dropped to his sides just as the car sped past, the driver not even glancing in their direction. London was like that - anonymous and cold. In the most part, people went out of their way to avoid involving themselves in anyone else's business. It was easier that way, but that unsaid rule didn't apply to *him...*

Everyone was involved in his business.

But he'd been correct. Despite being free to attempt an escape or shoot him, this woman remained where he'd left her. Except now she sagged against the wing of the car, all hope draining from her body.

Zane's eyes narrowed. He wouldn't fall for that either, but he'd seen enough to know force was no longer required. *And now he knew this woman's name…*

'So, Skye, if you're nothing to do with Marco, why would you try to contact him?' He raised an eyebrow and watched Skye arguing within her head how to respond. He didn't trust this chick. Nothing she said added up. She was lying. 'Furthermore, why have you been watching me?'

Suddenly, the connection dropped into Zane's brain. *Skye? The graveyard! That silver car had been there the same day he'd spotted the flowers on his father's grave with that name on the card.*

His eyes darted back to Skye who had taken the opportunity to sneak a look at him whilst his gaze was elsewhere, but the second his eyes made contact, she dropped hers to stare at her hands which were now wringing together.

'It was *you* at that graveyard! You left flowers on my father's grave,' he gasped. 'Why? Who the fuck are you? You've got two seconds to tell me what your game is!'

Zane's heart pounded and his eyes gleamed with rage. 'Why are you messing with me and my family? I'll ask you again, who the fuck are you?'

Tears sprang from Skye's eyes as she looked into Zane's face properly for the first time. 'Because... because he's my grandfather...'

'Grandfather?' Zane took a step back in shock. *Her grandfather*? His father was her grandfather? His heart thumped. This could only mean one thing: *Marco had a daughter*.

He felt sick. Was she lying?

Zane scrutinised the young woman in front of him. *She wasn't lying*. For the first time, he saw the family resemblance in the dark hair and the same piercing blue eyes all of them shared. The poor bitch - she'd gone looking for her father and found *Marco*. No wonder she'd been disappointed with his strangeness. Zane wouldn't wish that man as a father to *anyone*.

But now what? He couldn't let her go in case he was wrong and she *was* lying. 'You'd better come with me.'

Skye opened her mouth to speak but was silenced by the shrill ring of Zane's mobile.

Zane snatched the phone from his pocket in irritation.

…Leo calling…

Out of all the times it could ring, this was one of the worst. As he fumbled to answer, his head churned as to what to do with Marco's daughter, but he had to take this in case something had kicked off with Marco. Maybe Hazel had taken a turn for the worse? At least being here with the elusive silver car driver ruled her out as a current threat.

'What's up, mate?' Zane said, his free hand taking a firm grip of Skye's arm in case she bolted.

Suddenly his world tumbled over a chasm. 'What? Shit! I'm on my way!'

Erin had been shot? His breath caught in his throat and nausea twisted his guts. *Sandler…*

He pulled Skye towards the Transit where the engine was still ticking over. 'Get in,' he hissed. 'You're coming with me.'

That was the only choice because there wasn't a moment to spare.

Forty Four

THIS BRUNETTE was different to Marco's usual tastes, but right now a blonde with massive bazookas wasn't what he wanted. His urge to stick his dick into something the opposite of his cunt of a wife was needed to distract him from the ungrateful bitch.

He grabbed one of the brunette's small breasts and frowned. He wasn't sure how one with tits this small would fare with the film buyers, but now those Polish tarts had let him down, throwing his generosity back in his face, he hadn't the time nor the patience to spend days handpicking through queues of hopefuls with their sights set on being the next chick to top the bill at Luna Motion Films.

Marco stared at the gold plaque which he'd taken pleasure in ripping from the door lying face down on the floor in Hazel's dressing room. Waste of fucking time getting this room kitted out. He shouldn't have bothered, but at least he could christen some of *these*...

Shoving the extra-large black dildo into the woman, Marco grinned as she hid her discomfort with pretend pleasure. Even a smidgen of someone's pain deleted one line of anger Hazel had generated.

Actually, it didn't delete it, it merely placed it in the 'save for later' pile. And there were many things in *that* pile.

Furthermore, 'later' wouldn't be long.

'Enjoying this?' Marco asked, his mouth curling into a sneer. 'It'll get you ready for filming.' Filming that he'd purposely delayed.

Bending down, Marco snorted the line of coke from between the brunette's breasts, surprised the lack of them didn't cause the powder to fall either side of her rib cage. That would be a fucking waste.

Yeah, filming would begin the moment Sandler returned with the news he'd been holding out for. He couldn't concentrate until Erin Langley was dead.

An eye for an eye.

Zane thought he'd got one over by pinching Hazel? Well, the equivalent would be taken from Zane - the difference being that taking Erin would be *permanent.*

It was also amusing knowing the three men starring in this new film alongside Miss No-Tits were standing naked in Studio One until told otherwise.

Control was the best aphrodisiac.

'Are you going to fuck me now that you're single, Marco?' the brunette purred, her discomfort detectable only by the slight hitch of her voice.

Like the flick of a switch, Marco's mood morphed into rage. 'Who told you I'm single?' he barked. 'I'm not single! Why would that make a difference anyhow?'

Except it had for a while, he thought angrily. He'd been so controlled by Hazel, he'd actually wasted over a week of his life being available to her and her alone.

How bloody stupid was that?

Even worse, it seemed common knowledge that Hazel had left!

Delivering a stinging slap to the brunette's face, Marco yanked her off the illuminated dressing table to tumble to the floor.

'Marco!' The woman's hand flew to her reddening cheek. 'What are you doing?'

'It's Mr Morelli to the likes of you, you cheap slut!' Marco raged, the coke beating a fast rhythm in his speeding mind. 'I asked who told you I'm single?' Lunging forward, he grabbed the woman around the throat. Roughly yanking the large sex toy out of her, he shoved it into her mouth. 'This is what you should do to keep your filthy fucking gob busy!'

The brunette's muffled yelps failed to placate Marco's temper like it usually would in times of frustration. Hazel had ruined his trust in *everybody*. He'd treated her like a queen and look how the cow had repaid him!

Now this scanky whore believed herself good enough to jump on the bandwagon and speculate over his availability? 'Even if I could be arsed to screw you, which I *can't*, I wouldn't! My wife is my wife and always will be!' Marco raged.

And that was true. Hazel wasn't leaving him. *No way*. He wouldn't let her. *He* would choose when he became single – no one else. He would remain married to Hazel because that's what he'd decided was going to eventually happen ten years ago.

And he always got what he wanted.

Choosing to become a widow was different. After dragging the last bit of life from Hazel-bloody-Grimes he would still be married, but his reputation would be unsullied by the shame of being abandoned by his wife.

Pulling the naked brunette off the floor by her hair, he dragged her to the dressing room door, the plastic penis still firmly wedged in her mouth. Her stilettos slipped and slid across the floor and her muffled yelps combined with choking noises became louder as she grasped for something to steady herself.

'You're fired!' Marco snarled. 'Get the fuck out of my studios and if you've got any sense, out of London!'

He chuckled to himself. *That would give her bad dreams.* Not that he'd waste a minute on a worthless bitch such as her, but it was amusing from now on to know she'd lie awake at night worrying about it.

Single indeed? The cheeky cunt!

Getting a better grip of the woman's hair to throw her to the corridor outside, Marco yanked open the door only to come face to face with three men. 'Who the hell are you?' he roared. He was in just the mood to take these scrawny fuckers on, whoever they were.

It was then that he spotted the group of burly uniformed police officers standing to the left.

• • • •

ZANE HAD BEEN UNABLE to take a proper breath since hearing Erin had been shot. He still couldn't because he hadn't yet reached Mr Solenzo's Harley Street practice. The traffic was heavy and the stopping and starting; the inching forward; the snaking around the backstreets of London was pushing him past the ability to drive, let alone remember something like *breathing*.

His mind spiralled through every possible outcome. All of them bad...

Erin was alive when Leo called, but was she still? There had been minimal details given as to the extent of her injuries, aside from that she was bleeding profusely, but if it had taken Leo as long to get to Solenzo's surgery as it was taking *them*, things could have changed.

Christ, maybe Erin should have gone to the nearest hospital instead - *any* hospital. He'd rather risk the consequences of the barrage of questions surrounding a bullet wound than losing her.

All of the frustration and stress about Erin's recent behaviour disappeared. Even dealing with Marco and that bastard Sandler, paled into insignificance compared with facing life without her.

Chucking his cigarette end out of the window, Zane slammed his hand on the horn with the pointless notion that the blaring noise would force the traffic out of the way.

'Where are we going? What's happened?' Skye asked timidly, the first time she'd dared speak since being dragged into the van.

Zane was almost surprised to find Skye sitting there. His mind was so centred on reaching Solenzo's it obliterated everything else. 'To see whether the woman I love is dead,' he spat, barely able to utter the dreadful words. 'That's where!'

'Dead?' Skye gasped. 'But...'

'Be quiet!' Zane barked. 'I don't have time to deal with your questions now, so do as I say.' But he would have to deal with this woman - *Marco's daughter*, soon.

He forced a ragged breath into his lungs. The concept of breathing the same air as anything spawned from Marco made him want to be as far away from her as possible. But it wasn't her fault that she had *that* as a father.

He couldn't digest that right now. Not until he knew Erin would live. 'Fuck it!' he snarled, swinging the wheel. The Transit mounted the pavement, sending pedestrians scurrying out of the way.

'Oh my God!' Skye screeched. 'You can't just...'

'I can do what the fuck I like!' Zane roared. *And he would.* The only thing that mattered was Erin.

Seeing the familiar buildings denoting the Harley Street area, he swung back onto the road. *Almost there.*

Turning the next corner, Zane took a sharp left, leaving Skye to brace herself against the dashboard. Reaching a tall white building with an elaborate pillared doorway, he slammed up the kerb and came to an abrupt stop.

Launching himself from the van, Zane made to take the entrance steps three at a time before remembering he'd left something behind...

Backtracking, he yanked open the Transit's passenger door and pulled Skye from the cab. He couldn't risk her doing a runner and adding to his problems.

Skye prayed she didn't lose her footing as she was pulled

along by the arm. She fought to stay upright as Zane loped up the stairs to pound on the entrance intercom.

'Yes?' a tinny voice crackled.

'Morelli,' Zane barked and with the buzz of the door lock, he crashed through.

Ignoring the startled expressions of people seated in armchairs in the waiting area, Zane raced through the reception. He turned to the coiffured receptionist. 'Where is she? Erin?

He didn't wait for a response. He'd find Erin himself. Continuing to drag Skye along, he kicked open the first door he came to.

Nothing.

The same happened with the next room.

Somewhere in the back of his mind, Zane heard the receptionist shouting from a distance, but he didn't listen or wait. *There was no time.*

'Where is she?' he roared, sweat pouring from his brow. *Where was Leo? Tiger? Anyone? Was he too late?*

Suddenly remembering Mr Solenzo usually took 'special cases' to his basement rooms, Zane changed course. He knew where those rooms were. He'd escorted many of his father's casualties there to be patched up over the years.

'Come on,' he snapped to Skye as she skittered behind him, her feet sliding over the polished tile floor. He yanked open another door, revealing a long flight of stairs brightly illuminated by several small chandeliers.

In normal circumstances, Skye would be tempted to admire these exquisite lights, but this *wasn't* normal. Plus, she didn't want to lose her footing and tumble down the steps to end up a broken-necked mess at the bottom.

'Erin!' Zane roared as they reached the bottom of the stairs which opened out onto a large square area. Here, there were several further doors, as well as two corridors. 'ERIN!'

Zane stopped dead as a door opened and Mr Solenzo stepped out, his tweed suit covered with a blood-stained apron. 'Erin? Is she here? Is she...?'

‘Your lady is fine.’ Mr Solenzo smiled, his gold-rimmed spectacles pushing up the bridge of his nose. ‘She’s lost a lot of blood but she’ll live.’

Overcome with relief, Zane steadied himself against the wall. ‘Thank God.’

Mr Solenzo glanced at Skye with interest marked by a flick of his eyebrow, then placed his hand on Zane’s arm. He gestured to the room behind. ‘She’s through here.’

Forty Five

TURNING INTO THE CAR PARK at Luna Motion Films, Damon found himself singing along to Atomic Kitten on the radio. He normally hated their stupid songs, but he was in such a good mood their dire warbling failed to grate.

Parking in his usual space, he pulled on the handbrake and punched the air.

He'd done it. He'd wiped that nasty two-faced slut out of circulation. It just showed that it was a bad idea to play him for a fool.

Chuckling, he wondered what would be etched on her gravestone: Erin or Caroline?

Damon slapped his steering wheel to further embellish his mirth. He couldn't give a rat's arse what was on the bloody headstone as long as she was underneath it. And it was a certainty that she would be because Erin Langley was *dead.*

That he'd been afforded such an unexpected opportunity almost gave him faith in God. *Almost...*

Dead. Dead. Dead.

Ha ha!

Erin Langley was definitely dead. One of his precision shots to the chest hadn't failed to deliver yet.

Damon's mouth curled exposing his strange collection of teeth as he recalled the stupid cow racing towards him with a look of expectation. This had slowly changed to horror when she became close enough to realise it wasn't her lover-boy in the white van and there had been a gun pointing at her.

The thick bitch should have had enough nous to differentiate between a Transit and an Escort. It wasn't hard - the size difference alone made it bloody obvious.

Still, not his problem - only a fortunate benefit.

As she'd crumpled to the ground, his viewpoint had afforded him to just about witness the pool of blood fast spreading underneath her body as her life force flowed out of her like a knackered tap.

Shame...

Yep. Dead as a doornail.

Damon jumped from the van, grabbed his gun from under his seat and patted it gratefully. 'Nice work!'

He took up a jaunty pace towards the door, the Atomic Kitten tune still bouncing around his head.

Of course, he'd have preferred to plant a few more shots into the little cow, but being as Lady Luck had already shone on him with the power of football stadium floodlights by sending Erin racing into his path in the first place, there was no need. Also, that nutjob Leo Holland appearing, brandishing a sawn-off and taking potshots in his general direction, as well as other gun-toting loons doing likewise, Damon had been forced to make a swift exit.

Marco would not be pleased to hear that Zane was building his force up, but he'd keep that snippet of info to himself for now and only deliver the news that the woman he'd wanted dead by this afternoon had been accomplished.

Walking through the corridor towards Marco's office, Damon's chest puffed out in anticipation of the praise he would shortly receive.

Strange, he thought, wondering why there was no filming going on in Studio One. He'd been sure it was set to commence by 2 o'clock, so it should have been underway by now. He shrugged. The most important thing was that he'd done what Marco requested, so the second-in-command position was his. *No question about it.*

'Marco?' he called as he rounded the corner, unable to wait until he entered the office before delivering this most excellent news. 'Guess what? The job is…'

'Mr Sandler?' A man stepped forward in front of the police holding Marco spreadeagled and handcuffed on the floor. 'I'm glad you've returned. There have been serious allegations put against Mr Morelli and Luna Motion Films.'

Damon's eyes darted to Marco, his boss's furious face scowling as he spat obscenities in the direction of the uniformed officers. 'What allegations? *I'm* not involved in anything. I...'

'I didn't say *you* were,' the detective said, a hint of a smirk pulling at his lips. 'But your reaction that you *could* be accused of something is interesting...'

'What? No! I didn't mean...' Damon blathered, not missing Marco's stellar death stare even with half of his face embedded into the floor. 'Erm, I meant, nothing untoward has gone on here. Who said that there w...'

'Mr Sandler.' The detective held his hand up for silence. 'I cannot discuss this further. We're taking Mr Morelli into custody to help us with our enquiries. I suggest that you get in touch with his lawyer. I presume that he has one...?'

'Well, yes, but...' Damon's voice tailed off as Marco was dragged to his feet and held steady by the throng of well-built officers able to withstand his considerable strength.

Damon wanted to avoid looking at Marco as he futilely attempted to shake off being manhandled along the corridor, but there was no avoiding it.

'You'd best fucking sort this,' Marco snarled into Damon's face as he passed.

• • • •

THE MORPHINE had successfully dulled Erin's pain but it

didn't dampen her joy when the door opened. 'Zane!' she cried, moving to sit up but stopping with the searing flash of pain which reminded her to remain still.

Rushing over to the bed, Zane wrapped his arms around Erin, careful not to pull her against him like he yearned to. He wanted to feel her close and breathe in her scent, but he'd have to make do with the lightest of touches.

Bending down, he pressed his lips to hers, then pulled away. He ran a finger down her cheek and then traced it along her bottom lip. 'Thank God you're okay.'

'I'm sorry,' Erin whispered. 'I shouldn't have gone out. I thought it was you in the van and now I've made things worse for everyone.'

'No you haven't.' Lifting Erin's hand, careful not to knock the cannula, Zane kissed the end of her fingers one by one. 'What matters is that you're alive.'

Coming this close to losing her underlined how much he hadn't helped the situation which was driving them apart either.

Erin had been trying to help him, like she'd done for so long. She'd taken on board situations that most people would run a mile from. He now saw that *he* was also partly responsible for her recent behaviour.

Zane bit the inside of his cheek. Thinking it better to keep his thoughts to himself had driven Erin crazy and caused her to come to what had seemed like bizarre assumptions. If he'd realised he'd been making things worse, their relationship wouldn't have become so strained.

How would he have felt if it was the other way around? How would he have reacted if Erin was being cagey about strange men and disappearing off, not saying anything?

His lips flattened. He'd be ready to kill, that's what. His brain would have concocted all manner of things, just like Erin's had.

They were very similar.

Zane studied Erin's exquisite face, the truth slamming him between the eyes in technicolour. This woman would do *anything* for him. She already had, yet he'd considered walking away from this rarity?

Crazy!

The truth was, Zane had never factored anyone else into being party to the ins and outs of his business, his life or *him*. He'd never had to and certainly had never wanted to. But Erin was different. She was more connected with this chain of events than *anyone* in this room and firm, aside from him, so it was about time he afforded her some credit. 'Things will be different from now on,' he murmured, his eyes not leaving hers.

Erin smiled sadly. 'But I want you to trust me and you can't – especially now I just went against what you asked again. I shouldn't have left the works. I...' Neither should she have doubted him. Hazel wasn't a threat. No one was. Loyalty was Zane's trump card - it always had been and she should have known that.

'I *do* trust you,' Zane said. 'It's just taken me a while to realise that I've been shutting you out.'

'That's enough talking.' Mr Solenzo stepped forward. 'Erin is lucky that bullet missed her organs, but she's lost a lot of blood. Both these ladies need to rest.'

Mr Solenzo's use of 'both' and 'ladies' reminded Zane that Hazel was also present. He swung around to the bed behind him. Hazel's once beautiful looks were completely swathed in bandages, along with a strange contraption attached below her chin. 'How are you feeling?' he asked.

'Hazel won't be able to speak for a day or so as I have reset her jaw. She needs a bit of work done in her mouth and a few other things too, but she'll be fine – given time.' Mr Solenzo frowned. 'Your brother has a lot to answer for, does he not?'

Zane's skin prickled with the reference to Marco. 'Yes, he does.' *And that was something else...*

He'd told Skye to wait outside, leaving Leo with her to ensure she went nowhere, but starting as he meant to go on he turned back to Erin. 'I found the silver car and driver.'

Erin's eyes widened. 'That woman? Who is she?'

'Zane!' Mr Solenzo interrupted. 'I said that they need rest.'

Zane held his hands up. 'I know, but I have to say this.' He glanced first at Hazel and then back to Erin. 'The woman's name is Skye. She's waiting outside.'

Erin pushed away the familiar feeling of apprehension. She had to. 'You brought her *here*? Who is she?'

Zane frowned. 'She's Marco's daughter...'

Forty Six

MR SOLENZO had the good grace to step out of the room at Zane's news. He knew the Morellis from old and was onto a losing streak requesting no talking when a revelation such as *that* had been dropped into the mix.

He couldn't help but scrutinise the beautiful young girl standing dejectedly in the corridor, her uncomfortableness at Leo Holland standing over her plain to see.

She was a Morelli without a shred of doubt. Those eyes were the trademark in every member of that lineage. And Mr Solenzo had known quite a few: Giuseppe and his two sons all favoured the piercing blue. Even Giuseppe's brother and younger sister had them and no doubt their children had inherited the distinctive gene too.

Mr Solenzo couldn't help but look upon this young woman with pity. Having Marco Morelli as a father didn't bode well. 'Miss, would you like to go inside the room,' he asked quietly.

'Me? I...' Skye's eyes darted to Mr Solenzo and then to Leo whose eyebrows bunched with bemusement. 'I don't think th…'

'Zane has requested for you to go in,' Mr Solenzo continued. 'He wishes to speak to you.' He smiled at Skye and then nodded at Leo who stepped aside to give the girl free passage.

Swallowing nervously, Skye entered the room.

Zane looked up as the door opened. 'This is Skye,' he said. 'And Skye - this is Erin and Hazel - Marco's... erm... wife.'

Erin felt obliged to smile. The only time she'd ever seen this young woman, she'd threatened her, but she couldn't bring her mouth to move into the required position to greet Marco's daughter.

As much as she didn't want to be cynical, she couldn't help but feel resentful that this woman had put everybody through countless stress for the past however long, convincing them she was part of an underhand plan.

The other thing that was difficult to dismiss was that as Marco's daughter, wasn't it more plausible than ever that she could be involved and working against them?

Erin frowned, her mind spinning. There was no doubt this woman had the right colouring and characteristics to be Marco's daughter. Those eyes, especially. *Why hadn't she noticed this when she'd first seen her?*

'H-Hello,' Skye said, staying near to the closed door.

Zane now seated in a chair to the side of Erin's bed, ran his fingers through his hair. There weren't many circumstances that he found himself at a loss at how to handle, but this was one of them. 'What brought you here searching? Why now?'

'I-I always wanted to, but Mum...' Skye looked at Zane and then looked away quickly. 'My mother always concealed this from me.'

'I don't blame her,' Erin muttered and then vowed to keep silent as Zane cut her a look. He was right with what he'd said before Skye came in - it wasn't this girl's fault she had that bastard as a father.

'I only found out by chance after discovering a newspaper clipping in my mother's drawer about Giuseppe's death,' Skye explained.

Zane could see Erin's suspicion festering and had to admit

he shared it. 'My father died several years ago, so why *now*?'

Skye nodded. 'I didn't have any way of getting here until recently. Besides, there wasn't much point whilst...'

'But why follow Zane?' Erin asked. 'Why go to that trouble? You said you'd tried to contact Marco, so...'

'I'm really sorry if it looked like I was spying.' Skye's bottom lip quivered. 'I didn't know how to broach it. I still don't really. It's all so weird. Like, I mean...'

Zane ransacked his brain for any of Marco's past women with whom he may have fathered a child. It could be *anyone...* 'Does your mother know you're here?'

Skye's face dropped. 'No.' Her face reddened with embarrassment. 'She wouldn't like it. She's... she's not well. I doubt you'd recognise her now.'

'Do you think you should be trying to get in contact with Marco if your mother doesn't want you to? She might have good reason,' Erin said tactfully. 'I don't want to upset you, but you're better off not having contact with that man.'

Skye blinked. 'I...'

'Wait a minute,' Zane interrupted. 'You said that *I* wouldn't recognise your mother? It's unlikely I'd have ever seen her.' He smiled apologetically. 'Without being crude, Marco's had many women over the years and has never kept any around long enough for anyone else to meet.' *That was an understatement.*

Skye suddenly paled. 'I-I think there's been some confusion… My mother's name is Shirley Wilson. I only contacted Marco because I couldn't find you. Marco's not my father, *you* are.'

• • • •

PUTTING THE PHONE DOWN, Damon wanted to scream. His day had been going so well and now *this*? What the fuck was he supposed to do now, apart from wait?

He drummed his fingers on the desk in his office. He should be celebrating, not watching his hard work going down the toilet. But that's exactly where it had gone. It had gone so far down the sewer that it would be floating around the Hammersmith waterworks by now, along with every other turd this side of the bloody river.

'Christ,' he muttered. Getting up from his chair, he immediately sat back down. He didn't know what to do with himself. What *could* he do?

Damon stared at his watch, the second hand making its way slowly around the dial.

Had it fucking stopped?

No it hadn't.

'For God's sake,' he spat. 'How long does it fucking take to ask one question?'

Symonds, Marco's brief had promised to call back, saying as a solicitor he would be informed about *exactly* what evidence was held enabling Marco's arrest, as well as what it was about. It could be anything. But what? Who would dare to take on Marco Morelli?

Damon's eyes narrowed, betting it was one of those tart actresses who Marco had binned off during that staff cull not long ago. But would any of them actually be so stupid to think they'd get away with it?

Besides, surely someone couldn't be arrested for allegations of unfair dismissal?

Damon's forehead creased further. That detective had said, '*serious* allegation'...

It couldn't be those Polish birds, could it?

He shook his head. No. They wouldn't have the first clue where to start. Anyway, he'd personally ensured there were no leads back to this firm.

Even if Sonny Mitchell had attempted a setup using paperwork, Damon had removed that option. There had only been one or two dubious pieces of documentation that could perhaps count and he'd personally ensured they were destroyed. Even if Sonny had made photocopies, Damon hadn't put the contents of that man's desk through the shredder for nothing. There had been more to clearing every shred of Mitchell from the second-in-command's office than freeing up space for *himself.*

Damon had made sure no stone had been left unturned after Sonny's despatch in the event of a stunt like this.

Erin/Caroline hadn't had access to anything whilst she'd been snooping around either - purely because there *wasn't* anything, so it couldn't have been her.

A ghost of a smile touched his lips. He wasn't stupid, so what the hell was this supposed evidence? It couldn't be anything too bad, otherwise Marco would have been carted off long before now.

Damon snatched up his phone even before the first ring completed. 'Symonds? Did you speak to them…? What do you mean, it's not good? How not good is "not good"?'

He listened, his eyes narrowing. *Was that it? One of those Polish tarts had given a statement?* Damon almost laughed. 'It won't stick. Foreign bitches don't get any clout.' His mouth then fell open in shock. 'What? A photo? But how?'

How could the police be in possession of a photograph of women in cages and the 'Luna Motion Films' sign in the background? *What the hell?* There had been no filming and those Polish sluts hadn't a camera between them, so...

Caroline…

Damon's face screwed up in base fury. Caroline/Erin - whatever. It *had* to be her after all.

He dragged his hand across his face. That little cunt had got that photo to the cops quick smart! Good job she was dead.

But that didn't help the situation, did it?

Wait…

'Say it was part of a film?' Damon suggested. 'Explain it was a promotional shot for the movie. They can't prove th… *How* can you not be sure? Either it's feasible or... Right, so when will you get to see this photo?' He glanced at his watch. 'Then you'll call back? Okay, fine.'

Ending the call, Damon slammed his mobile down and stared at the wall. It wasn't fine. This was nowhere *near* fine.

Jesus fucking Christ! If that photo couldn't be passed off as a film still or something then...

Damon found his shirt getting clammy with a forming layer of sweat.

If the police and the powers that be decided that, along with the woman's statement, the photo was enough to use as hard evidence, then *he* could also be in the frame, along with Marco.

He jumped from his seat to pace the office.

Fuck, fuck, fuck!

Damon stopped, his smile returning. This might not be as bad as it looked. None of this meant that *he* would be charged. It was Marco's firm; Marco's film studio and *he*, thanks to Marco's reluctance to give him credit, wasn't in a position of authority.

The police could perhaps question him, but *charge* him with anything? No. That was Marco's gig to bear alone.

Damon's smile grew.

And *that* would open up a whole new world of possibilities...

If Marco was done over this allegation it would leave things open for *him* to take control of the business. All he would need was access to the bank accounts.

And that was something he'd ask Symonds about when he phoned back.

FORTY SEVEN

SINCE SKYE had uttered the words, 'you are', Zane had been in shock. As in complete and *utter* shock. Erin didn't think she'd ever seen someone look so thoroughly gobsmacked.

She watched him sitting with his brow furrowed and his chin resting in his hands. There was no point asking if he had been aware he was a father or even if it was a remote possibility. The shock and disbelief on his face showed the truth plain as day: he hadn't had a clue.

Zane raised his eyes to meet Erin's and then looked to Skye who was equally as mortified. 'I... I don't know what to say.'

'I-I'm sorry… I thought you knew...' Skye said quietly. 'I presumed... presumed you *must* know. I thought th...'

'You thought what?' Erin snapped. 'Does it look like he knew about this?'

Zane sparked up a cigarette, not caring if Mr Solenzo went crazy for him smoking in here. He needed a cigarette and therefore was having one. 'I did know your mother… It was a very long time ago... And yes, we were in a relationship for several months, but she disappeared. I don't know why. I never saw her again. All I know is that my father seemed pleased because it turned out that he had plans for me to eventually marry the daughter of a firm in Sicily.'

Erin stiffened. 'What happened to that plan?'

Zane shrugged. 'I got out of it for many years and then, as you know, I went to prison and my father died… *That's* what happened.' He turned back to Skye. 'Your mother told you that I'm your father?'

Skye fidgeted awkwardly. 'Well, no... She refused to talk about it... I did ask several times, but... like I said, she's not well.'

Zane frowned, his mind ticking over. 'So, how did you...'

'I started digging around a while ago,' Skye confessed. 'Bits and pieces and comments to start with and of course, the newspaper clipping. Then I learnt she'd been seeing you and everything added up.'

'How old are you?' Zane asked, his heart pounding.

'Seventeen,' Skye said. 'I was born in February 1984. That's why I couldn't come to find you before now.' She smiled sheepishly. 'I only passed my driving test two months ago.'

Zane's mind swam as he did the sums in his head. *February 1984*? Nine months back from then made June 1983. When did Shirley disappear? It was three weeks after Marco's birthday do. He remembered it well. Shirley was the first girl he'd introduced to his father and wider family. It was also that night that he'd realised Giuseppe had other plans for the future of his eldest son.

In all fairness, Zane hadn't been sure how he felt about Shirley. Sure, he'd liked her - liked her a *lot*, but marriage wasn't on the cards. He'd been sixteen, for God's sake. Not an age to think about marriage. And the level at which he'd liked Shirley now paled into insignificance compared with how he felt about *Erin*.

But that wasn't the issue. It was whether the dates added up. *Was he Skye's father?*

He looked at Skye standing nervously waiting for his response watching him with those eyes that so resembled his own. 'The dates certainly add up,' he said quietly. 'It looks like you were right...'

He glanced at Erin, wondering what she thought about this because he for sure didn't.

Christ, he was a father and never knew it?

Shock merged with anger. If he'd realised Shirley was pregnant with his child, he wouldn't have abandoned her. Whether he'd wanted marriage or to be tied down with kids before he was legally of age to even drink was by the by. He'd been brought up to shoulder his responsibilities, not to shirk from them. Shock and anger gave way to sadness that he hadn't been there for this girl who was his own flesh and blood. 'Why didn't she tell me?' he muttered.

'My mother never said a thing,' Skye admitted. 'She refused to talk about it. The only thing she ever said after I confronted her was that it was in the past and would never be discussed.'

'Where is Shirley now?' Zane wanted to speak with her. He wanted to ask why she hadn't told him and hadn't given him the option of helping out in whichever way she wanted.

Skye looked away. 'Well… erm…she's... erm...'

'I really must intercept now.' Mr Solenzo entered the room. 'I appreciate there's a lot for you to talk about, but Erin and Hazel need rest, so finishing this conversation will have to wait.'

Erin glanced at Hazel in the bed next to her. The woman looked as shell-shocked as she felt herself. As Zane left the room with Skye, promising to be back later, she wished Hazel could talk because she could really use someone to speak to. *Even Hazel.*

And as for resting - how was she supposed to do that? She could only imagine how Zane must feel.

Yes of course, she felt relief for Skye's sake that she didn't have Marco as a father, but what did it mean? The girl's mother – Shirley - would *she* want something from Zane after all these years?

And what had stopped the woman from telling Zane about

the baby in the first place?

Aside from all of this, there was still the issue of Marco and Damon Sandler hanging over their heads.

• • • •

WHEN DAMON HAD followed the detective down the corridor to the room where Marco and his brief, Symonds, waited, it was the last place he wanted to be. His first instinct when Symonds had finally called back instructing him to come to the station was to decline.

Didn't going there for an 'off-the-record' chat with Marco and his brief whilst those charges loomed all but suggest *he* was involved?

Damon believed so, but Symonds informed him in no uncertain terms that his presence was on Marco's specific instructions, which translated into: '*be here or else*'.

Or else what?

Marco could do little whilst being held at a cop shop.

Or could he?

Coming to the decision that Marco *might* attempt to pin the trafficked women thing onto him if he didn't comply was enough for Damon to swallow his cock and turn up as instructed.

And it had only got worse from there.

Damon stared across the table to where Marco sat with Symonds in the small grey room that he'd been shepherded into by the grim-faced detective.

He could see the pent-up rage simmering behind Marco's eyes and being in the same room as this lunatic, which he might add, was now locked, did nothing for his nerves.

Five minutes he'd been in here and no one had said a word. If this was a ploy to unnerve him, it was working...

Damon heard a strange scraping noise from the back of his throat as he swallowed saliva which had begun to solidify at the sight of Marco's icy-blue glare.

'In answer to the question you asked Symonds earlier, no -

I'm not willing to hand you power of attorney over the firm's bank accounts,' Marco said coldly.

Damon's face drained of all colour until it resembled a white paper napkin. *Symonds told Marco he'd asked that? Jesus!* 'I only meant until you got this business wrapped up. I don't want anything affecting the production of the new films that have been arranged and...'

'Bollocks!' Marco snarled. 'You think I'm that fucking stupid to give you access to my funds – to my money, so you can step into my shoes?'

Damon gathered by the rising pitch of Marco's voice that his reasonings hadn't placated the situation. He cut Symonds a glare. Why the hell had that fucking idiot told Marco what he'd asked. He'd only wanted to know if it were feasible to access the funds, not go and ask for bloody permission! *Christ, was the man trying to get him killed?*

The minute Symonds said it would be impossible to access the accounts without Marco granting power of attorney, Damon knew it was a no go, yet the fuckturd had gone ahead and mentioned it anyway?

'Furthermore, there won't be any production at Luna for the time being.' Marco's big hands curled into fists. 'And do you know why?'

Damon shook his head. No he didn't, but he suspected he was about to learn. All he could do was hope the reason wasn't pinned on him. He knew he shouldn't have come.

'Because,' Marco continued, 'until these wankers conclude their investigations and decide whether they can prosecute or not, they've slapped a ban on my businesses from operating.'

Damon's eyes widened. 'What? But that means tha…'

'It means I'll be more out of pocket than I am already!' Marco's fist slammed onto the metal interview table making the pen jump out of Symonds's hands. 'How did you allow this to happen?'

'*Me*?' Damon gaped.

Marco leant across the table, the words spitting from

between his teeth. 'I have been informed the evidence they hold came from that little cunt of Zane's. *You* were tasked with dealing with her, so yes, this is *your* fault.'

Damon blinked. He hadn't given Marco that news yet - the information which should have secured his promotion - a promotion for a firm that was now in total shit if these charges stuck. 'She must have brought that photo here the minute she left Luna,' he said, forcing his voice not to betray the crushing depression at his lack of future. 'Because that task was completed earlier this afternoon, as promised. That's what I came to tell you only to see the police had already arrived.'

'So she's dead?' A flicker of satisfaction appeared in Marco's blazing eyes.

Damon nodded. 'She is indeed.'

'I'll pretend I didn't hear that,' Symonds muttered.

'You'll hear what I *pay* you to hear,' Marco barked before turning his attention back to Damon.

In usual Marco style, his psychotic anger aimed at Damon flipped on its head. 'That's good.' He leant back in the plastic chair which was a damn sight less comfortable than the usual top of the range leather ones he insisted upon. 'So, Sandler. As you know, I'm not happy about your tardiness in carrying out the task I set. It has caused a blip to my business as well as to me.' He gestured around the cell-like interview room for good measure.

Damon frowned. 'I couldn't have done it any quicker and...'

'I don't want to hear your pathetic excuses.' Marco's eyes flashed dangerously. 'Like I was saying, even though you have caused me unnecessary bother, I'm prepared to overlook that and offer you a deal.'

Damon faltered. *Deal? What would that be?* That he should confess to the police that the trafficking was down to him alone and in return Marco wouldn't kill him? *Yeah, that was great...*

Marco held up three fingers. 'There are three conditions to my offer…'

Damon remained silent. *Wait for it...*

A sneer formed on Marco's face. 'One: work with Symonds to get me out of here by whatever method necessary. I don't want this going to trial, so I expect to be out of here within forty-eight hours.'

Damon almost choked. *Forty-eight hours?* How the fuck was he supposed to do that? Even Symonds looked like he was about to have a cardiac arrest with that ridiculous timescale.

'Two,' Marco continued, 'bring my wife to me and then... well, you know what needs to happen with her. And thirdly, deal with Zane.'

Damon remained motionless. *Not much then...?* 'What do I get in return?' Being as he would invariably end up dead one way or another within the next couple of days, he had nothing to lose by broaching the question. *What was his payoff for all of this? A package of chocolate buttons?*

A flicker of rage passed Marco's face which he pushed behind a fake smile. 'It's a generous offer, considering two out of three of my conditions you'd already been tasked with and because you were so slow achieving the other issue concerning Langley caused me to be in here... but hey, I'm a nice guy.' His smiled dropped. 'So, instead of pretending you're looking after my best interests with bullshit about bank accounts, get me out of here and I'll bring you into Luna as my business partner.'

Damon's mind emptied. All that fired the synapses in his brain was the loud ticking of the clock on the wall. *Business partner?*

He didn't want to be Marco's *partner* – he wanted to take over the place. But this was the only option he'd got. And one he'd hadn't expected.

Begrudgingly and a tad reluctantly, he reached across the table and took Marco's outstretched hand. 'Deal'

'Excellent!' Marco's handshake purposely crushed the bones in Damon's fingers. 'Now off you fuck and get on with it!'

Dazed, Damon rose from the table and banged on the door to be let out. He didn't have a clue where to start, but he'd better think of something.

• • • •

SKYE GLANCED with trepidation around the sitting room in Zane's house, unsure whether she was relieved to finally meet her father face to face after all of these years, or whether she had taken leave of her senses.

She managed a small smile as the man she knew to be Cav excused himself from the room, then glanced nervously at Zane. 'Doesn't that man want to stay in here?'

'He'll be fine in the other room.' Zane threw his jacket over the back of the chair and kicked off his boots. 'He's giving us space to talk. I think we need that, don't you?'

Skye looked away from the piercing blue eyes so similar to her own. Yes, of course they needed to talk, but after all the years dreaming of this moment and the scenarios she'd imagined of how it would be to finally meet her father, what had actually happened couldn't be further removed from how she'd pictured it.

Aside from the worst case scenario that this man could have refused to acknowledge her as his daughter, which he hadn't, everything else had been off the score.

Striding into the kitchen to fetch two bottles of beer, Zane cracked the tops off using his standard method - his teeth. He handed one to Skye. Seeing her face, he laughed. 'I don't think having a drink a few months short of eighteen will get you locked up!'

Blushing, Skye took the beer. 'It's not that. It's just...'

'Just not what you'd expected? That *I'm* not what you expected?' Zane shrugged. 'Being slammed up against a car and having a gun pointed in your face isn't how most father and daughter first meetings go, I guess?'

And how strange did that sound? *Father and daughter*. He had a daughter and he couldn't get his head around it. 'Like I'm sure you've noticed, your timing wasn't the best!'

Feeling slightly more at ease, Skye slipped into the chair

Zane gestured to. But what exactly was going on here bothered her immensely. The places she'd followed Zane too and the cloak and dagger furtiveness surrounding the behaviour and movements of the man who'd she'd discovered to be her father was far removed from the world she knew or what she'd been expecting.

But what *had* she been expecting?

That she didn't know. Was this why her mother was so against discovering her past and what had happened with this man?

Zane Morelli was a criminal, that much was obvious. He'd already admitted he'd spent time in prison. But those people being shot - those women... and his strange brother, her *uncle...*

Skye shuddered with the thought of the one time she'd set eyes on Marco Morelli. That was the only point she'd contemplated abandoning her quest. *What if her father was like that other man?*

Her brows knitted. Thankfully, apart from his looks, Zane didn't seem to be anything like Marco. He seemed... different.

But what did she know? This man - this stranger, whose house she was in all but alone, could be a psychopath.

Zane saw the fear and questions barrelling through Skye's mind. His brain was doing something similar, but on different topics. But whichever way he looked at it, they couldn't start discussing this now.

Pouring beer into his mouth, he slammed the empty bottle on the table and stood up. 'I'll grab some kit from the bedroom and then you can sleep in there. I'll crash down here with Cav. The others will remain at Solenzo's keeping watch.'

'What about your... your wife and the other woman?' Skye faltered. 'I don't want to make things difficult or...'

'Erin's not my wife but I think I want her to be,' Zane said, surprising himself with this unexpected admission. 'I'm going to see her again first thing tomorrow. Look, I know we need to talk properly and we *will*, but we also need to sleep. It's been a long day and there's too much we both need to know to begin discussing this now.'

'You're right,' Skye nodded. 'And thank you for not pushing me away.'

Suddenly impelled, Zane pulled Skye against his chest and hugged her close. 'Why would I push you away when you're my daughter?'

Skye clung to Zane's chest, the worry and dread draining away as the missing part of her jigsaw fell into place. She'd found her father and he seemed all right. Things might be good after all.

Forty Eight

'HE'S STILL IN THERE,' Tiger grinned. 'Plus, Luna is boarded up. Word has it down the Bluebell that the cops have banned all of Marco's businesses from trading.'

Leo grinned. 'That photograph did the job, then?'

'It did, but for how long depends on when Marco wriggles off the hook. Everything is temporary until he's formally charged,' Zane said. 'But at least this gives us breathing space. Things are already moving with my new men on Marco's territories and we also get a headstart to catch up with Sandler...'

'No one's seen or heard from that prick this last twenty-four hours,' Cav added. 'I put word out everywhere but there's been nothing. It's like he's disappeared into thin air.'

'Maybe he's already dead?' Leo chuckled.

'I doubt whether we'd be that lucky,' Zane muttered, 'but he'll wish he was when I find him.'

'And what about your latest surprise?' Tiger raised his eyebrows. 'What's happening with her?'

Zane chewed the inside of his cheek. 'Skye stayed with me last night and will continue to do so for the time being. I guess we need to get to know each other.'

But that was easier said than done. Last night back at the house had been awkward to say the least. How could seventeen years of absence be made up overnight? 'I still can't get my head around that she's my daughter!'

'I'm sure you'll do whatever needs to be done,' Leo said, watching Zane struggle within his own head. 'But why wouldn't her mother have told you? I mean, it's a...'

'I'll find out eventually – that I'll make sure of.' Zane got to his feet. 'But now I'm going to see Erin. There's something I want to put to Hazel too.'

• • • •

'WHERE IS SHE?' Zane walked into the room at Mr Solenzo's and frowned at the empty bed next to Hazel. He turned, about to apologise for expecting Hazel to answer with that thing over her jaw, but to his surprise he noticed it had been replaced with a smaller and less cumbersome dressing.

Seeing where Zane's gaze lay, Hazel pointed to her mouth. 'I only needed that other thing on for twenty-four hours. Erin's being checked over now.' She glanced towards the next door room. 'She shouldn't be much longer.'

Zane smiled. Although Hazel's voice was still muffled and she was clearly still in a lot of pain, she was much better and a lot brighter than this time yesterday. 'Anyway,' he continued, pulling up a chair next to the bed. 'I wanted to talk to you.'

Hazel paled. 'Is it Marco? Is he...?'

'Don't worry about him for now,' Zane said. 'He's been "detained". It's unlikely he'll be charged, but it gives us more time.'

Hazel's racing heart calmed. 'But for how long? And then what will I do? And Sandler - he's still out there somewhere. He'll still be gunning for Erin, as well as you.' She swallowed drily. 'He'll also be looking for me. Marco will never let me live.'

Not needing reminding of the scrote who had tried to kill Erin, Zane grabbed Hazel's hand. 'We'll sort Sandler. What matters now is keeping you and Erin safe and getting the firm running at full speed. You've got to concentrate on remembering that Marco isn't here for the time being and therefore can't touch you. Even if that period is only for a few days it gives us leeway to get things into place.' His mouth curled into a smile. 'Plus, the police have put the kybosh on any of Marco's businesses trading whilst investigations into the trafficking are ongoing.'

Hazel's mouth gaped before the pain made her clamp it shut. 'Oh, thank Christ! So he can't make films or hurt any more women?'

'Not for the time being. And that's what I wanted to talk to *you* about.' Zane released Hazel's hand and crossed one of his legs over his knee. Along with the unanswered questions and confusion surrounding his unexpected daughter, his night's sleep had been punctuated with what he could do to make a difference to the sick trade Marco had brought too close to his door.

He may not be able to eradicate human trafficking in general, but he *could* plough some money he held into a cause to make a difference to a small degree.

He concentrated back on Hazel who watched him with a mix of worry and anticipation. 'I believe I have an idea which might help both you and women like the ones down the corridor here.'

'Those women are improving,' Hazel jumped in. 'Mr Solenzo said only this morning that their wounds are healing nicely. It's just their minds which will take longer...'

'That's why I want to set up a centre,' Zane smiled.

'A centre?' Hazel frowned. 'What sort of centre?'

'I'll purchase a property that can be used as a refuge for trafficked women and...' His eyes trailed across the bandages scattered over Hazel's body, '...for women who have suffered domestic violence. Like you...'

Hazel blinked self-consciously. She'd never envisaged domestic violence as being part of her future. Not her - not Lisa

Tequila, the *star*.

But it had been.

Besides, she wasn't Lisa Tequila anymore. Perhaps she never had been? Perhaps she'd always been plain old Hazel Grimes - the woman she'd barely had chance to know?

But Zane's idea - actually putting money into something like this, rather than ploughing cash into getting rich off other's suffering or for criminal acts, showed there was a hell of a lot more to him than his brother.

But where did that leave her? She'd witnessed the love Zane had for Erin. It had been almost painful watching them yesterday. To have a man genuinely love her even a *tenth* of how Zane loved Erin was something she'd do anything for

But one thing it underlined was that she wouldn't get anywhere by taking Zane for herself. That part of her ostentatious plan had been just *that* – ostentatious, Lisa Tequila style.

'So, what do you think?'

Hazel pulled her thoughts back to Zane. 'I think the refuge is a great idea. It's very decent of you.'

'And you're happy with that?' Zane pushed.

'Well, I think many women will appreciate a safe place to...'

'I meant my idea of *you* running it,' Zane interrupted.

'Me?' Hazel cried. 'You want *me* to run it?'

'I take it you weren't listening?' Zane chuckled. 'Yes, I do want you to run it. It will get you away from this situation you're in. I'll station some of my men there as guards for you and all of the women in the refuge - starting with those in there.' He jerked his head in the direction of the corridor where the remainder of the trafficked women recuperated. 'Plus, you may not realise it, but you're savvy. Given half a chance, you'll be good at running a business - one that doesn't involve selling your soul. So, what do you say?'

Despite the pain, Hazel's mouth remained hanging open. *Her?* Running a business? One which would achieve something decent?

Could this be the opportunity to put right some of the wrongs? To give back some of the things she'd taken? Could she do something worthwhile as well as being free from Marco?

Looking at Zane, she smiled as much as her mouth would allow. 'I say I'd like to give it a try!'

• • • •

DAMON REFRAINED from crushing his mobile or taking the preferable option of throwing it out of the window of his shitty flat. It would be gone before even hitting the pavement, swiped by a robbing druggie bastard to sell for a couple of quid for a shot of meth.

Then, if Marco still had trackers on half the phones he'd 'kindly' dished out, the thieving fucker would get it in the neck rather than *him*. And, while they were at it, the junkie could also put up with Symonds's barked demands.

'Like I've just told you,' Damon repeated, forcing the tremor of rage not to show in his voice. 'Not as yet, but I will... Yes... Soon... I'm on it now. It's looking promising so far, so don't stress.'

Don't stress? Was he having a laugh? Stressed didn't go halfway towards how he felt at the moment.

'Yep. I'm more than aware. I'll keep you posted.' Ending the call, Damon tossed the phone onto the kitchen table and stared at it, wishing it would spontaneously combust before he did.

Yes, he was aware time was limited.

Yes, he knew there were only twenty-four hours left to meet Marco's demands.

And yes, he knew Marco wanted his release secured, Hazel brought to him and then killed. Oh, and for Zane to be killed too...

He also now knew that Symonds had done everything from his side to pave the way for Marco's release and that everything hinged on him accomplishing *his* side of things. Because he'd just had to listen to it. *Twice*.

And the first bit Damon needed to do to allow Symonds to move forward was get Hazel's statement about Marco not being part of the trafficking and that it had been arranged solely by her late father, Trevor.

That was Symonds's idea to get Marco off the hook.

Damon cracked his knuckles.

Being as he was on it and things were looking promising, that would be easy. It was obvious everything would be delivered on time…

Apart from the small details he'd lied about which included that he'd been working on things and that everything was looking promising...

A film of sweat broke out on the back of Damon's neck.

But that wasn't entirely true either. He *had* started to work on things. He'd gone to the penthouse at dawn this morning to round up some of the men, only to find no one there and the locks changed.

It was when he'd immediately recognised some men from the old firm – i.e. those under Zane, that Damon had beat a swift exit.

The relief that he'd driven away without a bullet lodging in the back of his neck had only lasted two seconds before it sank into his fried brain that Zane's men had taken over the penthouse. This disaster was further compounded after sloping into the Blacksmith's Arms for a swift pint only to hear the hushed words from a runner, who on hearing of Marco's arrest and subsequent detainment, that half of the men had abandoned ship.

Maybe more than half...

Damon picked his mobile back up and scrolled through his call logs at today's many missed calls. There were several from Symonds which he'd eventually returned, but a countless number from others - so many, he couldn't be arsed to count.

They were from Marco's men, so should he have answered them?

Probably.

Instead, Damon had raced back to his flat to think. And he'd remained there ever since.

What the fuck did he do now?

Here he was with Marco's stopwatch ticking at an alarming rate; Symonds on his case and the prospect of being Marco's business partner heading out of the window.

And no, he hadn't particularly wanted to be Marco's partner, but it sure beat being stuck as Head of Filming. Or *dead.*

But unless he thought of something pretty damn sharpish, then out of those three things, the only viable outcome would be the latter.

Damon cracked open a can of supermarket-own lager. It was the only can left in the fridge. His face screwed up at the taste, but he slurped at it regardless.

Like a horrible nightmare on repeat, the only available option was Hazel. He had to find her. If he made her concoct the story Symonds needed to make the police drop all charges, then Marco would be released. And if Marco was released, that was one thing out of the way.

Marco would realise that it had been so long since he'd got his own hands dirty that he wouldn't get far without having *him* on side. It was no secret Marco wasn't the best at thinking of ways to solve 'situations', so that reason alone gave more time to work on the other two outstanding tasks.

It was all Damon had, anyway.

Getting up, he necked the remains of his can and then chucked it on the floor near the bin.

Taking a deep breath, he grabbed his jacket. Hazel had to be somewhere. It was just a case of finding her.

EPILOGUE

'YOU LOOK A LOT BETTER than yesterday.' Zane cupped Erin's face in his big hands. 'How are you feeling?'

'I just want to go home,' Erin said, kissing Zane's fingers.

'Mr Solenzo reckons another day or so of observation and then you should be good to go,' Zane smiled.

Erin pursed her lips. Unless Zane was in it, being confined to a bed wasn't something she enjoyed. She'd see if she could twist Mr Solenzo's arm and get out of here faster. She'd recover better at home.

But then there was someone else at her house right now - someone she wasn't quite sure how to take. 'How are things with...?' She checked behind Zane to see if Skye was with him.

Zane plonked himself down on the end of Erin's bed. 'Skye's at the house with Cav. We didn't talk much last night - it was all so... Oh, I don't know...' He ran his hand through his hair. '... so unexpected.'

Erin bit down on her lip, reluctant to voice anything which might jeopardise the corner her relationship with Zane had turned since the shooting. She knew now that he loved her - *genuinely* loved her, and the wisp of hope that they could make a real go of this, despite the other factors hanging over them, burned brightly. But this Skye - this *daughter...*

Erin didn't resent Skye's presence. She didn't resent it at all. It was a shock, but she had to give the girl credit for having the balls to come looking. And against the mother's wishes too.

But something nagged and she was unsure how to put it without it coming out badly. If this girl *was* Zane's daughter, which from the uncanny resemblance and from what he'd said regarding the dates, it seemed she was, then what about Shirley?

As much as Erin wanted to push the thoughts away, they had prodded within her mind all night. She'd talked to Hazel, not able to get a response, but the mere feat of voicing her nagging concerns had helped. It hadn't helped with getting any rest, like Mr Solenzo insisted, but she hadn't expected to get that anyhow once this had come to light.

But whichever way Erin looked at this and tried to rationalise it, the fact remained the same: Shirley was a woman Zane had thought enough of to introduce to his family, so if she hadn't disappeared, what would have happened?

'Erin?' Zane traced his finger along Erin's hand. 'You're not saying anything. I guess you're upset that Skye is in the house when you're stuck here, but what else could I do?'

'She's your daughter, Zane. Of *course* you should want to get to know her,' Erin protested, horrified to think he'd thought she wouldn't accept that. If Zane had shunned the poor girl, *that* would have made her question him.

'Then what is it?' Zane pushed. 'I don't know what I'm supposed to do. I don't even know what to say to her!' He put his head in his hands. 'Christ! I'll have to go and speak to Shirley. I never thought that she'd do something like that.'

Erin's flinch gave Zane the answer he needed. He pulled her into his arms. 'I was sixteen, Erin. Me and Shirley... well, I liked her, but nowhere near how I feel about you.'

'It's not that,' Erin lied, not wishing to expose her glimmering worry that if Zane saw Shirley again it could reignite his feelings, especially as they shared a daughter. 'I just don't understand why she didn't tell you. Neither do I understand why she wouldn't tell Skye who her father is.'

'That's why I need to speak to her,' Zane said. 'I want to know why she didn't give me the chance to be in my child's life.'

Erin nodded. She understood that, but the fear remained. 'Then that is what you must do.'

Zane exhaled loudly. 'I was worried you were going to...'

'Accuse you of something?' Erin interjected. 'Nope! Like I said, I trust you.' *And she had to, come what may.*

Zane grinned. 'On other news, Tiger and Leo arranged some of our men to take back control of the penthouse first thing today. Now they're working on tracking Sandler down.'

Erin's eyes widened. 'That's fantastic! But Marco? What's going on with him?'

'For the time being he's still in custody, but we're moving as quickly as we can,' Zane said. 'I've also arranged something for Hazel, which she's agreed to.'

Erin glanced in the direction of Hazel's empty bed who'd made herself scarce so they could have a private conversation. 'Okaaaay…?'

'Never mind that. I'll tell you about that in a moment, but there's one other thing...'

Erin's heart sank. She'd thought this was going too well. Tensing, she braced herself for whatever bad news was about to come her way.

'Don't look so freaked out!' Leaning over, Zane pressed his lips against Erin's. 'I just wondered if you fancied being my wife?'

Erin blinked. *Wife? Zane Morelli was asking her to marry him?*

'I don't want to be without you, Erin,' Zane said. 'I know things are crazy, but I love you. I nearly lost you and I realise I can't live without you.'

'Then the answer is yes!' Erin beamed.

Screw Marco. Screw all the people threatening every part of their existence. She wouldn't even let the unfounded fear of

Shirley and an unexpected daughter cloud this moment.

Because with Zane, she knew she could bear anything that was thrown her way.

Next in this Series

TRUSTING BLOOD (SCARRED #3)

Hoping to build a relationship with an unexpected addition to his family, as well as rebuilding his firm up from scratch, Zane Morelli is counting on his brother remaining in custody long enough for this to happen.
But Erin is making things difficult. So much so that Zane is beginning to question whether they have a future after all.

Erin Langley didn't expect to find an ally in Hazel Grimes, but as it turns out, Erin isn't the only one who can see that more than one person could have an agenda.
But would anyone listen?

Zane's bloodline has already betrayed him in the worst possible ways, so it couldn't happen again.
Could it?

More From this Author

ALLEGIANCE SERIES:

TAKEOVER | FALLOUT | VENDETTA | PAYBACK

Daddy's girl Samantha Reynold hadn't bargained on unexpectedly needing to step into her father's shoes and take over the family casino business.

Pampered and spoiled, Sam knows nothing about the rules of this glamorous but deadly new world. She has a lot to learn and even more to prove. But she won't let her family down, especially when it looks like they could lose everything to their biggest rivals – the Stoker family.

Eldest son Sebastian hasn't got time to pander to pretty girl Samantha as she plays at being boss. Rumours are swirling around the streets of Birmingham that have the power to rip the Stoker family apart and destroy everything they've built.

MORE FROM THIS AUTHOR

RETRIBUTION SERIES:

AN OLD SCORE | FINDERS KEEPERS | THE FINAL TAKE

Three families... One prize...

Teagan Fraser had no idea what she was getting herself into when she took on an assignment as a live-in carer for Dulcie Adams – a retired dancer from a Soho club. Dulcie has waited forty years for her lover, Michael Pointer, to return, but she's been living in hope for a time that never came and left looking after something important, which Jonah Powell and his firm want back.

In addition to the notorious Powell firm, there are others wanting to claim what they believe is rightfully theirs and they'll do anything to get it back. If only Dulcie wasn't around it would be a lot easier, but she's difficult to shift...

A lot can happen in a short space of time and Teagan might wish she'd never become involved.

More From this Author

HUNTED SERIES:

THE STATUS DEBT | THE FAMILY LEGACY | THE TARGET OF LIES

Lillian Morgan would do anything to regain the status she lost by marrying beneath her and to cover the sordid details of her husband's death. This includes blackmail and the hand of marriage of her own daughter.

Tori thought her life couldn't get much worse, but someone is not being honest and secrets have the power to rip everyone to shreds.

Especially when life is built on lies.

*** This series contains written depictions of graphic violence, sex and strong language. It also contains some themes that may be uncomfortable for certain readers.***

More From this Author

DOWNFALL SERIES:

UNTIL THE END OF TIME | ESCAPING THE PAST | VENGEFUL PAYBACK

Dive into Seth and Jane's train wreck of a life, where drugs, alcohol and obsessional love means this downright dangerous pair will do *anything* to ensure nothing gets in their way.

They do bad things. *Very* bad things and their promise to love each until the end of time turns into a war against each other.

A war neither of them can win.

*** This series contains written depictions of graphic violence, sex and strong language. It also contains some themes that may be uncomfortable for certain readers. ***

About The Author

Over the years Edie has worked all over the UK as well as in several other countries and has met a lot of interesting people - several of whom have supplied ideas for some of the characters in her books! She has now settled back in central England with her partner and children, where she is pursuing her writing.

Edie writes gritty gangland and urban fiction for Boldwood Books and Athame Press.

Edie's series so far include her latest – the *Scarred* series; the *Allegiance* series; the *Retribution* series, *Hunted* series and *Downfall* series.

When she isn't writing, Edie enjoys reading and is a self-confessed book hoarder. She also enjoys crochet and music as well as loving anything quirky or unusual.

Visit www.ediebaylis.co.uk for the latest news, information about new releases, giveaways and to subscribe to her mailing list.

Edie Baylis

gangland | crime | urban

THRILLER AUTHOR

CONNECT WITH EDIE

https://fb.me/downfallseries

https://www.goodreads.com/author/show/17153586.Edie_Baylis

https://twitter.com/ediebaylis

https://www.amazon.co.uk/Edie-Baylis/e/B075FQHWCZ/

https://www.bookbub.com/authors/edie-baylis

https://ediebaylis.co.uk/

info@ediebaylis.co.uk

https://www.fantasticfiction.com/b/edie-baylis/

https://www.instagram.com/ediebaylis/

https://www.tiktok.com/@ediebaylis

https://www.pinterest.co.uk/ediebaylis/

JOIN EDIE'S MAILING LIST

Subscribe to Edie's mailing list for the latest news on her books, special offers, new releases and competitions.

https://ediebaylis.co.uk/signup.html

CWA MEMBER

ACKNOWLEDGEMENTS

Firstly, special thanks goes to the ladies (you know who you are) - who were brave enough to allow their names to be adopted by some of the characters in this story after winning a competition on Facebook. (I must point out that these characters are in no way anything to do with, or connected to, their namesakes in real life!) Just want to get that out there!

Also, many thanks to the people that kindly read my drafts of *The Price of Betrayal*. I appreciate your time and feedback.

As always, thanks to all of the supportive friends and readers who give me the incentive to keep on writing. And, of course, love and thanks to my family.

Thank you for reading *The Price of Betrayal*. I hope you enjoyed reading it as much as I did writing it!

If so, would you please consider leaving a review on Amazon and/or Goodreads. Reviews from readers are SOOOO helpful and especially important to us authors and without you we would have nobody to write for!

Thank you once again and hope you enjoy the rest of my books.

Edie xx

Printed in Great Britain
by Amazon

39850741R00219